I0760999

What the Giants Were Saying

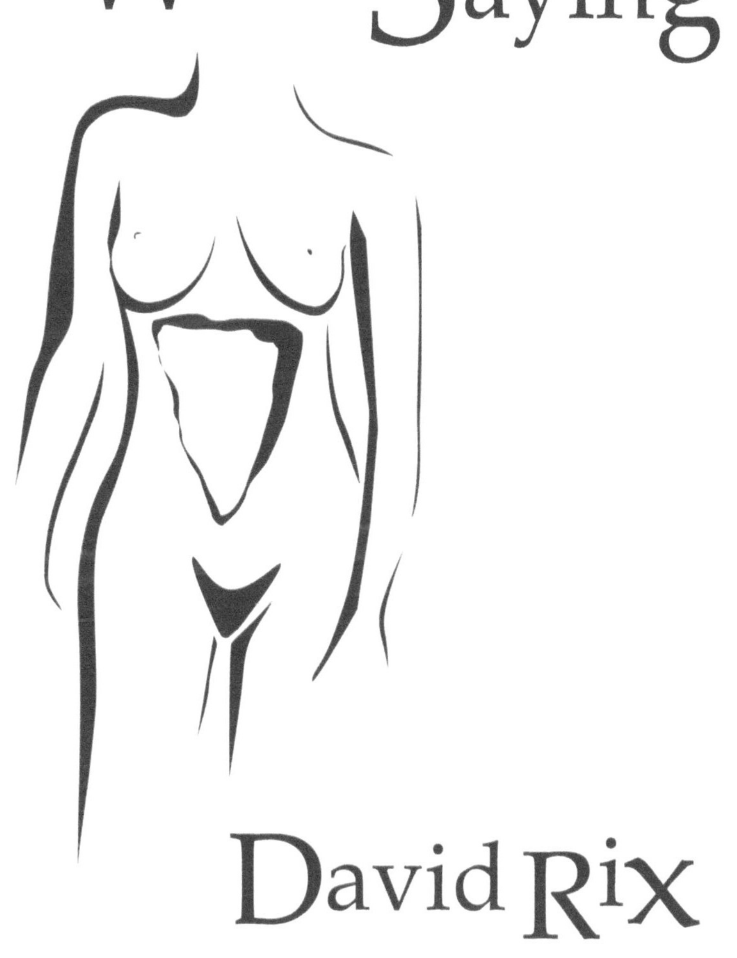

David Rix

What the Giants were Saying and Other Strange Tales
by David Rix

ISBN: 978-1-913766-26-9

First published in 2005
New expanded edition published in 2024

www.eibonvalepress.co.uk

What the Giants were Saying and **Red Fire** were originally published in *What the Giants were Saying,* Eibonvale Press, 2005.

Number 18 was originally published in *Strange Tales*, edited by Rosalie Parker, Tartarus Press, 2003

Duet was originally published in *Wordland 5: True Love*, edited by Terry Grimwood, The Exaggerated Press, 2014

A Taste of Casu Marzu was originally published in *Strange Tales 3*, edited by Rosalie Parker, Tartarus Press, 2009

Spiral was originally published in *The Monster Book for Girls,* edited by Terry Grimwood, The Exaggerated Press, 2011

Queen Rat was originally published in *Soot and Steel*, edited by Ian Whates, Newcon Press, 2019

A Taste of Canal Burgers was originally published in *Creeping Crawlers*, edited by Allen Ashley, Shadow Publishing, 2015

Henge was originally published in *Strange Tales 5*, edited by Rosalie Parker, Tartarus Press, 2015

The other stories appear here in print for the first time.

Contents:

Part 1

What the Giants Were Saying

When I developed my first book, in another life an impossibly long time ago now, it just contained the two stories *What the Giants were Saying* and *Red Fire*. Two rather contrasting pieces that nevertheless seemed to tread similar ground. Both are horror tales that I would now describe as quite extreme, or maybe extremely extreme, though I don't think I ever really set out deliberately to shock—they just deal with the similar subject matter of art and creativity in a particularly visceral context. Art of blood and body and madness with a hefty dash of the supernatural. They are stories about taking art into the deep places, with a certain implied 'message' about renouncing the sweet, pretty and mundane for bloody and extreme experimentation. At least as far as horror allows such a message before inverting it into a warning. It is a message that is familiar from a lot of rebellious art and, I'm going to say it, one that feels just a little tiresome to me now. It may help to see this not as saying "This is the way one should be", in the words of manifestoes everywhere, but as something on the margins of acceptability fighting for a toehold of the possible in an unsympathetic world. Maybe a bit of rebellious aggression is inevitable in the face of that.

These days, of course, I am pretty much opposed to renouncing *anything*—any genre or medium or style. If it brings you joy or meaning or pleasure, do it. Paint that landscape—write that erotic fanfic—give us that classic ghost story—tell that pulp tale. *Anything!* Whether I personally like it or not is entirely irrelevant if you do.

However, the rebellious nature of *Giants* does have certain roots in my own life. This book emerged directly from my own experiences studying the arts at a deeply experimental and alternate college—one very much open to unusual modes of expression. Performance art, performance writing, the weirdest ends of theatre and music, etc. I loved that stuff, not because I was deeply involved with it myself (though I have a few wild memories of fish heads, raw liver and playing music while being whipped with hazel) but because the act of doing this and what it could express seemed to reveal something very deep about human beings and their sense of play, expression, psychology and meaning. Nothing as drastic as *Giants* took place (obviously!), but the memories of all this permeate the characters I write about and my sense of what people are capable of to this day.

Looking back now, however, both these stories feel very alien to me, in good ways and bad. It is hard now to find the place I was in when I wrote them. One might imagine that I was a tortured soul back then to produce such dark and twisted writing without even really trying—and that may be true. But I don't think the readings on my torture meter have changed that much over the years. Perhaps paradoxically though, my writing style has mellowed and quietened a lot. The result is that while the occasional rough edge and sledgehammer philosophy in *Giants* might bother me, I am also kind of jealous of the ferocious expression that I managed back then. There seems a catharsis about it and I wonder what has happened over the years to lead me to restrain myself so. Reading through these old pieces again now, I am wondering what I can learn from them—whether the hysterically expressive old me can teach the tired, cautious new me a thing or two.

Of course, styles change over time. Things develop, values shift. There is nothing profound about that. With distance, I can look back and see these styles as they progress, and I am such a slow writer that whole chapters of my life can be represented by only a handful of stories. This is why, on deciding to bring out a new edition of this book, it seemed appropriate to expand it into a more comprehensive collection charting the entire span of such writing, right back to the earliest days.

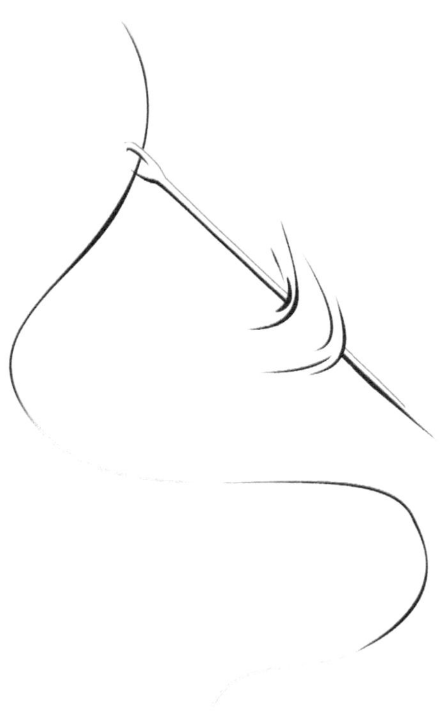

What the Giants were Saying

1

It was a grey day—a day that made you feel sad.

Filled with weariness, Don eased the car out of the remote moorland layby, where it had been parked for the last half an hour. Outside, the world was one of misty hills and looming grassy rocky slopes strewn with dead bracken and gorse, with the great dark masses of the occasional houses and trees and scrublands looming like smoke. The sun was going down in a cold, grey sunset and the sky was like an immense stone suspended overhead. He shivered beneath its weight as he pulled onto the road with a bump and drove, squinting ahead into the increasing gloom. There was nothing glamorous about this stretch of tarmac, for all its moorland setting. This was no wild bleak pass coiling through the gentle high hills. This was just a dreary strip of rough blasted land around which a few houses clustered.

From the radio trickled a stream of inconsequential classical music. The gentle warbling of Chopin probably. All trills and notes and prancing around elegantly with their noses in the air.

It did little to rouse him out of his deep gloom. And nor did the crumpled paper on the passenger seat, on which the rough lines of a pencil sketch wandered unfinished and unfinishable. The vague shapes of hills were visible—obliterated in an increasing overlay of scribbled lines. It looked like a violent storm had overtaken the land.

A mobile phone sat glassily next to the drawing—one of those fold-in-half jobs almost small enough to swallow. It was closed.

He slowed, leant forward and peered up at the sky, resting his chest against the steering wheel. If it was a stone up there, he thought grimly, then it had to be a block of reinforced concrete.

He sighed. There was a car coming up behind, and that forced him to accelerate again. Ahead he could just make out the silhouettes of the tall towers of the wind farm against the sky. That meant he would be home in twenty minutes or so. Then he could go in, shut the door behind him and curl up somewhere. Right now, that was all he wanted to do. Get indoors again—away from the light that he had fled into so thoughtlessly—away from the gazes of other people. Where he could curl up and lick his wounds, like a cat washing itself.

Then the phone rang.

He recognised the ring tone instantly and briefly closed his eyes—a knot of discomfort and fear forming somewhere in his stomach. He was very grateful for distinctive ring. At least you sometimes no longer had to pick up the phone in agonising ignorance of who was waiting at the other end. Way back when the world was younger, he had spent a few minutes trying to decide on this particular ringtone—it had to be a tone that fitted her character. Perhaps it had—but now the bright and vivacious little melody that beeped out at him sounded grotesque. Like the music to a cartoon featuring cute little animals cutting each other up with chainsaws…

Not recommended for small children or big babies.

Answer not answer answer not answer? The ring tone completed its tune, then started over again. He knew from vast experience that this particular ringtone played through twice before giving up and hanging up. So one more ring and the cartoon would be over and nothing left but dripping blood and American folk songs. Answer? He didn't know.

Not answer?

Answer?

Not…

"Shit," he muttered.

After all, if an olive branch was being offered, then why refuse it?

"Hello?"

Five minutes later.

Bad idea, he murmured to himself, brushing blood from his face and staring out into the grey. Bad bad bad idea.

His phone was still in his hand, he realised—it still read 'connected'—and a name—and he hastily pressed the hang-up button.

The sound of her voice had sent a burning pain down through his insides and the moment he answered, he regretted it. For a moment he had been unable to find any words.

Hi Don, Jacki had said, her voice filled with anxiety. *Where are you? Are you ok?*

He gazed out of the windscreen, down the bonnet and at the wrecked security fence, wondering if it was worth allowing himself to cry here and now or if he should wait till he got home. The November air was cold though—it seemed too cold to feel any emotion. Instead, he gazed up at the white monsters in front of him. It was not too cold for them, at least. Not cold enough to still the energy of the great towers. They spun and spun as always—huge sails whirling around, always seeming just slightly faster than they should be. That was a feeling that brought a small knot of discomfort somewhere inside him. The way those things turned reminded him of a dream or nightmare he must have once dreamed—perhaps when he was very young. Something claustrophobic yet vast—heavy yet light as a feather. But now the dream or nightmare was forgotten, just leaving the faint ghost of a feeling behind.

Yes.

Faintly, with the engine dead, he could even hear the sound they made.

Look Don, she had murmured, her voice one big apology. *I really didn't—didn't mean… I didn't hurt you did I?*

No no Noooo, he assured. *Of course not.*

After all, what does physical pain matter?

His finger had been itching over the hang-up button. Waste of time waste of time.

Outside the car, the giant blades cut the air, the huge white towers looking like ice in the cold evening. The wind turbines were facing him—spinning and spinning, and he gazed at them in silence.

"You bitch," he muttered aloud.

Don, she had said, her voice sounding so desolate that he wanted to scream. *What's wrong? Are you angry with me?*

What do you think? he said.

Do you hate me or something?

No—I don't hate you.

Then what's the matter? she wailed.

Nothing.

Look, she said, her voice breaking. *I know I lost my head a bit earlier—and you did too. I'm sorry—but what do you want me to do?*

Oh shut up, he had wanted to howl. You are a fucking artist and you are talking to me like a soap opera. He had stared ahead at the passing road signs. Want her to do? He didn't want her to do anything. Nothing. Ever again. The mere thought of her doing anything on his account, and thus putting him under an obligation, was intolerable.

He blinked. Cold grey filled his eyes and a splitting pain filled his head. With a groan, he pulled himself up and massaged his temples. He glanced painfully over his shoulder at the smeared pattern of hair grease and the minuscule blood smudge on the window that explained why. It looked as though a bird had flown into the glass.

You—don't want me to—come over perhaps? she had been saying. *We could have a quick drink of something before bed—or—I can't talk well over the phone. Are you on your way back? Or perhaps we could do some drawing? How about that? Just like we used to? Is there anything you want to draw me for? You drew me once. Why not again? Why didn't we repeat that? What happened? It almost seems as if...*

Drawing?

He remembered the 'drawing' in question. Not a particularly good experience, albeit not exactly bad either. And now what had she been doing? Offering her body in exchange for a meeting?

What happened was that my art died, he thought back to her. *That's all.*

It was a thought without much emotion.

He glanced at the mobile phone on the seat beside him. Yes. The snarl of wire fence crumpled around his bonnet seemed a fitting end really. The grey despair had given way to red panic, flaring like a flame. He had jerked the car back on course with a scowl, finally breaking away from her whining-induced reverie. Twice that had happened before he had finally come off the road. There was a crescendo of hooting. He had refocused his eyes on the car heading directly towards him and frozen. The twisted face of a middle-aged woman was there for a moment, gazing at him hugely.

He swerved away—too far. Then back… but not far enough, and suddenly there was one less security fence left in the world. One less car as well, very probably. The woman had just driven on, thanks a bunch.

He hauled open the car door and sat there, eyes closed, letting one leg hang out into the grass. It was a shock of cold, but he almost welcomed that. It woke him up a bit. And now, with the door open, the air was filled with the sound the great wind turbines made—the muted whispering, swishing noise. He realised that he had never actually heard them before. When driving of course, the sound was quite inaudible. Now they seemed to surround him, whispering at him, but try as he would, he could make out no words. With a first sense of peace creeping in, he tried to understand them, slowly and unhurriedly letting himself revive and trying not to think. Perhaps they weren't so discomforting after all. They were uncomplicated things and now they seemed to speak of a great calm. Perhaps there was something in there that could heal his throbbing head, he thought. In their gentle ululation was a curious dark spark of warmth. It made him think of the gentle buzzing of insects on a summer day, and smell the sizzle of frying bacon. The scuttle of wood lice and the patter of hail landing in the grass. Comforting sounds. Sounds that made you feel safe and happy with existing.

Somewhere below the level of the conscious, it reminded him of those dreams he sometimes had, where he seemed to be experiencing the most amazing vision—so powerful that it made him want to cry. And he could catch it—sure he could. It was all there in his head waiting for him to put it down onto canvas. But on waking, the dreams went and any memory of how to create that magnificence was quite out of reach leaving merely a sense of bitter loss.

He shook his head and scrambled from the car, clutching at the door to stop himself from falling. The cold, nearly-bonfire-night air cut into him even stronger, but he ignored it—barely noticed it. Perhaps he hadn't been driving home along solid tarmac after all, he thought. Perhaps he was driving across the sea, for it seemed every bit as fluid and as restless.

He rubbed at his face, trying to steady his mind—trying to force it to recover from the shock it had received. But why bother? It was safe here. Somewhere out there was a world of pain and grief, but this sea shut it out like a sealed window onto the storm.

He gazed out across the waves—the ocean heaving almost black under the heavy sky, his small craft waiting to ride before the wind. And he wasn't alone, he realised with a ghost of disappointment. There was a figure out there—in the distance beyond the opposite fence. The figure stood under the nearest of the turbines like an ant at the foot of a sunflower, rising up out of the water, out of the grass. He couldn't make out any details of it but seeing it there, he felt the real size of the things come home to him. Gazing up at the white giants, he was struck again by how magnificent they were. Just then, he would have liked to see the whole landscape made of these things. Every motorway with its string of turbines—every tower block crowned with one.

The figure seemed to be coming in his direction.

The phone rang then and reality came back reluctantly and painfully. His head throbbed—his stomach knotted. He staggered into the car again, reaching down for it. There seemed almost to be a hint of desperation in that ring—like a silly little cartoon appliance eager to pass on whatever message it had. "Mr Don sir Mr Don sir Message for you sir Message for you Message for you Message for you Message for…"

"Shut up," he groaned, his head bumping against the window again as he flopped back into his seat. He stared at the phone for a moment, then threw it feebly across the car. It clattered down into the back, still ringing, and he had to remain sitting there and listen as it played the Jacki tune one last time and gave up. "Oh sir Reproach Reproach Oh well Goodbye."

As he listened to it, he felt a helpless rage grow inside him and he closed his eyes. It wasn't even her fault, he knew that on some level. But still he wanted to take that phone and smash it on the ground, hurl it out of reach into the scrub of the moors, sling it over the security fence and never have to listen to its inane ring ever again. If only he could find the energy. His chest hitched in three great sobs before he managed to stifle them. Pain like a physical wrenching of flesh—as though his insides were being opened and spread. Edvard Munch's The Scream in lurid ultraviolet. It was not very rational, but it possessed him—tore at him. Jacki, he thought. The name was in his head like the huge lurid letters of a comic book explosion. Kablam!!!! Jacki!!!! Followed by a string of obscure punctuation marks. <<;*(&+#@)*&^(* #¬@‡?%))L!!!!! Of course all this was her fault, he wanted to wail. What was she trying to do? Ruin his life? He sobbed again, bathing in bitter misery as though sinking through the glittering green waters of a huge stagnant pool.

Liquid trickled down his face, and he opened his eyes with a flinch. However, now the comic book had turned red. The explosion faded to dull glowing thunderclouds. He rubbed for a moment, then gave up and watched the images on the page. The turbines still turned, but they stood now rooted in grim blood-coloured earth or sand—and they had transformed themselves into implements of torture and execution, for on each a tattered body hung, turning and turning, ragged entrails flopping and tumbling behind. They seemed to be secured there and tightly trussed with winds and winds of silver and copper wire surrounding arms, legs and chest. And on the closest turbine, Jacki hung, impossibly large, her mouth wide, her skin crisped as though from burning. As she spun she desperately kept turning her head to look at him, shaking the trailing ropes of her disembowelled stomach from her face. He gazed at her for a moment, feeling emotionless, watching as she turned forever, her eyes dying with dizziness. Overhead the darkening clouds boiled.

Two black birds sailed overhead, gliding carelessly into the heart of the storm. Towards her. They looked like ravens, maybe with claws outstretched, maybe not, and there was food aplenty here for them. Many morsels available to eager beaks. But then the scale of the image fractured. They were no bigger than dots as they circled round her. And with that thought the figures abruptly went away, leaving the birds to flap on across the moors. No interchange—no fade out. He was just no longer seeing them.

With a groan, he mopped the blood from his eyes and the world returned to normal.

"Fuck," he said and sat up, but the movement brought a violent lunge of pain from his head and he sagged down again against the headrest. He was still shaking, he realised. The car seemed very cold now and finally, with a weary sigh, he pulled the door closed. For a moment, he sat there staring out at the grey sky—at the lowering stone that mirrored the moors that it smothered—out at the great turning monsters that sat there like giant life-forms eating the air. The figure he had seen earlier was much closer now, he realised. Now he could see the long hair and small, angular face of a woman. Perhaps early twenties—perhaps older. It was hard to tell. Ragged looking. Her limbs thin and her clothing surprisingly light for this cold evening, seemingly nothing more than tattered jeans and a shirt a few sizes too large for her wrapped around her shoulders. Somehow she must have climbed over the fence, for she was on this side of it now. He watched her for a moment. Was she looking at him?

Well—who wouldn't?

He gave a grunt—reached over the back for his car blanket and hauled it over—draped it around himself. Turned the key and the engine shivered into life, finally drowning the sound of the whispering turbines. It sounded healthy enough as it started, and he eased it into reverse…

The woman had gone.

He stared out at where she had been, at the desolate moorland landscape filled with dead bracken and scrub, wondering if she had been real. She had certainly seemed real enough. Real enough to have untidy hair and ragged clothes. Maybe. Maybe not. It really didn't much matter.

His head was settling into a nice steady ache from the bump it had received—and now more than ever he wanted to get home and curl up—just lie down and sleep. He knew he should ring for help. He knew he was not in any condition to drive any more. But the mere thought of touching his phone right now made him shudder, and besides, there was something supremely comfortable about being alone. Home. Bed. Locked door. That was all he could think about.

The road was clear and he pulled out, bumping off the grass and onto the comforting tarmac. Home was no great distance away, and would involve no busy towns. Nevertheless, he struggled to keep the road from shimmering before his eyes as he snapped on his hazard lights, just in case, and drove slowly.

2

08/02/05 7.45AM

Jacqueline Adams: I remember that the only thing I was aware of at first was the light gleaming off it—the light of my torch I mean—it created a great blaze of copper—like a burning spider's web... Look—do I really have to?

Question: Please try. Can you describe a bit more about what the sculpture was like?

J: Sculpture? How can you call it that?

Q: That is the term that you used.

J: Was it? No... no no no, I'm sure I didn't. I am an artist. I know what a sculpture is. *[Brief pause]* Oh—well, it is what HE might have called it. Not me though. For me, art is to express beauty and emotion. Nature is beautiful, and who needs more than that? I always thought that he agreed with that, but lately I had been wondering if he was thinking the exact opposite.

Q: Yes indeed—but getting back to the description...

J: I mean—he was a landscape artist, for fuck's sake. What do landscape artists do? They catch and respond to the beauty they see around them. I told him that, but he just asked me "What is beautiful, then?" He was looking at a picture of a spider wrapping up a wasp at the time.

Q: Miss Adams, I am sorry, but I really need a brief description.

J: All right, all right. You want the details? I told you, it was all among the trees. Tangled there like a spider's web. All wires radiating. There was nothing random about it though. Rather it had a sort of organic feel to it, as if the metal had grown there rather than been tied. I remember thinking that... organic...

He arrived home and shut the door behind him. He didn't slam it.

He shook off his coat and dumped it on the floor, then tramped straight into his studio, his head a mass of throbbing pain. He poured himself a glass of warming coffee liqueur and made himself a big cup of sweet tea, then slumped down in his armchair with both and gazed woodenly in front of him at the picture-covered wall.

It was his entire collection of landscapes, still lifes and occasional gentle figure studies—those he had not sold, at least. He remembered the feeling almost of pride that used to go thrilling through him when he had sat in this chair and relaxed. Back when things had been simpler. Just him and his paintings. His landscapes had always given him a sense of accomplishment—a sense of warmth. They were a token of his love of nature—they were a philosophy.

He stared at them, feeling even more depressed. All that warmth seemed to have passed completely, lost amid nagging dissatisfaction.

It was not that they were particularly badly done, he thought. It was just that they seemed completely boring. Boring boring boooooring. They might even have been painted by someone else—anyone else in fact. There just wasn't anything personal about them—nothing that set them apart as his own work. The hills and fields and occasional buildings or rocks or rivers—they were nothing more than a pale imitation of a madness of reality that no artist could ever really hope to capture. Art was about more than just reproducing reality, anyway. Where was the point in that? Reality was there, everywhere, just waiting to be looked at.

And of course, there in the middle of them, that one figure study.

Jacki was an artist herself, though self-confessedly not a very serious or ambitious one. She had been like him, a painter of landscapes and amiable pretty things. What little he had seen of her work had rather left him cold except for the fact that it was her that had painted them.

His art. Her art.

Their art?

Well, for a while at least.

How often, he wondered, did friends slip into being lovers? Probably not very often at all. Bad move? Good move? There were no pronouncements to make there, that was for sure.

She staying late—working together into the small hours. Not on anything particularly significant.

She tired—the invite to sleep here with him—only the one bed in his small house.

She curling up with him like the friends they were—and going to sleep.

It was only in the morning, as they awoke together, that he gave her an affectionate cuddle—nothing more than a friendly hug round the shoulders…

She turning to him and responding…

He had half-expected her to run out of the house and never come back. He had half-wanted to do that himself. But she had just lain there, conspicuously naked now, looking at him with big eyes.

And above his desk, her portrait was also naked. It was a medium-sized work in oil paints—the only image of her he had ever done.

Maybe, he had thought, it had been love all along.

That had been… when?

It was hard to remember with a brain full of fog. Was it last month?

Last year?

He hoped not.

He tore his eyes away from the portrait with an effort. He remembered painting that all too well and it had been a strange fiasco. He had been restless and eager to try something new, even back then, so he talked her into posing for him. Tired of exploring hills and valleys of earth and rock he had wanted to try exploring the hills and valleys of flesh—and a classical nude had been as far as he dared go. She had stripped off uncomfortably and from then on everything had been lost in an elastic knot of tension and unease, her almost getting angry and he wanting to crawl away and forget the whole thing. It was strange, he thought bitterly. She never had any qualms about fucking him—but the moment he brought her into an artistic context it was as if her nakedness suddenly overwhelmed her, leaving her filled with tension and hiding behind the most stylised and stiff posing possible. But all that had been months ago. Weeks ago. He couldn't remember, but he had never asked her to repeat the experience.

"Love and art are synonymous," he remembered writing shortly afterwards in his *Morning Texts* diary. "They are all just part of the same basic thing. Why is this not working? Jacki is not a new art form."

He finished the liqueur—and tossed the glass across the room vaguely in the direction of the painting. He rubbed at his head and groaned, not just from the pain, but from the feeling of intense despair that was still welling up inside him. He looked round at his paintings and felt something close to hatred for them now. Nothing nothing nothing at all. Just self-indulgent daydreams with about as much substance as a piece of boiled sweet. And she was the most insignificant boiled sweet of all. She called herself an artist, and yet her brain had less capacity than that liqueur glass lying smashed on the floor. In his head, he swore at her bitterly. Swore at her for ruining things—or maybe, he was just honest enough to admit, for not helping him put them together again.

He had not put brush to canvas or pencil to paper for weeks now. Or was it months? And it was all her fault.

There was a knock at the door.

Speak of the devil. Think of the devil.

Don sat there without moving, save for an intermittent trembling that twitched through him.

The knock repeated.

"Oh please just go away," he said softly.

"Don?" came a voice through the door. It was husky and frightened sounding.

"Pwitty pwitty please—you don't really need me at all, you know."

"Don? The light's on. Are you in there?"

"No," he snarled through his teeth.

"Hello? Please open the door..."

Knock knock knock...

"No," he repeated, rising to his feet slowly, his lips stretched tight, cradling the remains of his cup of tea. He slipped into a corner of the room, retreating like a small rodent who hears a slithering in the undergrowth. "No no. No need to worry, my dear. No one home, you see. I'm out, ok. Just out. Don't come looking—no need to be suspicious. I'm just not here—still off chatting with the white towers as a matter of fact. Nothing to worry about."

There was silence—then his phone rang. It bleeped a very distinctive distinctive ring.

He jumped. She could probably hear it outside. She would at least know he had come home. He made a pounce to grab it and silence it, then stopped himself. That would blow his cover completely.

As if it mattered.

As if it bloody mattered.

Fuck, he mouthed silently—and violently hurled the half-empty cup at the painting on the wall. There was a shocking crash that must surely have been audible outside. A brown splash streamed downwards and he sighed. Oh dear oh dear. It looked as if Jacki had thrown up over herself. The revolting bitch.

How many rings was that? The maniacally cheerful little tune played through twice as he stepped neatly to the wall, grabbed the painting off its hook and smashed it over his knee. Glass showered the floor.

Who wrote these tunes anyway?

Finally there was silence and he began to relax at last, tension fading slightly, before…

The phone bleeped its answerphone message alert.

Oh sir Oh sir When you're ready sir…

He punched his knee hard enough to hurt—then punched the wall instead, a violent gesture bringing two more paintings clattering to the ground, where he quickly put his foot through them.

Could she have heard him here? The studio was at the back of the house after all.

Who knows?

Who cares?

There was no way he could know from indoors if she was here or a thousand miles away, but he didn't check. Instead he gave a muted, almost silent howl, ignoring the pain in his head—and continued smashing paintings.

Later, on the way up to bed, he looked at the phone, at the alert it was plaintively displaying for him like a good little boy who has done his homework (Oh sir please sir when you are ready sir when you are ready sir). For a moment he wanted to change her name on the listing in his phone book. 'Useless Bitch Calling. Answer? Cancel?' Then he burst out laughing at his own childish stupidity.

He slipped upstairs, stripped and slid into bed with a sigh. He was feeling better than before, but still rather dizzy and trembling and he pulled the bedclothes tight around himself. He wasn't very tired yet but bed felt the best place to be at the moment. The best place to lie and think about what to do next.

Although, he thought to himself, maybe there was a key somewhere in all of this. As he lay there, there was an image in his head. It was the first somewhat artistic image that had really come to him for a long time and it had been haunting him for most of the evening. Bloody bizarre image though. It was not one that he felt very sure about—but at least it was something.

A key, he thought. Perhaps. Would have to try and see.

In a way, as he dozed and brooded, he felt more awake now than he had for days or weeks or months or however long it had been.

From 'Morning Texts'—p68

I am so tired! So tired I wonder why I am even bothering to sit here and write. I know it is a habit I try and keep myself to—every morning get up and write a page or two before breakfast. A page or two of anything. But no habit should be binding, surely? There is no rule that should not be breakable.

The thing is, I dreamed last night—such a strange dream, and possibly relevant. Well, that sounds a blunt way of putting it really. It was just this endless sea of images and thoughts that would not leave me alone. Images of Jacki (no surprise) and the wind farm and... everything. I couldn't wake up from them either. I really hope I haven't done any damage to my head.

What am I going to do? I feel all dead and dry—it is horrible. I really have to get rid of that woman. Screwing someone was the worst thing that ever happened to me.

In a strange way I am glad I was stopped at the wind farm yesterday. I never before quite realised what an extraordinary place it was. I can remember them building it actually. 18 towers each over 40m high. People had been moaning about it—but people moan about anything. Did they have to have those things in the world, and even if so, did they have to have them right there? Right here? Shove 'em somewhere else out of the way! They seemed quiet enough though. Quieter than the road they were surrounding. Not that I cared much about it at the time. It was just another item in the newspaper and another monster building site to negotiate when I drove that way.

Yesterday it was as if I saw them for the first time. It is true, I think. I cannot forget them or the sound they made. I suppose if Jacki hadn't called me and shaken my world, then I never would have noticed.

I really want to paint them—but I cannot face just churning out yet another landscape—even with those towers in it. I am sick to death of landscapes. I must do something though. Those towers can inspire reverence—I don't know how, but they can! Like a modern-day totem pole or scaffold. Like some mysterious archaeological site 'of religious significance'—or indeed a place of execution. Does that sound fanciful? Well if it does, who gives a flying fuck? I am tired of being drab and rational. I am tired of being a landscape painter. I mean, what's the point? Let me be fanciful for a bit! I mean, what can I paint now? Forget all the silly elegies and gentle abstracts that I used to do! All I can see right now, if I let myself, is Jacki's face. So paint that? Perhaps—and I am in no mood for gentleness.

I remember that image that came to me in the car—the wind turbine torture instruments. Which I am now going to try and draw, just to see what happens. It is hard not to equate those towers in some way with older towers, and I have vague memories of great cartwheels hung on the tops of huge poles on which the ragged and broken remains of the condemned, their shattered arms and legs woven into the wheel's spokes, were left on display to die. Broken on the wheel. Broken on the windmill? On the wind turbine? Hey! Let the mind run wild! A futuristic society reduced to barbarism using the old but still working technologies of the wind farm to enact their ritualistic slaughter? While evolved creatures lurk in the trees? It is a strange image for me—but I feel a sort of perverse satisfaction with it. It excites me a little—perhaps however horrible, it is what I need to clear my system out. And whatever happens, I have to at least keep trying.

It is strange how fragile creativity is. It is something delicate—like an alpine plant that always has to be nurtured under exactly the right conditions; otherwise it would just die down to a useless invisible root.

I fucking HATE that!!!!!!!!

Key? he wondered, tossing the paper onto the floor. Was it?

He sat hunched over his coffee mug, staring without seeing at the broken frames and torn canvasses. Glass shattered. Wooden frames splintered, metal frames buckled—gentle landscapes and pleasant abstracts ripped to shreds by earthquakes and volcanoes of stamping feet and clawing hands.

This wasn't working.

In fact, it wasn't feeling right at all.

He finished his coffee and toyed with his pencil wondering what the hell to do. On the piece of paper crumpled at his feet, the image of a woman hung—a familiar woman—bound suspended from a familiar three-way shape.

Big deal.

The sketch he had done was like nothing he had ever dared draw before—which should have been good. Somehow, though, the result was entirely unsatisfying.

What am I doing here? the figure seemed to snarl impatiently. *Stop wasting my motherfucking time.* He stared at her and actually felt embarrassed. Yes—embarrassed. He kicked the paper away from him, aware that there was nothing profound about it whatsoever.

Hey, man, she murmured, drawling her voice like a hippie—like an art student. *This is so not cool. So Freudian. So sy-co-logic-al. Not.*

"Shut up," he grunted.

Wearily he took up another piece of paper and masking-taped it to the easel. Perhaps making this image could still help get him back on track, however strange and unappetising and sadistic it now seemed. That was what he hoped. Perhaps it was a key, after all. And, like all keys, not very important in itself. He must continue.

Really mate? she muttered—vaguely like a cockney accent this time, of all things. *Ooh boy. You think, like, destroying meeee is going destroy your own guilt? Hoooohhh-boy no way.*

He ignored her and drew grimly on. Hopeless. On the paper, the bloody clouds boiled once again, and the stark black outlines of the towers looked rickety and archaic. They looked as though they were built with raw wood. He drew in the rough grass of the moors, the low trees that clustered in the background. These were smaller towers though. Just a little bit taller than tree-height. Ideally scaled to fit the human body.

To fit Jacki. Is that it?

He stopped drawing and stared at it. That was the only thing left to add. The details of the figure.

Very slowly he sketched out her face. Then stopped again. Her expression had come out curious. The quickly laid out lines looked more like a smile than a scream, and he stared at her in dismay.

Kissy kissy, she said.

What exactly was he doing here?

He was feeling sick from it. The gruesome image sat at the base of his stomach like a meal of rotten fish. And, almost against his will, he became aware of a sad tenderness for her somewhere at the back of his mind.

He couldn't be missing her, surely?

Yes, my sweet, she murmured lyrically, her voice dancing through flowers. *Odd, isn't it. It must be springtime all of a sudden.*

A few memories came tapping at the door of his brain. Sharing dinner, her lighting candles and pouring wine into his chipped mugs. Opening the door to her grin and getting a full paintbrush dabbed on his nose. Driving through the moors at night, her half asleep, her hand trailing unconsciously against his leg. Watching her sleep—her eyelids twitching through a dream that he would never know.

Finally he slung another coffee mug across the room and buried his head in his hands with a yell. This was leading nowhere. Today's experiment:... Failed! Don't ask me what any of this means.

He groaned.

Was there any point struggling with this at all? Was there anything anywhere that felt right? Not this crude revenge, certainly. For a moment he wanted to take off his clothes and turn his paint brushes on himself—wanted to daub himself with great swirling lines and shapes. After all, he was the centre of this. Not some fucking hillside.

Why not?

Hey! Why not?

He caught sight of his phone and picked it up, ignoring the paint stain that smeared it.

Jacki had tried to call him three times already today, had even left another answerphone message, which he hadn't listened to. Thank god for caller display and distinctive ring, he thought again. He clenched his hands and groaned, his finger hovering over the 'call' button. Maybe he was being too harsh and stupid in rejecting her so violently. Maybe that was absolutely blindingly obvious, her punch in the face notwithstanding. Maybe, in fact, he was being a childish idiot.

Which was more important, anyway? His art or his love life? His art didn't seem to be worth anything now. So what? Scrap it forever and invite Jacki over for an evening of tender making-up? Eeeehh! How sweet!

Mmmmmmmm, she murmured. *Someone has a sweet tooth tonight, methinks!*

"Shut up," he yelled violently, beginning to tremble.

He vaguely remembered the two of them handling each other in bed; it had been as if they were made of expensive porcelain. And down there between her legs, something that felt almost incongruous and, now that he came to analyse it, not really very pleasant. Screwing Jacki? Hmmm. Imagine swimming in a small private pool—one of those things with ersatz painted tiles and water that killed all wildlife within a five-yard radius. Then imagine swimming down, eyes open against the stinging water, and there, in one corner, a small sea-anemone blossoms, tentacles waving. The poor thing looks lost and slightly embarrassed about being there, but still it waves gently, searching for food. Whatever food there is in that sterile place.

What balderdash.

The phone slipped from his hand.

"What the hell?" he shrieked aloud. "Maybe I will go and take a course in chartered accountancy. You know where you are with numbers. There is nothing philosophical about numbers."

Or maybe he would go out—take a bottle with him and go out—and sit on one of the hills he had used to paint so much and explain to it, with much detail and much colourful language, just why he would never be painting it again.

Or maybe he could visit the wind farm again.

He thought for a moment.

Maybe.

That place still attracted him, today's failure notwithstanding. He remembered the swishing voices of those giant white towers, and it was tempting. Anything was better than remaining here. Perhaps those great white towers would make him feel better, their whispering voices gently smoothing out his mind and soul. He remembered the oddly mixed emotions he had felt in their presence the previous evening. A curious blend of discomfort and calm. It was an intriguing mingling.

At the very least he could go there and perhaps take a few photographs. For future reference. For future paintings. For documentation and archiving purposes.

At least that was what he told himself.

Maybe these towers could become a symbol of something completely different.

And when he went, he would leave his phone behind.

Good idea.

3

J: It was like a burning cobweb, as I told you—but I don't mean it was a fucking neat spiral or anything. The thing I remember most—aside from its—its centre were the three great arms of woven wire. One vertically downwards and two radiating up either side of… of… yes, three great masses of wire. All on the same plane, if you know what I mean. For a moment I thought it was a crucifixion sculpture. I almost wish it had been—it might have made some sense then. You could have explained the whole thing away as some sort of kinked religious thing.

Q: But it wasn't that, was it? It reminded you of something else?

J: Yes—and that is what I mean. Because I would almost rather it was something horrible that I could understand than something that I just cannot. It just seems so completely pointless. I really don't understand… well… I don't understand why. Surely art should mean something?

Q: I couldn't say.

J: In my years dabbling with painting, I never paid much attention to meaning, to be honest. I just wanted to get on and do it and that usually took care of itself. But surely if you are going to adopt a symbol then it has to mean something? Doesn't it?

Now the weather was even colder. The clouds hung overhead flat and uniform—like a stone indeed, and he could almost feel the weight of it leaning down on him. It was a moorland sky and no mistake. The skies on the moors were like no other. They seemed closer and more alive—always changing—always unpredictable. When they wanted to be light and trixy, they were. And when they wanted to be heavy and oppressive… they were.

He drove onwards.

When the wind turbines came into view as black silhouettes on the horizon, they really did look like something alive. Like sea creatures sifting food from the current—like sea anemones amplified thousands of times and capable of swallowing a lot more than just shrimps. What did these eat then? Birds? Did they sift birds from the air and so grow larger? Or did they catch small aeroplanes and hot air balloons? Drawing them in and digesting the metal to build ever-stronger bodies.

He smiled to himself. What a picture. Maybe he could paint that as well. Let's hear it for surrealism! A little bit of Leonora Carrington meeting a ghost of Kit Williams. Yep!

But, these thoughts aside, he could not help looking at them as they approached. They were magnificent structures rising up out of the rough moorland grass, their triple blades spinning with that ever so slightly too fast motion. He felt a wash of aesthetic pleasure well up inside him, and he began to feel a little more cheerful. Just to sit and look at them for a bit, he thought dreamily as they approached ever closer. That would be great. Or just to be here forever amongst them.

Finally, with the huge shapes processing past like spinning ghosts, he arrived at a layby and pulled into it, killed the engine and scrambled out into the cold. Instantly the sound took over—the whispering voices that filled the air with endless susurration. It still almost seemed as if they were talking—to him? To each other? It was a good fancy and he smiled again. "I am an artist," he said aloud. "I am not a mad man. I am allowed to think things like that."

He grabbed his digital camera, crossed the road and began walking towards the nearest turbine, where it stood beyond the security fence. And as he walked he snapped photos of it, catching the ever-increasing angle and perspective as it reared above him. He wasn't trying to be very artistic; he just wanted to record the thing in all its glory.

"Documentation," he muttered, "Documentation."

He felt good now. He could not imagine why but their presence did seem to be soothing him a bit. Well—you take inspiration where you find it. And if this is inspiring, then three cheers please.

Finally, he arrived at the security fence and could go no further. Frustrated, he put the camera to a link and prepared one final shot through it at the caged monster within. If only he could get closer. Perhaps he should try and get in touch with whoever operated this place—the powers that be—and try and talk them into getting a guided tour. Or maybe not. Never mind. A few last shots up at the great tower, catching the sweep of the blades as a motion blur in the fading light, then away out of the cold…

Except…

He whirled round and stared at her blankly, his heart thudding with shock and his camera bouncing on the end of its strap. How she had got so close behind him without him noticing, he couldn't imagine.

"Hi," she said with a slightly shy smile.

For a moment he couldn't speak. He actually felt afraid and embarrassed—a thrill of terror born not from any oddity she possessed but simply from the unexpected presence of another human being.

"What are you doing here," the woman said, curiously rather than interrogatively. Her voice was somewhat hard-edged but frank and friendly and tinged with an unexpectedly lilting London accent. She gazed at him with blunt but uncensuring eyes.

He hesitated.

"I—I—I—oh bloody hell. I was just getting some pictures—that's all," he stammered, feeling the skin of his face prickle and flush.

"Not many people come here," she said. "It really is a quiet place, in spite of the road."

He tried to collect himself, half-appalled that he should have reacted so strongly. Really—he needed to get out more. She was only another person, standing there in ragged jeans and an oddly lacy-looking shirt several sizes too large, which hung round her in folds. Her eyes though grabbed and held his attention and he could not stop glancing at them, then sliding away as though he was looking at something forbidden. They were a rich brown—deep and very sharp and clear looking.

"What are you doing here really?" she asked curiously. "Why do you want the turbines? You were photographing them."

"I just want to—use them in a painting."

"You are an artist?"

"Yes," he said. "I think—perhaps. Well, trying to be anyway." He giggled stupidly. "I don't really know what I am doing at the moment."

"I know that feeling," she said, and smiled—a crocked but unrestrained smile that creased her cheeks. She had a wide mouth, he realised. A wide mouth, big eyes, sharply pointed nose—and dark hair that looked as if it hadn't been brushed after a restless night.

"I—er," he started. "I crashed my car here yesterday," he explained, immediately feeling foolish but anything to keep the silence from descending. "Then I had a strange sort of… dream about them. I just wanted to paint that."

What was he trying to explain? All of this was out of date, and anyway, why would she be interested? He gave up and shrugged, massaging his head, which had started aching again.

"Nice," she said. "But whatever you are planning, I see you rather like our giant friends anyway. Do you want to get up close? There is a way through."

"What—can we?"

"Sure, I will show you," she said, and took off, following the fence.

Don tramped after her, still wondering at her and her presence here. She looked like a tramp in her tatty clothes—and why she wasn't shivering and frozen he couldn't imagine. But she wore them with a certain sense of what they were—almost a hint of creative control. Her bare arms appeared tattooed with a vague pattern of what might have been plant leaves, though it was hard to tell.

They went for about a hundred yards, following the fence closely, until they reached an area of scrubby trees and bushes spreading across into the inside of the enclosure. She waded in without hesitating, slipping between the branches at though they weren't there, and he followed feeling far clumsier. He had not even noticed this thicket yesterday—a patch of scrubby woodland clinging to the moors like sailors to a life raft.

After a few moments of travel through the bushes, she stopped. "Here we are," she said, pointing, and he saw a hole where the mesh of the fence had been torn.

"But," he stammered. "Is it safe?"

"Safe?"

"Well—I mean, is this place guarded?"

She gave a dry laugh. "You joking? Well, if it is, they ain't spotted me yet. Now come on."

She turned and dropped down on her hands and knees, and as she did so her top rode up, caught in the branches, giving him a glimpse of her bare back. It seemed that she was tattooed here as well, as he had a momentary glimpse of leafy designs coiling about her flesh. Hints of what might have been a rough and rugged landscape of stones? Or sand? But it was like a space probe's first photo of another planet—tantalising, but impossible to really make anything out. Then she was down and wriggling through the gap.

She scrambled up on the other side and looked at her hand with a frown. It was bleeding slightly.

He followed her through, his head aching worse at the activity, and she grabbed his hand and hauled him to his feet. "There," she said. "Sorry, I cut myself on the wire."

He glanced at the smudge of blood on his palm and absently rubbed it away.

"You ok?"

"Yes yes, sure. Now, let's go and meet the giants."

He stared after her as she ran quickly off through the thicket. Giants? He smiled at her turn of phrase and tramped after her. They were giants indeed—great towering life-forms of metal—and he felt himself warming to her a little more.

It was a mere few yards until the trees gave way, but he found himself panting with the exertion. His legs were starting to ache and his head was filled with pain. Even his vision seemed to be blurring for a moment, but he hauled himself after her and they immerged into the open—into the moorland ruled over by the turbines.

Except that it wasn't moorland any more.

Don sagged on his feet, gazing around him in stunned amazement. Inside his head, the dull ache became sharp and he screwed up his eyes against the glare of light.

"No—fucking—way..."

He spoke the words distinctly, shaking his head.

"What?" she asked, glancing round. She stared at him. "Are you ok? Are you ill?"

"Where am I?" he said, his voice broken.

"On the moors. What do you mean?"

"But all I can see is... is..."

He broke off. He was dimly aware of the woman grabbing his shoulder.

"What do you mean?" she cried again, her voice changing. "Are you seeing... what?"

Now the great towers stood no longer surrounded by dead bracken and scrub. Now they stood up tall and proud out of a red desert of sand and rough, dry rocks. It stretched flat and open for as far as he could see, with no variation except for the white towers. It might have been like his vision of the day before, except that the sky was now a clear blue. The occasional stunted plant was apparent—ludicrous plants. Nothing more than a couple of long, twisted, leathery leaves sprawling out from a nub of wood. A cold wind blew—he could feel it ruffling his hair and he raised his hand into it in amazement. It seemed now that the turbines were not being turned by the wind—they were making the wind. The air was moving towards them, as though through a vast suction, and Don almost had to stop his feet from following it. The fans spun faster now—so fast they were almost blurring. And the woman was by his side, gazing at him with an intense expression.

"What do you see?" she asked again, gripping him.

"They are all turning to look at me," he murmured, trembling. And they were. Their great heads were all slowly twisting round. No matter what direction he looked, they were turning to face him, and as they did the air about him became more and more disturbed as it tried to go in all directions at once.

"They are looking at me," he repeated, still unsure whether he should be terrified or delighted.

They were, but not for long. After a few minutes of observing, they turned again, swivelling almost suddenly until they all pointed in one direction only, out across the desert. He followed their gazes and saw that the horizon was alive with black dots—moving. Black dots that streamed in their direction. He stared at them, feeling his heartbeat increase.

"There is something coming towards us—I can't see what though."

"Something?"

"Yes," he said. "It is coming down from the horizon—coming slowly—like a river. The turbines are all watching them now. I am sure they are increasing their speed…"

The wind was indeed picking up, blowing against him like a gale. Then he tensed, feeling fear run through him like wires.

"Oh fuck," he said. "I can see what it is now."

"What?"

"People—hundreds—thousands of people. I don't believe it…"

"What?" she cried again, getting increasingly agitated.

"It's a whole fucking army," he cried. "There's millions of them—and all running in this direction. I can see them now. Just. They look like wild men—and women. Long hair, ragged…"

They seemed to have weapons as well. He could see the sunlight reflecting off blades. Swords? Axes? It was hard to tell.

Presently the sound of them began to be carried across the hot desert air—brought here on the ever-increasing wind that the turbines drew. The distant murmur of a million shouting voices.

Now Don was terrified. He looked around, but all there was, wherever he looked, was desert. Nowhere to hide.

"Ok," he gasped. "We have to get out of here."

He started to run—away from the advancing horde. But he quickly found that he could get almost no purchase on the fine sand. He floundered forward a few yards, then flopped down on his face.

"Take it easy," the woman cried, grabbing him by his arm, but he shook her off and tried to get to his feet.

"I can see them properly now," he yelled over the ever-increasing roar of voices.

She grabbed him again and pulled him up into a sitting position.

"What can you see," she demanded, her voice high-pitched—almost yelling.

He gazed for a moment, then suddenly slapped his hands to his face and hunched away.

"Fuck," he said in a small voice, like a child. "I thought they were wearing armour!"

"What?"

He didn't answer, just tried to crawl away from them.

"What, for fuck's sake?" she cried, hauling him back. "What can you see?"

He groaned. "They have belts—and some have tattered capes. But—but—I thought they wore armour. They were shining so. But they are naked. There's wire in their skin…"

He shook his head.

"There's fucking wire—in their—skin…"

"Wire?" she said. "Did you say wire?"

But that was all he would say. He just lay there in the sand, twitching, before opening his mouth in a quavering scream.

"They are coming," he moaned. "They are—"

They came like a great wave, breaking around the outermost of the white towers. They came—a seething mass of humanity, the sun blazing off the reinforcing wire woven into every inch of their bodies. And they came, attacking the great white towers with terrifying energy. They seethed round the bases of the first towers, trying to climb them, hacking and slashing at the white walls, screaming in mad rage.

All this he saw before the throng swept up to him and over him. He curled himself up into a ball, lost amid the raging feet—but he was not touched. And when he opened his eyes and gazed up—

It happened so fast and so—almost the only word for it was casually, that he hardly noticed it as strange until it had happened. Hardly noticed when the great white tower he was looking at suddenly bowed—stooped over—swooping the great whirling fans down—to return the attack. And when they ploughed into the attacking mass of bodies, the pandemonium was indescribable.

He just moaned while the woman shook at him with futility. He ignored her, or didn't even notice. All there was here was the image of the great turbines swooping like dancers as they thrashed their whirling heads back and fourth among the army—their gigantic fans cutting through skin and wire, not white any more but spraying and splashing red—red that was caught and flung far and wide by the violent and chaotic winds that howled across the scene, sucking or blowing people helplessly to their death—while the bedlam of shouting and screaming rose and rose in an impossible crescendo.

"You…" he murmured, as she shook him.

"Come on Don," the woman said anxiously. "Wake up!"

He let out a muffled moan and clutched at his head, where a huge pain flapped like wings. He squirmed on the ground, gouging up the sand, gouging up the tough moorland grass with his feet. She held his head in her arms, massaging his skin with her cold fingers and gazing down into his closed eyes.

Eventually the pain passed.

"What did you see?" she demanded, her face intense. "Wire? Sand?"

"The desert… " he groaned. "I think there is something wrong with my head. I hit it… when I crashed yesterday…"

She regarded him in silence.

"The grass turned to sand," he said. "A desert. An army came—their skins bound in wire. I mean it was actually woven in their skin—like some reinforcement…"

"Fuck," she murmured. She looked away, and he noticed that she was trembling slightly.

"You saw a desert?" she asked finally. He just gazed at her, shivering. "Come with me," she said at last. "Let's go somewhere out of this wind."

She pulled him to his feet and gently supported him back towards the thicket. He leant on her gratefully, feeling unexpectedly conscious of her body touching his. They pushed in amongst the stunted trees again and together they tramped through the woods.

The light was going now, the cold sunset fading towards a colder night. It was a few minutes' walk, with the trees getting larger and the ground getting rougher, and it had cleared his head a little by the time she led him quickly over a small crest and then stopped.

"Welcome," she said, smiling, "to my garden."

He stared down at the sight.

When he was young, he had seen the places where children played. As a matter of fact, he had seldom played there himself, but he had liked to walk there and he remembered it well. Pieces of wild land, forgotten by most people, and which the children had made their own.

This secret hollow place in this odd scrap of moorland wood reminded him of that.

"I have never had anyone else here before," she said casually as she stepped down the slope into the midst of it.

Large bushes and trees grew everywhere and among them could be seen any number of small spaces—hollows and chambers. At first glance it might have looked a wilderness—but upon examination, it began to reveal a sort of order about it. This was wilderness subtly altered by a human hand. Many of the plants he dimly recognised as herbs—he could see a sprawling mint and some tall comfrey plants, rosemary, marigold and camomile, even some onions. And others that he couldn't recognise. They all looked faded with the autumn, but many still had leaves or drying seed heads. Here, a large bank of stinging nettles had been gathered together into a kind of impromptu hedge, shielding something that may have been a path, and tall burdocks stood in the centre of a bare patch of soil tramped hard seemingly by much use.

He followed her down. There were hints of creativity here as well, he realised, which added the finishing touch to the atmosphere of the place. His eye caught strangely intricate patterns laid out with various mundane brick-a-brack—fragments of metal, wood or wire. Delicate things woven out of twigs or leaves—or even things formed of the earth itself. And over all hung the whispering of the turbines—an unending presence in the air.

All this he took in and he watched the woman with ever-increasing interest.

She made for a battered old armchair at the far side. By the chair was a large heap of what looked like electrical wiring, some of it stripped from its insulation and lying in shiny coppery and silver coils. Seeing that brought him a flash of memory and he shivered. She regarded him in the deepening twilight and flicked an old cigarette lighter.

"Fire?" she asked. "Are you cold?"

He hesitated, but she was already rummaging in the tangle beside the chair, hauling materials into the centre of the clearing. On a bed of torn newspapers and discarded pornographic magazines she spread out a heap of twigs, and on top of that she dumped some larger branches and pieces of firewood.

"I like fire," she said, coaxing a spark from the lighter and touching it to the paper. "It keeps me company. It is always so moving and alive." Water-smudged print and images of contorted sex curled up in flames. The wood spat and complained. Casually, she ripped a couple of branches off the nearby plants and tossed them onto the fire. He stared at them, watching the leaves curl up and die and tasting the pungent scent of rosemary that filled the air. There were muskier tones too that he couldn't identify, drifting in from the other herbs.

"They used to think that burning rosemary would drive away evil spirits," she said. "It certainly refreshes the brain."

He coughed. "Is this going to get me high or something?"

She smiled and remained silent. The armchair was almost rotted away, but she sat in it anyway, leaning back comfortably. He took the opportunity to look at her in the increasing orange glow, and to wonder again who she was—or what she was. Tramp? Traveller? Eccentric? Survivalist? Whatever she was, her presence seemed to draw him. There was something about both her and this place that was intriguing him deeply. It appealed to his artistic side—the sense of bizarre creativity and sheer comfortable ease in the air. He looked her up and down, then sat down by the fire with a sigh of contentment and appreciation that would have been hard to imagine just a few minutes before. She possessed a wild and ragged beauty that he couldn't help noticing, and in the glow she even looked less pale—indeed she even seemed to be flushing in the heat. Gently she stretched her muscles as though waking them from sleep. She seemed to be listening.

"I love the sound of them," she murmured dreamily. "Those windmills—they were my key. Listening to those voices—it was as if they were talking to me."

"What did you say?" he murmured.

"Sorry—I am talking in riddles. Are you feeling better?"

"Yes," he said uncertainly. "But I have no idea what is wrong with me, for me to see something like that? It was horrible..."

She leant forward, elbows on her knees. "What you saw..." she said, "I don't know what it was... but it was a vision of some kind. You should cherish it—and use it. You are an artist after all. Everything is inspiration. But what kind of artist are you?"

"I do—simple stuff," he murmured vaguely. "I used to be a landscape painter. Now I am not so sure. It is all feeling rather hollow at the moment."

"Why is that? Because you want something else?"

"Perhaps," he admitted softly.

"Then why not take something else? Is it because you are frightened?"

She was watching him intently and he felt a touch of the defensive—but she smiled and shook her head. "Look at this," she said, and she dragged up the front of her top to her chest, revealing the tattoo that sprawled there—at last revealing more than just hints of twining plants. In the firelight, it almost seemed to move as he stared at it.

"Oh bloody hell," he cried. "That's what I saw. It was your tattoo all along. I hallucinated your bloody tattoo. Even the plants were the same."

"I know," she said.

"You…?"

"But isn't it great? What an inspiration."

The tattoo seemed to be of a grotesque figure in armour, riding through a barren landscape—a landscape of sand and stone and those same curious twining plants. The knight looked weary and exhausted, as through long searching—a cartoon knight with a lance. He seemed to be riding towards something, but whatever it was, it was hidden by the folds of her top. The figure looked familiar and he wondered where he had seen it before.

"There's inspiration for you," she said. "Look at it. Then look at the skin underneath. Then look at the flesh underneath the skin." She grabbed the backs of his hands and drove them, nail first, into the skin under her rib cage. He flinched and froze in alarm at the unexpected contact. "Then look at that flesh being eaten or rotting away—fading away to nothing. Then look at what grows from that rotting—look at the new flesh."

His hands were still buried in her stomach and he stared at her body as though hypnotised. She woke him up with a slap of the hand. He felt her fingernails scratching viciously across his skin and he recoiled with a gasp, almost ready to jump away. But she caught his head before he could retreat and caressed his smarting cheek softly.

"Feel it," she said. "Your skin is glowing—hot. It is sensation. That means you are alive. You have to feel," she cried. "You have to feel everything—you have to celebrate everything—life, death—everything. It is all glorious. It is all a fucking miracle. Pain is a miracle. Pleasure is a miracle. Eating is a miracle. Shitting is a miracle." She stretched out with a languorous motion and grinned up at the sky.

"I love the world," she said. "All the great teeming mass of it—humans—animals—plants—little microscopic things. All of them thronging and eating each other and fucking each other and dying. It is all a struggle—it's all wild and red and stinking. It is all rubbing your face in the blood and the soil. And that—is fucking beautiful. And I know you will never be a great artist if you can't feel that—that… that amazing beauty of living in all its rawness."

The fire danced like a living thing. He just continued to gaze at her. He had never heard anyone talk quite like that before. They were words that felt like solid objects that bit into his flesh and left him feeling the world around him with an immediacy that pressed up against him like the heaviness of the great sea waves. He glanced round the clearing—and shivered. A shiver of cold and awe.

Then she sat back, her eyebrows raised—and she grinned.

"I have been wanting to say that stuff for such a long time. Don, you have to come back here."

He still stared at her. She laughed gently at the numb expression on his face, stood up and reached out to him.

"Come, let's go, before you fall asleep. You are looking at me like a dead man."

"Huh?"

"Come on—you should go home to bed. But come back soon, do you hear?"

He scrambled to his feet, flustered.

"Um—yes—I—uhh—"

"You will, won't you?" she demanded, almost a hint of anxiety in her voice that caught his attention.

Even in his tired state, he found himself wondering why.

"Yes," he murmured, almost automatically. "Yes, of course."

She grabbed his arm and he let her lead him back towards the fence. He stared down, and shivered again.

If there had been a scratch on her hand, it wasn't there now.

"And when you do come," she continued over her shoulder. "Will you bring me a needle?"

4

J: Yes—it was a windmill—a symbol of a wind turbine I mean. You know—the big three-bladed electricity-generating... things. But why? That is what I want to know.

Q: You tell me that he had been... interested... in the wind turbines out on the moor for quite a while—is that right?

J: Yes. I noticed the resemblance immediately. I knew he had somehow adopted them as a symbol—partly because of some drawings I had seen earlier—which featured the wind turbines. And... well. Some horrible... claptrap of his...

Q: Not just the wind turbines, was it?

J: No—it wasn't. That's when I began to see what he meant about his art having died...

This time he slammed the door. Slammed it, then leant against it heavily. His head was aching from the drive home and all he wanted was to fall into bed and relax. Relax and remember. However, there was a piece of paper waiting for him on the floor under the letterbox. He picked it up and read it, feeling his heart sink.

Hi Don,

I have been trying to find out what happened. I have been trying to call you ever since whatever it was yesterday. I thought you had crashed, the noises I heard. But I can find out nothing – and you are not here – and

But look – PLEASE give me a call if you get this. Just to let me know you are ok. NOTHING else matters – just call me. I am in agony here !!!

Please

Just want to know you are OK

Jacki

What was she doing leaving him notes like this? He was still bemused from his unexpected meeting on the moors and he had to remind himself that Jacki had not left his life years ago—that she had not really left his life at all, yet. He drew a deep breath, hauled himself into motion and stamped upstairs, heading for bed. Absently, he checked his phone, where he had left it lying on the bedside table, set to silent. It listed forty-eight missed calls, and he groaned. What to do? He knew he should call her, should try and be sensible—but right now it seemed beyond his willpower. His brain was buzzing. Right now he just wanted to curl up in bed and remember while the mood was still fresh. Remember sparkling brown eyes that gleamed with reflected fire as their owner talked and talked…

There was something in that voice and that face that sang in his heart even now. A voice that gleamed like a flickering and elusive wandering light in the dark woods that were his chaos and confusion. She had been incredibly beautiful, he thought. Her sharp-featured face and pale skin had struck him hard. It was a shock that you got from people only occasionally—that bolt of awareness that came in at the forehead and rocketed down to somewhere in the pit of the stomach without paying much attention to the conscious mind. It was hard to describe. More like a force than a thought—and more like a touch in the dark than a sight. It was not a particularly sexual or physical thing, more this vast and unignorable thereness that made a person shine out among the crowd like a beacon.

He shivered. He hadn't felt like this for years.

I love this world, he remembered. *All the great teeming mass of it—humans—animals—plants—little microscopic things. All of them thronging and eating each other and fucking each other and dying. All—red and wild and stinking… the blood and the soil…*

fucking beautiful.

As his eyes grew accustomed to the dark and the faint glow from the window began to illuminate the room around him, he became aware of a very unusual sensation.

He felt peaceful.

From 'Morning Texts'—p73

She wants me to bring her a needle.

A sewing needle, I mean. A big one. The biggest I can find. Not just a simple cotton-threader.

It all feels a bit unreal. What the hell happened yesterday?... no, scratch that. It all feels TOTALLY real. It was just such an unexpected meeting. Her name is Feather, she said. A nice name. Is *that* real? She didn't say much about herself—she didn't say ANYTHING about herself. I don't know where she comes from or what she was doing there. I have no way of contacting her. Surely she doesn't live in that garden of hers? No way is that possible. But when she asked me to come back, she just seemed to assume that she would be there. Am I supposed to just haunt the turbines on the off chance? Hmm.

Last night I felt like I hadn't felt for months. I felt so... happy, I guess. I am still trying to work out why. I suppose meeting her was just what I needed in my current state of stupid braindead confusion. I have been so isolated, these last few days, or weeks, or years—and it is sometimes hard to function in isolation. You start spiralling. I just wish I could have held onto that happiness though. Right now it all seems to be crowding around me more than ever and I don't know what to think. Some of the things she said scared me, but even so—I feel strangely excited by her. She is a striking woman, with her tough, ragged clothes and the hints of tattoos. And her talk about art was interesting, I have to admit. It is true—what she said about needing to be a part of it—to taste it personally rather than just dreaming things up on paper. I wish I could do that. I wish I had a philosophy myself that I could rely on. All her comments, perhaps intended to be inspiring, only make my art feel more inadequate—more dead. I really do feel as if I should just give up on it and move on to something else—as if nothing I do will ever be worth anything. And what point is there in struggling and forcing it?

As I left, that strange 'garden' of hers seemed to be shimmering under the whispering voices of the white giants—those wonderful voices that don't talk philosophy, just simple blankness.

I wonder if I will ever see her again.

He put his pen down and leant back, yawning hugely.

Morning.

Bright winter sky.

Waking up feeling as though his muscles had set like jelly and his brain was deadened and worthless.

He sat hunched over an espresso, dumped two heaped teaspoons of sugar into it and wailed aloud with exaggerated and at least somewhat self-aware drama, stretching the muscles of his face. He massaged his head gently, feeling the swelling there. The taut skin felt hot and sore and he winced.

What for breakfast? Other than sugar sludge from his espresso cup. He could do better than that. Pacing through to the kitchen, he found and opened a tin of tuna and began to eat it with a fork. Then he grabbed the half-full bottle of coffee liqueur and took a long mouthful, gasped and punched the wall as the liquid burned down his throat. He tried to remember last night. He had felt under a spell of some sort. Tired beyond belief but comfortable and strangely happy.

Where was that now?

On the way back to the armchair with the bottle in his hand, he looked in at his studio, still lying in ruins, and felt nothing but a violent hatred for the whole concept of creating things. Anything. It had reduced him to an emotional ruin and now it offered him nothing. For all that woman's talk by the fire last night, he felt no better for it. Her words haunted him, but with the clear light of day and the nagging hopelessness in his brain, he found himself wallowing in feelings of inadequacy instead of inspiration. Whatever philosophy he had or had once had concerning his art seemed meaningless. The beauty of nature tasted of nothing in his mouth—the simple joy of painting things seemed obscene.

He tramped back to the armchair and sat down, vaguely wondering if the memory of the woman's ragged arse crawling through the gap in the fence was worth a quick bit of self-pleasuring—then decided that he couldn't even be bothered with that.

"Feather," he breathed, leaning back in his chair.

There was a paper pad on his lap and a soft pencil in his hand.

"Feather," he muttered again, and slashed a few lines on the paper.

He found himself trying to remember her face—her sharp yet smiling face, her gleaming eyes and untidy hair. "Feather," he said for a third time, "you are a crazy lady, you know that." He paused in his drawing and stared at the wall. What was it she had said? You'll never be a great artist unless you can appreciate the beauty of life?

"I guess," he said, taking another drink from the bottle. "That is why I was a fucking landscape artist. Nobody appreciates beauty like a fucking landscape artist. The gentle hills—the sweet pretty… beauty of everything."

But the sentence hadn't been finished—and until you finished it, it was completely trite. The beauty of life—in all its rawness. That was what she had said.

"Well—I can appreciate that life stinks," he said. "That good enough for you?"

Was that really true?

He looked down at the page on his lap. The heavy black lines formed a violent arrow or wedge shape aiming at a cloud of random squiggles. He chuckled.

"To the right buyer—hmm… couple of thousand, do you think?" He screwed it up and slung it across the room. "Well—someone else can be rich—because I am through."

He paused. The words had slipped out almost without thinking. Was that true? Was he really through with this? Was there nothing that could be salvaged?

Another big swig almost drained the bottle and he hauled himself to his feet, feeling very dizzy by this point. That liqueur was strong stuff. He swayed and caught himself with a grunt.

"Bingo," he said. "That's just what I need right now. Instant drunk."

He stepped across the room, pausing to down another mouthful. "Yes, indeed," he said aloud. "Finished. Bring on the classifieds—hello dole queue—I am just another of the scum unemployed now. The vile scroungers. The art is dead. Hey, don't forget—the funeral is on—Wednesday." He reached the wall and leaned against it. "Dress code—green and blue. No black allowed. Black is forbidden in landscape painting."

He half deliberately kicked at a table and a lamp fell over with a clatter. He laughed.

"And—and… bright yellow top hats," he continued. "And don't cry. Why would you cry? I am glad it's dead. The useless toxic bastard deserved it."

He paused, looking at the wrecked canvas of the Jacki portrait.

"Oh fuck this," he said suddenly, a tear trickling down his cheek and a sudden wash of despair welling up. "Alright," he muttered. "Perhaps I am allowed to cry. This is a fucking tragedy." He gazed around helplessly, by now feeling completely drunk. It hadn't taken long with nothing more than a tin of tuna to soften the blow.

"Feather, you bitch," he groaned. "What were you trying to tell me? And who are you anyway?"

Feather the crackpot? The renegade hippie?

Lost soul?

Or did she actually have something in that head of hers? Her and her crazy tattoo.

"Maybe I should become a tattooist," he said aloud. "Can't be that bad a job if you get clients like Feather and art like that."

He smiled to himself. He had never really thought about tattooing before, but now that he did, it seemed quite a comfortably direct and solid thing to do. Nothing up in the air about it—just flesh and inks and fine imagery. That, he thought, was maybe what art should be. You didn't get much rawer than a needle in human flesh.

"The art is dead…" he whispered, over and over.

Returning to his original armchair.

"The king is dead… long live the king?"

The empty liqueur bottle smashed against the studio door.

The phone woke him from a half-sleep, though he could not remember switching it back to ringing mode. His head was still spinning, and his muscles were still wobbly—he answered it without even thinking.

"Hur?"

"Oh," came the voice, sounding shocked. "Don?… um—hi. I was giving up expecting you to answer."

"Oh," he murmured. "Jacki. Of course." He slumped down in the chair and stared at the ceiling, his brain slowly waking him up.

"Are you alright? Where have you been?"

He drew a deep breath.

"Aaah Feather—I have been rather—out of it," he said haltingly.

"Eh?"

"What?"

"What's that about a feather?"

He frowned. "Nothing, sorry," he said. "So tired…"

"You sound terrible. Did you really crash your car? I thought you were in hospital or something."

"No—sorry. I am just a bit drunk still. That's all."

"Don—"

"I got a bit carried away and finished up my coffee liqueur."

"Why?"

"I really don't know what to do, Jacki. I guess I just need to sit and think for a while. Until something makes sense."

"What about?" she asked, sounding scared.

"Just—what I am doing. My art—or not."

"Your art?"

"I think it is dead," he said.

"What is?"

"My art is," he cried, suddenly feeling cross. "I think I have to leave it behind. Give up. Finish. End. Annul. Abandon."

"Don," she murmured, "I'm not sure you can just stop."

He sighed and flopped over, trailing across the chair like a tired cat.

"I am just not sure if it is even worth living without it," he said, his voice a pained whisper. He looked at the ceiling. Why was he even bothering to try to explain? He couldn't explain it to himself, let alone her.

"Don," she said again. "Can I come over? Are you home?"

He signed again. "Please don't," he said softly. "I—"

He hesitated.

"I need to go out."

"Oh?" she said, sounding glum. "Don, you are angry at me, aren't you? I mean, you'd be within your rights to be after I hit you, but—"

"No," he said automatically.

"You are behaving very strangely. I don't like it."

"Nothing," he said. "Just feel drunk and uncertain."

"But—"

"I have to go," he said.

"Don," she cried. "You are in no state to drive. I hope you are not…"

"Jacki—I'll be fine. Speak soon."

"But—"

"Please Jacki," he said heavily. "Give me some space here."

There was a long silence.

"Ok," she whispered finally. "But please be careful Don."

"If that is what is needed, I will," he muttered and hung up.

He flopped out again, hauling his legs up and slinging them over one arm of the chair. This reminded him of the way Jackie had sat sometimes. It always amazed him the way she could fold herself up into spaces that felt as though they should be too small, sit on almost anything—probably scratch her ears with her feet if she wanted. She'd been like a cat.

Not that he was matching her, he mentally added. It was quickly becoming uncomfortable and he reluctantly hauled himself up into a more conventional position. "Maybe I am unfit to drive," he muttered. "But that basically fits the pattern. I am unfit for most things I think."

Feather, he thought. He was certainly unfit for her. That woman seemed almost able to think.

You should go home to bed. But come back soon, do you hear?

Why?

"Can't imagine," he muttered.

5

J: I know. I have told you so many times... We hadn't been getting on very well by that time. We had been—together—for just a few months, but he really seemed to be taking against me. I knew it—it upset me so much. We had fought—I punched him in the face actually. It was just a heat-of-the-moment thing. I just—lost my temper. My own drawing was suffering, not that he seemed to care by that point. Selfish bastard. And—not that my dreams were ever up to much. At first, he had been so inspiring. I would draw him and we would work together. He never really drew me though. We tried once. I think I was a bit nervous. He wanted me nude—I did, but I felt so uncomfortable, I don't think it worked very well...

The weather had changed. Now the air and the sky were crystal—winter crystal. It was still cold—colder than ever, if anything. But now the sun gazed down at him small and pale as he drove. And against the already low sun, the silhouettes of the towers as they approached were black and terrible.

It was cold enough to clear away the lingering remains of his drunkenness and, as he grabbed the camera, scrambled out of the car and started walking across the moors, he began to feel more awake than he had all day. He pushed through the gap in the security fence, wincing as the wire tore into his clothes. His breath fogged as he scrambled to his feet and looked around, then he stepped in further and scrambled up into her garden and looked around. It was deserted. Somehow the place looked different to what he had remembered. It looked more…

He sighed. It looked more ordinary. The paths were just trampled meanderings among the bushes—heavy feet that maybe did not even belong there. In the distance, a crow called harshly. The wind bent the branches and sent his hair flapping against his forehead. The armchair looked forlorn and sodden, slumped like a corpse below him. He stepped down to it, scuffing at the remains of the fire that was nothing more than sodden ashes and crumbling leaves, and sat down heavily, wincing at the contact of the damp material.

Maybe it had all been a hallucination—just as the desert sand and the attacking horde had been. The wire by his feet was just dumped by a lazy workman. The paths were just kids playing. The herbs were nothing more than strays—or the ghosts of an old garden long-since vanished.

And where was he in all this? What was he trying to do? He rested his head in his hands. There was more to this than just artist's block and depression. If he didn't sell a painting soon he would be in the red.

Painting? What painting?

They still lay in shattered ruin in his studio.

Maybe he could palm off the ruin as some cutting-edge conceptual work and make a fortune. Anything seemed possible with the right marketing.

He could throw his phone in as a free extra.

Or perhaps it really was time to give up on art and move on to something else.

The sun came slanting through the trees again as a stray cloud moved away, destination unknown. He blinked. There was beauty here, there was no denying it. The moors lay skeleton-cold and clean under the crystal sky—a bleakness that made the heart cry. There was a beauty here—but there was no magic. Not for him anyway. He wanted something more.

"Sitting here dreaming about changing the world?" a soft voice murmured.

Don jumped violently and looked round—then stared at her, feeling shock and astonishment and confusion well up.

She was naked—wasn't she? It took a split second for him to be sure, she was so heavily tattooed. But yes. Not a scrap of clothing anywhere. It was such a startling site that for a moment he felt he was hallucinating again. All he could see was tattooed skin. Tattooing that held his eyes more than the skin did. It stretched from head to foot—literally. He could not see a single portion of her that was not covered with sand or stones or twining leaves—even her face was tattooed, he now realised, though it was such fine and simple sand as to be barely visible. And the huge design on the front…

"Hey—er…" he said rising hastily and clumsily to his feet. He gazed at her feeling as though he had received an electric shock. His eyes sliding around her as though forbidden to rest on any one place for more than a second.

"Hi Don," she said with a crocked grin. "How do I look then?"

He was silent.

"Weren't you curious about this tattoo?"

"Well—yes—I suppose…"

Her grin broadened. "I'm sorry, are you startled?"

He made an effort to collect himself. The grin on her face alarmed him a little—as if she was playing with him, and he felt a wash of defensiveness.

"Well, a little," he said dryly. "Middle of November. Heading towards evening. Probably frost on the ground tonight… yes. How come you are not blue and shivering… and dead?"

She smiled.

"I don't feel the cold much. This is very invigorating. You should try it sometime. Good for the circulation."

"I'm not sure I'm up to that," he murmured. "This is not my idea of naked whether."

"I am not naked," she said softly, rubbing at her tattoo. "I haven't been naked for years." She sighed. "Back then I was scared of it—then, when I could no longer be naked ever again I actually started to miss it."

"You got the tattoo to… cover, then?" he asked uneasily, allowing his eyes to rest on the figures that stretched across her stomach and chest.

She pulled a face. "No—not really." She shrugged and

plucked a mint leaf and popped it into her mouth, then sat down heavily in the armchair that he had vacated. He stared at her, fidgeting with his camera, feeling very uneasy. This was so bizarre as to be unreal and he felt her electric presence prickling at his skin. Her wild, rough beauty carelessly tossed into the wrecked armchair felt like an image that would live with him for the rest of his life.

"Now I have to make do with what I have," she said, with a hint of sadness.

"Er—yes," he said.

"It was worth it though," she murmured, looking down at herself.

"How so?"

She smiled softly and shrugged the question away. "Keys—symbols," she said with a hint of vagueness. "It is old now. Years old. But it is such an important part of me." She stood up again and turned round, and around again, displaying the stretch of desert landscape and the figure in armour riding through it. "Does it look familiar to you at all? I mean, aside from yesterday."

He stared at it. In a desert landscape the figure in armour rode.

"Don Quixote," he said.

The figure carried a long lance—was tall and gaunt. And the knight was riding towards…

"You see?" she said. "The figure was me once. Still is in a way. He comes from a book I read—as you say, the crazy knight Don Quixote. Now the figure is you. You even have the same name."

"Me? What—"

"Eternally on a quest for something ultimate—but not

knowing even where to look. And certainly charging at the wrong things. What artist hasn't felt like that?"

"He is riding towards a giant windmill," he said softly.

She waved at the great tower visible beyond the trees. "It's this place," she said simply. "It became this place. I know that it looks like an old-fashioned flour mill with four sails—but it is here now. One day soon I will update it so that it is a real turbine. I like these turbines—I think they are fitting descendants. If only the mad knight hadn't gone to it as an attacker."

He remained silent, looking at her. The windmill was huge—covering her entire chest, the great sails rising high over her breasts and onto her shoulders. The knight advanced grim and determined—and very very tired. The windmill seemed to watch him.

Nervously, he fumbled in his camera case. "I, er, brought you a needle. I hope this is what you wanted?"

She reached out and took it from him, holding it up to the dappled sunlight. It gleamed a metal gleam. Then she took up an end of the wire by the chair and threaded it through the eye. It gleamed copper as well and she smiled a lovely smile.

"Perfect," she said. "Thank you. Just what I needed."

"What's it for?" he asked, feeling a curious feeling at the base of his stomach at the sight. A not very pleasant memory.

"Stuff," she said simply. "Later."

She stood up again and tucked the needle into the hair behind her ear. "Let's go out onto the open land," she said. "Let's go and meet the Giants again. I want to feel the wind."

"What? Like that?"

"Yes, like that," she snapped. "Why not?"

He wanted to list some reasons but, but didn't, feeling rather stupid. He watched her as they pushed through the bushes, and it seemed to him that she was naked in a way that Jacki hadn't been. There was nothing fragile-looking about her. She was no peeled apple. She looked more as though she had been dusted clean rather than peeled.

She had picked up a small gouge on the back of her shoulder, he noticed, and she was absently trying to brush at it. A smudge of blood stained her shoulder.

"You cut yourself," he said, stating the obvious.

"Yeah," she muttered, trying to rub it. "I can't reach it," she said. "Will you suck it clean for me?"

"Will I what?" he said. Everything here still felt too unreal for him to actually be surprised, but he felt a throb of mingled hot and cold somewhere inside the pit of his stomach.

"Please," she said, with a half-smile. "Saliva is the best antiseptic."

He stared at her. For a brief moment, he wondered if she was trying to seduce him. There was something strange in the atmosphere, but it didn't feel sexual. The thought of actually touching her scared him almost as much as it attracted him.

"Are you serious?" he asked, taking her shoulder reluctantly, feeling her skin cold and soft beneath his hand.

"Yes—don't worry, I am not suffering from anything."

He rubbed at the wound, rather tentative and uncertain.

"Please," she said again.

He shrugged and shook his head, his mind a big shrug. He grasped her firmly and leant in—licked it—then put his lips to the wound and sucked. Her smooth, cold skin seemed to glow with the contact. He could almost imagine a flash of light radiating outwards. Her flesh felt firm and prickled with the cold—indeed, she was shivering slightly in his grasp. He sucked at her, relishing the soft flesh, the hint of a bone beneath. The flavour of her blood filled his mouth as he cleaned her up quickly, spitting away into the leaves. Then he released her and stepped back.

"Blimy," he muttered. His stomach felt as though it was full of swirling water.

"Thanks," she mumbled, looking slightly embarrassed. "Shall we walk on?"

He nodded and they did so. He kept a few paces behind her, feeling rather uncomfortable himself as well. There had been something rather contrived about both that exchange and this whole evening that he didn't like. A game was being played somewhere, he was increasingly sure.

They walked in silence for a bit, eventually emerging from the scrub and onto the open moorland. The sunlight met them with a welcome hint of warmth and he paused for a moment, listening to the voices of the wind turbines. He felt a mixture of nervousness and excitement out here with her, and he glanced round sharply, scanning for unwanted company and feeling painfully afraid of being seen. The scrub was between them and the road, but the moorland was flat and wide and it all felt very exposed. He wasn't even the naked one but her painted body was vicariously terrifying him.

He gazed down at the coarse grass they were ploughing through—the heather, the stunted, dying gorse—and shook his head. "You're nuts," he muttered, brushing the prickles from his socks and trousers. Even with his clothes on, his calves could feel it.

"I have tough feet," she said.

There was a brief silence.

"I am glad I met you," she said abruptly. "I was getting quite alone here."

"But what are you doing here," he said, finally asking the question that had been pricking at his mind ever since yesterday. "Where do you live? Surely not here?"

"It might as well be." She sighed. "I have been here for—well, for quite a long time now. Let me just say that I came here to escape from people. Except that nobody really wants to do that. It just means you want to find the right sort of people for you and get away from the wrong ones. Also it was to find my key to unlock what I really wanted to do. This tattoo was the key that showed me the way here," she said. "I was also an artist, though a bit of a desperate and uncertain one. I tried all sorts of different things, but none of them felt right. I got this when I realised that I was not separate from the art I was trying to do—that the art and me were the same. That I was not just some sort of factory, producing things for people to look at—I was the thing itself. The subject, canvas and brushes all in one."

"But the windmills? What do they… ?"

"It is surreal—but yes." She shook her head and the set of her chin ended the subject as clearly as words could have.

She stood for a while staring into the sun, then sat down on a round lump of moorland turf.

"Don?" she asked at last. "Are you an artist?"

"No," he said immediately and rather gruffly.

She looked at him and smiled slowly. "Yesterday you said you were," she said.

"Yesterday I was confused," he said primly. "If I don't feel able to do it any more then why should I force it?"

"Why indeed," she murmured.

"The last time I tried, I felt physically ill," he added.

"Don," she said leaning in close with startling intimacy. "I think we need to do something about you."

"What," he snapped, leaning back. "What do you mean?"

"You spend your life doodling pretty pictures and you think you know what this is all about. And then you think you can just shrug it off? Come on, I wanted you to see this tattoo of mine," she said, lying down quickly. "Now take a proper look. Use the camera LCD. It makes a good magnifying glass."

"But why," he protested uneasily.

"Don't be bloody squeamish," she said. "I want you to see it up close. This tattoo is the important thing here. Even more important than the Giants. Now get your camera."

Feeling miserably confused, and without saying anything, he fumbled for it and slipped the strap round his neck. He leant in and peered through it at her sandy shoulder.

"Don," she said. "I got this tattoo to remind me of the mad knight's unending quest. It made me feel better—helped me get on and do things again. Maybe it can do the same to you."

Looking at her through the camera LCD was like looking at another planet through a space probe. The landscape of her desert skin rose and fell beneath him as he passed over—now close to—now backing off—hills and valleys—alternately blurring and focussing as the camera's auto-focus struggled to keep up. It was a desert of sand and leaves that was dizzyingly familiar, but now it was a desert imprinted on the rough-smooth texture of human skin. At this range, the sight was extraordinary, he had to admit it. Skin and sand merged into one, the hills and valleys of sand moving and alive. He could not help touching her, leaning on her, bracing the camera against her. Her skin felt very cold to the touch—as cold as the desert imprinted on her.

"Look closely at him," she said.

The figure of the riding knight came into view. It was somewhat distorted by age—but he could make out a face in profile, picked out on the rough texture of the skin. He stared at that face in shock. Tried to say something, but the words hardly formed themselves.

The face was familiar—familiar from a thousand mirrors. He just stared at it in dumb astonishment.

And then the figure of the knight dismounted from his horse and tramped onwards across the desert on foot—towards the great looming form of the windmill. Every step was weariness—the feeling of a long journey over at last.

Below his feet, the sand was soft and smooth—soft and as smooth as a beautiful woman, he thought.

Don looked up at the tower before him. It was vast. It didn't look quite like the wind turbine—nor like a traditional mill. The great arms looked soft and tentacle-like against the evening sky. The leathery leaves around him moved fractionally in the cold wind that blew across the sand. The armour also moved sluggishly—only it wasn't armour at all. He looked down at himself and found that he was sheathed in wire, like in an insect cocoon.

Suddenly he was in shadow. The huge form of the windmill had blotted out the sun. Had it moved? Had it been looking at him like that before?

Why was it looking at him?

The pain in his head throbbed suddenly. The tower looked grim and oppressive. In it, he seemed to see himself—everything that was him. Everything that had been squashed out of existence. Memories came crowding in—soft and brittle like the flesh of a half-ripe peach. A child stooped through the long grass and lifted a fallen *For Sale* sign, the letters almost obliterated. Things fled from the sudden sunlight. A slowworm looked at him steadily. A pen writing on the wall—school. Driving a car—the hot sunlight passing by like rain. A woman getting a fit of laughter, then wiping, embarrassed, at her running nose. Reading alone in bed. Painting a picture—his hand shaking but unable to stop. Staring through the shocking verticals of a closed gate. The sky lit by a shining white glory—a pure white rainbow, spanning the low rolling hills. Children behind the prison perimeter of a school playground. A figure with blond hair, seen from behind. Walking away. A hawk moth at a flower, a barely visible moving blur. Waking up in the morning, crying and leaden, nothing to draw you out of bed. The full moon. Sitting exhausted at his easel surrounded by papers.

He dropped to his knees in the sand. Every part of his body was filled with the pain of exhaustion—his bones ached—his muscles barely moved anymore. He looked behind him—at the desert stretching off into infinity. The sense of distance travelled was overwhelming. All his life he had been travelling. All his life. And what had he been striving towards?

He looked back at the tower in front of him.

Slowly, the blades of the turbine began to turn.

Was this it? The thing that he had been looking for—that he had sacrificed his life to?

"It feels like that, doesn't it." It was Feather—by his side. "It is a bit of a parasite. You follow it. You think you can control it and use it—but it controls you. It makes you its slave and eats you like an artichoke. And as it grows, it consumes you until you are just an empty husk. If it survives, it will live on—but it will kill you to do it."

He gazed up at the tower.

"What do you think art is?" she asked. "Some kind of thing you do because it makes you feel good? A natural function? Because you want to try and—and say something to the world?"

The memories still held him. In this dream, it made perfect sense that this was his destination standing before him. What was Feather trying to prove? All this just made him feel angrier. In the past, faces looked at him, then passed on. Only one thing remained constant. "You bastard," he muttered. "You fucking bastard." He gazed at it.

"It's good to embrace it," Feather said.

"Embrace it?" he cried. "All my art is smashed to fragments now. I don't even have that left. So why should I embrace this?"

"You have no choice, Don."

"Wrong," he muttered, pulling himself to his feet. He stood panting. "I choose—" he coughed and spat out a bloody, sandy mouthful. "I choose! I followed—and I found that what I had followed for so long was an enemy. So I can choose what to do here without any doubt."

"Don—"

"Nothing," he cried, watching the blades turn faster. He felt angry now—the earlier sadness transmuting with ease into rage. He grabbed his sword, the handle of which was also bound in copper wire, and began to tramp forward again.

"I am going to destroy you," he said softly to it, "then I am going to leave. Go back."

The sand seemed even softer now, as though trying to stop him, but he tramped on steadily, following the long slender shadow cast by the tower, which now stretched to his destination like a road.

"Don," Feather called after him, her voice tight with dismay and anxiety. "Please don't."

"Feather, I have to," he said. "I am finished with art—and with playing games. Finished with everything."

"But Don—"

She didn't have time to finish though before, in an impossible gesture, the tower leant down gracefully to him and grabbed him neatly in its three arms like some vast sea creature seizing its prey.

Don tried to scream, but could find no air to. The suddenness and ease of the attack left him shocked to stupidity. He found himself enclosed. The pressure was terrible, but not lethal as he found himself spun upside down, vertigo spinning his brain, and then swallowed. He could think of no better word for it. The pressure flung him downwards headfirst, dropping him into a tube that opened up for him. The tube was red and vaguely organic and he slid down and down, layer after layer of it opening up like curtains of flesh.

And then, in the same way that, in dreams, perspective can be both inside and outside—in the first and the third person at the same time—he realised that it was not just the tower he was inside. This was too organic. Feather? He could hear her voice coming muffled through the surrounding flesh. "Don?" she called. "You madman. Don't try and fight me."

Down and down he flopped. His sword and wire armour had vanished so all he could do was thrash and kick and clutch at the soft surrounds. It really was as though he was travelling deep through her digestive tract—like a soft fleshy waterslide. Drenched with bitter-tasting slime, he allowed himself to be carried onwards.

"Let me go," he screamed, as loudly as he could.

"Don," the voice came again—huge and muffled—like the voice of the earth would be. "Don," she said. "You are a coward."

He stared wildly at nothing. "No," he cried. "No… I—"

"You have no choice in this. There is never any choice—not for any little decision that you make. When you realise that, you will be able to stop fighting. You will never have to fight again."

He shook his head, but could not speak.

"The only choice you have is whether to make the wrong decision," she continued. "And who the fuck wants that?"

The rippling sides pushed him onwards till he ran into a closure that hugged him tight. Like some kind of arsehole, he found himself squeezed through into the open in a moment of agonising suffocation. It was an atrocious sensation—the stomach-plunging feeling of a nightmare. Water—depth—his body swelling and flopping like a leech—his mother's eyes…

Grass hit him in the face—a hundred needles violating his tearstained skin. Somewhere in all this was an unspeakable tragedy. Something so vast it was like a waterfall—an ocean. He felt like a small creature—a tadpole or an insect—washed away—flushed down the toilet. No breath—air—he opened his mouth, coughed wildly—then howled like a baby and lurched back.

Grass—moorland—anxious eyes watching him. He felt her hands cupping his face—then a fluid trickled into his mouth and he coughed again. Acrid flavour—very familiar flavour.

Eyes full of pain and intensity.

"Drink, and don't fight me," she said in a tone of voice that boded no disobeying.

She pulled away nursing her wrist, from which a trickle of blood flowed. He stared at her. Blood—the taste of blood… and as he watched the trickle faded away like a time-lapse movie of a dying spring.

He slowly surfaced. Feather was leaning over him looking concerned. He couldn't have been out long, but it felt as though he had been asleep for several days and he tried to force himself clear of the great clouds of fog that filled his brain. "Feather," he whispered—half a question, half simply an acknowledgement of her presence there, as a child might point at something and name it. Slowly he raised his hand to his mouth, and even that was an effort. He rubbed his lips, then stared at the result with a queasy alarm trying to pierce through the swirling tiredness. His wrist was stained red. What did that mean?

He swallowed. "What the fuck happened?" he begged, a groan in his voice.

"It's ok," she whispered.

He pulled himself up into a sitting position—almost collapsed, but held himself there, staring at her.

"What did you do?" he said. He looked at her, his head spinning. A fear was beginning to creep through the bewilderment as memories returned. He stared at Feather with huge eyes—and she hung her head slightly and didn't meet them. He hauled himself heavily across to her, she watching his progress with an expressionlessness that nevertheless seemed slightly sad. He grabbed at her arm. She made no effort to pull away as he hauled her to him, just meekly allowed him to feel her flesh as he clutched at her arms, her legs, her side with a bloom of panic increasing inside him. Wherever his hands went, she was as cold as ice. "What the fuck is wrong with you?" he cried, rocking back on his heels and letting her sit back. His head was aching—a throbbing pain that bulged like a pillow inside his skull. His face was slimed with sweat.

"Don," she murmured softly. "Take it easy. It's ok. You are just suffering the after-effects of your crash. You hit your head, remember?" The tone of her voice was complex though—as though somewhere within it, she was apologising for the inevitable. She reached out, her hands finding his temples and she massaged gently.

He sobbed once. "Is that really all it is?" he asked. "Why are you so cold?"

"In this weather?" she asked with a wry smile. "Come here," she murmured, taking him in her arms and holding him close. "There," she said. "I am not so cold am I?"

He stared over her shoulder. She did seem warmer now—nice. It was nice. Nice to feel her there. Her skin—her sandy skin…

He felt himself relaxing a bit and hugged her in return. His hand encountered a touch of wetness and he pulled back and looked down. "You are bleeding," he muttered. "What's wrong?"

"It's nothing," she said in his ear, pulling him close again and holding her wrist away from his clothes.

She held him tightly just long enough for him to recover a bit, then she pulled away.

"Feeling better?" she asked. "You looked in quite a state."

"Yes," he said. "Thank you."

She lay down comfortably by his side.

"Why did you fight it?" she asked at last.

"Sorry?"

"I know what you were thinking," she said. "I could see it in your eyes. Nothing but anger and aggression. Is art really such a rotten business? I know it demands a sacrifice, and a high one—but isn't it worth it? Don, you are an artist—so you must embrace this parasite, right?"

"I—I don't know."

"Please don't try and tell me nonsense. It's not something you can escape from."

"Why not?" he asked, suddenly cross. "It has dragged me through the ditch backwards. Just why the hell should I embrace it?"

"You know that, though," she said.

"I don't understand you."

She sighed, and he was startled to see that her lips were trembling slightly. "It always feels to me like a living thing in its own right. Beyond all the moralist preaching and political activation and whatever dress we choose to put on it—it is still this same basic creature that comes from the same basic place. People dress it up in all sorts of different clothes—but it is still the same basic, stinking being. A creature that reeks more of shit and blood than of flowers—and cackles like a serial killer rather than sings pretty songs. Something totally elemental and raw. It's like trying to dress up a stinking, dribbling animal for a polite tea party." She chuckled. "Just like human beings really. Sometimes it even works, in a poor light."

"Then why do you do it?" he asked, feeling as though he was drifting hazily through a rather stormy sea of words.

"Aaah," she said. "That's the million-dollar question. Answering that wins you the cigar and a shag in a four-poster bed." She sat up. "Maybe that rawness is the most beautiful thing of all. Maybe that rawness makes you feel hot and dirty and alive. Because it feels real. Don't you think so?"

"Mmm," he said doubtfully. He stared at her. These were somewhat new thoughts to him. Sacrifice? Rawness? He hardly knew what to think on the conscious level, but somewhere at the back of his mind there was a barely acknowledged excitement building up in response to these words. He was aware of it, but as yet didn't know how to react to it.

"Don," she said. "There is so much that people can do. Please don't give up." She scrambled over to him. "Come on," she said. "Admit it to me. Tell me that you are an artist. That you always were and always will be. I don't think you would even be here if you weren't."

He looked up at her. Between her fingers, the needle gleamed in the evening sun.

6

J: We had a second fight. I told him I would kill him if he—if he... *[Brief Pause]*. I was desperate. But what I saw in his studio, it rather turned my head. He had smashed everything—it was in ruins—total ruins. And the images on the floor—they finally brought it all home to me. Surely you can see that? When I saw that, saw what he'd done, I finally realised what he meant when he said that his art was dead. His art had—had gone mad. It had degenerated into something base and degraded.

Q: Yes—I have copies of the images in question here. But can you tell me more?

J: *[Brief pause]*. I can't remember all of it. I am sure someone heard me—I was screaming a bit. He was completely mad but no one would have heard him—he was speaking so low I could hardly hear him myself. But his voice was as cold as ice. He tried to get me to leave—that's when I screamed at him that I would kill him. I was so angry and terrified. He never laid a finger on me—but I thought he was completely insane.

"Don," Jacki said shakily.

She rose to her feet from the darkness of the porch.

"I had to see how you were… what the fuck…?" she gasped, her eyes widening.

Don sagged against the wall of his house and gazed at her glassily. Who the hell was this person? For a moment, he really wasn't sure.

She grabbed at him, and he flinched away—it all hurt too much to be touched. She held on tight to his bloodsoaked clothes, however. "Don," she cried. "For fuck's sake—what happened?"

"Sorry," he mumbled. "I've, to get in—clean myself up."

It was a quiet street in a quiet town on a quiet night—but even so… across the other side, a woman was staring at them from her garden. A car passed—and slowed. It shouldn't matter—didn't matter. But even so, he fumbled for his key feeling a nervousness that annoyed him.

He was soaked with blood. His shirt front was a sodden rag and it had soaked down into his trousers. He rocked on his feet, the key following a wandering path in his fingers. She grabbed it from him, flung the door open and dragged him inside and into the studio—only to gaze round in even more shock at the devastation.

"Please don't come in," he whispered, aware that it was rather too late for that.

"What?" Jacki almost snarled.

"Please—not now. I must—I must…"

He stopped, giving up, staring vaguely at the wall.

"Don, stop being so fucking stupid. I am going to call an ambulance."

"No," he yelled, suddenly sharp. There was nothing but panic at that thought. She was producing her phone, but he grabbed it from her and flung it away, hearing it clatter. "Don't you—do that. No ambulance… I will be alright in a moment."

"But what happened?" she cried. "Did you have an accident? And your paintings? For god's sake don't be like this."

She reached for his shirt again, but he slapped her hand away and sat down heavily on the sofa as she watched with frantic silence. And it was then that she noticed the drawings.

"And what the fuck is this?" she cried, her voice rising in shock. She grabbed up one of the pieces of paper and gazed at the three-pronged shape—and the figure on it.

"Oh forget that," he said impatiently.

"But—that's me," she said. "How can you…? I mean… what did you do that for?"

He sighed.

"Why don't you just go?" he asked wearily. "I'm sorry, I know I'm not being much use at communicating all this but…"

"Huh?"

"I don't want you here anymore—can't you see that? Right now I just need to sleep."

She stood frozen. "Have you gone out of your mind?"

He looked up at her. "No," he said, and her face fell even further. That was a good answer, he thought. Just the one tiny word, but it encapsulated everything. *No.*

"No?" she murmured. "But—what's going on?"

"Please just let me sleep. I should have phoned you sooner, I'm sorry. I should have talked to you. But I couldn't. It's—whatever. It's over… it's—its—whatever you say at times like this."

"What's over?"

This really isn't good art, he thought. "Us."

"Are you serious?" she whispered. "What the hell has happened to you?"

"I just realised a few things, that's all. It's not your fault. I just..."

With a shrug, he opened his shirt. There was a flash of metal in the low light and Jackie flinched.

"Oh fuck..."

Spread across his chest, the three-pronged design of the wind turbine was marked in the surface layers of his skin, woven in dense stitching of copper wire.

"She gave me this. It doesn't mean much really though, it is all just a symbol. But still—it's an interesting start."

"She, who?"

"A needle in human flesh," he said, tracing the weave with his finger. "How much more raw can you get?"

He stood up, spreading his arms, enjoying the gleam of copper, albeit somewhat occluded by blood.

"Come and touch it, if you want. It's very real." He beckoned her closer, but she backed away, so he grabbed her hands and pressed them to his chest. He felt them squirm there like captured moths, fluttering in a feeble and ultimately meaningless attempt to escape.

"Please—stop it..."

All anger has left her voice now.

"Don't you like it?" he asked, still gripping her tight. "Well—perhaps not. It isn't much. Nothing very profound. But then—wasn't this what you were always afraid of? Blood? Flesh? What is underneath all the layers people clothe things in? Humanity seems to have spent its entire history trying to escape from that—trying to put clothes on things. And now look where we have ended up." He drew a deep breath. "No wonder I couldn't paint—and no wonder you couldn't help me to." Blood smeared her wrists and she again struggled to pull away—and he finally released her. "But yeah, this is nothing—just a doodle. We haven't even started properly. Let me show you something a bit more substantial."

He took out his camera and stepped to the laptop, open and humming on his desk. A quick fumble with a wire and it was connected and small thumbnail images appeared on the screen. He called one up large and stepped back, looking at her expectantly.

"Oh my god," she cried in a grating voice. "What the hell have you done? That just—isn't possible…"

The image of the winged woman glowed softly. She stood against the setting sun, barely more than a black silhouette, her cobwebby wings spread wide and glimmering softly. The wings were great weavings of copper wire running from the flesh of her arms down to the puckered skin of her hips. They looked like harp strings—held taut by her posture—each string plucking a small peak of flesh, giving her long rows and crowns of surreal thorns. Further wires threaded through the harp strings, creating radiating shapes, twisting patterns—an ornate cape built into her own body, a triangular wingsuit, a sugar glider's membrane, a visceral catwalk display. Her head was thrown back, her untidy hair glinting in the sun that silhouetted her. Jacki stared at it, but to his faint dismay, he could read nothing but horror in her face, even though no blood stained the figure. The woman was just clean white painted skin and copper but Jacki looked as though he had shown her a mangled corpse.

He sighed and clicked onwards through the images. They were harp strings indeed, as well as wings. As the images progressed, he crouched alongside her, his hands floating over them, stretching them into new shapes while she posed, an excided gleam in her eyes, the slightest movement altering her stretched skin.

"That's just not possible," she murmured again.

"Everything's possible," he muttered. "You can't give up. She was right. This," he patted his chest, "hurt like hell. It was an—an extreme thing to do—not very healthy under the circumstances. But it did serve as a reminder. It brought me back down to Earth and reminded me where this thing we do is really situated. Finally. Now please—I really need to sleep."

She flinched. "You're mad," she said. "You are fucking mad. And whoever that is, so is she." She looked from him to the computer screen to the sketches on the floor and back to him again, and then suddenly it exploded out of her. "You throw me out and I will fucking kill you," she screamed at him, staggering away across the room.

"Just leave me alone." By contrast, Don was quiet. "If I'm mad… I dunno, maybe I am. Maybe I had to become that to finally find a little hint of sanity in this mess."

She pulled herself up.

"Yes—I will go," she said. "I am going—and I will get a fucking ambulance—" her voice was rising "—and I will get you fucking put away for this," she sobbed. "Put away till you come to your senses."

She backed away, kicking at the drawings on the floor, turning her face away. She stumbled out of the studio, shutting the door with a bang and he glanced at the window. He was dimly aware of faces waiting outside. Astonished faces. Three of them now. And he hoped that wouldn't lead to trouble. They watched Jackie leave, presumably taking in the small bloodstains that now marked her shirt and hands. For a moment she stood still—then she walked quickly down the path and down the dark road.

The moment she had slammed first the studio door and then, fainter, the front door, uncertainty dawned in his face and he relaxed, dropping into the sofa again. His head sagged towards his knees, his chin pressing into the bloodsoaked material of his shirt. His eyes closed and his mouth turned down in a despairing grimace as he stared round the room at the devastation—at the shattered remains of pictures and sketches. He shook his head, his lips drawing back from his teeth.

"What am I doing?" he cried.

Two names sat in his head now. Two huge neon signs. He gazed at them feeling so torn in two that it might as well have been the rending of flesh and muscle.

He had kicked Jacki out almost without thinking. Was this his instinct in control? Was this what he truly wanted? He stared at the slammed door feeling a wash of bitter yearning.

Come back Jacki, he though. *I'm sorry—I don't want to hurt you…*

Bit late for that, isn't it?

Before Jacki had arrived on the scene, he had spent many years alone. He remembered that all too well. He remembered the days when even losing himself in painting couldn't quite calm the vast expanse of loneliness. That was a dangerous force. It was a force that could drive you to a rage of hatred or pining to fuck someone simply for the sake of it. Anything—just to prove the one thing that could never be proven… that you weren't alone.

Desperation—desperation…

Eventually he had shut his heart away somewhere deep and sealed, reluctant to think about such things too much, transforming into a coward. That was the default. It was easier not to think. And now, when there was no choice but to think and ask himself once and for all what he wanted, it was hard for his brain to wake up again. He felt agonisingly confused.

Into his mind there stole a vivid recollection of how it had felt when Jacki had first appeared—the tremendous sense of gratitude he had felt to her. Gratitude for being there—gratitude for… loving him.

But then—what did all this make her? Was all he had experienced with her nothing more than a desperation fuck? He screwed up his face at the thought. Maybe that was the problem. Maybe it had been doomed from the start. Maybe any human relationship was. And if that was true then she was better off out of it.

Why not?

But Feather on the other hand…

Feather.

He tried to remember her face—strangely difficult now. Nor could he completely visualise her body. It was hard to see it under the art that adorned it. It was that and the way she carried it that lingered. The animal-like comfort and carelessness. It was her concept that haunted him. The simple fact that she existed. But who was she? What did she want from him? There was a lot about her that didn't quite make sense. How had she been able to stand the pain of those wings she had had him sew into her? And he was sure that he hadn't imagined the scratches on her skin that were there but totally vanished a few minutes later.

Even now, the thought of her brought a throb of excitement. A stirring in the pit of his stomach and in the deeper places in his brain. Even the mystery titillated him—a feeling that this was something he had always wanted to find. Beyond any revolting desperation for human interaction, wasn't this a fundamental desire? For someone with this kind of strength and power and… wildness? Someone who… understood. Or at least understood certain things that felt important. No one else understood. Not himself, not Jacki, not anyone. He could sense at a deep level that Feather was someone who could show him things—really and truly. That was what stirred him to the depths. Her beauty, her careless attractiveness, was just a gloss on the surface and, below that, the rabbit hole descended deep and dark—further than the mind could plumb or the sound of a dropped stone could reverberate. Down at the bottom of that hole, there was a truth. A truth profound and uncompromising. And he wanted it. Or at least a glimpse of it. Even if that profundity was something he could never embrace. He clenched his hands. He wanted it so much.

Human beings were creatures built on compromise. He was slowly beginning to grasp that—perhaps slower than he should have. Everything they did was built up around their ability to lie to themselves, to pretend things were other than they were. To assign importance and aesthetic values to things based on little more than the arbitrary. But why? And, how to escape? Feather's words rang in his mind. Beauty in all its rawness. Blood and shit and soil—life and death—eating—dying—the taste of flesh between the lips. The crisp flavour of lettuce. The blood flowing into his mouth from the wound between her shoulderblades. The spider snaring its prey. The seed germinating. The scream of pain under your hands…

He brushed at his chest, plucking at the stiffening shirt fabric.

A needle in human flesh. How much more raw could you get?

"Feather" he whispered out loud, almost gloating over the word—clasping his hands across his stomach and squeezing himself tightly. He held himself for a minute then rose to his feet, reeling heavily from dizziness and reaching for his journal.

From: 'Morning Texts'—p77

Ok—this isn't morning, so I am deviating from my usual routine... so sue me!!! I am afraid that time is running out I wish she hadn't come I don't need ambulance I am fine—it hurts but it will get better. The bleeding is already stopping as I rub ointment into it

Why was Jacki so shocked? Feather told me she liked my blood. It was a sign that I was alive. It hurt a lot when she was doing it—she sat astride me still naked I remember lying in the grass in the sand whimpering and groaning. I felt like a sick man must have felt long ago as the surgeon got to work—crude tools no anaesthetic—just life-giving cutting of flesh—I think I had an erection—I remember it bumping against her arse then afterwards I remember her hugging me she called me her brave knight, though I am sure she was mocking a little. Of course she was. And I laughed. I remember that her body was once again cold not as ice but strangely cool. I wonder what she is? I might almost start to believe she was a ghost if she wasn't so solid and alive. And the place this world of sand and strange plants, the cold desert—the world of her tattoo. What hallucinations are these? Am I really Don Quixote? Somehow making my assault on the windmill stronghold. Perhaps I was wrong when I attacked it earlier—or whatever I did perhaps I am really trying to somehow get into that world myself. She said that the tattoo was a key—first for her... now for me?

I feel dizzy I think I have lost a bit of blood. I will be fine now it is almost stopped but I really want to lie down and rest for a bit—but I cannot can I? I fear that every moment Jacki will be back with her ambulance and I cannot let them take me anywhere. I will have to go back to the moors now tonight in the dark and get away until it is safe to come back here. I will take this notebook with me so I can write more if needed. Must just find the knife she wanted.

There are people outside looking in I think Jacki sent them I have to go I have to go back to feather

7

J: I was covered in blood—but he put that there. It was his. From that fucking thing on his chest. The windmill symbol again. I ran off because I couldn't bear to be in there any longer. I had lost him. I knew it. I had lost him completely. I was so... upset I couldn't even see straight. I just couldn't believe what had happened.

Q: And did you want revenge at all?

J: No—no—I am sure of it. I just wanted him back. I wanted him to stop those terrible things he was doing and come back to me. I meant to call an ambulance but my phone was left behind where he threw it. I had to run home. But then I just started thinking that perhaps I should just let him stew and if he fainted it would teach him a lesson. I still though he was reasonably in control of things and not very badly hurt. So I just shut myself in my room and cried for a while. It wasn't until later that night, after I had been agonising around and trying to phone him that I jumped in my car and drove back again. But he had vanished. His house was dark—the car wasn't there. So of course I followed him.

Q: How did you know where he would be?

J: I didn't—but it was the only thing I could think of. He had showed me that picture of the—the woman with the wire—and the wind farm in the background. That and the windmill design on his chest—well—it was just the only thing I could think of.

Q: And so you followed him there?

J: Yes—I found his car straight away. There's only the one layby. But I had no idea where he was. I just looked around. I couldn't find him at all. I just looked and looked. I felt as though I was in a dream—my head spinning. I would have just given up and gone home—

Q: And did you find him?

J: *[brief pause]* Maybe it did mean something.

Q: What?

J: That—symbol. The windmill triangle. It must have meant something to him. Even he couldn't have abandoned that. But what was it? I wish I knew. Perhaps you could never know what it was. Which surely still means that it failed? Did his last artwork fail?

Q: I repeat—did you find him?

J: Yes—how many times do I have to tell you that. I followed the fence, just in case. I guess it was the only physical line there was to follow. Found a hole. Went through. He was there—so was she, that—that freakish—person. And he was... he was...

They were in her garden now.

In the dark, lying on his back, stripped naked, with the cold November air floating over his skin against the glow of the fire, he was feeling better. The haze of faintness had faded now and his head felt clear. The fire of damp wood and newspaper filled one side of his world with a warm, comforting, moving light and the air stung with the faint tang of burning herbs. She lay up against him on the other, also naked, her chill body shielding him from the outside cold. Unnaturally cold or not, her touch glowed with prickling electricity and he felt content to just lie in that bifurcated universe, savouring the sensations, the presence, the life. In a very primitive way, it was as beautiful a thing as he had ever experienced to curl up here together, bodies against the dark, skin against skin.

In spite of that, however, he could feel a tension in her that he had not noticed before. He could feel her hunched up against him like a taut wire. She even seemed to be trembling ever so slightly.

"Don," she whispered at last.

"Mm?"

"It's a beautiful night. Fire in winter."

"Yes," he said.

After a long period, she rolled over and sat up—a separation of skin against skin. She sat up tall and flickering white against the trees and regarded him, a faint gleam of eyes in the firelight. He watched her back, content to study her with no particular need or agenda. The scars on her arms and hips from the wire wings had almost vanished, just as no wound seemed to linger long on her skin. But she had been doing other things to herself since they had parted. She had indeed been working on the tattooed windmill. It was now picked out in a wire design of three elegant arms like his—three superimposed on four—while an intricate triangular design on her stomach surrounded the figure of the weary knight like a frame. She sat there like a phantasm of skin and flesh and wire.

"Have you the knife I asked for?" she said.

"Yes," he said, reaching for his clothes and bag. He produced a small, long-bladed kitchen knife—serrated and sharp—and handed it to her. She took it and lay down again on her back, again forming that bifurcated universe of fire and skin.

"Yes, this is good," she murmured. "So now…" She squirmed over onto her side and moulded herself to him again, trailing the metal against her skin. "So…"

"What is it?"

"Are you any clearer what you want?" she asked. "I know where you started—and now I am wondering if you really do want to be an explorer?"

"Explorer?"

"Take a few more steps along the road of… of just how deep experience can go."

He shrugged, feeling a prickle at the words and watching her with interest. Her body was pressed up against him, but she wasn't meeting his eyes.

"Nothing I have found so far has ever made me feel as though I had really found anything at all," he said. "Maybe I was supposed to make rather than find. But obviously I didn't. And now… well…"

"Then perhaps," she murmured nervously, shifting and staring into the fire, "Perhaps…"

"What?"

"Perhaps we could make something," she murmured. "If you like, you could join me and… and be like me."

"You mean—join you out here at the windmills?"

She turned and stared at the towers, just visible through the small trees.

"I mean… well, if you like, yes. But I mean, I mean, I suppose… you can be like me. We don't need the windmills. They are just a symbol and you don't *really* need symbols. And if you were like me, then there would be no limit to anything. Together we could leave… go and sink into the city again—go where we please."

Don stared at her in the firelight. Her trembling had increased as she talked and her restless fingers played with the blade, trailing it against her skin. A small smile on her face that was almost shy, like a confused teenager asking if he would like to go on a date.

"But what about… well, everything?" he murmured. "What does *be like you* even mean?"

Even without an answer, there was an appeal to it, of course. Wasn't that what had been lurking in the back of his mind for a while now?

She smiled. "It's up to you. You seem ripe for a change—and I can give you that. I know you have been watching my wounds healing and my cold skin—but I don't think you know yet how far it can go. How far we can control ourselves."

The blade of the chef's knife slipped neatly into the skin of her stomach. It was such a simple movement that Don barely registered it for a moment—so little drama or reaction—but then he gasped in alarm and made to sit up. She just smiled, however, a smile that was trying to be reassuring. She reinserted the knife sideways, just under her skin, and slid it carefully upwards, right underneath the tattoo of the knight, using the woven wire frame as a guide. He just stared in disbelief as the knife emerged and the whole figure of the knight flopped loose. A few more cuts and it came away completely and she lifted it up and regarded it. On her stomach, a rough triangle of red meat had been left behind.

"It's up to you," she repeated.

Because no blood flowed.

"Look," she said, running her fingers across the red. They came away lightly smeared and she held them up to him. "We do not have to be slaves to our bodies—we can take complete control and nothing matters any more. Now look again."

Her face set in concentration for a moment, her eyes closing, her hands clasped across her stomach. Then, with shocking suddenness, there was a gush of red. Don drew in breath, watching as the blood flowed through her fingers in generous streams. She gave a huge trembling sigh and gazed at him, her face twisted with a sudden and very vivid pain. Even earlier as he had woven her wings, she hadn't shown any pain at all, and the sight sent a shock through him.

"And one last thing," she gasped, flopping onto her back and drawing her whole body tense and as taut as a violin string. Her hands clawed at the soil—her head twitched from side to side—and from her lips came a grating howl of intensity. He stared at her in terror, unsure whether to try to help her somehow or run away. But before he could do either, she screamed sharply, heaved against the ground—and the flow of blood suddenly increased dramatically. Spurts of it jetted out of her in various directions, some of them travelling over a metre. It settled on Don like rain and he cried out as he tried to shield himself.

But after only a moment it was over. She slumped down, drawing in huge gasps of air.

"Damn," she muttered, exhausted and trembling. "I really shouldn't do that. But I wanted to to show you…"

"We?" he asked, numb with shock.

"Yes," she said, sitting up heavily. "If you want. If you choose. It is simply a choice between one life and another."

He gazed at her, feeling numb, his head spinning, unsure how to even begin to process it. How could a body do this? Why wasn't she twisting in agony? Or bleeding to death in front of him?

She rolled over again and slid on top of him, encircling him with her arms. It was a wet embrace now—she was slick and he was spattered, and for a moment he cringed away from it. She held onto him tight though and he lay there staring over her shoulder, feeling the wound that had been a knight in armour slipping against his skin, moist and smooth and framed in rough wire, but no longer bleeding at all. This craziness was what it had all been pointing towards?

"Where I am, things matter less," she said, her voice soft. "I am free, or freer to explore to more distant limits of experience—and isn't that something humanity has always wanted? But what do you want? Do you want to taste this as well?"

He gave an uneasy laugh. "This is starting to sound like a religious conversion."

"It isn't," she said. "You told me yesterday that you were giving up? I know you were lying. But what do you want now? That's all. Go back to painting? Or explore something that not many people have ever known?"

"This is quite a sales pitch," he said. However, in spite of his shock, there was no denying the excitement, coming from somewhere deeper than his logical, questioning brain. If this was where things had been pointing all along, then…

"Fuck painting," he said, his voice almost on autopilot. "I… suppose I have nothing to go back to."

"No," she whispered, hugging him close again. "Not like that. Not looking back. Look forward." It was an amazing hug, filled with warmth and affection. He returned it and kissed her softly. Kissed her again. In spite of the taste of blood that flavoured them.

She smiled. "Yes?"

Flesh? Skin? Designs, possibilities. With a shock of realisation, ideas began to clamour for attention. Was this art? Could this possibly be art? Did it even matter? The thrill of excitement that was whispering somewhere deep down felt the same. It was similar to the way he had used to feel when the idea for a particularly urgent painting occurred to him. He drew away from her and started at her—her big brown eyes. Stared at her with a wash of tenderness.

"Feather," he said. "I want you to show me—everything. I want to explore this. I don't know what it is all about—but it seems to me that what you are, however strange, is closer to what is real than anything I have known before."

She smiled and nodded, then hauled herself up, still exhausted, and picked up the piece of skin—the last of the wandering knight, flapping loose and floppy on its red-smeared island of tattooed sand. "Sorry," she murmured, shaking off the leaves. "It's got a bit grubby." She held it out to him, trembling slightly, and even now he could faintly make out his own face staring out of it into the universe. "Look, this was you—the searcher. Always looking for something but never knowing what it was. Me too."

He took the skin from her, trying to repress a wince at its clammy texture. "Why are you giving me this?"

She hesitated, trembling again. "Don't panic when I tell you," she begged. "Not at this stage. You must eat it."

"Eat?" he cried, shocked.

"Hey," she said hastily, "I cut you the knight because it seemed good symbolism—but you have to eat a little of it if you want to be like me."

"Is this some kind of disease that I have to catch?" he said, his voice shaky. He gazed at the skin, feeling his own skin crawling. "Have you done this before?"

"No," she confessed.

"Then how do you know…?"

"Hey—give it here." She snatched it from him and fumbled with the knife. She seemed even more nervous now and her movements were jerky and tense. She sliced quickly, beheading the knight with one crossways gesture. "Here," she said, almost a hint of desperation in her voice. "Please? Just one mouthful—just the old knight's head. Just a little bit of skin. I can't think of any other way to give you some tattoo as well." She thrust the scrap into his hand, then shrank back, staring at him. "I made up my mind to try and feed you some of it a while ago," she said softly, "when I first realised that I… or we…"

"What?"

She stared at the ground, looking unhappy.

"Ok," he said. "Now let's just… hold on a moment here. Why are you so keen for me to do this?"

She backed off, still looking at him with big eyes.

"I thought you wanted to."

"Maybe," he said. "But—but—why?"

Silence.

"Feather," he whispered, reaching out and touching her hand. "I just want to know?"

"I hope you don't think you are about to damn your soul to eternal torture?" she said with a low laugh. "I suppose I can't really blame you. It's quite a thing to trust someone about."

"I don't know anything," he said softly. "I don't understand anything. This is all quite a lot to take in." He played those words back in his mind and laughed. "I mean… come on. Just tell me a bit more—can you?"

"Yeah," she whispered. "I'm sorry, I am not doing this very well. I try to be self-assured and think I know it all—but I am also just—confused and uncertain."

He lay down again, shuffling a little closer to the fire, and made an inviting gesture. If nothing else, there was always that bifurcated universe of skin and warmth. That at least was a simple profundity. She tossed some more rosemary branches into the flames and settled down beside him again, extending her hands with a slight smile.

"I can't even feel it now. But I am still human enough to reach for the warmth."

"Um—you're actually *in* the fire there. Does that matter?"

She snatched them out, swearing.

"This numbness has its drawbacks," she muttered. "You could break a bone and not even notice."

"So… you can turn off your feelings. And… you have to?"

"Only when I need to," she said. "I am too much of a sensualist not to want to feel the world." She brushed her stomach. "Right now… yeah, I have to. I need to do some serious healing this time. No more crazy stuff for a while."

"But if all your nerves and—whatever—are turned down… how can you still think? Or move?"

She grunted. "Fuck knows," she muttered. "I don't know how it works. I am not hibernating like a bear."

"Or are you still feeling the pain, just not receiving it in the brain?"

"I dunno. Perhaps."

He stared at her.

"Maybe this tattoo… maybe everything that happened is just some bizarre function of the mind. Maybe you could just call it magic and have done with it."

"I'm not sure I like that word," he said.

"Nor do I, but I don't know what else to use."

"Ok. So how did all this happen? Can you explain a bit?"

She shrugged and sighed. "It's all rather hazy. I'm a Londoner… I think. Yes. That's right. Nothing more exotic. I can't remember much. Can't even really remember how old I am. But I do remember growing up in the city. I remember… all I really remember is an endless sea of pain."

"Pain?"

"My head. Depression, I suppose. And…" She shivered, and he slipped an arm around her and held her with as much warmth as he could manage. "I remember being in hospital. I'm not sure. Suicide attempt? Or an overdose? Not sure. Not sure. But that's the foundation to it all. I felt like a tiny boat, being hurled around in massive waves. They chucked me everywhere. Other people seemed like great ships who could plough through these waters and… go places, but I was tiny and helpless. Couldn't even find an oar. I was just waiting to be smashed against the rocks."

Don was silent, feeling a swirl of emotion at the words, and he hugged her tighter.

"It's ok," she said. "After hospital, I do remember trying to get at least some control of that boat. At least to the extent of surviving. I remember slowly becoming aware for the first time of just how helpless I was, and also how little I understood—how little I had done or felt or experienced. There was no, I dunno, *sailing* that boat to find the calm seas of, of, of wholesome connections or fulfilling relationships. The storm just would not end. Just survival, with everything else out of reach. I didn't know what I wanted, as far as wanting things meant anything. It wasn't art—it wasn't people—it wasn't drugs—it wasn't fucking religion. All of them were starting to disgust me. That was when I got the tattoo. I empathised with old Don Quixote, or whatever image I had of him in my head—forever meandering through pointless quests and searching for things beyond reach. And I put him on my skin to remind me of—of everything…"

Around their little island of light, the darkness now pressed deep and primal and Don stared without seeing out into the trees, letting her talk.

"Well—that's the easy way of putting it," she said. "*I got the tattoo.* It would be more accurate to say that it found me. Or the guy who did it found me. And gave me a gift. And I suppose it really was a gift. He somehow knew that I needed something and… there it was. The offer was made. Why me rather than any other of the millions of people who desperately need… something, I don't know. Maybe it was just sheer random luck."

"But who the heck could do this? Some kind of… wizard or what?" It was an ironic word, but he also couldn't imagine another one that could possibly fit there, given what he had seen.

She shrugged. "He was a bookseller in London. Nothing very outlandish. And an artist, of course. But he could certainly do *something.*"

"Oh."

"Yes. It was based somewhat on the Gustave Doré illustrations. I liked the art—the tattoo art I mean. I could see the message in it clearly enough. And when I looked at it, I saw that it… that this figure had my own face."

"Hmm," he said, glancing at the scrap of skin.

"Yes Don, I know. You saw your face in it as well, right? Please don't ask me how the fucking hell it works." She sighed.

"Yeah," he said. "At this point, I believe in magic."

There was a long silence, in which Feather reached out and fumbled for some more wood, shoving it into the fire.

"I said yes," she continued. "It sounds nuts, but at the time I barely cared what happened to me. I felt on the edge of life, so any experience seemed to shine out like a beacon. And—there it was. Every inch of skin, Don. He went over every inch. Over quite a few days. Long… long and intimate. And it felt as though I was shedding my skin like an insect. As though with every stroke of the needle something fresh and new was being exposed."

Don listened in fascination—a singing sense of the otherworldly and the ineffable. Her face looked totally different now to the character he had first met. Now she seemed fragile and open and human—a figure tangled in memories and darkness and experience and power and magic.

She sat up again and took the scrap of skin. "Aah—the dear old knight," she said. "And now, after all these years, now I finally don't need him anymore. Whatever was in that tattoo has permeated me from head to toe. What he showed me he can also show you."

He took it from her slowly.

"But none of this really explains anything," he said. "None of this explains how this could have happened."

"What can I say?" she cried, with a shrill laugh. "I—" she shook her head. "I hardly know. I don't know what he did. I don't fucking know what this thing was that he drew on me. Later on, I looked for him. After the first hallucinations began, I was frightened out of my wits and didn't know what was happening or what to do. I thought my boat was finally going to crash. But I couldn't find him. He seemed to have vanished and nobody knew anything about him."

"You also had…?"

"Yes," she said. "I found myself wandering round inside the damn thing myself. It had a life of its own and I was slowly getting more and more tangled up in it. That great red desert— the windmills. Only in my case, they looked like an old renovated mill near where my parents lived. I suppose it was familiar. The sails there had been replaced by nothing more than beams of wood and inside it was a small museum. The museum was still there in my dreams—though I wish I could tell you about some of the things on display there. I still get them occasionally."

"I'm still not sure how I managed to… catch them? Are you *that* contagious?"

She smiled again and shook her head.

"Both times you had come into contact with my blood. That has to be the answer. The first time it happened accidentally—the second time I did it on purpose. Remember when I made a fool of myself making you suck that wound?"

He laughed softly. "I do. I though at the time that you were trying to… I dunno. It looked like some sort of clumsy pickup. Albeit a very odd one."

She frowned and smiled dryly. "So there we have it. This thing exists, I don't really know anything, I don't understand, and… I want you to join me."

"Ok," he whispered. "One last question. Sorry, but I have to. Why me?"

"Because… you're there," she said simply. "Because I don't want to be alone anymore."

She suddenly pushed him down into the earth in spite of his tentative protest and resuming her position on top of him, shuffling into a sitting position and allowing almost her full weight to hold him down. "I am so tired of being alone," she said, her voice almost a hiss. Then quieter and more thoughtful: "I never expected any of this—never really planned anything. I just wanted to talk to someone."

"Desperation?" he murmured.

"What?"

"Is that it? Desperation? It could have been anybody?"

"Oh fuck it all," she cried, bringing her fists down on his chest hard enough to hurt. "What does it matter? If I'd let that kind of thought govern me, I wouldn't be here now. If you think I'm chucking invites at the first person who will listen, then… hell yes. Because who the fuck is going to listen to this? Nobody, that's who. *Nobody* would still be lying here with me, after all that's happened. Everyone would have run away. Except you, for some reason."

Don sighed. No doubt that was true. And paradoxically he felt relieved. There was something very simple about that, and he had to admit to himself that maybe, just maybe, most human relationships weren't so different. The basic confusion that seemed to permeate all this, the fact that she had revealed herself to be as full of human anxiety and tangles as himself, was also comforting since too much certainly would have felt very dangerous here. Feather the self-assured teacher had long-vanished, leaving behind something much more real, something both strong and fragile, a more subtle equation of human existence. In spite of his lingering unease, the attraction to her remained—a blazing blend of sexual attraction, fascination and awe.

Then he frowned in yet further shock as he felt her body, the flesh that was pressed against him, distinctly warming up. It was the most amazing sensation—a glow of heat immerging inside her like an oven that has just been switched on. He could feel it in every point of contact and it made him realise with a jolt just how cold she had been before.

And simultaneously with the warming, he saw blood begin to seep from the already healing wound on her stomach.

"I am sure I can die," she said, her face dark. "I can bleed to death—but there is a lot of blood in a person. You wouldn't believe how much. Do you still think I am a monster of some kind? Do you believe me now?"

"Oh dear," he murmured. "I never thought that—but yes, I believe you."

"Do you want to join me?" she pleaded. Her voice already sounded weary.

"Yes."

"Then please eat it. My skin I mean." She picked it up again and pressed it to his lips. He faltered, staring at it again in horror. "It is just a tiny piece of flesh," she groaned. "Why should it be such a problem?"

"I can't," he cried. "Help me. I—I just don't think I can..."

She lay down flat on top of him, their two wire weavings rubbing against each other. It was a slick movement as his whole front was wet with her blood now. Shockingly and almost unbelievably, he felt himself beginning to get erect.

"Please," she begged. "I am starting to feel faint."

"Stop it," he cried, trying to push her off. "Please don't do this..."

Feelings churned within him but the horror and what he had to admit to himself was at least some kind of love balanced each other and created a vacuum that didn't know which way to turn. He shook his head and groaned. Her body heat was still increasing—indeed she was becoming positively hot. Too hot.

And with the heat, the sense of flowing blood was also increasing, throbbing against him with far too much pressure. She rubbed herself feebly against him for a moment, then gave up in exhaustion and lay still, draped over him like a sodden cloth.

"Oh god," she gasped. "I really am going to faint."

"Then stop it, for god's sake" he cried, panic rising like a siren. "Change back again—stop this fucking bleeding."

"No," she whimpered. "I'm sorry. Don—you have to do this…"

"Oh for fuck's sake," he cried. "You don't even know if it will work. Don't blackmail me into this…"

Her body felt like a hot mug of coffee now—not scalding, but definitely pointing that way, and with more heat continually creeping through to him. She was trembling on top of him, whimpering at every movement—as though her nervous system had been augmented as well, and with it all her sensation. Then, feebly, she reached for the skin scrap, bundled it up into a tight ball and popped it into her own mouth. Squirmed around again—and kissed.

He could not refuse that kiss. Whatever kind of love this was, if the word even applied here, the blaze of it dragged him onward, even through his panic. It was a huge kiss. He felt her gently licking at his lips, sucking with exhausted hunger—felt her hot tongue pushing in further… felt something else in his mouth…

He gagged and tried to wriggle away from her grasp, but she clamped down on him with an insistent moan, gripping his head hard enough to hurt. The skin was in his mouth—there was nowhere it could go except down. It was cold compared to her—cold and floppy. It would almost have been better warm. He felt his stomach heave. But no, he thought to himself. After all, why not? Why this huge refusal to admit this small piece of flesh? He still gagged—struggling grunts erupting in his throat. He tried to swallow. Feather almost screamed encouragement at the back of her throat, the vibrations of her voice thrilling through physically into him. He felt her heat, felt her lips, felt her body—and it snapped. In a wild plunge, he rolled his eyes up—and swallowed.

It almost stuck. For a moment he froze, limbs trembling—then it went down as easy as a bit of chicken skin. He remained clutching at her, and felt a wave of triumph. She sagged off him and flopped into the grass with a distinct squelch, clutching at her stomach. He sat up, feeling a tingling in his flesh that might have been from shock, and leant over her in a storm of anxiety. Not too late? Please not too late?

It took a few moments but she managed to get herself under control. The bleeding slowed and stopped. She relaxed back in the grass and regarded him with a tired smile.

"I feel like shit," she said.

Don sagged with relief—and then winced as he felt his stomach churn. He swore and clutched at his chest, where a burning sensation was creeping up his throat. It felt as though he had eaten too much fruit. He belched loudly, unable to help himself, and not liking the faint fatty, acid flavour that came up with it. The cold was eating into him as well now and he looked round feebly for his clothes

"Feather," he cried softly. "I think I am going to be sick."

She murmured something incoherent.

"Er—Feather?" he repeated. "Is this right? Did you expect this? I… very very quickly, really don't feel so good."

Feather grunted and sniffed loudly. "Dunno," she muttered, opening her eyes. She sat up heavily, and hauled herself to her feet. "Come on," she whispered. "Come out onto the moors."

He groaned and coughed. "Why?"

"We need the windmills now. Come on Don," she said, though there was a hint of uncertainty in her voice. "You are ok. Just keep hold of yourself. Don't throw up."

"My clothes," he murmured.

"Please don't worry about them."

"… so cold."

"You will be warm soon. I will light the fire again later. Come on, let's help each other."

She hauled him to his feet, then leant heavily on him. Her body was colder than he could ever remember it feeling before and it did nothing to warm him up at all. Slowly they began to walk. He looked back longingly at the fire they were leaving behind, but he hadn't the strength to object further.

Both of them were shaky and exhausted as they tramped out of the trees—and there the huge form of the nearest giant rose before them—black against a black sky, it's warning lights flashing and the blades turning serenely.

They headed up the slope. Overhead, the huge tower of the closest turbine loomed, turning and turning against the cold air. After a few moments he stopped.

"I'm freezing," he wailed. "It's fucking November. This is not the time to be walking about naked on the moors… at night… in the wind." He was shivering so violently that he could barely move. Feather gazed at him uncertainly, then around her at the bleak landscape.

Finally, she hustled him on a few more paces then dropped down into a small hollow sheltered from the wind. "Come here Don," she said. "This is far enough. We can see the towers clearly enough. Come here and I will give you some body heat. I suppose there is no alternative. I should have thought…"

He slipped heavily into the hollow and slumped shivering in the grass. For a moment his stomach hitched and he curled over to vomit.

"Don't," she said. "Come here."

He started at her blankly, then hauled himself across to her. She pushed him down into the grass and pulled herself on top of him, a comforting weight if nothing else, wrapping herself round him as best she could.

"I'm scared," he said faintly.

"My god," she said. "You are shivering so much."

"…feel sick," he muttered.

"I can't give you much," she murmured. "I will start bleeding again. I am shattered enough as it is. But you will be safe soon."

Did she know that, Don wondered, or was she just hoping?

Did she know anything?

As he lay there, he felt an increasing terror welling up within him. He could feel something happening to him—something he could not place at all. Shifts and changes, even though he had only swallowed the skin a few minutes ago.

"Feather," he gasped, his voice high with fear. "Feather… I feel—what's happening?"

"Please hang in there," she said. "It will be all right."

"But…"

"It will be all right," she repeated with determination.

The cold of the damp ground blazed up into him like a leaden fire, but at the same time, he felt her warming up slightly—marvelling again in spite of everything at the strange sensation. She never got hotter than normal body temperature this time, but Don hugged her greedily for it. He could feel the warmth slowly creeping into him and his shivering at last began to fade a little. Her chest and shoulders were against the side of his face and he could just make out the design of the huge old windmill in the darkness. That remained, even though the wandering knight had been removed, and he stared at the image, his head spinning with dizziness.

Overhead the giants talked softly. He could hear them above the wind. It was a peaceful sound. A sound that made him think of peace and restfulness. It made him think of the gentle buzzing of insects on a summer day, and smell the sizzle of frying bacon. The scuttle of wood lice and the patter of hail landing in the grass.

Curious associations, he though softly. But then again—why not?

He opened his eyes, gazing into the comforting skin of her shoulder…

And the sails of the great windmill were turning gently.

"Feather?" he murmured, staring at the giant where it reared above him across the sand.

There was no answer.

He stared—then began to tramp forward slowly. He felt as though he was in the presence of a thunderstorm. His body was tingling, flushing with a glow of heat now. With a careless gesture he tossed his sword away across the sand. The tower loomed higher and higher above him—and were the great blades bending down to watch his progress? He wasn't sure.

He glanced down at himself and saw that he was wrapped again in the copper wire armour and he began picking at it, unwinding it. It came loose in springing coils, which tangled round his feet as he scrambled out of them. He walked onwards, leaving a tangled trail of wire, and eventually he was free of it and stood naked, feeling the soft sand moulding round his feet.

He looked down at his chest, at the three-pronged design in gleaming copper, and he smiled, tracing the lines and looking up at the tower in front of him, almost as though for approval. Slowly he approached the base, where the white wall sprang up out of the red sand. He reached out a nervous hand and stroked the smooth surface. It didn't feel like metal at all. It felt almost like skin. It seemed to vibrate and pulse under his fingers like something alive. Alive and aware of him.

Eventually, he sat down comfortably in the sand with his back to the wall, settled himself there, and closed his eyes. Giving himself up to the voices.

Voices.

Voices.

Voices…

There were secrets here indeed. "Help me." he whispered. "I know where I am going now."

Hopefully that was true. Or true enough.

The world leant slowly and he tumbled backwards, gently as a dream, falling into the tower. This was different to before. While he had been plunged through a bitter and filthy tract, now he found himself floating as smooth as good sex through a delicious softness. It didn't last long though. He slid down the world and it passed away leaving him filled with a happy regret. Perspective swung this way and that. The ground was now below, now above him. And he was lying in the softly coarse grass of the moors again. As simple as that.

Hail was falling—small and cold. They fell as lightly as flower petals, and when they struck him, there was a flicker of cold and light. The grass stroked his skin. It was rough, but so real that he wanted to cry. This was earth in all its glory. A seething mass of questing roots and swarming creatures. And he could feel them all—as a great solid mass of life. This was a vision that he would never catch as an artist in the traditional sense, or maybe in any sense—that feeling before you wake up of seeing marvels that you could never pin down later. But it didn't matter. It didn't matter because he was experiencing it now. Nothing mattered any more except a gentle progression towards the unknown experience.

The giants were still there—the same old towers. They watched him placidly, with all the emotion or involvement of sea anemones. But he felt comfortable with them. Indeed, he remembered the sense of comfort he had felt when he first heard them whispering to him—and now he began to see why these towers had been such a key. Whatever fantastic tricks the human mind can play, this was the greatest. Somehow these white towers had become the symbol for all human creativity. And he finally saw it—and, with the hail falling around him like rose petals, he finally heard what the giants were saying.

He woke up to find himself back in among the trees with Feather sitting next to him, quietly stripping copper wire with the kitchen knife. It was quite dark now. He felt…

The lack of sensation was the first thing that hit him, and that came with a feeling of terror. His head felt clear and sharp, his lingering headache gone. But he also felt numb, as though his body was asleep. But even as the fear shocked him, he felt his body suddenly waking. He gasped and shivered, his eyes opening huge and his penis jumping erect at the flash of heat inside him. Like a swimmer taking his first floundering strokes through the water, he tasted his body. Sensations came crowding in—a vast overwhelming mass of them. Every blade of grass and moss and every leaf that touched him was a knife edge. The wind was a sandstorm. And every living thing about him rampaged like a dinosaur. He gasped and twitched and cringed away. No no—too much much too much…

And with that panicked thought, it faded—faded away to normal—then, before he could stop it, to complete numbness again. He felt like Alice lost in her Wonderland. Drink me. Eat me. Big. Small. This way that way out of control. With a plunge, he fled the numbness and once again the leaves became blades. He cried out.

"For fuck's sake," he wailed.

Then he felt hands touch him, and he froze.

"You can imagine this," she whispered, caressing his chest. The feel of her skin against his was incredible—like being licked by a burning tongue. He almost forgot the razorwire leaves.

Then she softly swung a leg over him and sat astride.

He felt her squashing into his pelvis, her pubic hair scratching at him, and he gazed at her unable to speak. Whatever electricity he had always felt at her contact was amplified a hundredfold. The sensation was so intense that he was tempted to flee it again, seek refuge in safe numbness. But he felt unable to move or respond.

Slowly and gently, so as not to hurt him, she slid down, lying flat on top of him again.

"Don," she whispered.

"Yes?" he said, and even his voice was a sensation.

Her lips descended.

Lips—tongue—burning—fire—

For a moment he struggled against it, terrified beyond belief at the sensations that ripped through him. His entire body was melting like ice in burning fire. Her lips flashed steam at contact. Her tongue, rough as sandpaper and as smooth as silk probing deep into his mouth. He gazed up at her eyes, and in them shone the depth of the vast rabbit hole that descended behind them. And slowly he returned her embrace, tasting her skin—skin that flowed like sand—soft and firm and glowing with lurid radiance.

Finally though she slipped away again, and his arms trailed after her regretfully. She grinned down at him and stood up to her full height, a tall white column in the gloom. She seemed to have recovered from her ordeal, at least, and her flesh was already well along the healing path. The wound on her stomach was sealed with a dense weaving of gleaming wire, which fused with the three-pronged design on her chest turning the windmill into one massive structure.

"Don Quixote… you are finished," she said, rubbing at her tattooed body, her eyes sparkling. She smiled down at him. "Did you dream well while you were out?" she asked.

"Yes," he murmured.

"Good," she said. "Now you must wake up. There is so much to do. There is one thing I must make, if I may?"

"Um—what's that?"

She grinned at him hungrily and gently swung the chef's knife.

"Are you ready to test out your new flesh?" she asked. "I want to work on you a bit."

He looked up at her, a flicker of unease dawning again.

"I… am… afraid," he murmured.

"Don't be," she said softly. "The sky is the limit now. I want to show you that so you will never forget it."

"You are back to your usual self, I see," he said with a smile. "Nothing if not the didact."

She hesitated, then grinned. Maybe still a little shy after all. "Yes, I guess so," she said.

"But I don't know how to control this yet," he protested plaintively.

"Don't worry," she said brightly. "We will find out."

8

J: ... he was... the—the figure at the centre of the wire... I—I just don't know how to describe it...

Q: But Miss Adams—you have to understand that...

J: No. You have to fucking understand. He was there. I don't care what happened later, I just know what I saw.

Q: The police...

J: Fuck the police. They never were much help and they certainly aren't now. They think I did it. Well—it was like—like an anatomical drawing—that is all I can think of. Or perhaps some cheap, overblown special effect in a film. It just didn't look real. The wire was everywhere—running through his skin—his flesh—his... *[brief pause]*... what had she done? And why? I just don't get it. He was in shreds—he was in fucking shreds—great flaps of skin caught and held splayed open by the wire... his stomach... his stomach was open—the... the insides... trailing out, stretched tight like the rays of a star—three-pointed star though I think—all held by the wire. Stars of skin—stars of flesh—stars of... of... It was all like those fucking windmill blades—everything.

Q: It is ok—you don't have to...

J: I can't get the image out of my head. I just would never have believed that skin... that the human body... could be so elastic. The way the wire had just... stretched him—great tent-like peaks and bat-like wings. His face especially—that was the worst star of all...

Q: Jacki—you really don't...

J: You want me to fucking talk. You are the one who keeps asking me fucking questions. And you are the one who won't fucking believe me. But I am telling you—he hung there in fucking... pieces. But he was fucking alive. His face... Just an elegant, pretty little flower of radiating peeled skin—and hair. I mean—the skill required to do that—a flower with a red skull in the middle—and two staring eyes... I thought he was dead of course—but when those eyes turned and looked at me...

Don never remembered how they got home. He woke up to find himself slumped in his chair in his studio. He groaned and clutched his hand to his stomach with a flicker of panic. The memories in his head seemed very hard to believe now in the confines of his familiar studio, but a moment's investigation confirmed them. He remembered the staggering sight of his own insides taken and spread—remembered pain—and its absence. Apparently he must have fainted. Yes—that sounds right. But now—he examined himself more closely—he appeared to have been sewn up again with all the skill of a surgeon, and now the heavy smells of flesh were mingled with the fresh scent of herbs. Copper wire ran through his skin—great turns of it—holding him together, it seemed. There was a moistness about the wire and the flesh beneath that suggested body fluids leaking—but it seemed slight. Very carefully, he leant back, feeling his body trying to obey his instructions. It felt loosely held together and very fragile, which was terrifying. Numb and dead to the world—and he shivered.

The door opened, letting in a gleam of light, and a figure stepped in. The sight of her brought the last vestiges of the past couple of hours crashing back, and he gazed at her in stunned silence. None of this was possible, he thought, fear flickering. All he felt now was a panicked desire to escape back to where things were comprehensible and rational. Feather regarded him with a very curious expression on her face. She looked cautious, as though worried how he would greet her after all that had happened. But there was also a glitter in her eyes—a satiated gleam of self-satisfaction. She was dressed again now in her jeans and that slightly incongruous lacy-looking shirt that hung round her like a curtain. She said nothing, just stood regarding the ruins of his paintings. Thoughtfully, she touched the crumpled sketch of Jacki on the turbine with her toe, then kicked at the torn remains of a landscape.

There was a crunch of glass.

Don wanted to shake his head in a general negation of the whole adventure, but he didn't dare move. It was curious to see her there though, in the mundane surrounds of his studio, he thought. It made her feel very real. She was not just some bizarre dream conjured up by a cracked scull.

Don sighed, and she looked round at him.

"How did I get here?" he asked, faintly. His voice both sounded and felt strange, as though his pipes had been configured differently.

"With a lot of help." She came over to him and examined him—still cautious. "How do you feel? Are you alright?"

"I don't feel very alright," he whispered, his voice flat and dreamlike. "I don't dare move in case something falls off."

"You will heal soon, though," she said reassuringly. "Very soon. And nothing is going to fall off. The human body is far tougher than people think."

He gave a harsh sigh. "You frightened me out of my fucking wits back there," he whispered, every word an exhausted and strained monotone. "Have you never heard of introducing new ideas gradually?"

She grinned broader. "Why bother when you can jump right in? You will be fine soon."

"But," he said, his voice shaking. "There is so much I still don't know. I mean, what is all this? Am I alive? Do I still eat? Do I still sleep? What…?"

"Don," she said reaching out to touch him, then thinking better of it. "It will be all right. And you know," she said conversationally, "it was a fine rich artwork. I just hope nobody who shouldn't gets a look at your camera. I feel good now. In the meantime—we must get out of here—and fast. I think we were seen. Remember?"

"Oh god—was that who I think it was?"

"I wouldn't know, but she seemed to know you."

"What happened to her?"

"She ran off—and so should we. We don't want to be around if she brings anyone back to start investigating. I know I haven't killed you or anything—but we don't want things complicated."

"How the fuck am I supposed to run anywhere?" he demanded crossly.

"How do you feel about driving?"

"Now?"

"I'll drive," she insisted. "I think I can remember how to. Had some lessons once. You just need to sit there."

"Very comforting," he growled.

"Well," she said. "We must get somewhere a bit private where you can recover. Then we can head on—wherever we want. I have already packed some of your things in the car—Laptop, camera etc. Now come on—give me your hand."

"Dammit, Feather…"

"You are stronger than you think."

She grabbed his hand and he struggled to his feet, and he was surprised to find that he could walk—just about, leaning heavily on her shoulder. Together they began to move slowly towards the front door.

"You can be revenged on me soon," she said. "There is something I want you to do when you are feeling up to it. You might enjoy it."

"Mm?"

"Before we left the moors I ate the rest of Don Quixote," she said, brushing at her stomach and the healed ghost of the huge triangular wound there, still encased in copper wire. "I don't know if that changed anything but… couldn't hurt. I was getting so tired of that fucking tattoo. So him and his desert is no longer needed, at least for me. I want you to get rid of him."

"What do you mean?"

She grinned at him.

"I want to be stripped of him. I want to be naked again. I really miss being naked. I want you to undress me."

He looked at her blearily. "But you are naked all the time," he said.

She sighed. "I mean," she said, "that I want you to cut this fucking tattoo off me," she said."

"Oh…"

9

Q: It's ok Miss Adams—please don't distress yourself. Take it easy—easy.

J: You don't believe me? Brrrr. Of course you don't believe me. *[laugh]* How could you? But he had fucking wire in his chest when I saw him the afternoon before—surely someone must have seen that. He had this small fucking windmill design woven into his fucking skin and he showed it to me—he was proud of it. And I just cannot forget what he was fucking saying to me.

Q: Miss Adams...

J: Look—I am not making it up. *[strikes table with fist]* I don't fucking care if it was possible or not—that is what it was that was... was... happened. I haven't done anything. You have to let me out of here—please. There's nothing fucking... nn... is nothing wrong with me. I haven't killed him. Please just stop asking so many questions...

Q: Nobody is saying you killed him, Jacki. We just want to find out what happened.

J: Oh fuck that. They go and... say that I am the only person with any motive for the crime, what crime? Her fault—fucking her... crime that there was. But what evidence is there? You tell me that? You tell... what evidence is there for anything? I know what you found—she... her... hurt him. That's who you should be looking for. Shouldn't be looking for me. Or perhaps you have already found him? Perhaps you have killed him. Did you? So you can prove I did it?

Q: Miss Adams, Please...

J: I know there is no fucking body. Because he was still alive. How many times do I need to say it? He walked away. Or she helped him to. What are you looking for? A corpse or a runaway?

Q: But surely you appreciate the contradiction? What you describe could be simple overreaction...

J: Oh fuck it all...

Q: Miss Adams, if you can't keep calm I shall have to call for help. I am not disputing that something happened—and nobody believes that you killed him as you keep mentioning, as we have no evidence for that at all. But you are pressing a complaint here against an unknown person for a crime of which we have no real evidence. Evidence points to some event occurring, true—possibly involving a third person. A small amount of blood and traces of human skin were found, among other things, but there is no sign of a disturbance of any kind—nothing to indicate forcible restraint or a struggle. Miss Adams—are you listening to me? We are as keen to find the person who did this as you are, but in order to do that we have to know what really happened. I am not trying to attack you—I am trying to help you.

J: *[Long pause]* You really don't have a clue, do you. And you won't find him now anyway—or her. He is no longer fucking human, after all. God knows where he is now.

Q: Miss Adams...

J: You stupid bastard—why did you have to... go and do... like this? Where are you? I don't want you to be... wherever you are. *[Tears apparant]* come back... please... just... fucking come back...

From: 'Morning Texts'—p83

Oh my god oh my god oh my god oh my god... this is really strange make no bloody mistake. What have I done? What am I going to do? I hardly know anything. I just feel like I am living in a dream—and I am not sure whether I want to wake up from it or not. I cannot even begin to describe what it felt like to skin her—while she lay there mildly instructing me what to do as though she was showing me how to peel potatoes. I don't know whether to throw up or laugh out loud.

I also cannot describe what it was like when she was working on me. It is such a strange feeling still—to be able to control all this—to be able to tell my body to shut down and speed up. I guess that it is somewhat instinctive—otherwise I would never have been able to survive her makeover. I can turn it up and down—it feels just like refocusing my eyes or something—and I seem to remember that it even happened without my consciously thinking about it. While she was 'working' on me, as she put it, then I just switched off as far as I could go. I was terrified out of my wits. I thought I was going to die. I even thought she had betrayed me. But I couldn't do anything about it except hang there.

But in spite of all, it just felt as though she was scratching an itch—deeper and deeper inside me. It made me want to sneeze... It was almost—pleasant.

After a few minutes I did allow myself to relax a bit. It had dawned on me by then that it wasn't going to hurt—that I wasn't going to die. That was when I started to get a little curious. I did let myself feel it slightly for a moment—though only for a moment and even then only a very slight flicker of it. I just wanted to see what it was like. And guess what? It was fucking horrible—it was agony. I seem to remember screaming aloud and fortunately my body took over and slammed the thermostat back down to minimum again while Feather gave me an odd stare with arched eyebrows.

And yet I wonder now how much that agony was real. When pain doesn't matter, do we cease to fear it? Does it just become another sensation? I wonder. Can you experience pain that goes somehow completely beyond pain—beyond a world where pain has meaning? It is almost impossible to describe. Pain as liquid? Pain as a flower?

Feather looked... magnificent standing there working, her face full of hungry concentration, her hand holding a smeared knife. It was as intimate as making love—a hundred times more intimate. It was terrifying—but at the same time, I remember feeling a glow of love for her even then. I know it is curious. But I have never felt like this before about someone. Perhaps nobody has in the whole history of time.

And the sculpture she carved from me? I have seen the photos. The light is bad—merely flash bulb and hence stark and ugly—but what it shows up makes me feel a strange thrill. The fact that it is me is scarcely relevant on one level. The important thing is that it is a sculpture—a strange, eerie yet oddly beautiful sculpture. What we are doing is art—of a type. I need convince no one—because the important thing is what I know myself. But even if there are only two of us (for now) it is still a form of artistic activity—as is any exploration. And—you know what?

It feels good!

Yes it does—now that I am finally getting over the shock.

Already my own mind is active. The memory of slicing the skin off her beautiful form was also an oddly liberating experience. I guess she was trying to prove the point again, but having done that I am now looking at both our bodies in a completely different way—even more so than after her essay with my own poor flesh. It freed me to relax a bit and to know that I can mould her how I want—as I suppose she can me. And, aside from these strange properties, I haven't really changed that much. It is great and refreshing to finally escape a bit from the castle of my skin—to find something rawer and wilder and less precious. And I look forward to the time when, through both our skins, I will finally lay my artist's block to rest. There are innumerable places to go and there is much to explore. No end in fact. That is the great thing about art. It never ends—always changes. Always there is something new.

Perhaps one day there will be more of us. Perhaps we will get ourselves an audience—viewers, readers whatever they want to call themselves.

The future is full of possibilities.

From here, the view was far and wide across an endless sea, not of sand and twining plants now, but of buildings. No mounted Knights in lost red deserts here. Don Quixote has come home.

The two looked out over London from the speeding car as it raced along the elevated motorway towards the west end. He ran one hand gently over her leg—carefully, for her skin was still a little fragile—feeling a little glow of heat from her even through the fabric of her jeans as she tasted the touch.

"You are beautiful now, by the way," he said.

"My new skin?" she said. "Yes—it is almost there. It feels great. So clean."

Clean and pure pink-white—untanned and completely unblemished. A few drops of blood appeared on her hands and she wiped them away absently, the heat fading. Her old skin still remained, folded and packed carefully at the bottom of his bag, where he had placed it after flensing it from her. Now the desert sand blew inert and unneeded and the twining leaves withered and died in long fraying strips, drying like herbs, to provide whatever mystery it possessed to others perhaps, should the occasion arise.

His own body was mostly healed too. Just a few lingering scars that hadn't quite faded. Soon even these would clear away, and then they would both be ready. Ready for the underground art scene. How much would a flensed skin design be worth to the right kind of collector? What secret and hidden performances would be possible? The ideas seemed limitless.

In his head, the first new design was taking shape nicely, all ready to be enacted on her skin. Gleaming and coiling. Hints of spirals and triangles—and leaves and great white blades. A cryptic map of a long journey.

Red Fire

1

Cal pinned the tattooed woman's skin to the small artist's canvas and stood looking at it, a tear trickling down his cheek. The room was still drifting with a faint smoke—the tang of burned meat, from where he had sealed her flesh.

"Feather, darling," he whispered, gently sliding his arms around her and hugging her, "Are you there? Are you alright?" He almost-sobbed once and hugged her closer. She was barely conscious and made no sound of response.

To him, her flesh always felt more like water than meat. As if at some point she had melted away inside—as if some tragedy had dissolved her flesh to tears. And now, limp and wrecked, she felt more like water than ever. She looked as though she never quite got enough to eat, and what she did get didn't provide much nutrition. But at the same time, there was a wasted and fractured beauty about her—her almost white hair contrasting sharply with the tattoos on her skin. Over her entire body they ran—from the nape of her neck, down her back, her chest; around her buttocks and hips, and down her legs to a trailing end round her ankles. She was a labyrinth from top to toe, and amid those endless intersections, all the stories of the world were written.

"Cal?" she murmured feebly.

He leant over her.

"You ok?"

"I don't know," she said, her voice hitching. "What did you… why… my god?"

He heavily ran a hand over her body, following again the maze, reading again the stories. Reading at least until he came up against the huge hole he had cut in them. It looked larger now, the flesh cooked and sealed—and there was still a hint of burned meat about it. It sat in the middle of her tattooed skin like a doorway—a doorway towards yet more stories inside her. Or maybe to something further. That was what he hoped, at least.

"I had to," he said simply. "I had to cut the stories."

She turned away and closed her eyes, her lips trembling.

2

Cal walked now. The grass parting for him to let him through. He could still smell the blood and the burning on his hands, even after a long shower, and he shoved them into his pockets and hunched down against the night.

Would that smell ever wash away?

Above him, the moon shone down, full and round, and around his feet the moths danced. He could see them. Great pale moths moving slowly through the grass—just white blurs. Their bodies hung upright, fluffy and oddly human—still points in the storm of wings—and he could see their eyes, jet black and staring. He stopped and watched them. Were they white or were they red? For a moment there was a flicker of colour at the corner of his eye—a red flicker and they seemed to him as little flames that moved and breathed amid the grass. Living flames.

He liked the moths—but in some ways, he felt almost too close to them. He was a moth himself, he sometimes thought—forever flittering round the light—but as soon as he approached, he would just end up burned and scorched. Creature of night but heading for the light. Light that would destroy him at a touch.

What light?

When he straightened up again, the moon also seemed to have flashed to blood red.

Cal felt sick.

3

Feather: face up on top of the black bed, her arms folded tight across her chest. Her small and fragile form was clad in loose trousers but her top was bare, except for the bandages. Her face was stained with tears.

Cal: sitting on a hard wooden chair, head resting on his hands, eyes staring at the floor.

"You have ruined me," she whispered. "How could you do it? Look." She twitched her bandaged body for him. "You have put a great big hole in all my stories. You have cut me in half."

He remembered the moths dancing, and for a moment he yearned to take her in his arms and hold her close and warm.

"Even that is part of a story though," he said placing a hand on her bandage. "I have just given them a new ending."

He almost wished that was true.

He remembered doing it—and the memory brought a strange deep feeling in the pit of his stomach. He remembered the sound and the sight as the smoking iron frying pan made contact with her. Remembered the explosion of steam, and above all remembered the terrific jolt that had travelled right through her body, as she bucked and heaved under him. Remembered the exhausted and panic-stricken shriek that escaped from her mouth.

"Read me then," she whispered, her eyes staring into his. "And see what new stories you can find there."

"What, now?" he said, staring back at her at last.

A moth had come in the open window, and with it had come a memory. He looked at her. This woman on the bed before him answered his earlier question easily enough. Here was the light that would burn him—the attraction that would scorch him forever.

Did it matter?

"I don't want stories," he said, watching the moth with careful attention. "Is there nothing else?" It was a smaller one than those he had seen in the field. Black blurred and fast as it circled the light.

"Why not?" she said.

"Because there is nothing real about them—that's why."

He ran his eyes over her. In the centre of the maze, a great plume of red flames blazed from between her legs. Was that some sort of final destination?

That would be pretty absurd. Feather's vagina nothing more than a literary device. The wound though was like a hole burned through a book with a blowtorch—a way through into a different world than that shown on the pages.

"Nothing real until I made something real there," he added with a petulant frown. "That," he said, pointing at the bandage that hid the area of meat in her stomach, "is real. I have simply replaced one doorway inside you with another. Where's the centre of the maze now?"

She glared at him, her face tight. "Alright you motherfucker," she snapped, carefully kicking off her trousers. "Tell me your 'real' new story then."

"Perhaps it is a story of redemption," he said. "Perhaps it is the tale of he or she who has escaped the cold red fires of hell."

"I am not sure I like your suggestion," she said.

He regarded her silently.

A young woman
A city
White hair and white skin
Tall buildings
A trail of glittering glass laid down like jewels on the pavements and walkways
Writing words on the walls
A doorway
Passes through

"And what was there behind that door?" Feather asked.

Slowly, Cal opened the bandage on her stomach.

"Nothing except meat… and water. You don't need anything else. Isn't that hot and alive enough?"

He stared at the wound—and it seemed to express something fundamental, sitting there like a great pitfall trap in the path of not just her life, but his too. It was easy to imagine the comfort of hiding behind fictions.

And, feeling a sudden wash of tenderness and fragility, he reached down—and kissed her gently, just on the lower edge of the wound…

"What the fuck are you doing?" Feather said softly.

"Feather—you…"

He stared.

"Your fire is moving."

"What?"

He screwed his eyes closed, then stared again. The flames that encased her lower stomach flickered gently—a quiet, blurred movement.

"What's wrong?"

In the stillness, the moth that had been circling the room flew downwards and settled on her stomach. On her wound. It lit there as on a flower, uncoiled its long tongue and began to feed.

Feather looked down, her head on one side and gazed at it in silence—but to Cal the insect had become a glowing spark of flame.

The room was also ablaze. It flickered at the edge of his vision. He gazed in silence, then slowly raised his hands to his eyes.

But the red fire remained with him.

4

In the field, the moths danced, their blurred bodies leaving trails in the air like tiny comets. There were more of them now—the grass was thronging with them. Cal stood and stared, feeling the gentle breeze cut against his face; the dark grass wet against his legs. They seemed larger now as well. Their eyes bigger and blacker. Every one that he saw seemed bigger than the last. He was sure they were looking at him. One moth landed on the sleeve of his coat. Its wings didn't look like moth wings—there seemed to be no scales or fur. Instead it looked like crumpled dry skin.

The moth made no move to fly away. And Cal just stood there gazing into those great black eyes. And the eyes looked back—the stare of an insect perhaps the strangest experience in the entire world.

At the edge of his vision though, the moths were burning.

5

Cal sat before the mirror. He was naked. By now the edge of his vision was entirely consumed by flickering red fire.

"And what about you?" Feather asked at last. "What stories do you have that I can read?"

She pulled herself awkwardly from the bed and hobbled over to him.

"Nothing," he whispered.

"Nothing?"

"Yes," he said. "Nothing. Is that a story too?"

"Then perhaps you can read me?"

He rubbed his eyes and looked at her. She leant on his shoulder, one hand on her bandaged stomach, and he was aware of the terrible and piercing necessity between them. It was impossible to imagine her not there. She was like a part of his own body—a sick part undoubtedly—cancerous—tumour ridden—but without it, he would die instantly.

"There is something wrong with my eyes," he said, rubbing at them again. "I think I have read you too much."

"No," she said. She dropped her dressing gown and lay back on the bed, her legs slightly apart, her arms spread wide.

"Where shall I start?" he whispered.

She gently brushed at her shoulder.

"And where shall I end?"

"Wherever it takes you," she said.

There were no walls to write on now
A girl sick—dying
Electrical wires
The blood running black and the skin fading to paste
What salvation is there in your own flesh?
A doorway…

He gave up, staring at the wound. It seemed a shocking intimacy to him now. What sort of perverted human interaction was this? Humans were made for more than just reading.

"I don't want your stories," he said, his voice shaking. "They aren't stories any more—they are a bloody fortress wall. Even you cannot find your way behind them now. That's why I cut a hole… I just wanted to let you out."

Cal hated to cry—it felt as though the muscles of his face were no longer under his control. He could feel them twisting like snakes. Like struggling moths.

"Cal," she said softly. "I don't exist. I never have. You know that."

He buried his face in his hands. "I think we have doomed ourselves," he said, rubbing at his eyes where the red fire still flickered. "In the story. In the life. That—thing made no difference." He touched the wound again with his finger and Feather winced.

"Can't you just forget the fucking wound?" she said heavily. "Can't you just read me?"

"It always made no difference—from the very start. And nobody realises that."

"Please," she said. "You fucking bastard. I have to be read. Use your eyes. The path carries on on the other side."

"To where?" he asked.

"To anywhere you want. My knee. My eye. My asshole. My toes. There is no limit to the endings a story can have."

He looked at her for a long moment. "Or maybe it continues on the inside," he whispered. "What do you think of that?"

6

"Feather?" he said in a voice so tiny he could hardly hear it. "Oh god—what am I doing?" He started at the moth before him.

It hung in the air. It must have been over four feet from wingtip to wingtip—wings of papery skin lost in a blur of motion that fanned a gale of wind in his face—wings that burned softly at the edges. But now the great black insect eyes had been replaced with human ones—brown—glittering—bloodshot. And the fluff of its shoulders had grown into long silky nearly-white hair.

"I never wanted to hurt you," he cried suddenly, tears beginning to stream down his face. He sank down on his knees in the damp grass, gazing up at the figure in front of him. The air was filled with smaller moths—a myriad of white/red blurs dancing in the darkness.

"Please believe that—I never—wanted…"

7

"What are you doing?" he shrieked.

"I am mending myself," she said.

"Feather, no."

He stared at her, watching her press the needle into her flesh. Red fire danced in her hair and flickered between her legs as she sewed. He just gazed at her in stricken silence.

"You cannot silence me," she said, her voice shaking with the pain. She held the skin down firmly, sewing with calm and methodical stitches.

"I must be whole," she said.

"Feather—don't," he said.

She shook her head. "Without this I am nothing. How many times do I have to say it?"

"No more or less than anyone else," he said plaintively. "What about me? I don't have any stories."

"For every book there has to be a reader—otherwise it is not a book. It is pointless."

"Stop it," he shrieked suddenly, jumping forward and grabbing the needle from her. She clutched at it, but he flung her hands away, grabbed at the skin and pulled. It came with a horrible plucking rip as the two sides she had attached gave way. It was worse, somehow, than the operation that had started all this, and he gritted his teeth, trying to keep himself from vomiting. Feather clutched after it and screamed at the top of her voice. It was a terrible scream—the hysteria of a tantrum. He tried to shut his ears and fight off her clutching hands that tried to punch and scratch him, flinging the skin away out of reach. She spat foul language at him, drops of saliva dusting his cheek as he tried desperately to force her back down on the bed.

Finally she gave up and lay still, breathing heavily with exhaustion, the fresh blood from the wound staining the bed. She opened her mouth and began to mewl softly to herself, rubbing at her stomach.

"Feather?" he whispered with desperation, but she ignored him, laying there as though asleep. He examined her wound. It didn't look much worse, in spite of the bleeding, and he busied himself in anointing it and preparing a new bandage for her.

Eventually, he stood back and stared at her anxiously. This felt beyond his knowledge of first-aid, even more than the first time. He sat down beside her and felt her cheek. It seemed hot and feverish.

"Cal?" she moaned.

"You ok?"

"No."

She turned over and looked at him, but he couldn't meet her eyes. Instead, he stood up and hurried through to the kitchen.

"Cal," she cried after him.

"What?"

"I am scared," she muttered in a small voice, as though confessing to a crime.

"Drink this," he said as he returned, gently putting a glass of water to her lips, then two small while pills. Painkillers. She slurped clumsily, then lay down again burrowing his face against his side.

"Cal," she whispered.

"Yes?"

"Please don't go."

She closed her eyes again.

"I won't."

"I'm sorry. I just don't know what I would do without you there—to read me."

"I'm not going anywhere," he said tightly, rising to his feet again. "But I don't know if I will ever read you again. My eyes are still… failing."

She clutched after him with a moan, but he slipped out of reach. Heavily he crossed the room and retrieved the skin. It lay limp and floppy in his hands and he tried to straighten it out.

"Sometimes I look at this and it seems to be moving. As if is it struggling to escape. What story is on here?" he wondered softly, staring at it.

A trace of glass…
A door…

"It is just fragments."

"I prefer the hole it left," he said pinning it back onto the canvas. It seemed to squirm under his hands, but he ignored it. "There is something very real about that hole. Maybe if I was to cut off your entire skin, then you would be complete again.

"You bastard."

He turned to her and sat down again by her side.

"Feather… I don't know what to think. I can hardly see—so you are losing your stories whether you mend yourself or not. And as you said, what use are stories when there is nobody to read them? Soon it is you will have to read to me."

She was silent.

"Can't we just forget all this?" he begged.

He ran a hand down her arm, following the patterns as best he could.

A man
A heart made of glass
Following a wall for guidance
Love
A doorway
Suicide dive
Passing through
The glass flowers fall and shatter
The sea washes in

A few minutes later, something landed in his hair with a fluttering sound. He clutched at it, his heart racing. "What is it?" he cried, feeling it moving around him. He struggled to see, but it easily kept outside his field of vision, lost in the swirling fire.

"Moths—" Cal cried. "Is it? Feather? What the fuck is it? I can't see."

It felt too large for a moth. He could feel the air moving as it circled him.

"A door," he cried incoherently.

Once again it tangled in his hair. "Is that what it is?" he cried, panic rising. "Feather, it doesn't feel like a moth. Feather—for fuck's sake…"

"What would you expect?" she said coldly.

He squashed the thing to a powdery smear and buried his head in his hands.

8

He started to his feet, feeling more afraid than he could ever remember. Everywhere there was fire. It was deepening almost visibly—creeping like a living curtain across his vision. He stared at the thronging insects, hands spread wide, his mouth open. Things queued up to be said. An incoherent desire to apologise for something—everything. Everything he had ever done in his life. He had to apologise for it. Sorry. Sorry for living. Expressions of a love so strong and a need so deep that it could tear flesh apart. Sorry for loving. A sense of total, irredeemable doom. Giant moths everywhere—their huge wings crowding him. He wanted to run. But all he could do was step backwards slowly and hopelessly.

It was not even worth running. Punishment only works if it is desired. And he knew that he deserved no escape.

9

The doorway within—must be opened.

"It's the fires of hell," he whispered. "That's what it is. Why did I do it all? I just wonder…"

"What are you talking about?"

"My eyes are burning," he said. "I can feel the heat—the flames. They will boil in their sockets—melt away to bubbling pus." He sniffed briefly. "I'm scared," he said. "I am actually—really really scared."

She was silent.

"This is your fault," he said. "Why did you drive me to this? And why am I being punished now? I just wanted to open a doorway into you."

"Why?" she cried. "Can't you leave me alone?"

"Do you want me to leave you alone?" he demanded.

She stared at him.

"You want me to read you? I want to read you. I want to read you—the real you—not some fucking story that is connected to nothing."

"Then read me," she begged, opening her night robe with a small smile.

Cal gazed at her, his eyes blank.

"You are not even listening to me?" he whispered.

"What?"

Cal drew a deep breath.

"I cannot see any more and you want me to read you. Where are you hiding, for fuck's sake?"

"I am right here," she snapped. "Cal—without these stories I am nothing. Without you reading them—I am nothing." And she added in a softer voice: "I love you so much..."

"Then be nothing," he cried. "I cannot read you anymore. Don't you understand? I can hardly see. All I can see is fucking red fire."

"Then I will read you a story then," she said, her voice suddenly high with fury. "I will tell you a new one—it is about an evil man who cut the skin from his girlfriend's stomach—"

"Feather..."

"He cut it from her with an artist's craft knife—then sealed the wound with a fucking frying pan."

"Feather... please."

"He pinned the skin onto a canvas because he wanted to gloat over it, but even he had to go to bed sometime—had to curl up and go to sleep. And then, in the darkness, in the depth—in the terror by night...

Skin
The light is green
Flying
A story is told
Death
The doorway is slammed shut
Red Fire

"Don't joke about that fucking fire," he cried shrilly. He stared at her through the small patch of vision left to him. He though about the moths—the light—him flapping eagerly for it—always so anxious to be burned… and this was where the stories ended?

Burned to a crisp in the fire that radiated from her cunt?

No way.

He couldn't even see where the fire was any more—it had swollen to fill everything. Where once the red flames had licked over her vagina, her pubic hair, now they consumed her entire body. Squinting his eyes he followed her flesh downwards until the burning stories passed under the bandage. There. He hauled at the windings of muslin, ripping it off her with a vicious gesture.

The wound.

He gazed at it longingly. That was the centre now—that was the only thing that mattered. It seemed larger still now—and dryer—a wound struggling to heal itself. A doorway struggling to close itself to prevent—what?—escaping.

Or entering?

Or was this just a dream as well?

"I told you we had doomed ourselves," he said. He clawed at his eyes with his fingernails. "Was it really worth this? Did you have to drive me to this ruin?" He felt filled with such a rage of self-disgust that he had to force down his heaving stomach. "You have a doorway, Feather," Cal hissed. "I know you have. I was beginning to believe you—think that you really didn't, but you have a doorway in there. A way into that shrivelled up, ruined heart of yours."

He hesitated, collecting himself.

"Everything you have thought for all of your life has been a complete—fucking—lie. Now please, for god's sake let me in."

Feather shrank back across the bed.

"The only reason I wanted to open that doorway was because I loved you. Why won't you let me in?"

"Keep away," she cried, but he hardly heard her. Through the dizzying blaze of his eyes, he caught the movement of her trying to get up, and he lashed out to stop her. He felt his fist collide with her watery flesh and bone. It was a tremendous impact—one which sent a blast of pain up his arm, but he saw her collapse back again like a doll, struggling to move.

"Feather," he cried. "Why won't you let me in?"

Something brushed past his ear, his hypersensitive nerve endings reacting to it like an electric shock. He clutched at it wildly—contacted—felt something dry and papery squirming in his hand. He waved it at her, trying to see what it was himself, but the red fire kept shifting and he couldn't focus on it. It certainly felt like the skin though—skin that flapped and wriggled in his grasp. "You bitch," he howled. It slipped from his fingers and he grabbed for it, but with his limited sight lost it completely. It was easy to imagine that patch of skin fluttering round him like a moth, always just beyond his tiny remaining field of vision.

Tears streamed down his face.

"Feather—don't you understand? Feather—I need your help. I need to get in. It is the only thing that can fucking save me."

"Cal—" she murmured dazedly, from somewhere in the glare.

"For god's sake Feather—you useless bitch."

His vision, desperately roving the room, suddenly spotted the artist's canvas. The skin was not there, he noticed, but this was hardly a surprise. On the shelf beside it though there was a flash of metal.

Stories… Doorways…

He clutched the craft knife.

"Cal—what are you…"

He screwed himself up into the most explosive entreaty that he could. "Please," he screamed.

"Cal, you fucking madman…"

"Let me in, you bitch. That's where your stories should have pointed all along, instead of playing horrible games."

"Cal—"

"Let me—in."

"You bastard…"

"And give me back my eyes—"

Feather howled. It was a horrible noise—broken, grating, exhausted, agonised. He felt her struggle—felt her try and kick at him

But at the last moment and with the last of his vision, he saw the trap into which he had been led, or had led himself. At the last moment as, with one last screaming wrench the knife tore open the doorway, and out from the doorway there exploded a storm of huge red moths.

They came crowding in. Cal screamed. There was nothing left. All he could see was a raging fire of wings.

This was it. This was totality. Cal was blind.

He staggered blindly about. His entire body was a mass of little touches—that might have been the brushing of wings or the scrabbling and clutching of small feet. They were in his face, his hair, his clothes… He thrashed around trying to get them away from him, but try as he might he could not catch them.

Beneath his feet, the floor also felt incorrect. It could almost have been grass again, he could feel the wetness of dew brushing against him.

But he couldn't see to check.

He crashed into something and sent it flying. The fire raged. He could almost feel its heat burning at him behind his eyes.

"Feather?" he screamed.

Another collision. His feet tangled in a wire and there was a tremendous noise as some heavy item was pulled off the table.

"Feather, where are you?"

He flailed around and suddenly felt the softness of the bed next to his leg. He slumped down on it and clutched at his face—at his eyes. He beat at the mattress—tore at it. Screamed and swore and raged.

After a long minute…

"Feather?" he whispered. "Are you there?" He listened, but could hear nothing. Not even the sound of breathing.

"Feather?"

He reached out, feeling blindly about him. Fumbled to the edge of the bed—and reached out into space.

It was there that he touched something soft, and wet. Something warm—a familiar soft watery flesh.

He opened his mouth—and closed it again. Then he quietly slid to the wet floor beside—her. Feeling onwards he found her shape, and followed it down to her stomach. That was when it began to feel unfamiliar. He felt the huge canyon that had opened up in her there and knew what he'd done. Felt with his hand—it was not water in there at all. It was meat.

It was a doorway.

10

Nothing but burning fire—red fire. Fire that seemed to resemble more and more the beating of a thousand blurred wings.

Cal lay on the floor and waited to die.

Part 2

Looking Back

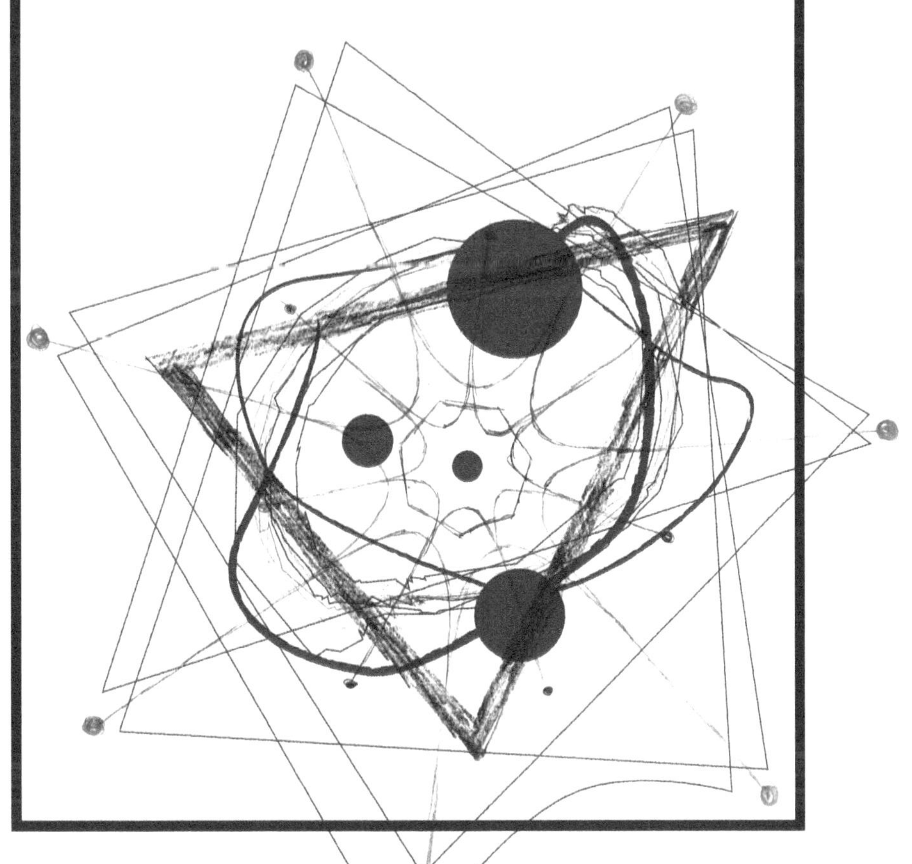

This section collects a few very early pieces that are nevertheless related to the main parts of this book—stories that might be called juvenilia. 'DVD extras' in this context. For the curious. Feverish prose poems and little horror tales, sometimes filled with heated Lovecraftian linguistic excess and loneliness.

Yes, it might surprise some people to learn that Lovecraft was one of my earliest influences, alongside a few other fairly familiar names like JG Ballard, Ramsey Campbell and Michael Moorcock. It is interesting to note, however, that while the Lovecraft influences in these fragments may be rather hilarious, it always seems to be the psychological side of his writing that I was responding to—the loneliness, the outsider, the misfit, rather than the overt horror or tentacled monstrosities. Sharing these here is rather wearing my heart on my sleeve—the sad, isolated kid getting a sense of fellow-feeling in a writer who always felt more of a lost and slightly mad outsider to me than a 'genre' author, and staring in dumbfounded wonder at such spectacularly and unashamedly overblown prose that was not so much purple as neon. *You can write like this? Bloody hell ...*

In spite of that excess, these are still little prototypes that provide a curious foreshadowing of the main parts of this book in ways that some people may not 'get' at all—and I'm not sure I do either sometimes. But there are some familiar *idees fixes* making their appearance, the feeling of a young me trying stuff out, and some of the earliest appearances of my recurring character Feather. Albeit without many hints of where she would end up taking me. These fragments include some of the very oldest texts that still survive, and I have resisted the temptation to edit them too much, save for a few direct mistakes and a few moments just too cringeworthy for human eyes.

Finally, this section includes the first story of mine ever to see print—in the 2004 Strange Tales anthology from Tartarus Press, though the story itself would have been written several years before that. Like the others here, I'm not sure I can really claim to 'like' *Number 18* very much these days, though its vicious surrealism certainly laid the foundation for stories like Giants and Red Fire. Be aware, this story is a grim exercise in child-rape and mental breakdown written when I wasn't that much older than the protagonist at the 'present' point of the narrative, and I'm not really sure where it came from. My own life has never experienced any major trauma from without (though plenty from within my own head!), so the topic must have been consciously selected. The ages in the story are not exactly spelt out but you can think of the 'present' character as a young-ish adolescent/teen who is dealing with all the changes of life, but coupled with truly toxic and traumatic memories of something from several years before.

These days, I find it weird just how bleak some of these earliest pieces can be. It feels as though I was one bruised and messed-up kid, though again due to no specific reason beyond having to exist in this world. But all that said, feel free to smile at them, or cringe a bit—don't take them too seriously. They are DVD extras after all.

The Execution

It must have been the heat—that awful humid heat, with the children shrieking outside in the darkness as I lay, drenched and dripping among the tangled chaos of my old quilts—that caused the moths to come. Never before and never again shall such a swarm beat before my broken eyes—wheeling and swirling about my room, the noise of their wings all but driving out the other sound of children playing at murdering each other—toy pistols flashing in the dark. Always there are moths of course—they come every night to me, attracted to the light that I can never extinguish since it comes from my own body—white and blazing. Never can I be rid of the wretched insects that float about me now, even as they did on that night so long ago. But now the walls are thick with them, almost hiding the dirty old paintwork. There are moths in the bed—fluttering about me as I move in an agony of caution lest their beautiful forms be crushed out of existence. The whole world is moths tonight—the whole world a storm of wings.

Except for the voices of the children.

They shriek on as always—calling and crying—as they have been for days now. And while they are there I can find no sleep. Their voices ring and echo through my head—smothering me in the jagged whiteness that is their playing. No one else hears them—I know that. They are ghosts, these children—and sometimes I think I hear them yelling my name amid the chaos—the sounds of wings and murder. *Bang bang—bang bang.* I put my head under the bedclothes—amid the dust of the unfortunate moths. But the sounds are still there—unchanging.

At first they seemed distant and I doubted my ears—but since then they have been approaching—always. They are in my own garden now—I swear it—yelling and yelling—yelling at me as they used to yell so many years ago—on the day I died. "Calvin—Calvin, you spoil our games—you spoil our games, our games—you annoy us—you annoy us—go away Calvin, go away home—go away Calvin, go away home." There were moths then as well—on that night. There were always moths coming to drink of the light of our bodies that turned the woods to day around us—but that night they were everywhere—the air heavy with them—clustering around us—around *her*, for she was as the sun is to the Moon—her light a blaze of glory. "Go away Calvin, go away home way home," they shrieked as I tried to join them—and then when still I haunted them in their playing, they all suddenly froze about me—all stood still on the instant—perfect silence—gazing at me. Then—then *she* said out loud, "if you won't leave us, then we'll have to kill you"—and two of them seized me and held me fast. They were all looking at me, a surrounding sea of implacable hate-filled eyes, and I shrieked with terror. I was going die—I knew it. This was no game—these people were no longer children—as they stood there grimly—their bodies aglow—as they, perfectly in unison, raised their toy pistols, training them on me as I squirmed and screamed—and they fired.

Bang bang.

Did I really die then? It would explain a lot of things. And all the rest was only the dreams of a ghost—running away from them, tears streaming down my face as they yelled after me—shrieking and whooping—and then I heard *her* voice. "Run, Calvin run—

you spoil our games so run away home away home—that time we let you off—but next time—"

And so I grew up in loneliness, and time passed—an incalculable passage—and now they're back, their calls growing and growing through the hours—endless—tirelessly—in the darkness of the night. The moths fill the room—endlessly shifting. Sometimes they seem to shimmer and change into other things, hazy and indistinct—things that whistle and vibrate in their excitement. Maybe when my light is finally extinguished they shall find rest—who knows? My body is cold and numb—I am less and less able to move. Tonight is the night—I know it—as the voices approach amid the storm of wings—and I will see their faces for the first time—the old familiar faces—the face of *her*. They grasp me and bundle me away into the world—the moths streaming behind me like a great wave—hustle and bustle my weary bones through the night to the fated spot—as they hold me up before that sea of eyes and the pistols reach for me and spit lines of vivid fire to break my flesh into red red ribbons—as the moths descend to drink my blood and my soul—

I sigh amid the drenched sheets of my old bed. My eyes have gone dark—the moths have vanished—but I hear them—I hear them still amid the chattering of children's voices. My room has gone—all the world is blankness. The voices fall suddenly silent. Are they coming? Are they here? All I can hear in these last moments is a great storm of wings.

Flesh

Come, strange woodland creatures, and moving forms. For me, for once be filled with strange wisdom and uncanny life—make your minds work as they should. You are never the same, you know. You are here, alone and just one of a kind—no mate, no love—just born to serve this accursed dell until you die, half-mad and dreaming dreams of flesh. Always it is flesh—flesh that trails blood and pus from hideous wounds. You have no place here, misbegotten things that you are—sexed but sexless—crawling slimily over the earth of this globe of insignificance—this planet of rock, half bare of trees. Come to me.

I sit here, watching you—I know each second's space and it thrills me more with horror than with joy because I ask myself, how long—how long will this go on for? Will nobody help me, or help you—or help themselves?

You flesh eaters—I will bring about your transition!

Here in this dell, the wolves howl—but yet tonight I can find nothing. Come to me! I call you—absurd creatures! Come to me. To me. Come to me!

And to think I thought this place, this nameless tarn, divine and measureless. When I first came here I gazed in awe, this rich dark life squirming among the decaying logs. I thought you could help me. I sat here watching the ages flow by me in a stately stream, watched the weird creations that clustered about me with a stifling, wraith-like noisomeness. Give me flesh, you wretched things. Flesh—living flesh. That is all I need. A spark of life to match my own. That thought drives me mad—so I turn my heavy thoughts away. And yet how can I still this yearning—this pain?

You tell me to brave it, this unutterable thing. You must. Time rages onwards maybe, but I feel so tired... nothing but darkness and abysmal voids, both inside me and without.

Can you create living flesh for me? I will crawl then—crawl into the mud. Let it fill me. Let it flow into my lungs. And then I will sit, silent and tranquil—in a world with a purer sheen—supernal.

Flesh—just living flesh...

Whirling in the maelstrom I see it all changing—transmuting into liquid flame.

The Hunted Form

Chased by nameless perils, he fled the town he knew—leaving, in that endless evening, that place of familiar streets where the lights stained the very sky a sinister red—and struck out along a deserted footpath. Ahead, he knew, was the real darkness—and only there would he find safety.

What he was fleeing from even he had barely an idea. He thought he knew certain images—images that drove him onwards even though they meant little to him. An image of something shiny and silver that lay and moved on the dark earth with sensitive slowness. And a man whose face was no longer as a face ought to be—glimpsed for one instant among vague and nebulous urban shapes and then lost, but still—always—following him. These images filled him with fear—but they were still vague—seemed even meaningless—and he knew not what to do with them. It was as if they came from some deeper dream—some older dream—whose fabric lay hidden and buried beneath the present.

Through a valley the path ran—merely one among many—and ahead he could make out the vast shape of the new motorway as it passed high above, carried mightily on a white bridge that was an engineering marvel. Twelve spans long—smooth and graceful in the darkness—and haloed eerily in the lights of the many metal vehicles that crossed it continuously. Beyond the bridge was the darkness—the place of safety in an oblivion of night. Away—away from this town where the light never faded—the town where the night never truly came. Safety—where even the man with the bad face could not come, for this bridge marked to him the edge—the edge of everything human—and beyond it all would be well again.

Twelve spans long was the bridge—and under those spans twelve ways passed—out into the wilderness. Roads, a river, railway tracks—and paths—many many paths. They all came here—all of them—for here was one of the few ways out of the town. They crowded together like sand passing through the neck of an hourglass—and then they were free. Free to spread out into the countryside. The bridge was huge, and there seemed room enough for all the paths in the world—all the good paths that led away, at least, he thought. No noisome allies, riddled with lurking shadows. No politely manicured paths where the trees are geometric and the very grass itself seems shaped by mathematical formulae. The bridge was huge, yes. He looked at it as he walked. Huge and airy—but with that, his eyes slid slowly leftwards—where the ground rose, and earth and concrete converged to a point—and he realised that some darkness could indeed be bad—the darkness made by humanity. Up there, where the spans narrowed and narrowed to nothing, there was a darkness that frightened him—and he would have to pass through it—for that was where he was headed.

He looked over his shoulder—he was always looking over his shoulder—searching for signs of his pursuers. He could see nothing—no tell-tail flash of crawling silver—no stealthy movement of the man with the bad face—but he knew that they were there. He drew a deep breath and looked again at the bridge. It was closer now, looming large—the bad dark was nearer—and he shivered, a slight memory surfacing. But did it matter? His pursuers were behind him—so he was told by every nerve in his body—not before him. Fear of that bad dark was meaningless, and darkness or no, it would be a matter of moments to pass through it—under that motorway to safety.

A sound behind him—

—and suddenly panic welled up—and for one moment he stood still as crystal. Then he began to run—pounding along the path and watching numbly as the bridge loomed closer and closer—and the path veered leftwards, ever leftwards, towards where earth and concrete met—towards the dark. It twisted and turned about—black tree branches meeting overhead—and the occasional street light, which gleamed like an orange ghost in the slight mist. He ran harder, his breath coming fast and painful—his teeth aching with the exertion. Not far now. The ground seemed almost to be twanging under his feet like running on the surface of a drum—bouncing—bouncing—even helping him along toward his destination—the soft earth nothing more than a skin—a skin stretched tight over worlds of strangeness—the worlds where the man with the bad face and the crawling silver had waited—waited for him—and now pursued him through his own familiar town. The bridge soared above him now—he was nearly there—and then just a brief dash through the dark—then free—forever.

Then—panting—he came to the point where the path forked—and he staggered to a brief stop. To the left, one branch rose up to the motorway, to where there was light—and he gazed that way with longing in his heart—for the light seemed safe. Even easy. But that was a false comfort and he knew it—for up there he would simply find himself trapped within the boundary of the road, which he certainly wouldn't be able to cross—and they would have him. So he looked rightwards—to where the other path dropped away down—into the dark. That dark was bad—he had never seen, never imagined or dreamed of such a darkness. And yet—

In this world there may be good darkness and bad—but at night it is the light that is unnatural—and so he made the choice that really wasn't a choice at all. He resisted the temptation of the upward path—the pleasant path that would lead to his death hemmed inside this horrible town. Ignore it—and embrace the darkness. At night it is the light that is unnatural. And so, with only the slightest tremor, he swung rightwards—and descended—and the night swallowed him—

Dual Carriageway

It had been a long drive, I'll give them that. A long drive after a self-induced bad night of farewell bingeing. A dumb plan from the start.

"Look," Jim cried. "Is it totally impossible for you to get this fucking car to move?"

I took my eyes away from the motorway for a moment to glare at him. "Why are you in such a hurry?"

He snorted—an unpleasant throaty sound that made me cringe. "You mean aside from wanting to get to college before the Christmas holidays?" He subsided scowling across the back seats and glaring out of the window. Outside, ahead, the road climbed up and up, a very long slope set in a deep cutting that seemed to vanish straight into the sun itself. No car could go fast on a hill like this, I told myself—lied to myself—especially as I could hardly see a thing in front of me. But while it was true that the entire dual carriageway had been wound down several miles per hour, everyone was still sailing past in an overtaking stream.

This old car was struggling.

"Would you prefer to walk?" I snapped. "I am sure a bit less weight could only be a good thing."

He clenched his fists. "In which case, my friend, I think you should let me drive."

I turned round again, furiously, but Feather yelped "Watch the road," and there was a grinding, vibrating shock as we touched the ribbed line of paint that marked the hard shoulder. I swore under my breath and pulled the car back in lane—but we had lost speed.

"I did wondering if this old thing would handle it," Feather began as I remained carefully silent. "But hey—it's true. No massive rush."

"It had better."

Ever since the struggle to get a sleepy and hung-over Jim out of bed this morning, I had regretted agreeing to give lifts. And now I was wondering what would happen if I were to just pull over, boot them both out and drive away, never to be seen again. Could one start a new life with nothing more than the minimal accoutrements intended for a college dorm and a clapped-out car? Maybe I could become a trailer dweller on the coast somewhere and forget about all this forever—live in one somewhat less pressured brand of poverty and learn to survive off my own handicraft.

If bloody only.

"Look," I said over the straining engine, "we'll get there. Soon enough. Just to the top of this hill and then it is headlong down into town, I think."

I wiped my brow. My head was aching, fuelled by lack of sleep as much as anything, but the sunlight streaming down on us was painful, shining and glinting through the windscreen. It was hot and the airstream from the four open windows was not much comfort. I have always found driving in bright sunlight painful and now the glare seemed to completely fill the cutting through which the road climbed, as if we were driving towards a blinding curtain. Indeed, we might have been driving straight up into the star's fiery heart for all we could see. The other cars sailed past only to dwindle in a shimmer of heat haze and vanish. Huge lorries went by, the slipstream making the car rock, before disappearing as dark square shapes against the glare. I reminded myself with desperation that it would not be long before we could get off this horrible road.

Jim shifted, lounged for a moment the other way across the back seats, shoving his guitar out of the way, then moodily demanded a can of beer, which Feather handed him with what felt like a lot of patience. She at least was quiet company and I appreciated that. Neither of us knew her very well—she was a subdued and rather isolated girl and our spheres had never really touched, but I couldn't refuse her last-minute request for a lift. And now I was quite glad she was there.

The car smelt of hot plastic, petrol fumes, hot beer and hotter people. For a moment, I felt a wash of dizziness and caught myself hastily before I drifted over onto the hard shoulder again. It seemed as though the car had reacted in parallel, because it was going slower than ever now. The engine raced but none of that racing seemed to be translated into speed.

"Are you all right?" Feather asked.

I glanced at her and tried to smile. "Just about. It's just hard staring into this sunlight."

"*Why* are we going so slow?" Jim demanded, tossing his empty beer can onto the floor. "What's the matter with this thing?"

It is probably significant that as the car struggled and began to fail, I was more disturbed by the prospect of Jim's whining voice than about any breakdown. *Please,* I was begging, *don't give that voice any more fuel—just get up this hill and all will be well.*

But no. The car was crawling more than ever. The accelerator was floored. The engine raced and roared but that was all. My heart sank horribly. The car was losing power.

"Well?" Jim demanded.

I drew a deep breath. "Just shut up," I said distinctly. He sat up straight and affronted and peered out between the two front seats.

"Is something wrong?" Feather asked, still sounding beautifully calm amid all this.

In my head, I was positively screaming. I worked at the engine, trying to get a response but nothing changed. The car slowed and slowed while the other motorists roared past faster and faster and noisier and noisier. The sun baked down, heat haze and impossible radiance filling the road—and at last, with a kind of sob, I gave up and steered the car onto the hard shoulder. It bumped alarmingly as it settled into the grass on the verge and I leant my head wearily on the steering wheel.

"What the fuck?" Jim began and Feather touched my sleeve. I glanced at her, only to receive a dazzling flash of reflected light from her glasses.

"Look," I said, blinking, "please just shut up." I gestured round vaguely, trying to indicate that we were going nowhere in the foreseeable future.

Jim thumped the seat in front of him. "Oh well, that's just brilliant that is. Absolutely fucking brilliant!"

I fumbled for the door handle and opened it carefully, for the racing vehicles were only a few feet away. I slipped out and was immediately engulfed in a tumult of noise, wind and motion. I screwed up my face against the storm and hurried around the car away from the road. But I could only retreat a few feet before I came up against the slope of the cutting, which was steep and stony—almost a cliff. Rushing air from the cars and heavy lorries sucked at me, blowing my hair all over the place. I felt like seaweed in the grip of a strong swell, pulled this way and that. The sound was continuous, though always changing—cars, lorries, even the occasional coach—and I felt trapped here in this steep-sided cutting. Trapped in a hell of sound and movement.

The passenger door opened and Feather followed me out. I looked at her and she touched my sleeve. "Never mind," she said with unexpected sympathy. "It can't be helped." She turned and looked at the car. "What's wrong—do you know?"

"That stupid vehicle, that's all," Jim commented as he also joined us on the verge. "I told you it wouldn't make it."

"Did you?" I grunted sarcastically. "When? All I can remember was 'Thanks for the lift—you saved my bacon'."

He snorted. "Well, a lot of use it has proved!"

"Very well," I said bitterly. "Next time you need to get across the country to college, you can take the train."

"I think so too," he said. "I would have been there long ago."

Feather forestalled my reply to that by quietly losing her temper. "Oh come on you two, shut up!" She looked at me. "Please stop arguing and let's think what to do. Do any of us have a mobile on us?"

"Well… no… I…"

"Then…" But instead of finishing she broke off with an exclamation, gazing up the hill.

"What?" Jim demanded.

She shook her head. "Nothing. Please, I don't like this sun. What shall we do?"

"No one likes the sun," Jim commented.

"Yes yes—I know that," she snapped. "But—"

I left them bickering and walked back to the car. Without much hope, I lifted the bonnet, to be greeted by a waft of hot, fumy air. I knew little about the mechanics of the thing. I knew how to change or refill the various fluids that needed changing and refilling, and the other weird rituals surrounding car ownership, but that was about all. Maybe it would start again and take us the rest of the way if we just waited a few minutes and let it cool off. That sounded too convenient to be very hopeful, but it was something for desperation to latch onto.

I slammed the bonnet again. Jim was strolling away, looking moody and defeated, and Feather was gazing after him with a downturned mouth. But right then I had little love for either of them, anyone or anything and I gazed out at the road instead. Brilliant flashes of sunlight from a myriad windscreens dazzled me and the heat radiated off the surface like an open oven. It was not a wide road—just two narrow, busy lanes on each carriageway. I had driven it before, and it always struck me as both odd and annoying that such a major route should be so small and tatty. Driving on it was a symphony of bumps from the tires as you crossed the black strips of old repairs or the seams between blocks of roadbed. Everyone drove fast, even now when you could hardly see anything.

I wiped at my brow, leaving a dark patch of sweat on my sleeve. I was uncomfortably aware of other such patches in my armpits and, in all probability, on my back as well, and I leant against the radiator grill and followed the cars with my eyes as they vanished up the hill. Engines racing—an endless stream, close-packed and impatient—probably all as bad-tempered as we were. The sun sat directly in the middle of the road and, looking at it, I began feeling dizzy again. There was something hypnotic and agonising about that light and I gazed at it until it seemed to waver and twist like mist. I blinked, with afterimages twisting against my eyelids—and now the inferno seemed to be all around me. Again I swayed like seaweed, but this time it was not air but light that pulled—light that seemed to plunge past me like waves. And that was when Feather gave a sudden shriek and I was jerked back to reality and looked round quickly.

But before I could even focus on her, I found myself faced with the image of Jim—flying through the air, his arms out like a superhero. That made no sense at all. It wasn't until he landed in a crumpled heap on the hard shoulder that I finally got it. I goggled at him—then at Feather, standing there with her mouth and eyes huge, absurdly clutching at her T-shirt—then out into the road where the cars roared unabated and oblivious.

I hurried round to him and Feather immediately grabbed at my arm and hung on tightly. She looked stunned and was babbling incoherently about the road, the light and something about a lorry. Jim wasn't moving—a smear of red. A bloodstained finger as I touched his face.

"The light," Feather whimpered. "He just fell under…"

"What happened?" I asked, but she ignored that.

"Can't we go," she moaned. "I don't like this road…"

Why, I wondered, was no one stopping? Surely they must see the crumpled body on the verge? Or was the sun and its dazzling light totally filling their eyes? I got up, intending to wave for help, but Feather dragged me back.

"Don't!" she cried and I looked at her.

"But I have to get…"

She shook her head.

"But—"

"I don't know what happened," she said rapidly, "I don't understand!"

"What do you mean?"

"I—don't—"

I tried to pull away from her but she stumbled after me.

"The light—" she murmured. "The light—pulled him under..."

She turned to look up the hill at the sun and gave a sigh. I followed her eyes, screwing up my face against the glare.

"You mean he was dazzled and blundered into the road by mistake?" I asked, but she said nothing. Her face looked unreadable—I wasn't sure if it was shock or something more. I guided her to the slope of grass and stones, and we sat together, one arm round her shoulders. She quietly leant her head against mine. And still the cars just raced past unceasingly and unheeding.

"This sun," she said at last, staring up—up the hill. "It's too bright—too—too... It flows down the road like a river."

"Right."

"The sun is—" she repeated again, still staring—then she pulled away from me, shaking her head.

"Are you alright?"

Gazing up the hill made my eyes water, forcing me to turn away and look down at the cars as they streamed up towards me. I would have to flag one down. Somehow. I needed help here. And yet, now I was suddenly nervous about stopping one of these racing machines. Why had no one stopped already? I felt alone among monsters, my headache was worse and I didn't know what to do.

"I feel sick," she muttered.

I scrambled up, heat haze rising on all sides, and shook my head. The back seat of the car was littered with empty beer cans, the relics of Jim's thirst—or whatever the word for it was—and for a brief moment they seemed haloed with vivid purple. I turned away with a start to find Feather still staring at the passing cars. I looked at her, seriously worried now. Her glasses reflected two dazzling points of light, hiding her eyes completely, but the rest of her looked ill. I made a movement towards her, then paused and stepped to the roadside. I had to stop someone. This was stupid. I extended my hand, thumb up—and then shrank back because my only response was a blinding flare of light. It seemed to be coming from where Feather was standing. I nearly stepped backwards into the road, but I stopped myself. Where her spectacles had gleamed dazzling white a moment ago, now they flashed and blazed with all the colours of the spectrum. The refracted light played around on the rough grass and in her hair, reflecting in the car's windows and dancing over my skin while an agonising pain hammered in my head. I cast one look up the hill into the inferno above, but that only made my stomach heave and I staggered against the car as waves of light flowed past. The world spun and flickered around me, and then I saw Feather moving. She flung up her arms—light shining through her hair, through her clothes, outlining her body inside them as though they had become as translucent as oiled paper. I still couldn't see her eyes because even when she turned her head, the dazzling glare was still there like twin stars. She appeared to be fighting with something and she staggered away from the road.

"Feather?" I called, horrified, for she was stumbling about as though genuinely blinded. I started towards her, for she seemed intent on climbing the cutting, which must be impossible. I tried to catch her, but all I managed to do was make her lose her grip. She opened her mouth and reeled backwards, tumbling head over heels down the slope, over the crash barrier and out onto the hard shoulder again in a flurry of legs and arms, landing in a heap on the ridged line that separated the hard shoulder from the main carriageways. Cars roared by just a foot from her head.

Again, I tried to reach her, still barely understanding what was happening—but then she stood up. The heat haze was all around her as she stood there on the line, her arms reaching out, not towards anything but away from that road. The cars thundered by—lorries whipping her hair in their slipstream—wing mirrors missing her by inches.

Then she slowly keeled over backwards. She lay for no more than a few seconds, trying to get up, before the whirl of metal caught her and smashed her down again. Her head broke with a crack against the tarmac and she sprawled in ways no one should sprawl as the wheels of an articulated lorry passed over her stomach.

The pain in my head was excruciating now and the air was filled with hints of odd refracted colour. I stared at her in utter horror. And… I was alone. Wasn't I? And then I was terrified. The light was everywhere. The sunlight. I looked about me. I was trapped here. On one side an unclimbable cliff and on the other a hell of moving metal. I didn't understand what was happening—what had happened—happening. There is a sense of unreality so maybe I am just dreaming. I made a dash for the car, clawed at the passenger door, then staggered over vomiting violently. Again I was feeling the seaweed sway and I reeled filled with dizziness, but eventually managed to get the door open, collapse in and slam it behind me. I scrambled across to the driver's seat, banging my knee painfully on the gear stick in the process, sat down and fumbled for my keys. I tried to start the engine in the hope that it might have recovered from whatever had been wrong before—but it still refused completely. Whimpering to myself at the pain, I rolled up the windows—all the windows, reaching over to the rear ones with difficulty, until the car was sealed. With that, the sound of the vehicles outside seemed remote and that was a small measure of comfort. The heat however was like a hammer, the light streaming through the windscreen as fiery as ever. I lolled back, sweat streaming down my face.

Feather?

I don't know what to say. I don't know what happened—I don't understand it. The light—she said it sucked him under—

In here, the temperature is really hot now—and the stink of petrol and plastic is overwhelming. I feel deeply unwell—my clothes are sodden and I am sitting in a puddle of sweat. But if I open the window—I dunno. Then what? In front of me—beyond the windscreen—I can see the cars, the endless, unchanging stream of cars, lorries, coaches, vans climbing up and up into the sun—

Too hot. They never stop—not until this road vanishes into the fire itself. They just shimmer in the heat and fade from existence. Still I can see the rainbow colours—everywhere. They flicker on the metal—reflected from a thousand windscreens—

Triangle

The copper wire continued.

This triangular building stood alone, with that particular kind of loneliness that you get in cities that has nothing to do with proximity or crowds. It was surrounded on all sides by a river of road and the building itself was little more than the support pillar of a huge bridge of weighty metal, across which ran multiple tracks of electrified railway. Whatever this building/pillar was or had been, it wasn't advertised, not even with ghosts. The windows were closed, the door looked as though it hadn't been opened for years and any decorations that might have graced the facades had long-since died and worn to grey.

The roads were busy, however—a split of carriageways and a major junction, with this island as the centrepoint. Many traffic lights, a tangle of pedestrian crossings, and yet as far as the passing eyes were concerned, the building was a thing that did not exist. The triangular pavement echoed to the tread of footsteps, but few paused to stare up at or wonder about this grimy block of forgetfulness.

However, along the pavement, in a triangle matching all the other triangles here, a single strand of copper wire ran. It was barely visible in the grime. Right round the building it ran, at one point, at one vertex of the triangle, it was tied off with a tight knot. This loop was trodden underfoot continuously, occasionally tripped over, kicked and sworn at, but like the building, few really gave it any thought. It was just another thing that the city threw up in the path of life, to be instantly forgotten when the inconvenience was past. Miraculously though, it had remained intact and unbroken.

Feather, though, watched it. For a long time. And from somewhere, she seemed to hear music. An eerie droning, dissonant sound with occasional jarring stabs of modernist melody. Tranquil but ultimately tense in ways that did not contradict. These grey windows had been ignored for years, but now Feather was trying to see through them. Because there was something inside that she should know about. The layers of grime made it difficult, but she could make out a room beyond—as grey and as dusty as one might expect. There was also a desk there, a small wooden office desk of classical design—and at the desk sat a figure. The figure didn't move. And Feather's skin prickled.

A shaking rumble overhead—the passing of a train. The silence in that room did not mean the absence of noise, but it was silent nonetheless—still—frozen. The figure still didn't move, though the music droned on—little flurries of notes cutting like thorns through the unending chords. Seated at his desk, the figure remained, holding a pen, ready to write who knows what on the dusty paper in front of him.

Then the other thing dawned on her. It was dark, but she could see that the figure was also covered in dust—old spider webs…

And grey—the cold grey of stone.

The wire circled round her—she could feel it like the coil of an electromagnet. Agonising. But time was passing. The city had fallen away. The land surrounding the crumbling triangular tower looking more like a rough desert—bleak and flat and treeless and wreathed with clouds that encircled everything like a crown. And as she watched, the stone man was weathering to nothing more than an outcrop of rock, adding yet more sand to the world.

After a moment, Feather bent and grabbed the long thread of copper. With a quick gesture, she snapped it and, still ignored by everyone passing, began to walk, winding it into a reel around her fingers.

The music was gone.

Casting the Chips

When I arrived at the little town chippie, it was already deep night. Most of the streets I had passed through were asleep in a dreary fog of silence. Nearby was a pub called Ye Olde Smack and a rock and shell shop, both shut down to black and closed, only this one island of light and food smells remained. Just a few metres away, on the other side of the massive concrete sea wall, the waves boomed on shingle and the darkness of the sky spoke of a world cut in half by coast. And this place—by day, no doubt, it was a suitably quint restaurant catering to the beach crowds. One of those large blocks of a building with white plastered walls and the wood frames painted green—adverts for ice cream and other seaside treats, swinging signs and paintings of seashells. Inside there would be framed photographs of sunsets over the sea, studies of shingle, maybe some shells collected and framed, or plastic starfish. That unique British seaside aesthetic now seeming rather incongruous with night. Now it was probably one last sad light in the darkness, a beacon to the few drunks or wandering teenagers ghosting the promenade. And hopefully a place not afraid to serve me in the small hours as well. Because I needed it. Oh boy did I need it.

It was empty of customers—no surprise. I could just see a figure leaning gently in the middle distance, behind the counter. Passing the night hours.

I swung off my bike with a grunt of relief and chained it up outside where I would still be able to see it. For a few moments,

I studied it suspiciously, making sure everything was in place. The rolled-up tarp, the bivvy bag, the solar panel draped over, the fishing catapult and gear, the small portable fireplace. Then I glanced down at myself with equal suspicion. These rare times when I interacted with the world tended to spark a hint of paranoia. Just what did I look like? I ran a comb through my hair and gazed down at my sandy clothes. But I was tired—very tired. So tired that I was neither thinking straight nor caring. I just wanted a plateful of something substantial and, above all, hot before I left this town of silence and ghosts behind me.

The young woman behind the greasy-looking chip fryer gave me a curious look as I stepped in. I was used to that—but I was relieved that my acute radar could detect nothing negative in there. There was a quiet smile on her face that became a welcoming grin, and the general air was almost one of contentment.

I looked around briefly. Again the classics—drinks fridges, illuminated menus, shelves full of vinegar bottles etc. There were indeed photographs on the wall, and what looked like a collection of ormer shells on one windowsill. Pretty, but I am sure not from around here. I studied the menu—though I don't know why because the menus are always the same. Various fish and chips and, because this place was obviously trying to cover more markets, kebabs served with salad and pitta or chips, chicken nuggets with chips, fried chicken with chips, weirdly red saveloys with chips…

"You look tired," she said, sounding at least agreeable.

I nodded—"Yeah"—too much so to really talk. Not that I am much of a talker at the best of times. There was still a way to go yet to get out of town and I hoped that I could make it. Fuel would be good. Warmth would be good.

There was an unusually gentle look in her eyes for someone working towards the small hours serving fast food to the wild night wanderers, and I couldn't help a tired smile. I wasn't used to that.

"Some cod and chips—please," I said. "Got any battered mushrooms?"

"Sorry—none of those left," she said.

I nodded. "No problem."

"Anything else?"

"I'll grab a drink if… if…"

"Of course, just help yourself."

All the options were sweet—but sweet is a good thing under my circumstances. Sugar is good and artificial sweeteners seem vaguely treacherous. Such are the inversions that can occur in life. Such are the perversions of luxury.

I took a carton of fruit-flavoured fluid, then paid her and sat down heavily at the nearest table, watching as she cooked. It didn't take long. And then I found myself watching an odd little pantomime. She held the plate up to the light, studying it with a quiet smile—a look of satisfaction on her face that seemed rather inordinate for such a basic white disc. Then she put it down on the counter and casually tossed a small shovel-full of chips onto it—nothing more than a handful. I was hoping that the portion I got to eat would be a bit larger than that, but she was just studying them dreamily—a quiet smile on her face. That same sense of contentment was in the air again—a sense of calm and homeliness that again seemed unusual for this place and this time. But then she shrugged and quickly loaded the plate with fried fish and a good heap more chips and delivered it with a smile.

"There you go, hope you enjoy."

"Thanks," I mumbled.

I could feel her eyes lingering on me with the same curiosity as she stepped to the door and switched the sign to 'closed', then retreated behind the fryers and sat down. But again, I couldn't be bothered to care. I just wanted food. And the food was good. Chips can be a lottery at the best of times—even more so at almost 1AM—but these were excellent. And I was conscious of a rather unusual feeling as I polished that plate off. Happiness.

As I sat back a few minutes later, sucking at that fruity stuff through its straw, she leant over.

"Want some more chips?" she asked.

"Hmm?"

"On the house—there's some left over."

I consulted my stomach. It wasn't hungry, but at the same time, the one thing you never ever did was refuse free food.

"Well ok—great, thanks," I said awkwardly, still hardly a good conversationalist.

She whisked out a plate and once again the ritual was performed. A small portion of chips was dished out as though to test them. She regarded it a moment, eyebrows up, then dished out a generous further heap.

"I always cook too much," she said, putting it down on the table. "The boss is always on at me about it. Our secret, OK?"

"Of course," I said. "I dunno who I would be telling anyway." I gave a huge yawn and ate a few more chips—the long ride still ahead of me only seeming to get longer and longer with every mouthful.

Then the tiredness and the present atmosphere in here led me to open my mouth when I would normally keep it closed. "Why do you dish the chips out like that?"

"Hmm?" she murmured, with a sideways glance.

"I mean… why the test-run?"

She smiled. "Well—I dunno," she said with deliberate obliquity. "It's just a thing I do. Why are you on the road? Cycling mile after mile, day after day? Why is there a solar panel on the back of your bike? Why don't you have a home?"

"It charges my camera," I said sleepily, before what she had said got through to me. I glanced up at her sharply, forgetting about the plate of food beside me.

"You are tired," she said. "But it is a nice tiredness, yes? Why?"

I just stared blankly. To be honest, all this felt like a dream now. I was definitely not used to people taking me this seriously.

"Just a thing," she repeated with a grin, then returned behind the chip fryer with a sigh. "Want any more?" she asked. "Look at all this lot."

Before I could think of anything to say though, there was an interruption. The door opened with a clang and she glanced round with a frown.

"Sorry—we are no longer serving food now. Unless you just want some chips."

The man who had come in didn't look best pleased at that. "Oh come on," he cried. "I'm fucking hungry."

"Sorry," she said again with an eyebrows-up smile. "All out of everything now—except chips. Can sure do you a plate of those."

"He's eating," he grumbled, pointing to me and I looked up reluctantly. He looked ugly with tiredness—and maybe with other things as well. "Can't you do me some chicken? Or a sausage?"

"Look mate," she said with a less friendly tone of voice, "I have been tossing these chips for ten fucking hours—my mind gets tired from all that mental exertion. Read the sign—we are closed."

"Look," he expostulated, "Surely you could…"

"Go on—sorry but you'll have to get out of here."

"Look," he growled. "I fucking didn't…"

She suddenly grew a very sweet smile and I stared at her in surprise.

"Alright—let's have a look at you."

I watched uneasily as she grabbed a plate and tossed a scattering of chips in her usual thoughtful way.

"Hey—more than that," he cried. "Come on…"

"Uh uh," she said sweetly. "Not sure that's a good idea. I'd say you should be at home right now anyway. Your girlfriend does know where you have been, you know…"

There was instant silence.

"What?" he managed at last.

She grinned. "Want the chips?" she asked, offering the plate. "It's all we have left."

"Why you fucking bitch," he muttered, making a sudden move towards her. I flinched and half stood up, but it wasn't needed.

"Yeah—do it," she cried, beckoning. "Great way to end the evening, getting some nice friendly police officers to chuck you out of here."

"Fuck," he cried, gave her one last bewildered look, then spun away and ran out of the shop. His eyes filled with some kind of panic and whatever she had meant, it seemed to have hit home.

She sighed and tossed the small plateful of chips away.

"So you're a bloody fortune teller," I said dryly—half joking, half too sleepy to question it much.

"You said it."

"You're a… a seaside chippie fortune teller," I repeated. "I like that."

"It's all in the patterns," she said with a playful smile. "It is amazing what you can tell from it. I shouldn't be talking about this though. I'll give the chip shop a bad name. Want any more chips?"

"Aaah," I said comfortably. "I can't—I won't be able to cycle a yard."

"Then the dustbin will have a good meal," she said forlornly.

"Maybe you should have a plateful yourself," I said.

She gave me a wry look. "Yeah?"

"Uhuh. Tell your own fortune. Or can't you stand the thought of eating them after cooking them all day?"

She smiled a crooked smile.

"It's much more fun to read the guilty horrors of other people. My own guilty horrors—I dunno."

I said nothing for a moment, mentally shrugging. I was too tired to regard this with anything other than a dream's logic.

"Aaaah sod it," she said at last. "Ok. Otherwise these damn things will just go to waste."

She grabbed a plate and I watched with the comfortable expectation of familiar events as she dished out a tiny helping. She stared at them for a moment.

"Well," she said. "They say—hmm…"

She broke off with a startled look—her eyes flickering to me with an expression that my tired mind certainly couldn't read.

"What?"

She glanced round the room, half smiling and still with that very odd expression in her face.

"I think you would be happier if I didn't tell you that one," she said.

"What," I demanded. "Have you seen me dying from eating too much, face down in your chips later this evening?"

"No no," she said. "Don't worry—" she gave a small laugh. "You are fine."

"Oh come on," I cried, unable to keep from grinning. "You have read two of my platefuls now and told me nothing. Ok—let's have one more—small. I doubt I can eat them but hey—tell me more."

She tossed some chips again, and leant over them dramatically. Theatrically, with a dark grin on her face.

"A long woman and a dark journey?" I asked.

"I am curious," she said. "The patterns—and your face. I have never met anyone quite like you. You are wandering—I can see that. You are cycling—you don't live anywhere. You have no home? Or did you deliberately abandon it?"

"Did you get that from the chips or from looking at my bike?" I asked suspiciously, gesturing at the vehicle tied up outside. She just gave an enigmatic smile.

"So what's the deal?" she asked. "You only sleep out of towns, where it is lonelier and safer? You have a way to go yet tonight? What's the deal?"

I sat back, suddenly feeling dark. "I will head out of town, yes. I am following the beach, so I will find a quiet lonely place out in the marshes and bed down there. Beaches are good places. In spite of people's best efforts, they are still about the only land left free."

"I'm impressed," she said. "But not tonight, ok? You can't cycle now, you look wrecked. Come on. We are going back to my place. You can sleep there—sleep in a bed for once, ok."

I stared at her, startled into a much more awake state by that offer. People just didn't do that to shabby strangers at one in the morning.

"But," I stammered. "But—you don't, I mean… you don't know me at all?"

"Don't I?" she asked with a wan smile. "I'm the fortune teller, remember. It's ok—just trust me here. Do I look dangerous?"

"I'm not sure about that," I muttered and she gave a sharp laugh. I quickly finished my chips as she bustled around tidying things up and preparing to shut down the shop. Then she grabbed my plate and washed it and soon we were ready to go. We went outside into the almost silent street and I unchained my bike. In the distance, some air-conditioning or ventilation unit whirred softly and under that I could just hear the sea on the beach. The familiar sounds of a small British town in the small hours of the night.

It wasn't a long walk to her house—just a few shops down the high street and a few metres into a side road of quiet terraced houses. Then she opened a gate and hurried up the path, key in hand. I followed, noting the non-descript garden: coarse grass and a few bushes that I couldn't identify, even though they seem to be in about two-thirds of all gardens. Then white paint—a blue gloss door opened into a short hallway of coats and shoes and a single painting on the wall. Something vaguely and indefinably ethnic.

"You can bring the bike in," she said, waving vaguely. She hurried in and opened a second door. "Here's my apartment," she said, switching the light on. Just run it into the front room here."

I did as she said, gingerly steering my bulky vehicle across the carpet and parking it against the wall.

"Now," she said. "I am going to put you on the sofa. Trust me—it's just as comfortable as my bed. That ok?"

"Fine," I said staring around. It was so long since I had been in a house—especially someone else's house—that I felt almost frightened of it. This place was alien and personal—her things scattered around. I watched dizzily as she quickly made up a bed for me.

"Now—are you going to be ok?"

"I am used to sleeping on shingle or sand—so whatever this is will be very much ok."

I sat down gingerly, kicking off my shoes, releasing a trickle of dirt, which I looked at guiltily. I was reluctant to move too much in case I somehow damaged this strange personal space and I watched uneasily as she slipped away into the other room. There was a flurry of clothes sounds and she reappeared in a dressing gown.

"Um," I murmured helplessly.

"Just make yourself at home," she said. "Please. Just flop out and don't worry about anything. Tomorrow you can have a bath if you want—and wash your clothes."

"I—uh…"

I was struggling to find the words to express gratitude, but they weren't coming. It was so long since I had had any reason to be grateful to anyone.

"It's ok," she murmured again. "You don't have to say anything. I'm the fortune teller, remember?" She hurried into the bathroom and there were more sounds. Running water. Brushing teeth. A trickle into the toilet.

"Can you really read the chips," I asked sleepily when she returned, "or are you just exceptionally good at reading me and my bicycle?"

She gave a sly grin. "Answer that one and you may just solve all the mysteries of the world."

"Then what did those chips say to you? That you wouldn't tell me about?"

She coughed. "Oh, they said something about—*tonight I would sleep with a perfect stranger*. Or am I just reading myself now?"

"Ah," I murmured.

"Kind of threw me for a minute," she said. "But that's life—you never know where you will end up or what anything really means. Never say never and all that. Of course," she murmured with a chuckle, shaking her hair. "I thought for a moment this, uh, image meant something a bit more than you crashed on my sofa."

I gave a dry laugh. "At this time of night, after a week's solid cycling… and three plates of chips… I think I would be a disappointment."

She grinned and I lay down gratefully on the sofa.

"What will you do tomorrow?" she asked at last. "Just—continue?"

"I suppose," I said. "It's not so bad."

"No?"

"Well—I may not have a home, but at least I am out in the fresh air, reasonably independent, no bills to pay—not spending my time sitting in front of a computer getting fat or working a nine-to-five until I am old before my time…"

I broke off.

"Like me you mean," she murmured.

"Um…"

"It's ok—you are right. That's another reason I don't like to eat the chips myself. All they tell me is the pointlessness of life—over and over."

"Mmmm," I said, suddenly seeing her point with some clarity.

She chuckled. "So now the chips say what? *She sat back and stared at the ceiling, an agreeable fantasy in her head of joining him on the road, like in some old fairy tale…*"

"Yeah?"

"*But no*, she thought quickly enough. *She likes her comfort. She may die young but at least she will die in bed. We hope. Though the lingering doubt remains—even beds aren't seeming such a given these days.*"

I gave a sad sigh.

"Anyway—I will let you sleep," she said. "The chips say I can't keep my eyes open—the chips say *no earthly need to get up early tomorrow at least.* The chips say *if I don't shut up soon, he will pass out on me.*"

I gave a sleepy chuckle, almost under my breath now.

"Goodnight," she whispered. "I will be dreaming of chips, I know it."

I rubbed my stomach. "Me too probably."

She snapped off the light and I was left in the dark, save for the few tiny LEDs from somewhere that lit up the room—unusual constellations for me now. I glanced at the bulky shape of my bicycle against the wall, then closed my eyes.

Number 18

The orange sodium light fell through her window, imprinting the shapes of the frame on the wall opposite her—many shapes, layer upon layer—one for each of the street lamps that marched along the road outside. The room was bathed in a soft glow that only served to make the shadows darker, plunging her old familiar surroundings into mystery and strangeness. Pepper lay on her back, clutching the bedclothes tight under her chin in spite of the heat. Her eyes were wide open, gazing intently into the gloom, and her face was drawn and haggard. How, she wondered, could a room that she thought she knew as well as she knew her own body, look so alien when the night held the world in its hands? It was as if the orange glare from the street lamps had cast a very subtle projection of something else over it all—a world where anything was possible. Sometimes she thought she caught movements out of the corner of her eye—brief flickers of shadowy white or red—but when she looked—nothing. The world outside was far from silent. Occasionally, from the street below, there would come the sounds of voices, cries and whimpers, drunken moanings and shrieks—and always, from the distance, there was the sound of traffic, roaring like a furious beast about to descend on this town and smite it out of existence, and every evil force therein along with it.

Pepper groaned aloud and turned over. Her head felt strange, as though full of warm cotton wool, and her body was as dry as stone between the sheets. The heat enveloped her like a giant hand, curling among the furniture and around the bed, an invisible mist in the darkness. Her eyes felt huge—and even they seemed dry. She blinked—screwed her face up—rubbed there with her fists, causing bolts of colour to flicker inside her head, and a dizziness enveloped her. The bed creaked loudly as she did so and she froze and lay still. She thought she heard a noise outside—a scuffle of leaves from the garden, and she stared urgently in the direction of the window. There was a white shape there, looking in at her and she expelled her breath slowly in stark terror—before realising that it was only a shadow of moonlight. Trembling slightly, she relaxed and drew the covers around her neck again and gazed at the ceiling. The light cut across it in a great triangle, as distinct and clear as an ice cream wafer—and as she stared, it seemed to flicker, as though what was outside was not the old familiar street lights that marched down the hill bobbing and swaying like something out of a cartoon, but a great fire that filled the world in a lake of glowing orange.

Pepper closed her eyes, and from out in the road, there came the sound of raised voices—a man sobbing. As it slowly faded away in the distance, she cast the eye of her mind out through her window and into the empty street, trying to visualise the houses—no. 10 with its privet hedge, the lawn scattered with children's toys—no. 12 with the bricked-up window like a blinded eye in the shadow of the holly tree. There was no. 14 and the dog that barked as you went past—and no. 16 with the weedridden garden. And then there was no. 18—and she stopped herself. She had no wish to remember that. The house was empty now, and the image of the man's face that floated up before her was a thing of the past.

She drew in a deep breath—and again there came a sound from without—a hedgehog in the garden most likely, she told herself, but she gazed at the window intently again for a while, just to be sure.

The image of no. 18's bland white-washed front drifted again before her eyes—the door, painted dark red like blood, standing open—the blank windows. She tried to chase the thoughts away, her mouth turning down at the corners in a painful grimace. The bedclothes seemed very heavy about her now and she pushed them away, running her hands over her skin and feeling its dryness. It seemed as if most of the heat was coming from within her body, radiating from her as though she was an electric light bulb. It was unendurable. She wanted to get up and go through to the bathroom, there to hold her hands under the cold tap and then rub them all over herself to try and induce a bit of moisture—to bathe her parched face in it—to drink it by the cupful. She wanted to. She could almost feel the slosh of the cold water over her skin—and yet she didn't dare get up. Instead, she gazed round the room, her heart racing. Everything was still now but for the ever-present traffic—outside, the last drunk seemed to have gone—and she drew in a long slow breath of misery. Her bed was a place of sanctuary, a place where she was safe. She could see herself bent over the sink, rubbing the water over her face. The world would be full of splashings—her eyes would be closed—and who knows what might happen? Who knows what horrors might creep up behind her, grab her ankle or pinch her arse? Or who knows what her eyes might meet on raising her head.

She turned over again, hiding herself in the bedclothes—and, unbidden, the face of the man rose up in her mind—standing at the door of no. 18—his arms extended beckoningly for a hug. She shivered—and then found herself wondering for the first time, exactly what had happened to her rubber lizard on that day now getting on for four years ago. Then she shivered again. That business was over and done with, she told herself—the house empty and the garden weedridden. Perhaps, she thought suddenly, her lizard was still there somewhere hidden under all that long grass. The thought made her go tense all over—was it possible—after all this time? She tried to recall where it had landed. It had been a hot day, she remembered, but the road was deserted. She had been playing by herself, playing animal games, tossing that lizard higher and higher into the air—when she had suddenly bungled the throw, and it went sailing off to fall somewhere in that garden. She had sworn to herself, and hung over the low brick wall, trying to see where it had landed. There had been no sign of it, she remembered—and she had been wondering whether she dared to climb right in, when the door had opened and the man had looked out—

She pulled up the train of her thoughts sharply. What the hell did her lizard matter now? Impatiently, she kicked at the bedclothes, sending them onto the floor in a heap. The fresh air was pleasant, but now she felt painfully exposed and she wasn't sure which was worse. The sounds had begun in the garden again—the hedgehog was still there hunting for whatever it was that hedgehogs hunted for. Worms, slugs, snails. Maybe? She spent a few minutes trying to remember what little she had ever known about hedgehogs, then gave up and violently grabbed for her quilts, hauling them over herself again in a complex tangle. She spent a few moments kicking at them until they had taken on a form that was vaguely usable, then shut her eyes—and winced as her mind threw up a brief image of that upstairs window—and the face. Why couldn't she sleep? It was all right when she could get to sleep. Determinedly she tried to think about hedgehogs. What exactly, when you got right down to it, *was* a hedgehog? A hedge pig? A pig that lived in the hedgerows? A bizarre creature when you came to think of it. Cute—but bizarre. She listened to the sounds from outside—and then froze in terror as it finally dawned on her that they had changed. Now they seemed closer—far too distinct to have come from the garden. For a very long time she lay there, face down, goose-pimples jumping all over her skin and quite unable to move. By the sound of it, what was making the noise was only just outside her window—and for one absurd moment, she found herself wondering whether hedgehogs could climb. But then it finally dawned on her just what the sound was. Familiar enough. A plastic bag, she thought—a plastic bag caught on the drainpipe—or—or something. It certainly sounded like the rustle of plastic. That familiar crackly noise that a carrier bag makes if you scrumple it up. She ought to go and look, she thought—at least it would set her mind at rest. But her body seemed to have frozen solid. She lay there wishing, not for the first time in her life, that she was a thousand miles away—a thousand miles from no. 18. She might be able to relax then. The rustling continued and she gritted her teeth in despair, unable even to turn her head for fear of what she would see.

What at last got her into motion—shocked her out of her immobility, if you like—was the man's face as it appeared for a moment amid her chaotic thoughts. For a moment they had gazed at each other, his eyes as sharp as two icicles, making her quail slightly within—then he relaxed.

"Lost your toy?" he asked—and now he seemed just an ordinary person—a friendly neighbour ready to help.

"Er—yes," she had stammered. "But I don't see it."

She resumed peering, and he spoke again.

"Then you had better come in and look," he said, stepping out onto the grass, and Pepper had gratefully opened the gate and stepped through. They had searched together, but the lizard seemed to have vanished from the face of the Earth. They had both been bathed with perspiration by the time they finally gave up—and he had invited her in for a drink to cool off—

Pepper turned over and looked towards the window. The sounds still continued, but there was nothing visible except darkness and orange, so she scrambled out of bed. She trod heavily on the buckle of her belt and hissed in pain, biting back a yell. It would not do to risk waking her mother—more than once, Pepper had been slapped for causing a racket in the night—including that one time when—

Limping and annoyed, she approached the glass and peered out.

She gazed in silence at the face—and the face gazed back at her. She did not scream, but her breath escaped her in a whistling gasp. A bag, she had thought—and she had been right. It hung there exactly as she had predicted, caught by one of the clips that fastened the drainpipe to the wall, flapping gently in the breeze. And yet there was a face in it, as if the thin plastic was moulded about invisible contours. The eyes were tight knots under the sharply raised eyebrows, the mouth a crinkly dark hollow. The orange light glinted off it, throwing it into a sharp relief of light and shadow. Just an ordinary carrier bag—she could even see the word 'TESCO' traced across the thing's cheek and right eye. She recognised that face instantly. He had invited her in for a drink to cool off—and then, several days later, on a night as silent and as lonely and as sleepless, she had seen—

Very carefully, she opened the window and peered out, then cast her eyes down the road to where Number 18 stood amid its own personal darkness. The upstairs window was blank. Not surprising, she thought—and if thoughts could be considered shrill then hers certainly were at that moment. The eyes seemed to watch her—no, they *were* watching her—and, in that dark orange night, time stood still as they each gazed at the other—

—and then she snapped.

She slammed the window shut and staggered back to her bed. She flopped face down on top of the covers and buried her face in her arms, clutching the fabric beneath her in a white-knuckle grip. About her, the world had gone vague, her thoughts chaotic. Outside, the rustling continued, but she didn't look up—she knew what was there now—and she began to shiver.

The door of the house had stood open like a mouth with him in the doorway, arm extended welcomingly. Inside all seemed dark, but she thought the invitation the most natural thing in the world. So she followed him in—and from that moment, things were very vague in her memory. Her mind had drawn a lace curtain across all that had followed, throwing it into confusion. The world shrieked in a spiral seeming of nightmare—dark rooms that shifted about her in a maze before her dazed eyes—fragments of vision, each as clear as crystal, whirling in a high-speed dance—a ceiling with a naked light bulb—an expanse of carpet—a child's doll—the legs of an armchair—a thick dark curtain. And over all the man loomed—his claws holding her tight—seeming to have grown to giant size—she was hanging upside down—and there was pain—but she couldn't scream. She remembered her mouth hanging open, as though struggling for air, her legs kicking feebly at nothing—

And after that, he had killed himself—she knew he had.

Later, that night, when the cars with the blue lights had come, she had watched from her window. The lights had flooded the road with alien colour, blue and orange mingling. The blue uniforms walk grimly up to the front door—but there is no answer—there is never any answer. The door breaks—the blue uniforms enter and vanish—and he is dead. She never knew how he had killed himself. He had held on to her weeping—she had never seen a man cry before, and it shocked her—and, kneeling on the floor amid his tears, his face twisted like nothing she had ever dreamed of, he had spoken almost unintelligibly. The words were meaningless now, but she had felt the pain, violence, conflicting things that warred in his soul like fighting cats—vast things, coloured purple, and she didn't understand them at all. That was the worst bit—before it, all else seemed to pale into shadow, and she had finally pulled loose from his feebly clutching hands and fled back into the outside world. Leaving him to kill himself. She had watched them carry him out as a shape in a bag—load him into a vehicle—and drive away—and that was that.

Finally she stirred herself and glanced around the room again. All appeared normal, and she wondered for a moment whether she had imagined everything—that the bag outside her window had just been a bag, nothing more, nothing less. Even the sounds of it had fallen quiet now. Her body felt cold while still hot, the dryness of her skin twisted up into goose-pimples, and she lay for a long time without moving. Her eyes were smarting again and she blinked—and for a moment it almost seemed that she saw the man's face hovering in the air before her, not the impression of it in plastic, but the real thing—an image from memory. His face had haunted her, that twisted expression of utter despair. All night it had hovered over her, keeping her from sleep until she came to dread the night time—dread that in her dreams she might be forced once again to live all that confusion and pain again.

Her mother had been shocked of course, and irate—at least there was rage directed somewhere, though she could never quite figure out where. But that had been no comfort to Pepper who found her well-meaning attempts at sympathy and comfort all but unendurable, bringing an instant atmosphere of claustrophobia down over the house. It seemed as if she couldn't really believe what had happened—not deep down, where it mattered—and she had eventually left Pepper alone with barely concealed anger. Pepper had lain that night as she had lain this one, with the orange light from the street lamps tracing patterns across her walls. Outside, the beast that knows no sleep had purred gently to itself from the main road, but nearby the world had been quiet enough. Not even a last drunk making their way laboriously down the hill, migrating to who knows where. The image of the house had been in her mind, and the face of its occupant. But he was dead, she told herself over and over again—the house was empty—it was over. Except it hadn't been—and never would be. The face had gazed at her through the darkness from the upstairs window—and she had recognised it instantly. She gazed at it for a long time with the night breeze blowing through her hair as she leant out of the window. It had been vague, indistinct in the distance, and for a long time she had been unable to make up her mind whether it was a face she was seeing, or merely some unexpected fold in the curtains. Her eyes began to water from the effort of staring and she screwed up her eyes and drove her wrists into them to clear them—and looked again. The expression it wore seemed to pierce through her mind like a spear of ice—even at this distance—and, before she knew what had happened, the world had gone red and she had started to scream. She pitched away from the window and collapsed, more by instinct that anything else, onto the bed. And then she had fallen suddenly silent, her senses reeling among vast twisting shapes of red—blood red. The house had been roused, but she hardly noticed—her mother burst in, face furious. She had probably tried to demand of her what the matter was—Pepper had vague memories of questions—but she had not answered—and then she had been caught and turned over without ceremony—pressed face down into the bed—and she had felt herself smacked hard, and then again. Then she had been free—she tumbled over among the quilts, her face wet—and she had looked up at her father standing before her as her deliverer, and her mother, restored to her senses by a sharply restraining hand, standing uneasily beside him. That was another image that had seared itself into her mind—those two standing over her so tall and confused, like two ancient giants, their hair tousled and the expressions on their faces distinct in the ugly orange light as though engraven in stone. Actually, the pain inflicted with those two slaps had helped to bring her to her senses somewhat—at least enough for it to finally dawn on her that she had no clothes on—that she had been sprawling before them as naked as a peeled apple—and she feverishly scrambled under the covers, and her tears came like a summer thunder storm as the world closed in about her in darkness.

Again, from outside, there came the sound of rustling plastic, and Pepper tensed in the darkness. What was happening to her? She wondered this question in despair, and there was no answer. Since that awful night, the man's face had never left her. She had never actually seen it again until today, but she had always been conscious of its presence, like a grey cloud in her mind, its eyes wide in despair and its mouth agape. In her dreams, it would be before her, seeming to fill the sky and causing her to wake drenched with icy sweat, her heart pounding and her stomach filled with a blankness of terror. Many were the tears she had shed during the dark hours, uncomfortable but with nobody to comfort her.

Her face was blank as she stepped from her bed and crossed again to the window. She had to know.

She took hold of the sash and pushed it up, letting in a wash of cool night air. It rippled over the fine hairs that covered her body as she leant out into the night. The bag still hung there, limp and flapping against the drainpipe, but now it was just a bag—just a sodden bit of plastic with 'TESCO' written across it in large letters. She studied it carefully for a long moment, and then turned her eyes to Number 18. Its windows were blank, but it seemed to her haunted brain that the very house glowed in the darkness—a soft green light that bathed the surrounding bushes and trees in an eerie glow. Pepper watched it with a heavy heart. The lack of sleep sat on her like a great log of wood—her head felt heavy, as though full of water. Would this night never end? Outside, the silence reigned, as far as it ever did in this world. The road still purred in the distance. In those cars, she told herself, there are people—ordinary people. She found the thought vaguely comforting and she wondered what they could be doing driving about at this time of night. Were they simply night workers, heading off to start a shift in some all-night factory, or heading wearily home to their sleeping families with nothing in their heads but the thought of a nice bed? Or were they people like her, unfortunates to whom the idea of sleep had become a torture? Such thoughts went round and around in her mind as she leant out of the window, her eyelids heavy and drooping.

But then there came a sound from the room behind her—the familiar rustle of plastic. She whipped round, straining her eyes into the gloom. The rustle came again—and she caught a glimpse of movement amid the dark shadows, a flicker of white. Her breath escaped her in a thin whistle, and she stood like a statue. *In her room—it was actually in her room.* The thought spun over and over in her head as her eyes gradually pierced the dark to reveal the face, the old familiar face, its contours thrusting out from the old carrier bag she used as an impromptu rubbish bin. The eyes gazed at her steadily without moving, filled with appeal, two points of a yet deeper blackness than anything that surrounded it. *No*—she thought wildly—*no, no, nooo!* Then she shook herself—shook herself violently—and drove her fingers into her eyes. Pain flooded them, and she moaned aloud, but when she looked again the face had gone. She sat backwards onto the bed, gasping for breath and clutching her hands across her stomach as though to hold her aching insides inside her. She sobbed loudly, but just once, and then she simply sat there as still as a statue as the minutes slowly passed.

Then the sound came again, and again she whipped round—and again, there was the face, gazing at her from another bag—a tatty brown paper bag this time. Then even as she looked, it dissolved and was gone. And then a third time—a movement caught her eye and now it was staring down at her from the curtains, the smooth fabric twisted into a knot. At that point, something seemed to snap in her mind—like a blinding flash—a bolt of electricity from a severed cable. She did not scream—she had no desire to be spanked again—but she bounded to her feet like a firework, and hurled herself at the curtain. Her hands plunged deep into the fabric of the face, and she hauled at it. There was a crack as the curtain came away from the wall and descended over her. She flailed at it, eventually got free and hurled it across the room—but it was just a piece of fabric. Whatever face there might have been was gone now. Red lights danced before her eyes, as she leant against the wall. The shadows of the room seemed to shimmer and shake all around her—and there was the face again, gazing up at her from a pile of her own clothes. Sobbing silently to herself, she bounded forward and landed astride it, clawing at them and tearing a great rent. But the face had gone—yet again it had simply vanished. She gazed wildly about the room—*where was it?*—and soon found it regarding her from the fabric of her satchel. She made a few feeble steps in that direction but then stopped, plunged towards her bed and flopped down on top of it, burying her head in her hands. Inside her mind, chaos reigned. Again she saw her lizard sail through the air, black against the sky—sailing so inexorably beyond her reach—saw it engulfed, as though by clutching hands, by the bushes of the garden. She saw the door standing open like a mouth, and through it came drifting the man's face—the real face of flesh and blood. Once again she was held—hanging upside down—and once again came the pain. And there was his face again, stricken now and begging for something that only she could give, and his eyes were huge. She had given him nothing, she didn't know how, and the eyes filled the world, engulfing her—becoming two wet mouths—or two huge upside-down pools of grey water descending out of the sky on top of her. The eyes swallowed her and she found herself swimming through redness—she was filled with the taste of blood and she could not breathe. She was fighting for a surface, but the red was spiralling downwards, down to a point like water running out of a bath, and again the face was before her, but now it was dead and black. It stuck up out of an ocean of sand like a rotten mushroom and, even as she watched, its eyes began to swell outwards, and then slithered down its cheeks—two mushy pieces of grey jelly—and, out from the empty holes that now stared at the world, there flooded a great tide of dark life like nothing seen in the waking world—things with eyes that were round and mouths that were human—things that wriggled wetly on the sand, the grains sticking to them all over like a swimmer freshly crawled from the sea—coming towards her—smothering her and filling her world. She sank down backwards—upside down—blackness trailing about her in wisps—and then she was in bed again—and again she was being spanked. The fabric pressed suffocatingly into her nose and mouth, and she could make no movement to escape the pain that was inflicted on her. Her buttocks seemed to have inflated to an immense size under the repeated blows, as though blown up like a rubber glove, and the pain blossomed and shimmered there grotesquely like a flower—a great red flower with many petals. The flower grew, spreading itself luxuriantly through a world of darkness. It heaved and swelled—and finally opened to reveal a waving bunch of filaments surrounding a soft slippery-looking tube that led off into the distance, and into this she plunged—the memory of her own pain swallowing her—as she sank into the darkness.

She opened her eyes and gazed fearfully around her, but the face seemed to have gone. She sat up, shivery, her eyes huge. Sweat had replaced the dryness now and her hair was plastered with it, her skin sopping. The orange light still flooded in through her window, spraying a dozen shadows of the frame across the wall opposite her. All was still and silent, but she knew that the face was not far away—it would be back. For a moment, she wondered to herself just what the time was—whether dawn could be that far off now. Somehow it seemed to her that, if she could just survive through to the light of day, then she would be safe. She thought of her parents—but they were no use to her. There was nothing in this world that was any use to her—not them, not the people in the neighbouring houses, not even the anonymous drivers of the cars that still purred in the distance. She gazed out of the window, and there, beyond the orange haze that lay always over the city, she saw the stars and the infinite blankness of the sky. With that sight, there came a feeling of insignificance, but she fought it, knowing that it was of little use to her either. Tears ran down her cheeks, and the man's face hovered in her memory again. With a mind that was completely blank, she tried to recollect exactly what it was that he had done to her—but she couldn't find the details. *Maybe*, she thought to herself, *if I can remember then it might cure me*. But those images, beyond the precious few that haunted her dreams, seemed walled off in her mind. What had he done? Some sort of rape, she supposed, but beyond that was just confusion. And it was then that she felt the bedclothes move beneath her. She looked down—and there was the face, gazing up at her from between her legs.

No—her bed was too much. In an instant she had plunged from it, staggering across the carpet and fetching up against the wall with a painful bump—and then, for one long crystalline moment, all was perfect stillness. Her mouth hung open and, as she stood there frozen, a thin rill of spit trickled slowly down her chin. Her body was tensed like an animal's, the muscles of her arms and legs standing out like boards. And then the face moved. It rose up, tilted towards her as though to see her better, pulling the quilt covers up into a small peak. The mouth trembled—seemed to gape wider—and then Pepper got into motion. She blinked twice and shut her mouth deliberately—then she gathered herself up and hurled herself through the air towards the bed, jumping half the width of her room in one huge leap and giving out an inarticulate cry of effort. It seemed to go on forever, that jump. Pepper saw, amid the clamouring red shapes that swarmed before her eyes, the face growing larger as she slowly plunged towards it—saw the mouth gaping—a great cavern of darkness—growing and swelling—to engulf her—

And then she landed on the bed. She flung herself upon the face, hands clasping it to her, pounding and flailing at it—and immediately it dissolved under her fingers, only to reappear again a few feet away. She whirled towards it and grabbed, but the whole procedure was simply repeated and she spun round again. But her feet seemed to have got tangled up in the chaotic quilt covers. She tugged at them furiously, while the face reappeared yet again. By this time, it seemed to her crazed eyes that it was glowing—picked out with lines of pale green fire—lines which danced and twisted themselves into impossible knots. The rest of the world had become just so much black chaos, chittering and whistling at her—but she paid no heed to that. Her whole consciousness was fixed on the face that glowed and gazed at her and now seemed to laugh even through its despair. Once again she hurled herself at it—but her feet were tangled and she tumbled flat on her stomach. It was just out of her reach and she floundered towards it, pulling the covers with her in a heavy tangle. She flung out her hands, but again the face only dissolved and appeared again—this time behind her. She looked about wildly and tried to turn, but the tangle impeded her movements and instead of her hands, she landed on it face-first. She saw it coming towards—and at the last moment, its mouth seemed to open in a great gape. It closed around her head, and she thrashed wildly—but she was stuck. She kicked and struggled, but the fabric held firm. *This*, some part of her brain thought hysterically, is my own bed—I've slept in it all of my life—*it's just not fair!* The face—the real face now—floated before her mind's eye, bulging forward through the red that clamoured there, and its mouth was also opening—growing huge—closing about her—she could see its tongue extending in anticipation, its teeth glistening in readiness to chomp down and up through her red-filled body, tearing bones to splinters and squirting her intestines out all over the place in a sticky stream—and that was when she finally panicked completely—and, for the first time, she screamed. Better a thousand blows, she thought with surprising clarity, than this, so she opened her mouth and howled as loudly as she could. The sound inside her head was deafening, and yet she knew—knew as clearly as if she had been standing there listening—that outside this, her own personal nightmare, it would be virtually inaudible. It would be nothing more than a muffled moan. She began to struggle furiously beyond all reason, but she could not succeed in loosening the fabric that clung tightly around her head. Indeed, the more she struggled, the more tangled she became. She felt her bed wrap itself around her, fold after fold, and she opened her mouth to scream again, but could find no breath to do so. All there was was fabric, swirling about her in a steadily tightening spiral. By this time, her legs were pinned and immovable, and in a few moments her arms were likewise captured. She could not breathe. She opened her mouth and made a frantic effort to suck in some air—but all that happened was that the fabric entered her mouth. She choked, but had no breath to expel it again, instead it just entered her deeper and deeper with every helpless attempt to breathe, pressing even down into her throat. The pain was excruciating—she could feel it inside her neck—to drown in fabric—

The redness filled her world now, clamouring about the image of the man's face, flooding out of its mouth as its jaws finally closed about her, cutting through her body like an axe through a twig. She saw his throat before her—a red and black pit—she was sliding headfirst towards it and she feebly struggled to check her fall, but all was moist and slippery and she found nothing. She watched the lower half of her body disappear into the depths, gulped down greedily by the living flesh that surrounded her—a pathetic thing—just two legs linked together by a pair of buttocks—that was all. Around her, the red pulsed and changed, and the hollow of that throat was like a black well of nothingness—growing—blackness flooding her vision, blotting out pain, terror, despair and confusion in a vastness of oblivion.

Part 3
Strange Tales

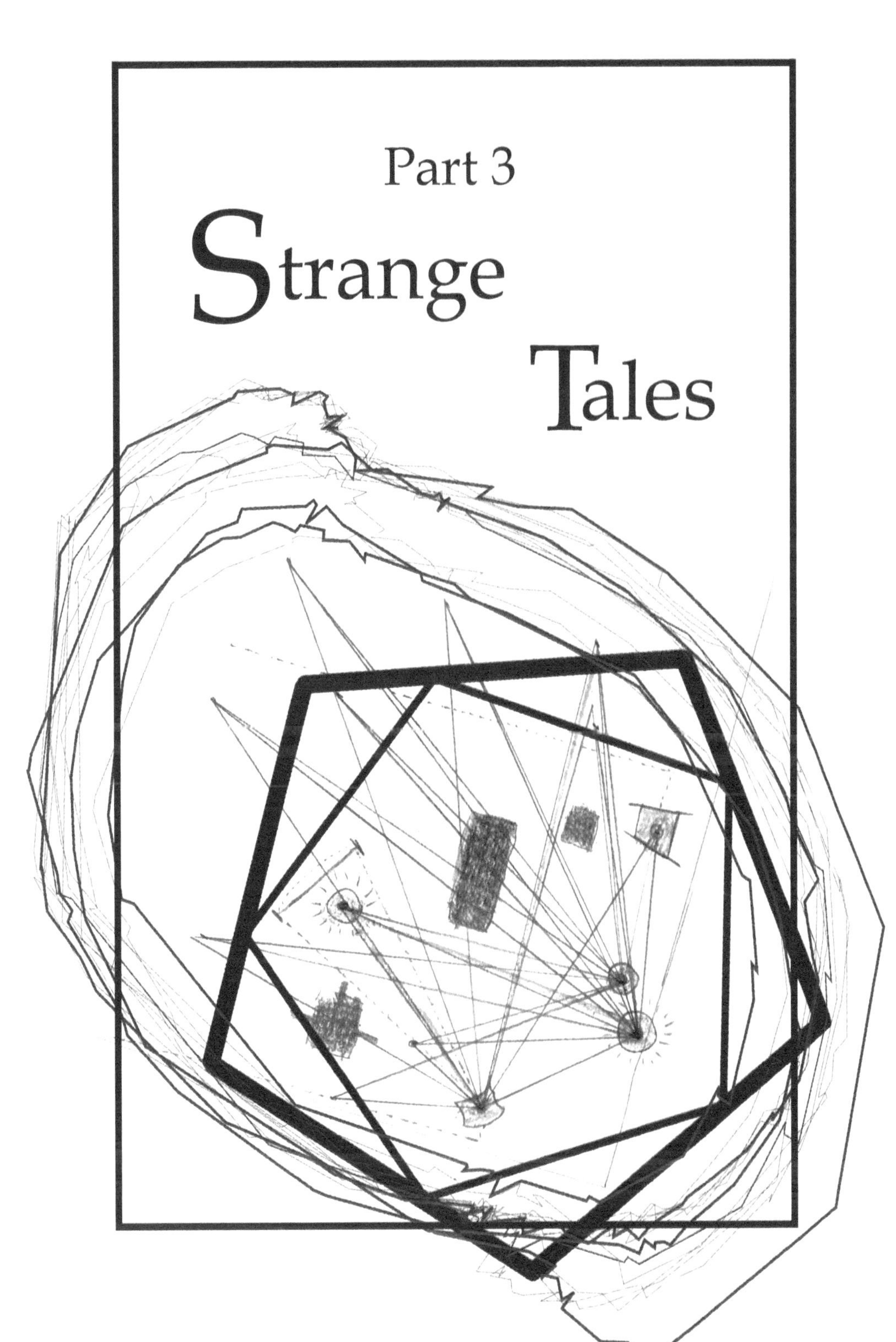

With this book, as we move into quieter and hopefully more mature territories, I feel as though I am signing off on and finally putting to sleep a part of my life—a younger, wilder part. A part that spewed lurid phantasms that I can barely imagine now, that opened its heart maybe a bit too much, that expressed the horrors that lurked in the minds of the broken then felt innocently sad when the resulting protagonists were unlikable and twisted. These were the dark and stormy nights before I began to lean more towards speculative fiction and a different kind of expression. The final part of this book includes stories that are starting to become more familiar to me from the place I am now standing in, moving from hysteria towards melancholy, from remote wilderness towards city, from extremity of some kind to a subtlety... of some kind. And some of these stories still have a special place in my heart, as they say, however much I may change.

These stories appeared in various anthologies since the early two-thousands—notably the *Strange Tales* series from Tartarus Press. That makes this book a companion to the rather more structured collection *Feather*, and together they house pretty much everything of relevance from those times, as well as some more recent pieces and oddballs. It's a slim output, but I have never been prolific and probably never will be.

All in all, this has been a curious book to put together, with a different kind of emotional investment to most. This is not about me struggling and struggling to put together the most polished text I possibly can, something I can feel vaguely comfortable letting out into the world—it has been more like an exercise in curation. Weird though they sometimes are, shaky and flawed though they sometimes are, they were very much a part of my life, and a vital part at that, and so… this book came to be. *For the curious.*

Duet

As the months passed and turned into years, he tried his best to forget about Marija upstairs. For a long time she had been there as life passed by down below. He had not approached her door or looked in since the night it had happened, only left it sealed up and abandoned. It was hard to imagine a truly hidden place in London—a city full of swarming eyes and where privacy is as rare as loneliness is common. But in this case, that room had lingered, unvisited and unused—even unopened. There was something shockingly untenable about this—about a dead woman upstairs—but, as the years came and went, she continued with what might seem almost a beautiful stasis. And he was the murderer, the man with death in his fingers. So why was he still alive? He would also have asked why he was still free if freedom had ever existed.

There is an energy in the violin that you don't get in many other instruments—maybe that was why the violin has always been associated with the devil. Play the cello or the guitar and you are caressing a beautiful woman—the flute and you are a fluttering bird or dancing satyr—but the violin, gripped under your chin while the bow flails with savage energy… maybe then it feels more like a weapon.

So was that what was going on here, he wondered, as two bows flurried the air? A duel of two strange weapons? That wasn't what music was about. The expression on Amy's face certainly didn't seem friendly though, and he could sense her pushing at him, competing with him, restraining him as the complex music coiled round them both. It was Henryk Górecki: Sonata for Two Violins—bitter, cold and aggressively modernist yet very beautiful as well. As the harsh tones filled the room, he found himself zoning out, forgetting her, forgetting himself as well, as his fingers danced and as flicking black light played at the corners of his eyes. It was a music that resonated some other more esoteric set of strings deep inside him, its frozen irregular shapes sweeping him away. Music of crystal patterns and organic growth rather than heartbeat or pulse. It would count onwards in a stream of ones or twos or threes, increasing or decreasing tension, dragging you onwards or pushing you down. Music that took you on a journey. Energy, ferocity, serenity, silence—like human life itself, sometimes a matter of slow inevitable development or emotional turmoil, or sometimes total shock out of nowhere…

Finally it ended, with some last stabbing chords like lashes from a leather whip. And the bows were still.

"Wow," she said, drawing a deep breath. "That was intense—you were leaving me behind a bit there."

"Was I?"

"Yeah. Maybe we can tighten that up."

"Funny," he said. "I was feeling exactly the same thing."

She gave him a thoughtful look.

"We need to come together more, yes," he said. "We need to be as one."

"Hum—yes, I suppose," she said awkwardly.

"Again?" he asked, turning back to the first page of the score.

She gave a restive sigh.

"Enough for now," she said. "I'm getting tired. It's not exactly a relaxing piece…"

"It's not?" he asked, with a small kernel of genuine surprise. "Very well—let's sit down—and listen to the silence instead."

Amy settled rather primly on the sofa and he studied her for a moment. Smartly and reservedly dressed with formal-looking black suit trousers and a severe-looking blouse, her hair long and brown, falling straight over her shoulders. Almost as though she was performing in some imaginary concert, even here and now in his dark wood-floored home.

She looked around the room. "I must say, you have a rather nice silence here, for London."

He nodded. "Yes," he breathed. "I sometimes think that if you can't hear silence, then you can never hope to hear sound."

"You're weird, you know that," she said with a smile.

He shrugged with a faint hint of defensiveness. "Well it just strikes me as funny. Music is everywhere—and yet so little of it seems to, well, ever listen to the silence it is supposed to be replacing. It's as if there's a war going on instead."

He sat down beside her, feeling slightly uncomfortable. Now there was a parallel pressure—to keep talking for the same reason. To prevent the all-powerful silence crashing in again. And yet why should that be? The silence when the last musical note has sounded is probably among the most profound sounds that can ever be heard. The silence after sex—the silence after sound—the silence after death… and he found himself watching her again, wondering what thought processes were active behind those reserved-looking eyes. Something he could never know or touch.

"Strange house actually," she said at last, a twinge of jealousy in her voice. "It's a pretty amazing place to just—have. I live in a room stuck behind a freelance hairdressing studio in hackney wick. I mean literally, you have to go through the studio to get in and the shower is hidden in the corner behind the barber's chair."

"Well," he said, feeling a slight twinge of guilt, "I gucss I was lucky. I inherited it. It used to be a tiny factory—I didn't convert it much, just cleared out most of the equipment. If it wasn't for this place, I don't know what would have happened to me."

"You'd probably be in my place," she said with a rather humourless grin. "Not much silence there."

He nodded simply. "Probably. I could not face being anywhere other than London. Beyond the boundary of the city, there is nothing but darkness. I would rather die than be forced out—so yes, very lucky."

She was staring at him with a blank look in her eyes. He gave a sudden laugh. "Sorry—I didn't mean to be depressing. I will get you a drink. Would you like some wine?" he asked. "I have some rather good Australian Shiraz here."

She laughed. "Ummm—actually, no thanks. Though don't let me stop you."

He studied the bottle a moment on the shelf, then shrugged it off. His eyes briefly searched the room for the moving black shapes, but they seemed to have gone now. All he could find was a blurred pale shape up by the ceiling—a moth trying to navigate this weird roofed world. There always seemed to be moths. And always then the merging of the black and the pale…

"So what do you think?" Amy asked, a hint of doubt in her voice. "Think we can pull this off? It's a hard piece."

"I think we can manage something. We could perform it in the old warehouse cave room I suppose—to the usual audience of six. But we need to come together. We need to find that union otherwise music doesn't happen. There needs to be one music, not two. One body, one mind, one instrument… The question is how."

He gave her a thoughtful look, narrowing his eyes slightly—and now she looked even more uneasy.

"What do you mean?" she asked.

He was very well aware of the vague kind of innuendo in his words, but there seemed no other way to put it. No other option. That's what music was. You either come together with a sense of intimacy and melding rarely experienced in human life—or the music crumbles and fails.

Studying her now, it suddenly seemed a very remote possibility.

"Maybe we need to try some bonding exercises," he said evasively, beginning to feel awkward again.

"Hmm—I'm not sure…"

There was another silence—a less pleasant one than earlier. He glanced round the room absently.

"The moths are active tonight," he said.

"Moths?"

"Yes—they always come around at night when I play—the Black Sheet Moth and the pale. They are everywhere."

She gave him an uncomprehending look, then shifted uncomfortably. "Right—must be the warm weather. Um, look—I, er, I'm sorry but…"

Her eyes flickering around the room towards the door.

She coughed. "I'm not sure myself. Sorry, I don't think I can do this. It's a nice idea, and good to try, but…"

He was silent, his face falling.

"I just don't think it will work."

"Oh?" he said, hoping that his face was not reflecting his mind too much.

"I'm going to have to go as well I think," she muttered, "it's getting late—and—and I need to get home before…"

"Oh right—of course," he said expressionlessly.

"So—well, thanks," she said, putting her coat on. "And—um—sorry. I'll see you around sometime."

He was dimly aware of her letting herself out, looking red-faced and even more awkward—even a little resentful. The door opened but did not close again behind her. He sat down, feeling a prickle of shock and stared into space. It was a rejection—but maybe she was right. It sometimes seemed a waste of time to hope for any kind of true music any more.

Not now.

Like true love, you only ever get a certain number of chances before everything subsequent begins to taste bitter.

He finally reached for the bottle and poured a glass of wine.

Maybe it was time to check upstairs at last…

And now—then—years ago—Marija, also playing the violin. Her fingers dancing like spider feet, her face ferocious with intent, her body moving like wire. Marija—playing with a delicate passion like no other. Intricate. Complex. Harsh. Beautiful…

Going by her name and the brief programme he had picked up, she was one of the many immigrants from somewhere out east—spat out by the Yugoslav wars no doubt, given the time when this had happened. Largely ignored in the political climate of London, both then and now. She had been performing in an old warehouse space in the East End, where the massive brickwork suggested something of docks or canals in the distant past—hints of crane and pulley and transient merchandise. The dingy vaulted roof curving overhead reflected any sound like a cauldron as he waited patiently for the concert to begin—the slightest movement of his foot or chair. It was like a cathedral of industry that crouched black and oppressive over the island of light in the middle of the floor. It was going to be one of those underground concerts that hopeful new artists might put on before the world crushes them to dust and forgets them—hidden and never-known geniuses in the underworld of the contemporary classical music scene. Lone soloists or edgy ensembles in crumbling and abandoned industrial rooms—basements, converted warehouses, old cinemas, even abandoned residential spaces occasionally. Sometimes the intrusion of the city would be all too apparent—the rumble of trains in the middle distance, streaming traffic, revellers in the room next door, bustling machinery overhead. Or sometimes, like now, the silence would be more profound than any church or concert hall. Audiences would be small—but fanatically dedicated. Or drunk and mystified. You could never know.

Or even, as seemed to be the case here, non-existent.

He stared round in increasing agitation as the time ticked on towards the appointed hour. Surely there would be someone else? Surely he would not be the only person who had bothered to turn up for this obscure little event? These concerts were always rendered rather bitter by their circumstances, but that would be heart-breaking.

It was unmistakably a shock to her as well, when she finally walked on into that light island—a pained and unhappy shock. And he felt he could read every little flicker of despair in her mind perfectly. She actually hesitated, gave a confused glance round the room, her eyes focussing on him, sitting alone in a chair at the front, the one and only audience member…

The one and only audience member…

And he looked back, feeling a kind of frozen awkwardness within himself as well—something between a desperate apology and a wry grin on his face. For a moment it looked as though she was going to speak to him, but then her classical training kicked in and she just gave a small formal bow, the twist of her lip saying that she was well aware of the absurdity.

However, whatever awkwardness there may have been—his nervousness, his consciousness of the echoing empty space around them both—quickly faded as she took up her position just a few feet away, cold light bathing her skin. So close he could almost reach out and touch her. Lines were etched into her face and her hands skinny and wrinkled beyond her age. She wore rough city clothes—black scruffy jeans and a black and gold waistcoat in some jarring deferral to classical traditions, a haircut as jagged and harsh as her music, short and hairsprayed severely out of the way of her violin—a tattoo of a black flower visible on her bare arm. And he watched—as the bow floated in the air a moment with a prickle of anticipation—and as the first sound rang out, long and rich. As that music developed, the rest of the world faded—the sense of emptiness and loneliness faded—even she faded—and all that was left was the harsh and passionate notes invading the world.

It was a programme of Ligeti, Penderecki, Schnittke and others he had never heard of—modernist composers with an Eastern European flavour. Complex and experimental, but filled with a cold and angry passion. It was a concert of music that stretches the pallet of sounds and notes and harmonies and techniques as far as possible. Music that seeks the last and deepest possibilities of expression. Music that counted in fives and sevens and thirteens as much as threes and fours—or maybe counted with nothing at all. Music that was shaped rather than numbered. But more importantly than that, this was a type of music that had grown among those who felt everything the keenest yet were persecuted the harshest, seeded by two world wars and eternal political turmoil. The ghosts of pogroms and purges and splits and bloodshed still felt here in the chaos of the 90s when everything, there and here, seemed grey. It was music where you could still feel the fury of civil unrest and protest, even now—then—years ago—as another war raged in Eastern Europe. It was music where the ghosts and anti-intellectual flounderings of powerful children whose greatest fear was intelligence seemed very close. And also the cavorting mad humour of art that is stifled and sent underground. It was a kind of music that still ran wild in an attempt to find some kind of expression that nothing else could provide. Some kind of balm for wounds nothing else could ever heal.

When the silence finally came crashing in like ocean waves, Marija gave another formal-looking bow, obviously far from happy, eyes flickering to him and away again several times. And yes he actually clapped his hands awkwardly a few times, an embarrassed smile on his face.

"Wait," he said, as she turned to leave. She paused and glanced back. He nodded thoughtfully, looking at the floor. "That was great—really," he said quietly, seriously. "Magical. Thanks for playing."

She hesitated one last moment, then the formal façade gave way.

"Oh fuck it," she said, her voice as deep as her lowest violin string, her accent as heavy and harsh as her hair. "Thanks. I'm… glad…"

She gave him a look as awkward as he felt, still wondering whether she should be maintaining the barriers inevitably erected between performer and audience, author and recipient—then she dropped down in an empty chair with a twinkle of humour. "Joj—what a disaster."

"Not a disaster," he said. "Not for you anyway. For them, maybe." He pointed at the empty chairs with a grin. And then the conversation slid deep and long and smooth into all the esoterics of modernist violin music, first in that deserted venue, then later in the cold East London streets, and finally in a quiet bar in another converted industrial space nearby…

…and about a fortnight later, the two violins played together for the first time. The musical notes coiling and exploring—uncertain, like your first fumbling attempts to explore another body, yet blazing bright, dazzling, almost painful, like no other he had ever experienced. Each instrument the forever incomplete and hungry gamete demanding fulfilment and union. A meshing together on many levels, every level, from the most physical as they breathed and moved in agitated unison, to the most ethereal as the surrounding world faded away to nothing…

It was all a fog anyway—but one thing was certain in his mind. He was a murderer.

The door wouldn't move, he knew. He had made sure of that. So he armed himself with some tools from the kitchen cupboard and set to work breaking the seal. It was hard—he had done a thorough job, even filling the cracks and keyhole with epoxy and foam. But after a lot of gouging and leveraging, it moved with a sharp crack and he flinched away. He stood frozen for a moment, then slowly opened the door further, half-expecting to see a flood of black light radiating out—but there was nothing. No visual, audible or olfactory extremes, just a faint musty smell and shadow. He peered in, then stared down for a moment at a pair of shoes sitting neatly together just inside. Familiar comfortable trainers, covered with a sheen of dust.

Those trainers nearly caused him to choke with their agonising familiarity. But beyond them, his eyes soon found the one thing he didn't want to look at, barely visible in the dark…

The bed looked ruined—a sagged shape, half rotted away where she had rotted away. But the rot and dissolution had been limited in this dry room. Now everything was desiccated—as was she. She lay there in exactly the posture he remembered leaving her in—as though sleeping. But now she was only dry and dusty bones.

He stepped into the room and quietly opened the curtains, letting in a glow of city light and revealing an anonymous view across London's rooftops to the distant railway. As the glow drifted in, he glanced round uneasily for flickering black hidden in the corners—but there was nothing. Nothing to do but stare down at her, feeling as though water was flowing and heaving within him. Vast water, like the ocean. What did it matter that he hadn't meant any of this? What did grief matter? Such was the way the world worked. And whatever fundamental unfairness may lie in that was not really relevant here and now. He just stared around the room in infinite sadness.

Maybe it was time to start disposing of this once and for all. Just a bit at a time, ground to a powder in his mortar and pestle maybe and cast to the winds around this thronging city—until this guilty secret was no more. Until Marija was finally as vanished as her music.

A pale blur caught his eye then and he looked round. The moth bounced against the ceiling. It looked stupid and useless in this dead environment, barely able even to navigate, but he still watched it with keen eyes. Pale. In his head, it seemed as though the violin bow was moving again in anticipation, string stretched taut and exposed over the bridge—strangely like a human form itself, stretched, bent with tight skin and awaiting the most erotic touch. And the contact of the bow—a hundred resined threads picking up the string, the skin, vibrating, grinding out notes that were deep and slow and intense. And the room shimmered slightly, the faint glow from the distant street lights picking out the swirling motes of dust in the air.

And then what could only be a dream. The long-faded bones sitting up and reaching out towards him, fleshed again in translucent black, even as more moths flickered round the room. Some of them pale—some of them black. It was not horrible—more like a hint of the tenderness and affection that she had never been able to display in reality. Never in the world beyond her music anyway.

He just stared at her. Then accepted the hug, dropping first to one knee on the bed, then flat on his face.

There was a bang in the distance.

"Hello?" a voice called. "Are you there? Look—I'm sorry I ran off. Maybe I was over-reacting a little. Are you ok?"

The sounds of footsteps blundering about below. A light flicked on beyond the open door. He stared vaguely, with little idea what the distant voice was even talking about.

"Where are you?" Amy called.

He glanced down at the bone-black arms around him, as footsteps came pattering upstairs. He could have pulled away—could have done something—but this was a special moment. Some hugs you just didn't break. Instead he simply watched the figure put her head round the door, long brown hair trailing. She stared in for just one moment, then lightning struck.

"Hey—what are you… oh my fucking god," she gulped, strangely casual in tone, her eyes widening stupidly, then she had jerked away as though yanked on a chord and was gone. There was a tremendous clatter on the stairs and the door banged in the distance.

What did it matter?

He looked down again to find bones littering the bed around him in an untidy pile—her restful posture finally disturbed after all this time.

Surely there was something significant here that he should be realising. But everything seemed beyond thinking about. All he wanted to do was continue to exist within this emotional sea that swirled around him—as though London itself was drowning. Fragments of pavements and railings tumbling in water. Buildings leaning and shifting in the swell. The sea bigger than the sea should be. And the female figure out of memory that gave him a friendly greeting from the watery chaos before him.

When the long long journey of notes was finally over, they had just stood in silence save for heavy breathing—Marija looking at him with a small smile, then rubbing the sweat from her forehead. It was an extraordinary silence—one of the most powerful he had ever known—and there was no need to break it. No need to speak or use words to communicate. Indeed, in that silence, any sound, even more music, would be an intrusion. There was an energy in the air—connected to the music, to her haunting eyes staring at him, to her flushed and sweaty skin and hard breathing, to her bedraggled hair, to her bare feet on the rough wood of his floor. The whole room seemed black with faded music in ways he had never seen before—the violins almost feeling warm to the touch.

Touch.

Only one sense could possibly exist in that hot silence—touch. And both knew it. With an actual slight tremble in his hand, he reached out towards her. It was the first time he had ever touched her, even casually, and that came with a weird prickle and glow of correctness. With what seemed infinite slowness, his hand progressed towards making the connection. She glanced round at him—a curious, uneasy but welcoming expression on her face. Touch—the most obscure and restrained yet powerful of the senses. Her hand also rose up in response, not aiming to touch fingers, but to link arms, each hand grasping a shoulder in a heated and affectionate hug.

But that warm gesture was never quite reached.

Contact…

His fingers touching her skin first—and a violent black flash arcing between them. It snaked like black lightning from instrument to instrument. It was impossible to say in which of them it originated or which direction it was going—but it stretched up her arm, through her chest and shoulder and into his hand, then down across him to his own violin. It was gone in a fraction of a second, but the nasty all-encompassing snap it made stunned him. He stared without feeling as the violin fell from her fingers onto the sofa—a smooth white expression on her face—before she slowly leant and fell, hitting the floor with a tremendous crash.

His own violin felt hot in his hand now—very distinctly. And it glowed with a black light. They both did. Still without feeling, he put it down, vaguely aware of a faint noise coming from it as the strings thrummed to themselves. Without knowing why, he picked up her violin as well and placed it alongside his own. They sat there a pair—thrumming with dark. The Black Sheet Moth. It was there. It streaked round the room—agitated movement in stillness—long black antennae feeling ahead in a flurry. *Marija*? he murmured to the fallen figure. Later he had her lying on his bed upstairs—heart still and chest still and nimble fingers still. And he stared round in confused terror. On the ceiling, a pale moth was moving, a bouncing blur. Others were at the window. Black and pale everywhere. But inside there was already an ocean—an ocean that heaved and expanded and would never go away. There was nothing he could do here. Instead, he went downstairs. Her shoes were still standing in the doorway, politely side by side. Small and unpretentious trainers in black. And still moths. Even with the windows closed, they were somehow managing to find a way in. His hand touched his mobile phone for a moment—then removed itself. They would think he was the murderer. He was the murderer.

Finally, much later, he pushed her shoes round the door of that upstairs room, then locked it. Then tramped downstairs and spent the rest of the night staring at the corner of the kitchen.

And the next day he set about attempting to seal the room. Epoxy went into the cracks in the window, then the curtains were closed. And finally the door was also sealed, then locked shut. Then even the keyhole filled. A bookcase obscured it from view as though it had never existed.

Every day he expected someone to come. He gave up answering the door or the phone. Parcels that wouldn't fit through the letterbox had to be collected from the sorting office. He communicated through answerphone and email.

But nobody did. That was the weird thing. Nobody knew—or cared.

As far as the world was concerned, Marija the refugee violinist had never existed.

Slowly disentangling himself from the old bones, which clicked and clattered dully, he stood up. His hand brushed at his face, barely conscious that he was brushing away dust and smuts that were once her. His jacket was filthy but he ignored that as well. There was something that needed to be done now.

He picked up her violin and put it to his chin. It was time to play a threnody.

It was as dusty as the rest of the room—a dust that was thick and oily. It also looked slightly warped, but still intact. Still somehow glowing as it had so long ago. The bow touched the strings with a flaccid scrape and he quickly tightened the tuning pegs. And as he did so, as sound slowly found its way into note, darkness flickered again—an undulating film of black. This was a different kind of music. He was playing from no score, following no system. He just allowed the notes to come, sounding like bells, sliding sombrely from one to another, even microtones. Long-breathed, free, random, vibrating—each one somehow containing all the emotion of a whole life.

The tone of the strings had degraded rather but even that seemed appropriate under the circumstances. Tones whispered and shadowed in dust—the dust of a pain hidden for aeons. The Black Sheet Moth didn't seem to mind either. Sheets and tendrils, strange swirling shapes, like a black amoeba or many-headed planarian worm, a manta ray with moth tentacles or a sheet swirling in a stream… slow but with great exuberance and sharp movements, the Black Sheet Moth danced, excited to be aroused again after so long. And he played to follow, and to lead—to find again that perfect musical union where both terms are meaningless.

With a despairing noise, a string suddenly snapped—then almost immediately another. The two lowest strings, G and D. He frowned in shock. The coiled steel had deteriorated but he paid no heed, just continued scraping at the remaining two, the threnody soaring to higher pitches. But the Black Sheet Moth heeded. It flinched in real pain and twanged/flickered across the room. He watched it forlornly. The Black Sheet Moth was no enemy—

Another snap and he was reduced to just the highest string—a shrill almost painful final sound, wailing like an animal vocalisation. Then that failed as well and the wood of the old violin warped back in ecstatic freedom and fell from his chin. The neck and the fingerboard separated into two layers—different woods built to be under tension from the strings that filled their lives, now unable to cope with their absence. And the energy that was the Black Sheet Moth was cut.

Marija's violin was dead.

There were tears in his eyes as he stared down at the scattered bones and forlorn dumb maple, spruce and ebony wood. The first tears ever. He stared down at the ruined violin and tasted that feeling.

Salt.

Oysters.

◇

Noise is no fundamental. Only silence is fundamental. And any noise intrudes… a strange philosophy for a musician…

There was an inevitability about this. Sooner or later an ending had always been bound to come. Even as fists hammered on the door below. He crossed to the window and peered out, taking in the uniformed figures in the street, guarding the main entrance.

Shouting voices behind as well.

"Too bad," he whispered sadly.

Bluestone

Merryn must have passed the old junction stone a thousand times since she came to live here in the wilds, but it wasn't until it vanished that she really noticed it. It had always been just another part of the scenery—just a small brownish-grey rock, about a foot high, resting in the rough heathland where the steep path to the sea branched away from the almost derelict coast road. It must have been lying there for many years—the hole it had left behind in the ground was not one of flattened or decaying grass, it was pure soil. A rich brown hole into the earth lined with roots and worm tunnels. Why the stone had been there, she wasn't sure. It looked too well-placed and distinctive to be natural, standing like a miniature marker where the paths diverged; it looked too insignificant to be deliberate, just some random rock in a world of rocks. But now, something or someone had ripped that stone out of the ground—uprooted it—and it was gone.

It was strange the way some things became part of the scenery so insidiously that you didn't even notice them until they weren't there—whereupon they left an unexpected hole in your mind. It was a hole that equated well with that raw hole in the earth.

Merryn looked around the wild hillside. The coast path climbed steeply down below her, vanishing into the dense bushes that framed the beach. It was a steep slope, one of rough grass and occasional rocky outcrops, hollow scrapes where rabbit droppings and the shells of obscure heath snails accumulated. She was not sure why it even mattered. Stones were always moving and the world was always changing, but instinct pricked at her with a wry smile. That rock was a marker point in her mind; it should be there to complete the world. As a woman who had lived alone for most of her life, Merryn was used to following such thoughts without too much questioning.

Fortunately, it didn't take long to find it. As she stared down the slope, she caught a gleam directly below her, one easy roll and tumble downwards. Cracked stone—the brighter hue of pure fresh broken rock gleaming in the evening sun. She scrambled down, picked it up and turned it over—then a moment later found the other half. A rough crystalline grey spotted with patches of white like snowflakes. In her mind, it was easy to see the rock descending, bouncing down the slope, striking other rocks as it passed, picking up speed, bouncing higher, until it met the other stone that killed it. Right there—a tough-looking lump of granite still bearing a smudge of dust and shards. She held the pieces for a moment with a wry sigh, then put them together again. The fit was almost perfect, save for one small area of damage, presumably the impact site. And it was a shame. It had been a nice rock. Standing proud in that wormy soil for all its small size.

And furthermore, the broken face had revealed what it was. Dolerite—Bluestone. Something she had never seen around here before. And Merryn always knew the rocks.

Without thinking much or with any particular agenda, she put the two halves of the stone in her bag. She even grabbed a couple of the small scattered fragments and slipped them into her breast pocket. It seemed worth fixing this—if not for any direct ideals, then just because it felt right. "I am the rock collector, after all," she said aloud with a smile, as though in justification. She hoisted the bag back onto her shoulder, feeling the increased weight dragging at her, and scrambled back towards the path.

Arriving back home in the lowering evening, Merryn went straight to her wood- and stone-scented workshop. Home was a rather remote one-storey cottage tucked below the railway tracks, but the workshop was separate—a large shed placed alongside the stream that kept her company on its way to the middle-distant sea. It was a tranquil space of rickety home-built wooden machinery, boxes of stones and a generous scattering of mud and rock dust. In the tumbling water outside, a small waterwheel turned, shaded by one of the few groups of trees in this rough heathland. Everything in this shed was powered by water—the large rock saw and lapping wheels, which were geared from the drive shaft, and the small generator that powered the lights, the vibrolap machine and three tumblers running quietly in the background. It had taken years to set this up, but the feeling of increasing independence from the world had made it a labour of love. In the vibrolap, rock halves jostled with a gentle rumble and a sea-on-shingle sound as the flat surface was polished to a mirror shine. She watched them with fondness. Sometimes there was nothing more comforting and peaceful in the world than a lump of rock.

She cleared a space among the pieces of stone she was working on—geodes, agate, rhyolite, marble etc., cut in half or carved into elegant shapes—and unpacked the broken bluestone. It was a big specimen for her, well over a foot long when together. It looked good—it looked imposing. It was a stone with significance.

Fortunately, it was not impossible to fix a broken rock.

The technique is simple. Epoxy resin is spread over the cracked face of the stone and the halves put back together. The crack may stand marked in gleaming fluid, almost as though the rock is bleeding, but that can be rubbed off with a cloth or a toothbrush. Spare fragments of rock can be pounded to dust in a mortar and then mixed with a little more resin and used to fill any cracks that are still visible, or rubbed into the surface to dull any lingering traces. Then the stone is secured tightly with bandages and allowed to cure hard. It was a job Merryn had done many times, though it always felt strange to physically bandage a broken stone, as though it was alive and wounded.

With all that done, it was pretty much dark and she carried it back into the house and left it on the table to harden overnight in the warm. Looking at it, she felt an odd twang of poignancy, wondering what to do with it now. Keep it? Put it back? It was a nice specimen and one she would like to have around. The fact that the material was dolerite—bluestone—and not native to the area was interesting. Maybe it was a glacial erratic—or maybe not. This was a type of rock that had fascinated the early people of Britain. They had used it for parts of Stonehenge and elsewhere and maybe saw in it something special. So had someone sometime put it there? Just as they erected the massive blocks of Stonehenge miles from where the stone naturally formed? But if so, why? Was this little rock just marking the junction where the path to the sea branched off from the coast road? Or something more that she would never know? Maybe she was the first to even pay attention to this little rock in hundreds of years.

Outside, the rush of a passing train cut through the silence, no doubt a simple four-carriage sprinter heading west. It was a sound of movement, however familiar, and it roused her from her musings. She helped herself to a glass of fruit juice and settled down at her computer, preparing to get on with more mundane matters. There was an order to deal with for a set of marble spheres she had carved, and another for a few polished thundereggs. Then there were online auctions to check and fight for—a rare Brazilian marble, a nice piece of Mexican Cold Mountain rhyolite that would make a great large cabochon, a few ancient thundereggs from Albaum in Germany in which the conventional beauty had long-decayed but the alternate beauty of aeons and stories remained. Hard to sell but she found them fascinating. And time passed with the quiet comfortable slowness of an unpressured existence in the wild lands. Time that you could not hear, yet whose weight was like a fuzzy blanket. The deep familiar time of the country night beyond the reach of the warm lights of the fireside.

Later though, as she worked, the peace was broken by a soft tap at the door. She glanced round with a frown, unsure if she had even heard it. No one ever called here unexpectedly. But then it repeated, a soft double knock and she sighed and rose to her feet. A broken-down car? Someone lost in the back roads? Getting involved with a problem felt like the last thing she wanted to do this late at night, but isolation carried with it a certain responsibility and she twitched aside the curtain that covered the door. She could see nothing through the glass, so she opened it and peered out—and gave a small hiss of shock as she found herself staring down into a white face under wild bedraggled hair.

A face that made a low, miserable breathy sound that was almost words.

Her visitor was a small woman dressed in some undefined white garment that looked tattered and torn and damp—those were the first impressions. She was crouched on her doorstep as though she had collapsed there with just enough energy to reach up and knock. As Merryn opened the door wider, the figure slumped into the gap and would have ended up on her face if she hadn't reached out and caught her. There was a faint sigh and Merryn could feel hands clutching at her with almost no strength at all.

"What… what happened to you?" she demanded, glancing round the dark garden and road, her heart racing and chills breaking out all over her skin.

The girl cocked her head on one side theatrically, as though about to speak, but at that moment the rush of another train came sweeping in, noisy in the night, and Merryn gave up, shaking her head. There were blood stains as well, she realised, scattered in various places around her clothes. Her feet were bare and covered with mud.

"Oh shit," Merryn muttered. "Come in—can you walk? Come in and I will get help."

Her visitor half scrambled, half crawled inside and she helped her over to the sofa. Merryn stared down at her, feeling dreamlike. She was definitely flesh and the weight of her was substantial, her skin cold and damp and covered with mud—but it still felt unreal. Merryn had to drag herself back down to Earth, to stop herself staring and actually do something. She grabbed the landline phone—but before she could dial, her brown-haired visitor was moving again… sitting up and reaching out…

In one sharp yank, she had ripped the wire from the wall, snapping the plug.

"Hey," Merryn cried, but the girl just shook her head, speaking just too much effort. "But surely I should… what the fuck did you do that for? Aren't you hurt?"

In defiance of all appearances, the girl shook her head. Merryn gazed down at her, filled with caution, trying to decide whether she should be frightened. The stillness of the wildlands still seemed absolute, but she crossed to the front door and shut it with a bang.

"What happened anyway?" she asked.

The girl gave no answer, just stared with unnervingly penetrating eyes.

"Look," Merryn said, "I really think I should…"

The emphatic shake of the girl's head and horizontal gesture with her finger was answer enough. She returned the now-dead handset of the phone to the cradle and stared in puzzlement. Her visitor hadn't said a word yet—not even a grunt or groan that was beyond breath. Was she a mute? Or was she just exhausted? In shock? Watching her relax back into the cushions, Merryn also realised that she had no idea how old she was. She looked barely into her twenties, but at the same time her face seemed too thin and worn and her eyes looked as though they had seen far more than twenty years. She was short. Her body was solid and thick-limbed, but that did not mitigate a sense of frailty. Merryn gave a discomforted sigh. In her head, all sorts of things were clamouring now—was her visitor running away from something? Or someone? Was she in trouble? Was she victim or criminal? As far as that meant anything. She looked out of the window, searching for any other signs of activity out there in the dark, but she could see nothing. There was hardly any wind stirring the trees and the only sounds she could hear were the stream, the hum of her computer and the girl's tired breathing.

Merryn tried again.

"Do you need… is there anything I can do? First-aid? I don't know much but I have some kit. I'm sorry, but you look a mess."

The girl just stared at her for a moment, then ran her fingers over her body and legs in a long fluid movement—spread her hands in a gesture that was half shrug and half tragedy.

She must be mute, Merryn thought, feeling even more discomfort. The gestures she was making and the ways her hands moved seemed too expressive to be made by someone used to mere speech.

Her hand reached out and grabbed at Merryn's arm for a moment, as though making sure she had her full attention. Then she simply peeled the white gown she was wearing off over her head. It was a shock and Merryn flinched—partly because of the sheer lack of concern or self-consciousness but mostly because of what she revealed. Her body was covered in bruises and scratches, mud and blood stains—the Celtic-type white of her skin occluded from head to toe by brown and black and red. She gazed down at herself forlornly, running her hands over her skin with quick delicate gestures as though drawing attention to specific wounds, even trying to brush them away. Even the most dedicated nudist could hardly have seemed so careless and there was something frightening about that. Maybe she really was in shock.

Merryn backed away towards the kitchen, aware of narrow eyes watching her over a thin smile. Those eyes were extremely intense—deep dark brown pools—and she broke the connection with them with some difficulty. A quick rummage in a cupboard produced her first-aid box.

"Here," she said, running back. "It's all I have. You sure you don't need a doctor?"

The girl sat up and gave the assorted bottles and tubes a confused look.

"Um…" Merryn picked out a tube of antiseptic cream, trying not to show how disturbed she felt. "Try this. Just rub it on—good for cuts…"

It seemed ludicrous, given the state she seemed to be in, to just offer a tube of cream, but she honestly had no idea what else to do. The girl took the tube, opened it and sniffed it, pulling a face of distaste.

"Look," she said. "Are you absolutely sure you don't want me to—well… to get you to a doctor? We could drive—right now. And sort out…"

The girl shook her head and smiled—the first proper smile since she had arrived—and made another gesture, reaching out to touch Merrin's chest, then fluttering her hands down over herself as though brushing away all her injuries. Merryn wasn't sure whether she was asking her for heeling or suggesting that the process was already underway. Then, dropping the cream unused, she just curled over on her side and closed her eyes.

Merryn sat down at her desk. The sense of unreality was still washing over her and, now those eyes were closed, she realised she was trembling. In the shock of the last few minutes, she had just followed the sequence of events through with barely time to think, but now as she sat and watched, the sense of something wrong was sounding like a gigantic bell. This couldn't be real. The clothes she was wearing didn't look like clothes that a person might wear under normal circumstances. It wasn't what people wore when out in the hills. It was just a big piece of white fabric, with a hole for her head and slits for her arms. It looked elegant and well made—possibly sleepwear, possibly some airy modern dress design, but she wasn't sure. She glanced at the computer screen, where mundane internet matters looked back at her—then at the clock—then at the dark window—then back at the figure on the sofa. What did you do in a situation like this? No doubt some would just call the emergency services regardless and let them sort it out. She looked longingly at the broken phone, then at her computer, telling herself to just open up the right program—make a call, send a message—make this someone else's problem. But she couldn't. She had lived alone for too long to do that. She couldn't go against what seemed a direct request.

At least not yet.

Finally she tramped through to the other room and unearthed her spare quilt, which she draped over her sleeping visitor, who gave a sigh and cuddled it appreciatively.

Later in the evening, Merryn was awakened from a half-doze by a sound. A bump and a sharp hiss of breath that sent a prickle down her back. A dull thump unique to the sound of human flesh—and a hiss like sand falling onto a drum. She scrambled up and grabbed her robe, then pushed the door open.

"Hey," she called. "You… ok?"

The room was filled with voiceless gasps and sighs. The girl was asleep, she realised, but she was twisting around under the covers in a flurry of limbs. Merryn grabbed her bare shoulder, the twisting figure gave a jerk, then came up out of the nightmare with a much louder hiss unlike anything she had heard a human make before. She came lurching up in a flurry of quilts, naked, hands outstretched, face twisted, punching and clawing. The energy was astonishing, especially given how weak she had seemed just a few hours ago. Merryn backed away, any reactions short-circuited in the face of nakedness and fury—but she only dragged her attacker with her. She shrieked aloud in confusion and pain.

Then there was a staggering stop—eyes at last registering who she was. The girl stood frozen for a moment, then made a weird sound that was half sigh and half voiceless laugh and backed away against the wall. Merryn rubbed at her face, glancing at the smudge of blood on her fingers, then down at her torn night robe.

"What the fuck was that all about?" she demanded, too shocked to keep the shrillness out of her voice.

The girl didn't reply of course, just remained staring with the same feral look in her eyes, as though waiting to see what the reaction would be. Then she dropped to her knees and made a curious apologetic spiralling gesture with the first two fingers of each hand—rolling, over and over.

Merryn sighed.

"I had better find you some clothes, hadn't I," she mumbled, desperate for something mundane in all this. But the words that were coming out of her mouth were starting to seem ridiculous. A trite useless kind of expression that she wasn't sure meant anything at all. She stepped back into her room, grabbed a pair of pyjama trousers, a shirt and a pair of knickers, and hurried back but her visitor was already on the sofa again, eyes closed as though nothing had happened. Merryn watched her for a moment, unsure if she was really asleep or just pretending. Then she left the clothes on the nearby chair, covered her body with the quilt again and retreated to her own bed in the next room.

She didn't sleep. Her unease about her guest kept her lying there, scanning for some noise from the next room—some sound of stirring—some further nightmare. Scenario after scenario played through her head. Maybe it had all been fake—some crazy elaborate plan to gain admittance to the house. Maybe her visitor would now be ransacking it for valuables. Maybe she was a serial killer searching for her next victim. Maybe there were more outside, just waiting to be let in. In the face of these dizzying thoughts, time just drifted until a familiar sound came—the first passenger train of the day passing west over the rails above her house. A soothing rush of familiarity. That sound signalled morning, even though the window was still dark. It was enough for her to give up on sleep and stand up, still listening. Then she opened the door and peered into the next room. It was even darker in there, but there was enough light to reveal an absence. The sofa was empty. Just the quilt piled on the floor. The original torn garment had gone as well. The clothes she had left for her hadn't.

She switched the light on and stared round. All the scenarios turning over in her head were coming back to her, but there seemed no sign of anything missing. She checked her spare keys—all present. She checked over her small stash of money—also undisturbed. None of her rocks were missing, or anything else that she could see. The door was closed and locked. She was just gone.

In the end, she forced herself to put the mystery out of her mind, trying to calm the knot deep in her stomach. She checked the bluestone boulder she had brought home yesterday, undoing the bandages and inspecting it carefully. It had set well, though she realised with annoyance that there were a few patches of gleaming resin visible on the outside. A scrub with a dose of acetone might fix that, though it was a bit of a blunder. The crack itself was almost invisible, but the remaining scrapes and scratches were not. They were a problem. She could smooth them out easily enough with her equipment, but the stone's weathered brownish outer layer was damaged, revealing the green-grey interior of the rock. It would bear the scars of its tumble down the hillside forever—or at least for many more years. An alternative would be to deliberately saw a flat face on the stone, removing the damaged part, and polish it as a display piece. When finished, dolerite has a very appealing dark marbled pattern with a nice speckling of white. It was tempting.

She stroked it. In contrast to the marble she worked with, this stone almost seemed warm to the touch. Maybe that was another reason the material had appealed so to the early people who used it. She took the stone outside and placed it in the early morning sunlight, admiring the hints of greenish colour showing through. Then she retired to her shed. There were more rocks to cut and grind on the big spinning wheels. Orders to fulfil. Specimens to prepare. A massive red-banded Dulcote agate from Somerset that was destined for her own over-full shelves. There was a big Lucky Strike thunderegg from Oregon that looked like a surrealist rock pool. There was a box of Septarian nodules to cut and see what, if anything, was inside. Best case scenario—a beautiful geode of calcite crystals. Worst case scenario, a ball of dull brown mudstone that she had paid a lot of money to ship round the world. Lost in the hypnotic action of the wheels, she finally began to put her visitor out of her head.

One reason she had been so happy to retreat back here to the west was because other people always left her feeling tense and nervous, unsure how to interact with them and what they expected from her.

Here though, the rocks were eternal and demanded nothing.

After a day of work, her hands and arms were aching and she finally shut down the machines and went back indoors to change out of her working clothes. After a bath to wash off the mud and dust, she hurried to the fridge, looking for food. However, now at last, with a shock and an accelerating heart, she found what her eyes had been consciously or unconsciously searching for all day—something was indeed amiss with her house. Something had changed.

The fridge had been disturbed. A tray that had once contained lamb chops—raw lamb chops—had been ripped open and all that was left was a few stripped, chewed bones.

Merryn frowned. When had this happened? She hadn't noticed it earlier. She was sure…

It was hard to hear much when in the bath, or when polishing…

She shut the fridge door and stared round, listening for any sound. She could hear her vibrolap jostling in the distance of the shed—the murmur of her heating system—the fridge—the sounds of water and nature outside—her own clothes rustling. Nothing alien. She stepped to the door and looked out, trying to pierce the dark garden. Trying to map the place in her head, searching for anything that shouldn't be there. The night air smelt crisp, with a faint tang of fast-flowing water. Familiar.

And yet…

A tiny hint of movement.

And there she was.

She was half-sitting half-lying propped up against the grassy bank below the railway line.

Merryn stepped outside. "Um…" she managed.

The girl opened her eyes and gave her an oblique smile, as though she was an old friend and this was all completely normal.

Merryn shook her head and sighed. It had been hard enough in the past talking to ordinary people—faced with deciding what to say to a seemingly feral girl who had just raided her fridge for raw meat, her social skills shut down completely.

"You're—ok then?" she asked at last.

The girl nodded with another smile.

After a moment, Merryn just sat down in the grass alongside her with a weary sigh, ignoring the cold dampness that soaked through her thin trousers and content for the moment to play along. Whatever thoughts were storming through her mind, this figure didn't seem threatening. Certainly, any idea that this was just a normal person in abnormal circumstances had long gone but in the face of the aching hole that left behind, the complete impossibility of working out what was going on, it seemed easier not to think at all. Living alone, you tend to lose the habit of questioning things—you forget the panic that the loss of social norms can bring. Should she be afraid? Fascinated? She had no idea. Stories of children growing up wild in the forests or reared by animals were trickling through her head, but that was absurd. Not here in the British hills. There was another, more likely possibility. Maybe this was all deliberate. All some kind of weird performance. As though she should be glancing round for hidden cameras. There was a college in the city not so far away—maybe she was an art student. Art could explain almost anything, she knew that much.

"I wish you could tell me what happened to you?" she said softly.

The girl gave her a curious look—then suddenly grabbed her. Merryn flinched away, memories of the hissing thing that attacked her last night strong in her mind. But she was only trying to show her something. She tried to symbolically drag her across the slope a few yards, then grabbed a stick and held it up—furiously miming burning gestures.

"Fire?" Merryn asked. The girl stood tall, holding the stick in the air with a dramatic frown on her face. "Torch?" she cried. "Burning torch?" The girl grinned, then the pantomime continued. She grabbed at herself, enacting some sort of struggle, kicking and fighting with an invisible opponent. It was a little awkward for she was still hurt and limping, but the message of an attack was conveyed. Then she was on the ground. She curled herself up into a tight ball, grabbing at her feet, knees to chest. A tugging gesture indicated that there was no choice—her hands and feet were bound. Merryn stared in amazement as the figure struggled, glaring up at her with terrified eyes. Then she was up again. She jumped a little way up the slope and mimed a dramatic shoving gesture—then she bent over, almost putting her head between her legs. Again she grabbed her knees and toppled forwards, tumbling head over heels downwards. It was a clumsy and untidy fall and she finished up in the grass, still curled up, still grasping her ankles, knees still to her chest.

Hints of meaning were getting through but it was all too fantastical for Merryn to glean much information from.

"This is the dream you had, right?" she asked, rubbing her cheek. "You were thrown down a…?"

Silence.

"Is this real?" she asked at last, her skin starting to crawl. "Is this… somehow… what happened to you before… you came here last night? Were you attacked?"

The girl shrugged.

"If so then I really had better phone the police…" Merryn began, but the response was a shake of the head and a finger drawn across her lips in an unmistakable shut-up gesture.

"But…"

The girl gestured sharply again—almost aggressively this time.

"Ok, ok," she said. "I won't phone anybody—I promise." She flinched slightly as the girl leant across, but she only planted a little kiss on her cheek and grinned a broad grin.

"Where do you live anyway?" Merryn asked. "If you can tell me."

An expansive gesture circling round her, ending up pointing at the grass between her feet.

Here.

Merryn looked at her feeling a wash of unease. "Indeed?" she murmured.

The girl sat down again with a bump, trying to be graceful but still rendered clumsy by her pained legs. One hand reached out to the bluestone boulder. She studied it for a moment, then rather sadly ran her hands over the damaged surface.

Merryn reached out and picked it up, pleased to change the subject. "Don't worry," she said with a smile. "I will make that better tomorrow." That got another big grin. It was amazing how expressive her face was—amazing but maybe not surprising if the most familiar avenue of communication was not available. "In fact… I'll show you," she said, scrambling to her feet.

She carried the stone into the shed and set it down on the worktop, the girl immediately reaching out and stroking it again, running her hands over the healed crack. Then she looked round at the machinery and her face changed a little—a puzzled look. A hint of worry. That sensitive hand reached out cautiously and touched the big diamond blade, then she picked up a recently halved thunderegg and stared at it.

Merryn watched her, feeling discomforted. The girl seemed disturbed now, and that in turn disturbed her. The rock studio was such a fundamental part of her life that any hints of a negative reaction came close to hurting her feelings.

"Yes," she said, brushing the damaged area. "I can cut all this off and polish it up nicely. It will look beautiful.

The girl gave a frown, as though trying to understand something—then grabbed the bluestone from her and cradled it in her arms. She shook her head decisively. There was a tense silence for a moment, then she backed away out of the shed.

Merryn followed her down the garden and caught up with her as she approached the road.

"Hey," Merryn called, some anger in her voice now. "Don't run away with my stone."

She tried to grab it, her heart racing again—but there was none of the aggression of the previous night this time. There was just an upset and frightened grimace as she wrestled the bluestone from her grasp.

Merryn frowned.

"I don't know what you are doing here or what performance you are putting on—and I don't really mind. But please don't mess with my rocks," she said. "These things are valuable."

The girl just stared at her, and she was surprised how genuinely pained she looked. She felt a wash of guilt, as though a momentary loss of temper had led her to kick a cat. To swallow that, she ushered her back inside under the light, turned the rock over and examined it again, grabbing a wire brush and briefly scrubbing at a few lingering patches of resin.

The girl followed her forlornly—and yet again reached out to brush her finger over the broken surface. Merryn smiled, anxious to make it up to her. "Don't worry," she said. I'll make all that shiny and bright. It will be beautiful. In fact… I will do it now. I'll show you."

Why not?

She mounted the bluestone in her huge rock saw and adjusted the complex clamp, angling it so the blade would cut a perfect flat slice off it. Then she glanced sideways and winced at the expression on that face. Something was definitely wrong, but she felt a need now to prove herself and her machinery, so she threw it into gear. The massive diamond blade began to turn with a dull wooden rumble.

The girl grabbed at her arm with an almost strengthless gesture. She was miming something again, drawing her hands in sharp gestures across her chest and stomach, then circling them urgently.

"It's perfectly safe," Merryn said soothingly. She reached out and touched the cutting edge of the spinning wheel, then held up her unmarked hand. "It won't hurt you."

All she got in return though was a panicked look and she sighed, beginning to feel more annoyance. Was this really nothing more than some crazy performance? Should she be taking any of this seriously? She checked the angle of the bluestone again and tightened the wing-nuts holding it in place. Even this basic rough cut had to be a work of art and, done right, it would remove about 20% of the rock's mass leaving a beautiful specimen piece for polishing one flat face.

"Look," she said. "This is how it works."

She slid the rock and clamp into position and began the cut.

The spin of the blade was nowhere near as fast as a lapidary saw or tile cutter of course, but that didn't matter. Instead it cut slowly and powerfully. All Merryn had to do was apply pressure and guide the rock forward as the blade bit in, cutting a slot-black groove. The air was filled with a roaring squeal—loud and painful. The eternal hardness of rock protesting at this assault. Muddy water from the cooling system splashed and trickled everywhere and the bluestone shook and vibrated under her hands. It could indeed be a traumatic process, cutting rock. Violent—shocking.

A long way from the perceived calm of the finished product. So maybe it wasn't so surprising that the girl reacted badly. She screwed up her face and clasped her hands to her ears. Then she made a sound. It was the first sound she had ever heard from her, clearly audible over the sound of the machinery—a small high-pitched squeal of protest that sent prickles down her back. She grabbed at Merryn urgently—that same 'something to show you' gesture, now imbued with desperation, but she shook her off.

"Don't," she snapped. "You'll ruin it."

The girl backed away out of the shed and vanished into the dark.

Merryn gave a groan of confusion and ran to the door, watching the white figure run away up the steep garden towards the railway tracks. She wanted to follow, feeling guilty without any real idea why. She hadn't meant to frighten her, only wanted to show her some of the magic of working with rocks. That moment when the stone opens to reveal its interior. She wanted to follow, but she couldn't leave the machine unattended. The stone was still yelling at her from the clamp. It could break, or even damage the machine if she didn't get back to it. She felt a throb of fury. This whole strange charade and performance had been almost agreeable for a while, but now she was fed up. She was beginning to wonder again if there really was something going on in the mind of this person that went far beyond art or foolery or trauma.

She hesitated over the mechanism, wondering whether to shut it down, then she impatiently grabbed the rock again and continued the cut. With the machine roaring at her and water flying everywhere, cutting a rock came with a lot of impetus. Once started, it was something that had to be finished—only then could the monster be silenced, the job done. She frowned and leant a little more weight on the bluestone, rocking it backwards and forwards, trying to hurry the cut along—watching the blade sink deeper and deeper. Trying not to think about her resident mad girl.

Just as soon as this was finished, she would go inside and make a phone call from her computer. It had to be done.

This was farcical.

Inch by inch, the blade sank deeper until, after about five minutes, the cut was complete. The rock parted. This was always a special moment. The last few millimetres give way suddenly with a little rush and the two halves fall apart, revealing that first glimpse inside—a secret that had never been seen before. Sometimes it would be a spectacular pattern of agate or chalcedony, sometimes a crystal geode in all its intricacy, or sometimes, as now, just a beautiful stone surface—but it was always a moment of magic to see it emerge from the seeming mundanity of a rock. She put the thin piece aside, splashed the main specimen and held it up to the light, examining the cut face. Gleaming with water from the cooling system, it looked beautiful—dark and marbled with white spots and patches like snowflakes. Then she reached out and shut off the rock saw, the clunking, growling machinery falling into relief-filled silence at last, leaving a ringing void.

Except that the world was not silent. Somewhere in the distance, she realised, a sound continued. A familiar wailing voice. No words, just a high-pitched cry, half way between pain and singing. As theatrical as everything else about her visitor seemed to be. She put the stone down again and stared outside.

"Where are you?" she yelled into the darkness. "Come back here for gawd sake." The voice stopped. Merryn stood for a moment listening to the silence, but any smaller sounds were masked by the rush of yet another train approaching—one of the last passenger trains of the evening, heading west. She sighed and glanced down at herself, realising that she had not changed into her usual working clothes and that her light top and trousers were now covered with water and mud. She switched the light off and made for the house—but as she did so, the approaching train sounded its horn, which was unusual. She paused a moment. The horn sounded again—a long long note that didn't seem to want to stop. There was a squeal of brakes. Merryn felt her skin freeze. Train… stopping. Emergency brake. The slowing of tortured metal…

And she knew what it meant.

'Something to show you'… spinning wheels… diamond wheels… train wheels… rolling… downwards… broken…

Merryn gave a yell that was not really any kind of word and dashed up the garden. She could see the moving lights approaching down the track—then passing, still with the brakes screaming. Slowing and slowing. In those lights, she could see people looking round uneasily—staring out the windows—bracing themselves. Then it all finally came to a stop. She scrambled through the fence into the hallowed and forbidden territory of the railway, her eyes darting everywhere, unsure where to look first. A faint smoke could be seen rising from around the wheels—the smoke of brakes.

It was amazing just how big a train was when you stood next to it, below it—massive wheels gleaming almost at eye level…

And there, amid the under-train darkness of machinery, ventilation grills and heavy metal, all wreathed in that same light smoke, was something white—and red. A glimpse of the incongruous blend of mangled meat and human face, hair trailing, eyes looking barely more than asleep…

Merryn gave a long groan.

"Hey," a voice called and she flinched, looking round. The terrified driver had jumped out. "Oh gawd," he called, running breathlessly in her direction. "Oh fuck—I think I hit something—someone. Did you see…?"

Merryn gestured under the train. But it was then that the impossible happened. Impossible, yet she saw it so clearly and mundanely that it was only after a few seconds that the impossibility kicked in.

The girl was vanishing.

It was as if she was melting into coils of something that seemed half-smoke half-liquid, which sank downward into the ballast. Patterns roiled within like ink drops in water, slowly dissipating—little weather phenomena in miniature. A few faint gleams of light, barely brighter than fireflies, flickered and died.

"There was someone crouched on the track," the driver said, arriving at her side. "White. With her face in the fucking ballast. Where is she?"

Merryn just stared. Any hope of speech had left her.

The driver leant in and frowned. "Where?" But there was nothing but ballast and sleepers. Not even an obvious stain. The driver stared around in confusion, this way and that, flashing his torch towards the back of the train, running a little further. Then returning with a huge sigh of relief.

"I could have fucking *sworn…*" he muttered.

Merryn still said nothing.

"You alright?" he asked. "It's ok—I, um… there doesn't seem to have been an incident after all—so…"

She blinked. "Yes," she managed.

"You sure?" he asked. "You're in a bit of a… well, have you had an accident?"

Merryn stared at him in mystification, then glanced down at herself, remembering the mud all over her clothes.

"Oh. No," she said. "I'm ok. Just... working. I just also thought..."

She shook her head. Coldness and confusion filled the world. She couldn't talk.

"Um—ma'am?" the driver continued. "You shouldn't be here. You're trespassing..."

She turned away without a word and ducked back through the fence.

"Um—ma'am?" the driver called after her anxiously. But she ignored it—didn't look back as she stumbled down into the garden again.

After a few minutes, she heard the train get into motion again with a drone of motors and a chug of diesel—but she didn't look at that either.

There were patterns in the world—even though sometimes you could barely accept them or believe them. At the junction where the path to the sea branched off the coast road, Merryn stood in silence. She had been standing there for almost half an hour, but there was nobody around to wonder what she was doing. There rarely was out here. The junction stone was back in its place, standing again about a foot above the rough grass and again providing shelter for the small creatures of the soil. Now though, the gleam of a smooth flat polished surface reflected the sunlight. Merryn had finished it—eventually. The feeling was of intense regret at ever having cut it at all, and for reasons she could hardly allow herself to accept or believe—but having done so, finishing it seemed the only thing to do. A saw cut couldn't be repaired, even if a crack could—it was far more destructive. So she had ground the surface smooth with silicone carbide, then polished it with her water-driven felt polishing wheel. But now, out here, the polished face seemed far from appropriate—it looked almost like a gravestone…

She stared with intense exhaustion down the slope towards the unremarkable bushes that separated it from the beach. It seemed a long way down. A long way to fall. A long way to roll. And even further beyond that to the gentle whisper of the sea.

A Taste of Casu Marzu

Amid a proliferation of cheeses, Richard Jarvis raised his glass. "Ladies and gentlemen," he said. "Well—lady and gentleman. Both of you. One of each, to be precise..."

Feather and Calvin grinned.

"...I hope you have had enough."

"It has been an education," Cal said.

Plates covered the small dining table. Plates with crumbs of Pecorino Sardo, Bocconcini, Podravec, Paški sir, Anthotyro xero, Metsovone and several other cheeses from Italy and the Adriatic—along with the remains of bread, Italian ham, pršut, mayonnaise, olive oil, Serbian ajver and other dips. There were also several bottles of Cannonau wine—also mostly empty.

Red-haired Richard Jarvis and the equally red-haired Peacock regarded their guests happily. It was a relaxed and comfortable gathering in Richard's eccentric living room—which meant being surrounded almost from floor to ceiling by collected oddments. Richard Jarvis was the Procurer—a man who could find almost anything, one way or another. He was notorious for it. And this room was stuffed with everything from rocks and thundereggs and preserved insects to certain sculptures and books. Lurking in one of the more shadowy corners, there was even a rather eerie Jenny

Haniver[1] in a case, staring down at the gathering with shrivelled eyes. This was a place where the collector's instinct had run wild and where the room was filled with a sense of life and love because of it.

And cheese.

He and his partner Peacock made a curious pair and both looked as eccentric as their room. She had the sharp eyes, prominent cheekbones and hard-edged accent that spoke of Central or Eastern Europe, while he looked like an English gentleman from a past age—though comically and slightly ironically so in a respectable faded suit and even a pocket watch for the occasion. He was like something from the grand old days of the Victorian eccentrics—tall and rather gaunt, but with a very eager and enthusiastic face, with a mischievous grin contrasting curiously with his very intense eyes. That energy made him look boyish, though that was belayed by the well-defined streaks of grey through his red hair.

"I hope you have saved a little space for our special finale, however?" he said, gesturing at a small wooden crate still sealed in plastic. It looked just big enough to contain a human head. "I haven't opened this yet," he said. "So what follows is all part of the great unknown."

Cal and Feather stared suspiciously at the box as he tentatively picked it up and broke the seal. And what happened next was quite spectacular. It was invisible—silent—insubstantial. But it almost felt as though it shouldn't have been. There should have been a noise to accompany that smell as it came radiating out. A crackling or fizzing sound perhaps. It made Feather, Cal and Peacock sniff suspiciously and flinch. Three pairs of eyebrows went up almost in unison. Ancient milk shot through with the

---

1 Constructed from the desiccated corpse of a skate, carved in such a way as to give it enough of a human form to make it suitably cryptozoological and mermaid-like.

acrid burn of ammonia. A shivering tang of odour like a knife in the air. A smell of the creatively dissoluted.

"This took some finding, I can tell you," Richard said, carefully lifting out a rather doubtful-looking pale brown, blotchy sphere…

"What is it?" Cal asked. It didn't look much, but the smell was making his hair prickle.

Richard didn't answer. He placed the cheese carefully on a plate, as though nervous that it would explode, and for a few moments everyone just sat and stared at it. Then Richard picked up a knife with a flourish and carefully cut the top off—scalping it neatly. A few small worms scattered on the table and Calvin winced. They were white and tiny and almost glassy…

"Oh dear," he said with a laugh. "Woops. I hope that wasn't valuable." He leant forward to sniff, then backed away again sharply. The soft, almost liquid interior of the cheese was a squirming mass of maggots.

"Oh dear," he repeated with rather more feeling.

Richard nodded in satisfaction. "Perfectly ripe," he said.

Cal blinked at him.

"This is Casu Marzu from Sardinia," Richard explained. "The famous maggot cheese."

Cal stared at the squirming mass.

"Is it?" he murmured faintly.

"Yes. It's not exactly legal—but I had to try it. Not exactly easy to get into the country either…"

Feather shifted. "How did you…?"

Richard tapped his nose and nodded. "My methods are intellectual property of the highest order. The closest of close business secrets."

He took a hunk of bread and cautiously examined the cheese.

"Now," he said. "According to what I've read, you just…"

He dug out a wriggling forkful and anointed the bread with it. A few of the worms actually jumped off, scattering on the table, and he rolled it up quickly. Then, shielding it with his hand he raised it to his lips… and paused.

"Well?" he demanded. "After all the work I have gone through—are you going to just sit there and stare at it?"

After a moment Peacock also took a forkful and rolled herself a sandwich.

Feather shrugged and followed.

"I've eaten stranger things," she said.

There was a brief silence while people considered that one, then Cal cautiously dipped a fork in the squirming centre, regarded the resulting dab carefully to make sure nothing moved, then licked it off.

He made a curious noise, ending in a choking cough.

"Oh bloody hell," he coughed. "It burns my nose." He drew a deep breath and puffed urgently for a moment. Then quickly took a drink of wine.

There was silence.

"Want some bread?" Richard asked, without much hope.

More silence.

Richard nodded. "Ok—you won't join us then? Feather? Chew it well. Don't swallow anything alive. That can lead to… complications."

"Now he tells me," Cal grunted.

"And shield your eyes," he continued. "These things can jump."

In perfect unison, Richard, Feather and Peacock chomped their bread. In perfect unison there were three explosions of breath, coughing and dabbing of eyes. Cal watched in sympathy.

"My skin is crawling," he complained. "I am tingling all over. What the hell is that stuff?"

Richard sat back. He seemed to be perspiring slightly.

"Kind of smarts, doesn't it," Cal said dryly.

"There are no words…"

Feather gave a high-pitched giggle and consumed the rest of her sandwich.

"I like it," she said. "It reminds you you are alive."

"I dare say," Cal growled. "I have never seen a cheese so brimming with life and vitality."

Richard dabbed his eyes again and laughed. "Oh Feather, I wish I could sell you in 200ml bottles. We would all be rich."

Cal shivered and rubbed at his arms. "My nose is still tingling," he stated. "What have you done to us?"

"I am tingling as well," Feather said, squirming in her chair with a short shrill giggle. Peacock drew a deep breath and also drained her glass of Cannonau. She also seemed to be struggling to maintain her composure.

"I think another round of wine perhaps," Richard offered.

Another bottle was opened and more Cannonau flowed and was drunk.

"There's a lot of world out there," Feather said wistfully, staring at the remains of the feast. "All these cheeses—and all from different places I have never seen."

"Oh yes," Richard said. "These cheeses come from places where the wine and—and the olives and figs grow. Where the blue sea basks under a far too painful Mediterranean sun. And you can taste it."

"Hmmm?"

"I love the south—central Europe," he said. "The land—the people—the pretty girls… In Zagreb. Dear sweet Ljubljana.

Sardinia. Down in Dalmatia. The endless Croatian islands… riding the railway down towards Split…"

Peacock gave a small smile. "Mr Jarvis would collect them if he could," she said.

"Who?" Cal asked. "The islands, the railway or the girls?"

"All of them," Richard cried. "I want them all in my museum…"

"Sounds rather dull to be stuck in a museum," Feather said.

"Well—" Richard gave a mischievous grin. "Define museum. You have been in my museum for years."

"Does this cheese count as a museum then?"

"Well—why not. A brief and fleeting one true—but why not?"

Peacock grinned and spat on the floor.

"Perhaps mercifully, I think. More wine yes?"

Richard distributed Cannonau, then raised his glass high.

"I think we shall have fine dreams tonight," he said. "And I hope I am in all of them."

Laughter.

"Have some more cheese," he cried.

There was a faint whistle of a train in the distance, making him hesitate and listen. The local railway line? It was a breathy steam whistle, not a horn.

"I love trains," he said. "Remember Tolkien? *The road goes ever on and on—down from the door where it began. Now far ahead that road has gone, and I must follow if I can…* Somehow that seems trebly true of the railways. That same railway line rides down to Split. Rides across Siberia. Bears the thundering weight of the Shinkansen…"

Cal was looking uncertain and hazy from the rich wine. "Cheese everywhere," he muttered, brushing at his suit. "And my nose can still feel that. How much of that stuff did I eat? Where did that cheese go?"

"I like tingling," Feather said, rubbing her face against the soft fabric of the chair. Cal gave a snort of laughter.

Richard glanced round the room, blinking. Everyone looked relaxed and contented now. Feather was sprawled out and basking in the glow of the wine—a huge grin on her face. Even the usually gruff Calvin was smiling openly. Outside, in the world, things may be complicated and tiring but in here, in the here and now, things were pleasantly simple. That was just another power that a collection of loved objects in a comfortable environment could have. With a smile, Richard Jarvis helped himself to another portion of Casu Marzu. Feather followed him.

"A loaf of bread—some wine—a... a rather large number of cheeses... and thou. What more do you need?" he murmured, sniffing appreciatively.

"What?"

"Just thinking," he said. "Travelling. Perhaps it is time we went back to Sardinia... Peacock?"

She leant sleepily back in her chair. "Mmmmmm," she murmured.

"I should like to see it," Feather said.

Something outside was rumbling, and Richard stared round uncertainly.

"What is that noise?" he demanded.

"It sounds menacing," Peacock said with a wicked grin. "Maybe they've finally caught up with you."

"Who?" Feather asked.

Peacock shrugged. "Just 'Them'. Those who chase and pursue anyone who spends fortunes importing rotten cheeses from the ends of Europe."

"The Anti-Eccentric-Collector League?" Cal asked, smiling. "We all know they exist."

"Sitting in a white room…"

"Plotting new government measures to make life hard for people who are actually interested in something…"

"The Measuring Men?" Feather asked. The rumbling was getting louder. It sounded as though a lorry was negotiating the small road outside Richard's spiked gate.

"Who?" Peacock demanded back.

Feather gave a sigh and buried her head in the chair.

"The people who watch and measure you and…" She waggled her finger scoldingly at an imaginary victim. "Tut tut," she said. "But never mind them. I wish that noise would go away. It is disturbing the cheese feeling."

Richard rose to his feet. The sound almost sounded as though it was in the garden rather than out in the road.

"Damn," he muttered, making for the window.

That was when the whole outer wall gave way from floor to ceiling in a huge cloud of steam, cutting the lights out in an instant and dropping the room into blackness. But the light was quickly replaced. Richard found himself staring directly at a huge white glare filled with swirling dust and steam—a glare that framed him like an animal caught in headlights. The roar was deafening. He gazed into the flaring inferno for a moment longer, then dived away on instinct.

The steam screamed.

Cal and Peacock jumped from their chairs, yelling aloud as the light blazed in. It came from a dazzling point that approached slowly through the dark, barging through the last of the wall. There was a glint of metal there as well. Very large metal. Advancing slowly.

Richard staggered across the room gazing around stunned as his collection was demolished. The last of the Cannonau wine spilled on the carpet, followed by the squirming Casu Marzu, which landed and smashed, shedding worms everywhere. Shelves came down, strewing collectables and beautiful things across the floor. Everyone was frantically trying to find somewhere to retreat as the intruder finally came clear.

It was a locomotive. A gigantic black steam engine with one huge headlight, which slowly and solemnly slid through the living room, mashing the furniture. The boiler was immense and black and gleaming. The front quickly passed out again deeper into the house, taking the opposite wall with it, the huge slowly turning wheels ploughing up the floor. The smoke stack blew the ceiling away in a storm of plaster, which rained down on the stunned quartet. But it was still many panicked seconds before the driver's cab appeared. In there it was night time—so dark you could see nothing save for flickering embers. Soon that too passed out. The tender solemnly passed by—and then the first and only carriage, where lights also shone in a blaze that hurt the eyes and where shadowy figures could just be made out against the glare. And then it was gone again, leaving a ruin where there had once been a room. A collection.

The roar faded away to silence and nobody moved. Everything had been flattened into stunned passivity.

Finally, Richard Jarvis shakily pulled himself to his feet out of the devastation of his shelves. He picked up a piece of the crust of the Casu Marzu and stood staring at it like an actor on stage about to produce a soliloquy. Then Feather came out cautiously from behind an armchair and Cal picked valuable limited edition books off himself and sat up.

The cheese party was over.

A glare of light came.

Richard gave a muffled groan and clutched a hand to his temple. He turned over and dug sharply into something warm—something that gave a moan of protest. It was all too much for a morning.

"Peacock?" he managed. "What are you doing here?"

She gave a sleepy grunt, propped herself up on her elbows and stared with hatred at the open curtain, which was casting an early beam of sunlight across them both.

"What happened?" she asked wonderingly.

Richard didn't have an answer to that.

Eventually she got up out of bed, stumbled to the window in her underwear and slammed the curtains closed. She looked pale and sick. Richard stared round the room. Feather was lying curled up on the floor in a corner, her clothes folded nearby. And there was Cal, still dressed in his black suit, stretched out on his back next to her, jacket and flies unfastened, mouth open and a worried frown on his face.

Richard screwed up his eyes, looking as though it hurt too much for the brain to function or analyse the situation. A brain full of crawling, eating things—just like that cheese—the Casu Marzu. Break open his head and it would probably taste just as bitter…

Peacock found her clothes on the floor in a corner, grabbed them up and hurried from the room. The door shut with a bang behind her and, with that sound, Feather roused suddenly, sitting up with a small sigh and rubbing at her face.

Richard gave her a small good morning smile and sat up in bed. This room was like the rest of the house—filled with more odd specimens and things on display, and Feather gazed round curiously, as though seeing it for the first time. Richard Jarvis forlornly picked up a case of small meteorites and stared at them as though they could explain something. After all, sometimes a lump of rock can be the most comforting thing in the world.

Then the door opened and Peacock peered in again. Dressed now.

"Richard?" she murmured rather grimly. "There are dead worms all over the living room, an empty shell of cheese that stinks to the high sky and two broken glasses. Just how many bottles of that wine did we get through last night?"

Richard put his head in his hands. "I don't remember," he said. Then he gave a small grin. "It was worth it though. What a cheese."

Peacock sighed and tramped back downstairs.

Richard and Feather exchanged glances.

"Our dear Peacock is not amused," he said softly with a tiny smile. "Our dear Peacock has a headache."

Feather grinned. "I like that cheese," she said. "It brought strange dreams."

Richard nodded guardedly—still looking puzzled.

"Maybe we should have got aboard," she said, and he gave her a sharp look. "Maybe it would have taken us somewhere interesting."

"Maybe we should," he said at last, but she wasn't listening to him. She leant back into the corner of the room, glanced at the sleeping Calvin a moment, then settled to comfortably staring at the ceiling.

Footsteps returned and he heard Peacock entering her own bedroom. The door shut sharply.

"These things are great," he said, mostly to himself, opening the case and taking out a pebble. It was the sort of thing you would completely ignore if you saw it on the beach—small and knobbly and nondescript. Except that it wasn't. The surface looked tortured—fused and burned a very different sort of smoothness than you get from the sea.

"Stones left over from before the Earth was even formed," he said dreamily. "Perhaps some of the oldest solid stuff there is… around here. Impossible to really imagine how old… and it just keeps reminding us that the world is—more than we can ever imagine."

Feather nodded and touched the rock curiously. Then leant back again.

"Richard," she said, "I want you to find another of those cheeses. I want to ride that train."

She drew a deep breath and gave a long sleepy groan.

"My head feels funny," she said.

"Don't worry," Richard murmured. "I have something for that—a little remedy of mine that I found…"

But she wasn't listening. "Far far away," she said faintly. "Far far away… The rails go ever on and on… and I must follow… if I can…"

One Rainy Autumn

I'm not an expert, this wasn't really a science lab and I suppose, when you get down to it, the Doctor wasn't a Doctor. That's a good start, isn't it? But what can I say? It was a converted shipping container somewhere in the middle of the marsh—a type of accommodation that can flip from nice to excruciating very easily, I think. Little more than a fridge and some plumbing at that point. And my job was to wire the basic electrics of the place—to provide enough 13A sockets for a sparse life, a sparse computer and some sparse monitoring equipment.

Oh and the Doctor was, as far as I could figure out the details, still studying—to be a doctor of entomology. Not helminthology, you will note, not medicine—entomology. The study of insects.

It was striking how soon all this became meaningless...

This little place may have been far off the grid, but I was enjoying the job. To be alone, with a relatively simple task to do, nobody staring over my shoulder or trying to micromanage—it was pleasant. Several mysterious keys had been signed over to me along with a whole load of materials, and then I was on my own. Alone to find my little adventure down tiny country roads, about half a mile of dirt track, barely functioning gates, and finally a rough causeway/flood barrier that stretched deep into the marsh itself.

All around were water channels and areas of reeds, a place some might see as dreary. But the flatness, the vast sky, the birdsong, the insects, the solitude and the sound of the rain together had their own magic. Maybe I am a wilderness kind of person at heart, even though not so much in practice, and the bleak tranquillity here was a welcome change from pretty much the entire world. Even the rain, which had done nothing but stream down ever since I arrived, was pleasant in some ways. The sound of it was continuous—a patter becoming a hiss becoming a roar becoming a patter again, while grey upon grey filled the hemispherical sky. And this eternal white noise cast a strange sense of the static and frozen across this expanse of water and mud and plants.

To the south, some distance away, was the sea. The haunting estuarine sea of the far lower Thames. Nearby was a small river that tangled and split and joined and lost itself in this marsh. In the distance, to the west, when it was no longer hidden by rain, I could just make out the distant towerblocks of some town in the commuter orbit of London. Somewhere inland was a village. But I could be forgiven for forgetting there were any other human beings around at all. Even my old and rather feeble phone wasn't working out here. There were some flickers of signal in the surrounding area, but out in the wildlands, even this close to London, nothing can be taken for granted.

And in the middle of this marsh was a concrete wharf, seemingly without purpose. Maybe the tangled channels had once been more open, more navigable, but now it sat lost in weeds and mud, invaded by buddleia bushes and banked with watersoaked debris. In the middle of that wharf, looking even more abandoned and out of place, the cuboidal shape of a single shipping container, though one converted with doors and windows. There were three rooms—a bedroom, a workroom with a separate kitchen area and a bathroom that was far too small to contain an actual bath. Instead, a single wetroom contained a showerhead, a sink and a composting toilet, while a drain in the floor opened eerily into the depths. Out the front was an awning and some chairs so you could sit and watch the marsh in shelter from the eternal rains. And yeah, I wouldn't have minded being out here, doing whatever it was the sciency bods were going to do.

As I finished bolting the third solar panel into its mount on the container roof, as I scrambled down the wet ladder, I caught the sound of an engine above the rain. I lingered under the awning, looking around the marsh for its source. It was not exactly strange, however precarious this place seemed to navigate, but this was the first sign I'd had of another person since coming here. And it didn't take long to spot a small boat, approaching from the direction of the sea and picking its ways through the channels and islands towards me. Two figures, one a young man who seemed to be piloting, and a woman in a raincoat standing beside him, hunched against the weather. Various boxes and cases were stashed on the deck and covered with tarps. As the boat approached the wharf, I felt a small sigh somewhere deep inside at the prospect of having to deal with humans again. But I chased that away and stepped forward to greet them.

"Uhh—hi," she said, scrambling out with a stumble that told me she wasn't really used to the boating life.

"Hi," I said with a smile. "Delivery?"

"Uhhh," she repeated, staring round at the piles of gear and cable trunking and tools under the awning—then through the open door to where naked and unconnected wires trailed. "What's going on here?"

Her tone of voice wasn't exactly hostile, but it came with enough potential for hostility that it put me on the defensive immediately. There was a whiny quality to it that I didn't like. "Just wiring the place," I said, keeping my voice amiable.

"But—but that should be finished now. I am supposed to be moving in. Is this… now what am I going to do? Are you running late?"

I thought quickly, double-checking my memories. Out here, my mobile may have almost no signal and time may blur into a strangely static span, but I did know what day it was. "Nope. Not running late," I said with a slight frown. "I think you are running early."

"I was distinctly told today," she said sharply.

"And I was distinctly told to be done by tomorrow afternoon," I said.

She gave a sigh. "Oh... well—ok, I suppose there had to be a fuck-up of some kind. At least it's not my fault. How long will you be?"

I watched her, feeling a little more annoyed than I maybe should. She was young, but she packed enough arrogance for one multiple times her age. By and large, I liked and respected scientists but this one did not seem to be returning the favour. "Sometime tomorrow afternoon," I repeated. It was a little short, I admit, and I turned away and grabbed an armful of aluminium cable trunking.

She sighed and stared round, then crossed the concrete and peered inside—and I could almost see her mood dropping by the minute. I could understand that—this little marsh hutch could go either way in terms of perception very easily. There was nothing glamorous about it, especially at the moment. Nothing comfortable. This was no doubt going to be her home for some unspecified period of time, and right now, she was having *thoughts* about that.

She pushed open the door to the bedroom and I felt a kind of annoyed embarrassment as she stared at it, taking in the stuff I had left there—and the tiny little bed that filled almost all of it.

"Problem?" the young man on the boat asked as he followed her ashore.

"Yeah," she muttered. "There had to be a fuck-up. Look, uhh…" She turned to me again. "Can I at least unload? Are the cupboards available? And there's a bit of equipment…"

"Yes—go ahead. The left side of the room is fine. There's just no power yet. The bedroom is finished as well, though…"

"Hey Steve," she said. "Let's bring it all in. I'll sort it out later somehow."

"Ok, Doctor," he said with a grin, and I noticed the word with interest. I had only the vaguest idea what this place was going to be used for but obviously this was one of the persons who would be doing it.

"You need a hand?" I called.

"No no," she said. "It's ok. Just finish up, please."

I stepped back inside and returned to mounting the wall parts of the trunking. Flat strips that the main channel clipped onto later to make a neat tube. Holes drilled into metal and sealed bolts. There were so many 13A sockets here—a whole row of them, and each had to be connected by trunking. I was trying to ignore her going back and forth behind me, her hair and clothes getting wetter and wetter, and happy to leave her to be fed up in peace. I was watching though, out of the corner of my eye, as the equipment piled up. I had no idea what most of it was, but as she opened boxes and dragged stuff out, I did recognise computer gear, a digital microscope and what might have been a mercury vapour lamp for attracting insects. I was curious what my installation would be powering and trying to form a very off-the-cuff assessment of whether the system could handle it. I'd been given my instructions, of course, I hadn't personally planned any of this—but given how well things were working out, I was wondering whether it would be sufficient and how this *doctor* would react if it wasn't.

There were also various nets on long handles being stashed in the corner, a bicycle and a canoe stowed outside, and, perhaps the most surprising of all, a simple diving suit with a snorkel. There was a flash of pink among the black neoprene. This hardly looked like a prime diving location—but what did I know?

Eventually, with a few last words exchanged in the rain and a hug that looked friendly rather than romantic, the boat was shoved off, made a cautious turn and picked its way back to where the channels and waterways were that little bit wider. She stood for a while under the awning, watching it go—and there was a bleakness to that silhouette against the rain. A dark and ineffable hunched shape that filled me with gloom.

Then she turned, shook the water off her coat, and stepped inside. She looked at me for a moment, then back to her gear in stony silence, so I just ignored her right back again and continued running wires. I knew that if she was depressed, it wasn't at me personally—and hey, I get it. I remember the day I moved into my college halls for the first time, staring at the small white cubicle that was to be my home. And I remember the feeling of the bottom slowly falling away from my world. But even so, it didn't look as though we were going to be friends any time soon. With slumped shoulders, she began putting stuff away, filling the cupboards and the fridge, while larger items were arranged on the worktops.

"You want anything to drink?" she asked at last. There wasn't much in the small kitchen. I had brought a few scraps to keep me going, and to those she had added a few packets of flavoured noodles, some tins of soup, pots of salt and pepper, a bottle of cooking oil and other things. The tiny fridge had been stocked with a few bottles and cartons, though it wouldn't be keeping anything cold until I had got the power going.

"No thanks."

She poured herself a cup of presumably warm orange juice and downed half of it. "I can see I will have to go and do some shopping—nearby village, right?"

"Yes, there's a small shop there, but it doesn't stay open as late as they do in the city."

She seemed slightly less frosty now. Maybe it was thanks to the orange juice or maybe she was just starting to settle in. I gave a wry grin. Even though it seemed easier to be amused than annoyed at the evaporation of the peace I had been enjoying, there was nothing to do except get back to installing the trunking. There was still much to do.

"Tomorrow, I think," she said. "I'll live on the basics until then." She drank the rest of the juice in a second big gulp, then leant over for her bag and rummaged, producing a map. "I guess if you are still working, I will nip out while the light is good and have a look round—see what's living out there."

She put on her damp raincoat, reached for one of her nets and stepped outside into the rain. The grey swallowed her in a million jewelled drops as she wandered away down the path through the marshes.

When she returned a few hours later, she was looking more cheerful. I even got a smile out of her as she stepped in and dragged off her coat, dripping water all over the floor. And yes, it's amazing how much a smile changes a face.

"This is a wonderful place," she said. "So much life. The water's very high though. This rain must be swelling the waterways all across the county."

"Yeah," I said, putting down my screwdriver. I was getting a bit tired by this point. Evening was drawing in and I felt fully entitled to knock off for the day now. Had I been alone, I might have lounged under the awning watching the light fade, or just gone to bed with a book. "It was raining when I came—it's been raining ever since…"

"And it will probably still be raining when you go again," she finished. "I am starting to wonder whether it will still be raining when *I* go."

"How long are you here for?"

"A month," she said.

"All alone?"

"Yup. And that suits me just fine."

I shrugged, glancing round the room, unsure what to do or say next. The sound of the rain on the roof filled the silence with a cosy patter.

"I admit, the bedroom feels a little claustrophobic," she added. "But I'm sure I'll get used to it. It will be a nice little hole to curl up in when I'm done poking through the mud."

She picked up her phone again and studied it. "Not much signal here, is there."

"Mine's offline entirely. You got something?"

"Yes, just. The battery is almost gone though. I'll be able to charge it tomorrow, right?"

"Yes. And the internet will be on as well." I indicated the router—then hesitated. "Um—where do you intend to sleep tonight?"

"Hmmm—I wasn't expecting to share the place," she said, opening the door to the bedroom and leaning in. She studied my tangled bedding and few supplies as though they were a species of life form she'd never seen before. "How shall we do this? I have bedding, but…"

I sighed. I could see where this was heading so I might as well just dive right in. "I guess I can sleep in my van," I said. "I've done it before."

"Thank you," she said with a hint of relief. "You can… take your bedding as well and I will make the bed afresh."

She crossed to one of her suitcases, bent and opened it—and that's when I saw it. The small patch of blood on the back of her leg, staining the fabric of her jeans. It hardly looked anything serious but I spoke up anyway.

"The first-aid kit's in there," I said, pointing to a cupboard.

"Huh?"

"Your leg—just in case you need it."

"My… leg?"

"Back of your calf," I said. "Cut yourself?"

She twisted round to examine it, then stared at the smudge with eyebrows up. Then lifted her trouser leg.

What was revealed sent a massive prickle over my skin from head to foot. It wasn't a cut—something was embedded in her flesh. Something small and thin that wriggled and squirmed at the centre of a small red mark smeared with blood—and even as I looked, it seemed to penetrate a little deeper.

She made a weird noise—*hiieeggh-gh-gh*—then grabbed at it, but I had to admire her reaction. She quickly swallowed her shock and just stared, touching it with caution. It was obvious that she didn't dare yank at it in case it broke—and a dead broken thing in your leg is probably a lot worse than a whole live thing. She just grasped it and applied a very gentle pulling pressure. For a while it seemed to be resisting, but in the end, the steady pull worked and it popped right out. It had been embedded almost a centimetre deep.

She held it up, her hand shaking slightly.

"In that cupboard there," she said quietly. "Specimen bottle, please."

I hurried to get one and she slipped the thing—it looked like some kind of worm—into it, shut the lid and sat down heavily in one of the few chairs.

A massive shiver ran through her.

"Oh boy," she muttered. "Fuck it—I didn't even feel…"

"What is it?" I asked, studying the thing. It was nothing more than a whitish or translucent thread, maybe three or four centimetres long. A nondescript hair of life with no visible head or spines or legs. Even I knew that worms still had anatomy and features, but none were visible to the naked eye this time.

"I don't know. I'm an entomologist—this is some kind of worm. I didn't even know you got this kind of thing in the UK. It was trying to burrow into my fucking leg." Again a small shiver, and again I could see her swallowing it with an effort. "I'm going to have to ID this later—it's pretty fucking bizarre."

She set the bottle down and grabbed the first-aid kit, dabbing a little antiseptic onto her leg, then pausing.

"Uuhh, excuse me a moment…"

She hurried into the tiny shower cubicle. It was a tiny cubicle with barely room to move, and several bumps and thuds came through the wall as she, presumably, stripped off and checked herself over for any more thread-like invaders. I listened, feeling more shaken than I maybe should. This place had seemed so peaceful just an hour or so ago—a calm waterworld where I could relax and watch the time pass, not where things would try to eat their way into your leg. What with that and the loss of my bedroom, I was starting to look forward to driving my van back out of here along that causeway.

She stepped out of the cubicle again, looking rumpled. "Ok, emergency over," she said, reaching for her cup and pouring another glass of orange juice. "I wish I had some vodka to chuck in here," she muttered. "Nice welcome to the marsh. Nothing like saying hi in the most dramatic way possible."

I laughed, feeling relieved at the slight clearing of the air.

"If I'm to be stuck here," she continued, "the last thing I need is for it to be boring, right?"

"So what are you actually doing?" I asked, grabbing another length of trunking.

"Oh… well," she said with a small grin. The first real grin I could remember seeing on her face. "I guess I chose this, but I still think I managed to annoy my supervisor somehow. Some people go off on nice glamorous internships like moths in the African jungle, or studying ants that navigate using polarised sunlight in the Sahara Desert, or the medicinal properties of beetles—but I got myself shunted out here to basically watch a salt meter for a month."

"Why?"

"Well—the sea is pushing in here more and more. The tides are higher, the salt water is getting carried further and further upstream into this wetland. Things are changing here pretty drastically—and I suppose it's important. Species are dying out and other species are moving in. But even so…"

"Give some poor sod 'work experience' out here because no one else really wanted to?" I asked.

"I thoroughly resent that," she said with a sour laugh. "And… I did choose it. I think. But it's probably true."

She stepped to the door and opened it, the eternal hiss of the rain falling on the roof supplemented by the non-metallic version from outside forming a two-tone harmony. The light was starting to fail by this time and the sound of water somehow only emphasised the intense silence. No human noises drifting in from far off—no cars, voices, laughs, cries. And at this time of the evening at least, no natural sounds either—no bird calls, no insects, no scuffles or splashes. It was a time of day that I enjoyed a lot—a curious liminal period that was neither day nor night.

"Ah it's not so bad," she said at last. "Quite nice to rest up out here and study—and I do love the marshes."

I made some polite sounds that were presumably some kind of agreement as she drifted away to the edge of the concrete, leaning down to examine the plants where the light from the door caught them. Then she paused.

"Look at this."

I joined her under the awning and followed her indication—and could quite clearly see a small worm twining there among the stems, high off the ground—thin and moving with a quiet determination.

"Another one. Keep an eye on it." She ran for the hutch and reappeared in a moment with another specimen bottle, then quickly plucked the worm out with her bare fingers and slipped it in. "What the fuck is this thing? I don't know much about worms. As soon as the power is on, I must do some checking. Any chance of internet today?"

"Sorry," I said, spreading my arms. "Tomorrow. I need to get the panels and the battery unit wired up before I can bring everything online."

"Ah well," she muttered. I watched her for a moment as she took a packet of tissues out of her pocket and soaked one from a bottle, before adding them to her two specimen jars. Presumably to keep the occupants moist. She then moved into the bedroom and began dismantling my bed, bringing all my bedding out and piling it in the main room of the lab. With a small and hopefully inaudible sigh, I gave up on the wiring and gathered it up, carrying it outside and tramping or squelching across to the van. I watched the surrounding plants suspiciously, but surely I was safe on the path itself?

I had grown to quite like that little mattress. But what could I do? It was her hutch.

Reaching the van, I arranged the stuff as well as I could, and then returned to find her bending over the microscope.

"Want to see our vicious little friend?" she asked without looking up.

"Sure."

I leant over and she made way for me. This was somewhat unfamiliar gear for me, though not entirely since as I kid, I could remember playing with these on occasion, looking at the weird world that is pond life or soil or my own skin. I looked through it and adjusted the focus.

The worm still looked featureless—so much so that I was struggling to even find words for it. As formless a thing as I could ever remember seeing. It was long, and thin, as you would expect from a worm, but that was about it. It was just a translucent tube. Turning the wheels, scrolling along the length of the thing, I could see what might have been a faint groove or marking running along it—and on reaching the end, a small triangular notch presented itself. Though whether it was head or arse, I had no clue.

"So what do you think it is?" I asked.

"I have no idea. Worm. Just a fucking worm of some kind. Nematode. Flatworm—I mean, planarian. Or… maybe not. Who knows." I didn't express any surprise, and I'm not sure if I was even thinking it, but she gave me a slightly annoyed glare. "It's not my speciality. Look—scientists can be dumb outside their areas, ok. And I'm an insect girl."

In spite of everything, I had to smile. Not at whatever kind of dumbness may or may not have been involved but at her choice of phrase. Being an insect girl sounded—really rather wonderful.

"You want to know what that micromoth over there is, fine," she grumbled. "But micromoths generally don't try and burrow into my fucking leg. Maybe I can find out more if you can get the internet going."

"Tomorrow," I said. "We're almost done. Just need to finish the connections and check it over before I bring everything online."

"Cool. In the meantime, I guess I'm going to bed. Do some reading. Are you going to be ok out here?"

"Yeah, I'll be fine. Done it before."

She smiled. I think she could read my discomfort easily enough and appreciated it, but also felt a certain satisfaction at the conquest of the bedroom. Well—whatever. I wasn't going to let it bother me.

I spent another half hour or so installing the last of the trunking, connecting the wires to the inverter and the big battery unit, then finally called it a day. A rummage in the warm fridge and I grabbed a handful of edibles, things that could be eaten easily enough out of the packet, then took a drink of water and stepped outside.

The darkness here was intense. When the hutch was online, no doubt the lights would shine out at least a little, but for now there was nothing to be seen beyond a few very distant pinpricks. Far off houses or the even more distant town. All washed by rain. Switching on my torch only made the darkness beyond far deeper and I followed the path with some caution and climbed in, shutting the door behind me.

Yeah—just one more day's work. Maybe less than a day if I hurried. And I was quite ready to hurry now. She was welcome to this place.

And sitting, sprawling in the reclined seat of the van, the hiss of the rain just increased and increased, until it was a roar.

Next morning, it was still raining. I could tell even before I opened my eyes. The stream of sound and water continued as an eternal drone accompaniment to life. I liked the rain well enough, but right now the van seemed cold and musty and I rubbed at my eyes with a sigh. I hadn't slept well and I was feeling grumpy. Whether her majesty the Doctor was asleep or awake, I was going to get on with things and be out of here as quickly as I possibly could now. Then she could have all the solitude she wanted.

What was there left to do? A few last connections. Checks. Finally connect the solar panels, and test test testing all around…

Then I sat up… and everything froze.

There is a particular type of dream, or nightmare maybe—I don't know if everyone gets it, but I certainly have on occasion: a vast expanse of water where water should not be. The flood horror, in essence, in which you are completely trapped and overwhelmed by an alien environment of mirror water to the horizon. My van was now right in the middle of such an expanse, stretching off into the distance. As though my van was a miracle able to drive right across the water's surface and into the clouds. An endless filigree of raindrop ripples. Trees and hedges interrupted that infinity, of course—increasing with distance—but even so, it came with a deeply weird feeling and I just sat there for a long long minute or so, staring.

Marshes change. Water changes. Even when humans try to tame them, they can never be trusted. A path stays only as long as nature permits—and when it chooses, it can snuff out human presence in a moment. And now, the causeway had simply vanished. I could see the hutch, sitting on its slightly higher concrete wharf, now like a boat itself. I gave a shaky sigh and glanced at my phone, but the reception was no better than it had been. What the hell was I supposed to do now? Who do you call when the land itself has vanished?

I scrambled out of the van and fortunately the water only came up to my ankles on the causeway itself, but it was dark and occluded by the endless ripples. I grabbed my night bag and splashed quickly in the direction of the hutch. To my relief, the causeway seemed to be still there, just below the surface. The route at least was reasonably clear, marked out by fringes of drowned grass stems. It felt rough and unstable though, as though being slowly eroded by the soaking. My feet sank into mud or stumbled into invisible holes, but I made it to the wharf without issue and splashed up onto dry ground with a gasp of annoyed relief, then looked back at my van sitting forlorn and lost in the water. I suppose maybe I would be able to walk the other way as well—walk whole length of that drowned causeway to safety—but the thought was not appealing. Who knows what lay beneath that dark water? Too many visions of feeling a sudden slump underfoot and going straight down into a quagmire. And also…

I bent and quickly examined my legs, taking off my shoes and rolling up my trousers, begging the universe not to have seeded any flaming red coin-sized entry points on my skin. But it seemed fine. And so… I just started work again. How to get out of this situation, I had no idea, but having the power and internet on could only help. So I grabbed what I hoped would be the last of the trunking and prepared to attach them to the wall—the last conduit feeding the last 13A on this worktop.

After a moment of banging around though, the door to the bedroom opened and the Doctor came out in a rush, wrapped in a robe. I glanced round, preparing myself not to lose my cool if any kind of complaints about the noise were on the way.

"Um, hi," she muttered. "I—I…"

Something was wrong.

"What is it?" I asked. "Have you seen what's out there…?"

"I… no. I think I need some help," she muttered, her voice very tight.

I put down the trunking again and hurried over, my grumpiness forgotten. "What is it?"

She tugged at her robe, showing her legs—and I immediately saw several distinct wounds on her skin. Familiar. Red and swollen. Similar to the mark yesterday except that there was no worm hanging half-out of them. She stared at me, her face pale.

"In here?" I said, my voice feeling very strained.

"I can... feel, I think, feel something under my skin," she said with extreme, terrifying calm. "Can you please drive me... I dunno. I need medical help."

I drew a deep breath. "I can't."

"You what? This is serious."

"No, I mean..." I rubbed at my face. "Look outside. The road's out."

She stared at me, then darted to the door.

"I was going to say. The causeway has flooded... washed away. Not sure. We are on an island.

"Oh no," she murmured. "This is starting to feel like a bad dream. I can feel them under my skin."

I swallowed, trying to repress a wash of my own terror.

"Yes, in here. They—they got me while I was asleep," she said. "So that means they must have... come in. Somehow."

I stared around. This was a nice little building for working in, but it had never been intended to be a hermetically sealed clean room. It was old after all—just a basic metal shed, not far off the end of its natural life. There were joins, gaps, ventilators, unsealed ducts, holes I'd cut for wires and not yet sealed, a draughty doorway.

These were heart-sinking thoughts.

She urgently dug her phone out of a bag and plugged it in.

"There's no fucking power," she yelled, the hysteria slipping out for a moment. "Of course there fucking isn't—that's what you are here for… ooohhhhh gawd." She drew a deep breath. "How's yours? Any signal now?"

I shook my head.

"Right… ok. Ok. Ok. Then can you please finish the power system here as soon as possible so I can make a phonecall? In the meantime, I guess I'll have to take care of this myself. As far as… I can…"

I stared at nothing, trying to map out what I needed to do, though my brain still felt sluggish and stupid. Never mind the testing, just get some kind of fucking wire running between the batteries and the solar panels. And then, this endless rain and endless grey notwithstanding, we might be able to get some kind of power into her phone. I stared up at the ceiling—at the hole I'd previously cut into the metal to let the cable through. Rain had seeped in and I swore under my breath. It shouldn't matter to the wires but everything about this place was starting to feel broken. Then I hurried to the battery unit.

Meanwhile, she dragged the first-aid box out of the cupboard, and then another small case from her own supplies. When she opened it, it revealed a host of small tools—blades, scissors, pics, hand lens, tweezers.

"What is that?"

"That's my entomologist's dissection kit," she said, her voice still frozen. "You just—just get on with that wiring, please. At least something basic so I can charge my phone and make a call."

"Right, right…"

I hurried to work, opening up the battery unit and preparing to connect the cable, while she sat down at the tiny desk. I watched her grit her teeth and make a small incision in her arm with the blade—then another, digging deeper. Then she was poking around in there with an angled pic. And almost immediately, she hooked something long and white. It came out in a little ooze of blood and she flung it into a bowl with a wince.

"That was easier than I thought," she muttered, then looked round. "Hey—are you ok?"

And now it was my turn to freeze. Was I? Somehow, I had forgotten about that. Having been splashing through that muddy water, it was a very unpleasant thought.

"Go and check," she ordered.

I abandoned the cable and stepped into the tiny bathroom. This was the first time I had really had any chance to stop and think and an attack of something like panic caught me immediately. The magic of nature is all very well—even the magic that can eat you can be amazing and beautiful when you are a safe distance away and in control of the situation—but when the magic of nature starts burrowing into your skin, it starts to go dark for even the most determined nature lover. I dragged at my clothes, yanking them off and trying to examine myself with the help of the tiny mirror. But to my immense relief, I could find no trace of any violating wound.

"Nothing?" she asked when I emerged again. "Maybe there was no way for them to climb up your van wheels. They seem to have been able to get in here easily enough. I found a dead one on my bedroom floor."

I stared at her. She had shed her robe and was sitting there in her underwear and vest, and four worms were now squirming in the bowl. Four precise cuts to her skin, now hidden under plasters. As I watched, cringing, she started a fifth, her face taut, teeth clenched.

"I—I might need your help," she whispered. "I—think there's a few where I can't reach."

My heart sank even further into the dreamlike.

"But I don't know how to..."

"It's easy enough," she said impatiently. "It's right there—just beneath the skin. Just make a cut." She dragged off the vest and turned round, indicating her shoulder. "Can you see it?"

I could—another of those red swellings surrounding a small pinprick of deeper colour.

"Alright," I said. "I suppose there's nothing for it."

I grabbed the scalpel, which felt agonisingly small and refined, still hesitating.

"Just do it," she cried, with a flash of real hysteria.

I cut.

I mean... not so different to some other delicate bit of craft. Cutting into a wire to split the strands. If I could just forget what it was that I was cutting into, it would be nothing. Nothing at all.

Blood flowed from the wound—I'm sure more than when she was doing it herself. I could see no worm, however, and there was no choice but to carry on, slowly slicing a little deeper at a time until I spotted movement. Then the finest carving out, cutting around it until it was exposed enough for me to pluck it away with her hooked pic.

Easy peasy.

She watched it join its mates in the dish with a frown. "And one more here please," she said, standing up and indicating her thigh. And I repeated the process with gritted teeth.

"Right," she muttered. "I counted nine wounds—and we have nine worms. I really hope it's that simple."

We both stared at the wriggling worms, still smudged with blood—then I threw the lot into the toilet while she busied herself with liberal doses of antiseptic.

"I need a drink," she muttered, finally putting her robe on again. "Oh boy I need a drink..." She opened the fridge and stared grimly at the emptiness within—then shut it with a sharp exclamation. "There's one on the floor," she snarled. In fact, there were two, looking lost on this vast flat surface. She picked up a spare shoe and quickly whacked them one after the other, with great precision. Then we opened the door and stared out—and soon enough spotted another one twining among the grass stems at the edge of the wharf.

"Ok, so there are lots of them around, we know that," she said, her voice as frosty as ever. "No idea what they are. I should... probably go out and have a look around. See if I can find out anything more about them."

She sounded reluctant, however, and I almost laughed. Not, obviously, at her reluctance but at the mere notion that there could be any option other than reluctance. While we were awake and watching, they didn't seem very dangerous—rather helpless if anything. But pushing through wet and flooded vegetation seemed a bad idea nonetheless.

"Also—they're coming in. They can't survive in here for long, it's too dry, but they keep fucking coming in."

"How are you feeling?" I asked.

"I dunno," she muttered. "I am shaking a little, a slight pain in my stomach—I even feel a little dizzy, but I think that's shock. The wounds hurt and feel inflamed but I suppose they would. I should like to get checked out as soon as I can though."

I stared at her, still bemused at the clinical way she was describing it all, even as her hands shook and her voice quavered.

"Maybe you could get on with the wiring?" she suggested.

"Oh—yes of course." I made an effort to wake myself up. There was something almost hypnotising about the way she was dealing with all this. "I can have something ready in about half an hour… enough for a phone anyway."

I started work again as fast as I could, finishing connecting the cable and running the other end out through the hole near the ceiling… into the rain. No need to worry about trunking now—let the wires hang everywhere. Meanwhile, she was sitting hunched in a corner, or rising to her feet and grabbing her shoe to whack some intruder.

"Ok," she said at last. "I have an idea—a stupid one maybe but who knows."

She ran to the cupboard again and dragged out a box. I stared in amazement as she pulled out her diving suit. Then she dragged off her outer clothes and scrambled into it, zipping it up. It was a simple skin-hugging scuba suit, decked out in curved areas of pink in some bizarre deference to gender stereotypes. It left her hands and feet bare, but she quickly fixed that by dragging her boots on again and slipping the cuffs over the outside, taping them down firmly with black tape. A pair of thick gloves and more tape finished the job.

"There," she said, straightening up. "Let's see them get past that. But—what about you? I don't suppose you would fit in this thing, even if I had two?"

Yes, what about me?

"Well, you stay here where it's reasonably safe. I'm going out to see what I can find. I want to know what's going on, if I possibly can."

She stepped outside, looking even more surreal. Then she had left the concrete behind and was poking around in the flooded bushes and grass.

"There's hundreds of them," she called and I stepped to the door and looked out. "And if I touch them or approach them, they go for me. They seem to be very much aware of me in some way—I can see them reaching in my direction. Moving towards me. Maybe it's the movement, or maybe they can detect something else. Some smell or chemical in my skin. Maybe my body heat. They can't get through the suit though. For fuck's sake, don't walk out here."

For a while, I watched the dreamlike image of her wandering round in her diving suit, poking with a stick, skimming her net through the water and examining the contents, bending over and swirling the murky water with her hands. I felt content to just stand there and watch, to let the performance play itself out. And it took a certain effort to drag myself back to work.

If I could at least get one solar panel online…

It wasn't long before I was interrupted again, however. I'd run the ladder up to the roof and was about to run a cable through to the charge controller when there was another sound from her in the distance—one that stopped my work in its tracks. Somewhere between a call and a gasp, different to her usual crisp scientific detachment. I looked round, then slid down the ladder as the diving suit figure returned to the concrete, flicking a worm off her leg.

"Um," she said, "Could you please hand me my longest net—the telescopic one behind the door?"

I leant in and did so.

"There's… there's a body in the water," she said with a sigh, eyebrows up, her face blank.

I froze. Then followed her to the edge of the concrete. There were a few worms here, but it was easy enough to avoid them or stamp on them if they got too close. I watched as she splashed off through the marsh in the direction of the central channel, then leant over, reaching out with the net to where I couldn't see. She hooked something and dragged it towards her, then along in parallel back towards the wharf. And yes—a sodden mass lolled in the water. I could see a rucksack, jacket and colourful leggings—as well as long dark brown hair.

And finally, she reached down with gloved hands. I joined her, squelching through the grass and helping to haul the body into the sodden shallows.

I appreciate the scientific approach, I really do. In the face of something like that, there is a massive comfort in just forcing the horror back down, drawing a deep breath and just being coldly rational about everything. I could see her doing exactly that as she examined the corpse. This seemed such an intolerable disruption of the normal—more so than anything that had gone before.

"Worms," she muttered. But even I could see that there was not just one wound, not nine wounds, but what might have been hundreds. She was riddled with them, a grotesque puffy mess, some with worms still making their entry. The reality of this, flesh inflamed, punctured and bleached bloodless by the water, was trying to send a crack right through me, but I hung on somehow. She lay like the most relaxed sleeper possible—or as though she had just surfaced from the deepest massage or meditation. It wanted to be beautiful, that carelessness, and it might have been if hadn't been the carelessness of death. The Doctor just remained, leaning over her, examining without touching, sometimes using the net to move some part of her, or her clothes, or the weed that covered her. Then she finally straightened up.

"What can we do with her? I don't want to leave her here. In case the water rises. I dunno about taking her back to the lab. It just… I mean, it feels… in case she… releases… sheds… in case more worms…" she drew a deep breath and stared around, for the moment frozen.

"There's a little patch of high ground behind it," I said. "Probably the last place the water would get to aside from our roof. That might be safe."

"Yeah… yeah. I guess… so."

I watched as she hooked her with the net again and we both towed her through the sodden grass and plants. She was heavy—that heaviness of the human body that always surprises you when you are confronted with it. It was an awkward journey—a squelchy, slithery journey, but we eventually made it to the small tuft of soil and plants that rose up out of the marsh. We stretched her out and stared down at her again as she lay in what looked quite a comfortable position. Hopefully a peaceful, if remote place to be.

"I don't understand," she whispered. "No—for a moment I was thinking the worms had killed her, but surely not. She must have died some other way. Maybe the flood caught her and…" She swallowed. "There is no fucking way that a human being can be overwhelmed by worms. That would be absurd. You just can't have some tiny slow-moving creature defeat something thousands of times its size that can pluck them off or just… step away. Unless you're asleep or… It's not possible."

She broke off and flicked a few off her diving suit, then twisted round to check herself over as well as she could. That brought me back to reality with a shock and I glanced down. And yes, there were a couple on my trouser legs now. White threads on the coarse fabric… on my skin.

And that's when I suppose I lost it a bit. I slapped at them, sending them into the grass, then bolted the few metres back to the concrete wharf.

"Easy," she called. "Don't panic."

Even the concrete didn't feel safe, however. There always seemed to be more of them making their way across the wet surface. She was right. This whole thing was indeed starting to feel like a nightmare. So I ran on back to the hutch and burst into the small bathroom, dragging at my trousers. A few more were revealed—some even surrounded by little rivulets of blood. Small red wounds. I gave a wail and slapped again.

She stepped in behind me. There was barely room for one in this tiny cubicle, let alone two, but she grabbed my arms and restrained me. "Easy," she said again. "Calm down. Let's just deal with this…" She reached for a water bottle and sloshed it over my legs, then leant down. "There are… I see three small wounds," she said. "Did you get them off you or did any get in?"

I have a cringing groan, realising with horrible clarity why keeping calm was so important. I couldn't remember. She squeezed at the skin around each wound, examining it with the care of one trying to read secrets in a crystal ball.

"I think you're ok," she said, though how much because she was sure and how much just to reassure me, I didn't know. "I don't think there was enough time for… But we have to keep calm. Otherwise…"

"Yes," I muttered. "I—I know…"

She looked round the room and stamped on a worm that was struggling on the floor, then showered it away with the bottle.

"How's the wiring?"

I gave a long groan. "Every time I try to start that, something comes along. It's starting to feel like one of those dreams. Those futility dreams where you have one simple task to do, yet never manage to…"

"Yeah, I know, but… can we get on with it?"

"Yes of course," I stammered as we stepped back into the main room of this hutch, trailing water across the floor. "Just a minute… I'll, I'll finish it off."

I sighed and looked around, scanning for worms. Surely… they might be able to get in here but surely they wouldn't be able to get up onto the roof?

"They're just everywhere," she said. "I don't dare to stop or even sit down…"

"How do you think I feel?" I growled. "For some reason, I didn't include a diving suit among my electronics gear."

"Ok—ok—let's just hang on and get out of here. It'll be fine."

"Yes—yes… I just need to get this damned solar panel working. Never mind all the testing and details. I wish I hadn't wasted so much time on the trunking now, the cable channels, but how could I have known that…"

I hesitated. The building was firmly on concrete and that at least should be solid—the only way in was across it…

And the idea came.

"That damn trunking," I said.

"Huh?"

"There's loads of the stuff—I was using it to wire up… hang on a moment…"

I grabbed a piece of it and held it up. You can think of this as a simple aluminium tube with a square profile—one side a removable flat strip intended to be fixed onto the wall. It was the other part, with its roughly C-shaped cross-section, that was of interest here though. I turned it over in my hands, while the Doctor looked at me, her eyebrows a question.

"If I turn this on its side, hollow facing outwards… can you see worms being able to climb over?" I asked.

She stared at it. "Hmm—maybe not. At least, the vast majority not. A snail might, but not a worm."

"Anything trying to climb up would just hit that lip and end up coming down again, then stuck in open air."

"Are you suggesting some kind of small fence?"

"Yes."

"What about under?"

"I have some rubber sealing strips as well—will screw them in too."

"Cool," she said, with a gleam of excitement. "That sounds a great idea. Do it."

"I'll just finish the solar panels…"

"No no—do this first. I… I want to see."

I gave her a puzzled look, then shrugged. Whatever the logic of this dream was, I was just along for the ride at this point. However, that was when the obvious problem of the idea occurred to me and I swore. "To have any hope of doing this properly, I will have to go back to my van. I'll need my masonry drill for this one."

"I'll go," she said. "I'm fine in this get-up. Give me the keys."

I hesitated, but that was no doubt true. The diving suit was perfect protection. Again, we stepped outside. I was sure the van had sagged rather in the water and it was leaning. One wheel had sunk and the front right corner was now submerged.

"It's open. You'll find the case in the back. A big green plastic box with a red handle. I think there's a full charge in it—I hope so."

I watched her walk slowly and carefully along that drowned causeway, the heavy sky reflected in the rippling water like a dream. Occasionally, her feet sank down over her knees and it was obvious that a lot of the structural integrity of that earthen bank was failing. I wished I could take a photograph of her there—diving suit, drowned van, water, heavy sky. It could have won any surrealist photography contest. Then she held up the case with a question and I responded with a thumbs up.

She splashed back and I took it, opened it—powered the drill on and was relieved to hear that it was running as strong as ever. There had been little need for it so far in my work, so the battery was still full.

"Right," I said, feeling quite happy to have something so directly useful to do. And I immediately started work, drilling holes in the concrete and metal. *Why?* It was actually quite a quick job. Holes drilled, plugs added, rubber strips and aluminium trunking laid hollow side outwards in a tiny fence, then screwed down through the aluminium to hold it fast. In the meantime, the Doctor in her diving suit was on hands and knees, scrubbing the floor, dealing bristly death to any worm still inside the perimeter. The last stage was to go round it, sealing any corners and gaps with calking—and then I was staring at the fence with some satisfaction. That would take some removing. No doubt it would still be there long into the future, confusing the occasional visitor to this lonely place.

"How are you feeling?" I asked.

She gave a shrill giggle.

"Fine actually," she said. "A bit sore—in fact this diving suit is a bloody nightmare. But I think it's ok. Hopefully I am not infested with something horrible."

"You could probably take it off now," I said.

"Yeah. I could. Though… I am tempted to go out again. I never got very far the last time." Again, a small giggle, which gave me a pang of unease. Hopefully the calm wall of scientific detachment wasn't starting to crack under the strain.

"I'll just finish wiring," I said. "Just a few more connections now then I can uncover those panels."

"Ok."

I rushed to work, half-expecting yet another interruption in this futility-dream, However, she just sat and watched me with a vacant stare, still in her diving suit. I ran a last wire up from the charge controller onto the roof, literally out of the open door, connected it, and then finally removed the cover from the solar panel, which was the very simple way of 'switching it on'. And at last electricity was flowing. Even from this grey sky.

"Try plugging into the socket by the desk," I called, scrambling down the ladder again and flicking a last switch on the inverter. There was an immediate blast from the shower unit as water sprayed across the cubicle and out of the door. One of us must have left it switched on and I hurried to shut it off. The fridge hummed into life—and she gave a whoop as the screen of her phone lit up.

"Thank goodness," she said. "It's working."

I sat down feeling more exhausted than I probably should, content to let her deal with things. It was her phone after all.

She sat for a moment, her finger hovering over the screen. Then she shrugged, touched and put it to her ear.

"Hello? Hello? Oh hey. Stan? Yes—we've got a fucking situation here. Need to—need to abort. Can you come and get us off again. A bit urgent, sorry. Um—is tomorrow the earliest you can do? Yes—no, we're fine. That's fine, I guess. No problem at all, we're fine. Just… things going on. Thanks."

I stared at her blankly as she hung up again.

"Looks like we're here for the night again," she said.

"Is that all?" I asked. "Tomorrow?"

"It's fine," she said, her voice bright with brittle cheer. "We're safe now."

I looked back at the 4-centimetre fence I had built and felt a momentary sense of satisfaction. She was probably right.

We sat outside under the awning, watching the grey rainy evening fade down to dark. And watching the fence. It seemed to be working. There were one or two worms slowly exploring the wet concrete on the other side, but none had made it beyond the trunking fence.

"That was a good idea," she said with a smile. "Who knows—I might even be able to sleep."

"Yeah," I mumbled. "Sleep. Sleep sounds nice." *What about me though?* I certainly want going anywhere near the van this time. *Is it really safe? Really?*

I suppose it was. It certainly felt good now. Thanks to me.

What the hell?

She lounged back in her chair and stared at the sky. "My beloved marsh," she said. "In spite of this, it's still my place. So much life—such a poetic bleakness."

I nodded slowly.

"You know, I'm fairly sure there's nothing normal about this," she said. "If this was regular UK wildlife behaviour, I'd have heard about it. And it just doesn't make sense. It's not *right.* What are they looking for? What are they expecting to find here?"

"How do you mean?"

"There are so many—and presumably they need some kind of host. Like, well, an animal of some kind. But what is there here for them? Just a few seabirds. There's no cows in this marsh—or any other large animals. Even if some got us, they would almost all just die. So it doesn't make sense. It has to be some kind of freak event."

"Or maybe if even a few find a home, it's enough?" I suggested.

"But then what? They lay eggs somehow? Do we shit them out of us into the sewers? Do they just kill us or leave us again when they are ready? Either way, our world is too, too, too sanitised to sustain something like that for long. And that means… whatever they are doing, they are going to fail. There's nothing sustainable about this."

I nodded slowly.

"The world is always changing," she said gloomily. "Soon this will be a salt marsh—parts of it already are. As the world changes, all sorts of new things might turn up. We aren't very good with changes—people I mean—but… Inevitable."

"You think it's some kind of alien?" I asked. "An introduced species?"

"It's very possible. Can't say yet though. I should probably go and have another look around. It would be good to see if they are any more or less active at night."

"You sure?" I mumbled. "I'll be happier when we can just get out of here."

"Yes. You stay here—I'll be fine in my diving suit."

"Ok," I whispered, shaking my head. If she wanted to go and science, that is what she should do. I watched her grab her net and her powerful torch and make her way into the water again, splashing away down the drowned causeway. For a long time, I could see her light, flickering this way and that, now here, now gone, now here again, illuminating the marsh. I watched her feeling a dreamlike sense of peace now. Occasionally my eyes found the fence again, but it also seemed to be fine. It was intact—nothing was getting over. Everything was safe and under control.

I even felt a wash of fondness for her now, when I thought about it. She had started off by getting right up my nose, but now I was deeply glad that she was there, looking after things. And hey, she was the expert. The Doctor. It was nice to have been useful as well though, with my trunking. Science meets craft and all that. What are we but an interrelated web of dependencies and skills? And blah blah blah.

In the middle distance, I could just make out the form of the woman we had left on the small area of higher ground. A small figure lying, seemingly peaceful now. And I wondered who she had been. A local? Someone out enjoying the countryside when things had gone very very wrong?

Don't worry—we'll soon get you home.

Maybe death wasn't so bad if that level of bodily peace was possible. It looked like the ultimate relaxation of sleep—beyond any meditation yet devised. Something almost enviable.

But then the peace was broken—a very small, very thin sliver cutting through it. A distant cry, wavering and uncertain.

I sat up, blinking. Trying to work out what I had heard. The light was still visible in the distance. I could see the rays moving through the raindrops, swinging around in an uncertain arc from water to sky and back to ground again. Had I even heard it at all? Maybe it was just another part of the great dream in this heavy, hallucinatory marsh darkness.

Then it came again—a touch harsher. It wavered in a long thin note, then jolted into a hint of panic for a moment before returning. Now here, then far, then gone, then here again. And I froze completely. This was one of those points when your brain realises that it is not dreaming a dream at all, but a nightmare. Looking back, I remember a mixture of terror and stasis. As though the stark chemical fear was blended with an indolence that barely allowed me to care.

I scrambled unsteadily to my feet and stared round the marsh, trying to work it out. As the light ray from her torch again lanced from ground to sky and back, casting a cone of white through a fog of water drops.

"Hello?" I called at last. "Are you ok?"

Silence—and I swore to myself, trying to chase the tiredness away. So far, analysis hadn't given me any excuse to sit down again and resume drifting and I stared at the dark drowned grass in annoyance. I could see the occasional worms clearly enough, scattered and twining through the stems. But I would have to go through them. Surely, if I kept moving, there was little that something this slow could do to me?

Whatever. It was fine.

I grabbed another torch and jumped off the concrete and into the water. It splashed and squelched around my ankles, then my calves, as I ran with deliberate speed and high bounding steps along the causeway, past my van and towards the light. I had never before been so conscious of the plants as I ran—every touch of a seedhead or weed stem like a whip.

"Where are you?" I cried. "Are you alright?"

There was a strange moan in response.

The perilous flooded ground almost got me on a few occasions—sudden soft quagmires beneath the water, submerged branches to trip over—but somehow I managed to keep moving, finding my way along a line that felt like a maze until I found her and came to a complete halt in astonishment. And the dream took over because, like a surrealist painting, she was naked, spread out in the drowned grass in a white X, the water lapping around her and drops pattering on her skin. The diving suit lay crumpled some distance away, her underwear flung into the marsh plants.

"Who painted this?" I asked her—a lunatic question that fortunately she paid no attention to at all. Fortunately, that lunacy got through to me with a freezing shock and reality came back, at least partly. In the beam of my torch, blood flowed in tiny threads in the rain, worms writhed like sentient white hairs… and the expression on her face was so strange that in spite of all, it entered my memories and will live with me. Distraught peace—despairing tranquillity—agonised comfort.

"What's happening?" I asked stupidly. "Can't you move?"

"Nnnnn…" A long sigh of negation. "I… want… to…"

I grabbed at her. The only thing I could think of doing was to pick her up and somehow get her back to the hutch—to the safety of my mighty perfect little fence. But *now* she moved. She thrashed around, flapped at me, punched at me, tried to wriggle away, tried to crawl away…

"Don't touch me," she wailed, still with that breathy, empty voice.

There wasn't much strength in her, however.

"What are you talking about?" I yelled, feeling very close to losing it myself by this time.

"Hhhhhrrrrrrrrrr…"

For a ridiculous moment I almost obeyed her—almost let her go again. There was a fog in my brain and my thought processes were so simplified that it seemed right to just leave her there if that was what she actually wanted.

Then her head turned and she stared up at me, her eyes huge.

"... heeeeelllp..." she managed—and it was fortunate that she did because that got through sufficiently for me to try again. I caught her under the arms. Again, she slapped at me, strengthless but enough to make this almost impossible. It was like trying to handle a floppy and uncooperative cat, only far far heavier. For a long few minutes we floundered, she moaned wordlessly, me I think swearing at her without much coherence. Worms were flying everywhere—scattered and washed away. Picking up a human being who isn't helping you in any way is a crazy hard thing to do—another of those things I'd never quite realised before. But finally I could gather her up, my arms locked around her, half hauling her to her feet, half carrying her and we made tangled and floundering progress back to the causeway and towards the distant hutch. We were both covered with mud, there were worms everywhere and after such a long time in the diving suit, she stank.

"Over your shoulder..." she managed, a touch more rationality in her voice—maybe even a touch of that familiar scientific detachment. "Put me... over your..."

I realised she was right, and with a massive strain, hauled her up. She hung there, arse in the air, flopping around my shoulders, arms trailing. I think this is called the fireman's lift, or as far as my inexpert hands could manage it—totally unceremonious but at least I could move again and start making some kind of speed back to the hutch. My feet coming down in the water like the blows of a pile-driver—splash... splash... splash...

"Your... your legs..." she muttered and I glanced down, knowing what I would see. Blood spots and white threads. And not just on my legs either. But there was no point worrying about that yet.

"Shower," she ordered as we stumbled inside. I hurried into the shower and let her slide to the floor with a thud. Then I turned the water on and washed her down, washing away the mud and the wandering worms that hadn't yet got a hold. She shrieked at the cold—a complaining childish wail rather than an adult's shock. There were still dozens of worms embedded in her skin though, little white wriggling tassels hanging out of her flesh. And how many had already worked their way right inside?

There was nothing to do but try and get them out.

"Slowly," she said, sounding more coherent now. "Take it slow—just… ease them out, remember? Don't break them. And you too," she said, pointing at my legs. "Don't let them get into you…"

What followed was almost ridiculous in the cold light of day—no longer a surrealist painting but something more like a medieval hell, as two naked people sat together, crammed half-in half-out of the cubicle under freezing water quietly pulling worms out of each other—sometimes with the aid of her dissection kit. She had way more than I did, of course. Mine were mostly in my legs and arms with a few making it onto my torso, but I had to go all over her. There were worms under her arms, worms in her face, worms in her arse, worms between her legs, worms between her toes… we didn't exchange any words at all once it was underway, just sat there as the cold water washed the blood away. And when the worms were gone, as far as we could tell, we still just sat there, still naked, shivering, bleeding, clutching each other, eyes glazed and totally shattered.

It was going to be ok. She had phoned… someone. Right? Phone call—would… boat—out—escape…

"I don't know," she muttered at last, crawling out into the main room on all fours, grabbing her robe and laboriously putting it on. "I don't know what happened."

"Tell me—if it helps."

"I just—I just couldn't bear to be in that suit any longer. I knew I had to be alone—and I needed the fresh air. I remember—just taking that damn thing off…"

She shook her head.

"And it felt so glorious—cool and fresh, after all that heat and sweat."

"But you were calling for help," I said. I hadn't dressed again—I had no robe and I was terrified of what might be living in my clothes. Nothing to do but sit there and worry about nakedness later. The cold water seemed to have woken me up a bit, however—woken us both.

"Yeah—it was weird," she said, sounding almost normal. "We have such complicated minds. Some part of me knew what was going on. I tried to get up—lay down again—up—down. Get up—lie down and go to sleep. And fortunately it got through to me somehow. When I yelled, I was just lying there. It seemed… easier." She looked at me. "I wasn't paralysed," she said. "I *wanted* to lie there. I didn't want to move—because everything was ok. It was all so restful. Yet I was also terrified out of my wits. It was like… I dunno. Can you imagine being on a very careful diet for some medical reason? You know very well that to eat this… this thing, this binge, or drink this whatever, or take this hit of… it could very well kill you. And you're terrified of that. But you also *cannot* stop yourself—the impetus to drink that drink or eat or shoot up that… that thing is so incredibly strong. That's kind of what it felt like."

I rubbed at my face. Her voice was quiet—rational—comforting.

She gave a sudden laugh. "I dunno—maybe some people wouldn't have a clue about what I just said. They'd think I was nuts. But some will know exactly what I mean."

"I think I get it. You mean… addiction? Kind of."

"Addiction," she murmured, closing her eyes. "Yeah. Maybe for a moment there, I was addicted to that tranquillity."

"Were… you… in pain?" It was hard to talk clearly.

"No, I…" She shifted awkwardly. "No, it didn't. Wasn't. It felt… odd. I could… write a whole paper about what that felt like. An'… maybe I should. It felt… kind of… good. Though I also really didn't want to be touched."

"Mm."

"I… don't have Haphephobia or anything. But… right then I just couldn't stand it. Couldn't stand being *disturbed*."

She stared dreamily off into the distance for a long few minutes. "I will write that paper," she said. "Strange… sensations. I feel so high. Even now. And… I seem to be aware of it. I can feel myself very clearly. As before. Right now—I can feel it. I can… Not many scientists get to feel… for themselves. Stuff. Especially this. There's… no shortage of parasites that can have weird effects on their hosts. You know… offering yourselves to be consumed, directed to certain places, going to your death in very specific ways that… that they need. It's… kind of fascinating."

"What… are you talking about?" I felt a faint chill and for a moment I found myself thinking about whatever strange, theatrical and socially-awkward deaths these worms might have directed us to if we hadn't been alone.

"Oh… I mean ants. Snails. Um… caterpillars. But that must take millions of years of evolution. We're…" Her voice rose a little in a complaining wail. "We're too young for this. Too… young a species. We're… just babies. Who've barely started to learn how to wipe our own arses. So… what are you *doing?"* She stared at the door and out into the night, a petulant frown on her face. At that moment, I had no ability to keep up with this conversation, so I just hung on, content to let her expound her wisdom.

"I wonder if we're supposed to do anything?"

"Hm?"

"You know… to finish the ritual. To pass on the seed. Maybe we're supposed to go somewhere specific. Or get into a certain position. Do you feel anything? Any needs?"

"I just want to lie here."

"I wonder if her… if she… out the back. Did she go somewhere specific for them?"

"You mean… if they don't come and rescue us?"

"They?"

"They?"

"Uhhhhhh..."

A long silence while she stared thoughtfully at nothing.

Then she moved so suddenly that I almost yelled aloud. She lashed out and hit the wall of the container with a huge booming thud, then rubbed at her face, then came snaking over and grabbed my arm. "Slap me," she screamed.

"What?"

"Do it, please. Just slap me in the face."

"But I… I…"

"Do it."

Whatever.

The flat of my hand hit the side of her face. It wasn't that hard—instincts tried to put on the brakes, deep taboos against physical violence screaming at me. But it was hard enough to ring out with a sharp sound and make her rock and blink.

Then she retaliated, hitting me hard enough to make my head ring.

"What was that for?" I demanded stupidly. "You asked me to..."

"What are we doing?" she cried.

"Ummmmm...?"

She jumped to her feet, grabbed her phone where it was still charging on the desk and almost threw it at me. "Call triple nine—right now!"

I stared—and something in my mind did go *click* at that point. Not profoundly, but on the level of a quiet realisation. A numbed *oh yes.* I took it, stared at it. I also felt addicted to peace, and nothing about this phone was peaceful. I really should have just let it drop again—really should have. But the smarting pain burning on my face forged a direct line to whatever part of me was still vaguely functioning.

Her eyes bored into me as I jabbed the dreaded three digits, making sure that it actually happened, then she curled up on the floor with a sobbing wail.

And when I had finished my confused and no doubt very confusing call to the emergency services, I joined her. We just curled up together on the floor—two broken human bodies waiting for rescue. I locked an arm round her and she grasped it tight, holding it to her chest with a grip that wasn't going to let go any time soon. In some strange way, whatever emotions were in me, brought to the surface by whatever had happened to us—some ultimate rawness of feeling that may or may not have had any kind of reality—I didn't think I could bear her not being there. I hugged her tighter than I think I'd ever hugged another person and I almost felt in love.

And so time passed. And the rain on the roof drummed on and on… a white noise in between the spaces of our souls that seemed it would go on forever.

Islington Tunnel

At least the boaters get to go under London instead of through it, albeit in a deep and oppressive world of quietly slopping water and brickwork. Down here, where Regent's Canal tunnels deep under the city, under the hill crowned by the Angel of Islington, it is as dark as anywhere humans have built. No lights beyond the distant tunnel portals, no towpath, nowhere to walk, just the water of the canal and the arching roof that always seemed lower than it should.

The rules are fairly simple: one boat at a time. This dingy bore is too narrow, even for narrowboats to pass. So switch your main lamp on and look closely as you approach. If the far end of the tunnel gleams like a star of daylight in the black, you may proceed. If the light is occluded, dimmed, like a planet transiting in front of that star, or if you see another light moving, then wait. Ignore this and you will end up bow to bow in the darkness. When two trains come face to face on a single track, it is called a cornfield meet. Down here in the dark, there were definitely no cornfields involved—more like two earthworms meeting in a tunnel, sensing each other suspiciously. And after that, nothing left but a classic bickering London row.

"Please reverse," the woman on the yoghurt pot said with chilling politeness. Her voice sounded refined and well-modulated—and so very very polite. That very specific kind of totally reasonable, reserved and utterly contemptuous politeness that some parts of British society are so good at. "I'm not sure you should even be here, you know."

The Heartsease, it was called, apparently—a classic fibreglass cruiser, somewhat luxuriously fitted out.

"What did you say?" Crystal demanded with a weary sigh as she scrambled along the narrow ledge on the outside of her narrowboat to the front deck. Her own accent was no less well-modulated, she knew—it sometimes felt too BBC to be entirely comfortable—yet it might as well have come from another country, simply because of the way she used it.

"I believe you heard me."

Crystal drew a deep breath, trying to still the feelings of dull rage—a rage that was not without the roil of the socially anxious. For a moment, she wanted to do just that, just for the sake of a quiet life. Yet it felt farcical. She had been here first, she had right of way, her own boat was much larger and harder to manoeuvre—a heavy residential narrowboat named The Wandering Eye, fifty-two feet long, painted black and adorned with a glare of street art that she herself and various friends had contributed at one point or another. It stared down at the small yoghurt pot in a way that ought to have been intimidating, yet the self-important Madam Heartsease seemed oblivious to that. For a moment, she was tempted to just jam the engine to maximum and charge, barging the yoghurt pot before her, but quite apart from anything else, river and canal boats were made for quiet lives. The centre of a canal tunnel a quarter of a mile from daylight in either direction was not a place for a wreck.

"I presume you know the rules," she said, her voice low. The angrier she got, the quieter she got. "See this?" She grasped the binoculars around her neck. "That is how I know the tunnel was empty when I got here. You'd have seen me in here if you'd bothered to look. So *back the fuck out.*"

Madam Heartsease had gone stiff with rage as well now, in the glare of the Wandering Eye's one headlamp—a glowing disc almost the size of a dinner plate. "I've just about had it with you canal rats," she said. "You lazy scrounging clots clogging up the waterways."

Crystal shrugged, again telling herself firmly not to lose her temper any more than she already had. Be a rapier, not an explosion. That yoghurt pot was no residential craft. Madam Heartsease certainly didn't live down here on the water. She didn't wander the network as a modern-day nomad, searching wearily in the rain for somewhere to empty her shit. And that was fine—until you crashed up against insults like this. "You don't know who I am," she said. "Though I think, in the here and now, in this fucking tunnel, we both know which of us is more responsible for everything wrong with the world."

Not a particularly helpful thing to say, but at this point Chrystal felt little desire to be helpful.

The two boats, narrowboat and yoghurt pot, sat in silence, facing each other, headlights trying to outstare. Around them, the darkness seemed absolute—cave darkness, albeit a man-made cave. The same music of slaps and pops and drips and swirls as the most isolated places you could find in the earth. Maybe it was just a simple brick tube hidden deep under the lively and at least fairly clued-up Islington, but it was an inhuman place. Only ever seen by the waterfolk and even then only while passing through to more comfortable places. High overhead and nearby was a small mall and the nearby Angel tube station, where thousands of people went about their business with this water as far from the perception of most as the Lost Rivers of London.

Crystal stared up and down the tunnel, as far as she could see over the bulk of The Wandering Eye. No doubt there were other boats queuing up outside, getting more and more irate. No doubt telephone calls would soon be made to the Canal and River Trust... *Hey, why is Islington Tunnel blocked? What's going on?* By any measure of sense, she should just back out of it, prove her superiority in a way Madam Heartsease would never understand and then send the yoghurt pot on its way towards Hackney with a few well-chosen words. And nobody could choose words as well as an East Londoner.

But she didn't want to. It was a minor thing in the face of the world, but it was as if years of this stuff had finally caused a small trip switch in her brain to snap. In a quiet, lethal and very implacable way, Crystal had seen red. No way was this posh-voiced bitch going to force her into a retreat by pulling class.

So instead she shrugged and smiled, said "Oh well," opened the door to the interior and stepped down inside. Heedless of Madam Heartsease's angry yell behind her. The sounds of it echoed around in the tunnel sounding a lot more dramatic than it should, but she simply busied herself in the small kitchen, making a quick lunch. Various things went onto a plate—some bread, a few slices of meat, some dollops of dip and a couple of olives. Then a glass of wine was poured and she climbed back up onto the tiny front deck.

"Still here?" she asked, placing the plate on the small table.

"Of course," Madam Heartsease said. "For heaven's sake, we can't stay here forever?"

"No need to," Crystal said mildly. "Just follow the rules of the waterways and back out and we'll be fine."

"I thought I had made myself quite clear. You are bigger, you are slower, you are the one who shouldn't be here... you are the one who should have given way, and you are the one who will give way now."

The sound of her voice was maddening but Crystal just shrugged and sat down on a bench and took a sip of wine. "What time is it?" she said. "Almost evening. I might even head to bed soon."

"Oh fuck you," the other cried.

Crystal chuckled. "Oh hello hello hello… not so posh now, are we?"

The woman on the yoghurt pot gave a grating yell of frustration.

Any minute now, she'll snap, Crystal thought. "Just back up. It's not hard. I presume you know how to put that thing in reverse?"

At that moment though, they were interrupted. A deep thud echoed through the world, deep enough to make her ears ring briefly. Crystal put down her wineglass and stared round. There was a plink and plunk as a few fragments of brick and cement fell from the ceiling and into the water—a scattering pattering sounds like a bass-amplified egg in a frying pan. And something about the faint light changed. The tiny point that was the end of the tunnel in the distance behind the yoghurt pot had flashed brighter. Changed colour. The evening tone replaced briefly by an icy white.

"What was that?" the woman on the yoghurt pot demanded, the sneering anger on her face fading.

"I… don't know."

The sound was still continuing, as though the initial thud was continuing to echo like thunder—dissolving into a long rumble.

"Maybe a lightning strike," Crystal said, though without much conviction. It sounded too immediate for that. It sounded too much as though it was within the ground for that. She glanced at her phone, but of course there was no reception down here. "Or maybe… the Northern Line tunnels are just a little way in that direction…" She waved at the tunnel wall, leaving the rest of that unsaid. Something about that thud had felt deeply significant.

The sound finally echoed its way to silence. Deep silence. But then a movement. The powerful headlight of the narrowboat picked out something approaching in the water—a solid line of darkness. She stared at it puzzled. Then…

"Hold on," she yelled. Madam Heartsease stared at her blankly—but then her boat reared up and she grabbed at the railing with a shriek. There was a tearing crash as the canopy on the back of the yoghurt pot hit the tunnel roof and then another as the bow was rammed into The Wandering Eye. Crystal also grabbed hold as the wave swept through. It wasn't particularly high—just a couple of feet—but on a canal, that was massive. Her much heavier boat resisted being tossed around as much the yoghurt pot had been, but it did slam hard into the tunnel wall. Her dinner and wine went flying, and from inside came the sound of things smashing and falling. She swore and hung over the side of the boat, trying to see back. She could see almost nothing of the hull in the darkness, but for now it seemed to be floating ok in the agitated water.

Madam Heartsease was also frantically checking her boat. The canopy was in ruins, the bow dented, but it also seemed to be floating ok.

"I'm out of here," she muttered at last.

"You sure?" Crystal asked. "I don't like this. What the fuck just happened?"

The light at the end of the tunnel still didn't look right. The bright white had only lasted a short while, and now everything seemed to be tinged red. A red that was deepening as the seconds passed. It was hard to read much info from what was little more than a star but it was all telling her very strongly, very clearly, that something was wrong.

In reply, the yoghurt pot's engine roared into life and the boat backed clumsily away down the tunnel, bumping occasionally into the wall as reversing boats are apt to do in any narrow space. Crystal stared after her with a sigh. That was technically a victory—she could proceed again as the rightful first enterer of the tunnel and all was well. But she had no interest in that now. Instead, she just stood there, watching as the Heartsease dwindled into the distance and eventually vanished into daylight that now seemed to be verging on red. Then, unsure what else to do but with every instinct screaming, she bent down and began collecting her spilled dinner and chucking it overboard. At least it would feed something, even if it was only the crayfish. Then she hurried inside and examined the boat from bow to stern, checking for any water where water shouldn't be. Various things had fallen off shelves, toppled over, and one bookcase had come loose from the wall, shedding its contents across the carpet. But at least it was dry.

The silence down here was always intense. In Islington Tunnel, the chaos and sounds of the city withdrew completely. She was used to that—as used as one could ever be—but now it seemed terrifying. On the stern deck, she stared back eastwards at the second tunnel exit, and that, half a mile from the first, also looked strange. In both directions, the light was fading yet further, through dull brown to almost black. As though the outside world had ceased to exist. She smelled the air, but for now there was nothing but the scent of old wet bricks.

Feeling a dull terror that was entirely new to her, and with no idea what to do, Crystal stood there watching as the two lights dwindled to nothing.

Spiral

in Svartavatn lake. A very strange place tha
remember seeing several rather unusual and sev
striking shell specimens there. All were at
least a few inches long and unusually thick te
Unfortunately I had no room to carry extra so
idn't stay long anyway—my schedule left no

What a bloody fool—so obsessed with walki
couldn't even stop to look when he found somew
All I can say is it might be worth someone one d

Fragment from a page of the Conchological Review, letters page, June 1998.

The air was easily the first thing that we noticed when we arrived at Svartavatn. Over everything hung a pall of faint scent—wiffs of rot and sulphur and less definable odours that I couldn't identify. I hadn't expected that. I knew it was a volcanic lake, but I hadn't expected the sheer physicality of that air. It wasn't entirely unpleasant—it was powerful and earthy, maybe even somehow primal. But even so, it was like walking into an alien atmosphere that was just a little thicker than it should be.

Somehow, even in those first few minutes, that air made hard work harder and muted the flurry of activity as we dragged our stuff from the helicopter. It didn't help that my legs still felt wobbly from such an unfamiliar mode of transport, and Lydia also looked a bit unsettled; for the moment we just dumped the equipment into a pile. The pilot gave us a wave—I remember that—then lifted off and abandoned us. We both stood watching the craft go. It all seemed very casual—just a quick goodbye and the roar fading away like the vehicle itself until it was just a dot in the sky. And there we were—alone and hopefully self-sufficient somewhere deep in the inner lands of Iceland.

Lydia rubbed her face and gave me a brief resentful look, which I was left to try to analyse in silence as she turned away. She had been doing that increasingly of late, since we arrived in Iceland. I gave a small and weary sigh, wondering why—remembering how eager she had initially been to accompany me on this bizarre trip.

For a long while, we just lingered and stared at the scenery—putting off the boring task of getting the tent out and erecting it. And indeed, the scene demanded our attention. It was not that Svartavatn was overtly strange—it was no fantasy landscape, at least not here in a land filled with fantasy landscapes. On some level, you could even have called it insignificant—little more than a dark crusty looking pool of about a hundred feet across lurking in a low-lying area, surrounded by rough rock and scrubby grass. But there was still something about it that made you stare—something about it that marked it out. The whole lake steamed gently in the cool Iceland summer air, sending otherworldly streamers of mist drifting over the surface and, when we descended to the edge and reached down to touch, the warmth was pleasant. Through its dark-stained water, the rocks were clearly visible, highlighted in a murky but vivid orange. Around the edge was a layer of light brown encrustation, encasing both the rocks and the dead vegetable matter—a dull crystalline growth laid down by the water as it cooled and evaporated. It glittered slightly in the low sunlight.

In the shallows, there was a mess of scum and mats that looked like a dirty garden pond but here made me think of extremophile bacteria and exciting scientific discoveries.

Of course, I am not exactly a scientist—nor is Lydia. Let's get that cleared up right away. This is not exactly a scientific expedition. I am an amateur conchologist—an obsession with shells—and I have a certain working knowledge of the natural world. Lydia's obsessions covered volcanism and the wild lands, which was even more appropriate here but just as non-professional. When we first heard of this lake, with its hot volcanic water and vague references to shells, it jumped out as a perfect obscure and fitting place to visit as a break from normal life. Way off the beaten track—way out there away from civilisation and etc. etc. Looking around, I was beginning to wonder if anyone else had ever been here and taken a close look at it before.

I stole a glance at Lydia and registered the glitter in her eyes that had wiped away any sullen expression.

"Well?" I murmured with a smile.

"This place is amazing," she said. She seemed to be smelling the air as though it was an old lover, tasting the volcanic gases. Then she bent, scooped up a handful of water and took a sip, then spitting it out and pulling a face.

"Shall we go for a swim?" she asked with a bright smile. "You going to join me?"

I glanced without enthusiasm at the pile of supplies that was still awaiting our attention—practicality warring with self-indulgence—then shrugged and grinned. There was still plenty of the day left after all. Aside from the scummy edge, the water did look rather inviting. Substantially deep and warm in this cool Iceland air.

"Yes," she said. "I promised myself that would be the first thing to do when we got here. The best way to say hello to any water body. Just it and your skin."

She didn't waste time—simply kicked off her clothes and splashed into the lake, wincing at the rocks underfoot.

"It must be full of minerals." She sat down and scooted herself out into deeper water, guarding her arse against the rough deposits. She lay back and floated. "I feel very buoyant," she said. "I think this is slightly denser than usual."

I joined her and we relaxed, surrounded by steam.

"Some other mineral springs have dark and strange tasting water like this," she said, swirling it. "There's a black mineral spring down in Slovenia—Moravske Toplice, or something—that people think is almost magical. Maybe this place also has health benefits. I must get some samples."

I felt the water swirl around my legs, as though subtly thicker than water usually is, and tried to work out whether it was pleasant or not. But then—healthy and pleasant always did dance a strange dance together. As we drifted further out into the lake, the temperature increased, radiating up from below until it was just verging on painful. Below us, we could see the orange-stained rocks descending into the dark water until hidden and I realised that the lake was actually quite deep—deeper than we could see or feel. Below our feet was nothing and I began to get a slight eerie feeling, imagining the water far below, superheated and raging amid the hot rocks—black and unknowable. As though at any moment my feet might be boiled by a geyser or we might be suffocated by an eruption of gas.

I gave a laugh. "I think I will get out and start putting things together. I'm feeling rather dreamy."

"Ok," she said. "I'll come with you."

As we splashed to the shore, I thought I saw a small red dot moving through the water—the first sign of active life here in Svartavatn—but when I tried to focus my attention on it, I couldn't find it. I spotted something else lying in the shallows though, almost as though the red dot had been pointing it out. It was a shape that caught my trained eye in a moment and I darted down and grabbed it. It was a shell—broken but obviously part of a large water snail, several inches long at least. I turned it over, pleased to have found something in my own area of interest so soon. The size of this thing was pricking at me and Lydia stared with interest.

Sometimes, when you work with nature—even an amateur scientist like myself—instinct can play a very large part. Of course, instincts have to be backed up with some very rigorous checking and research that can take years but sometimes things can happen very fast—when you see some insignificant looking fragment and you 'just know' in a split second that you have found something important. The thrill of excitement that you feel at that moment is not something that is easy to communicate. If you can't understand why the sight of this fragment of shell was like a slow electric shock that left my heart beating just a little faster than usual, then you will have to take my word for it—and call me a nutcase if you like.

"It's a..." I hesitated. "It looks like a *Lymnaea*—like the common large pond snail. Or related to it. But it's the biggest fucking *Lymnaea* I have ever seen—but..." I didn't like to express the excited thought that had already germinated in my mind—that this could be a new species—but I had never seen or heard of anything quite like this before. "Look," I said. "The way the body whorl flares out—almost like an ear. And as far as I can tell, the spire is very concave..."

I stared eagerly at the water by my feet. "There must be a whole one here somewhere—even a live one. I would love to have a look at the anatomy."

Lydia chuckled.

"I'll have a look, shall I?" she said, obviously keen to get back in the water. She ran with a cautious, wincing gait to the heap of equipment and unpacked a pair of goggles and a pouch, which she strapped round her waist. Then she splashed back into the lake, gave me a wry wave and disappeared under the surface.

I waited in the cooler shallows, filled with eagerness, but soon started shivering. The summer air was warm for Iceland, but still chilly after that hot water, and I quickly scrambled out and shook off as much as I could, rubbing myself down with my trousers and getting dressed.

There was a splash in the lake as Lydia came up for air and dived again. Then, a short while later she appeared in the shallows. She scrambled out of the lake, her face radiant with excitement, her skin looking pink all over, waving a massive shell. Almost five inches long and a beautiful polished brown—and alive. I took it, almost dropping it in my excitement.

"It's incredible down there," she said breathlessly. "The visibility is quite good—dark water but clear, like a herb tea. But I can't see any bottom to that lake. It's just like a funnel—it curves away down until it's lost. It's fucking hot though."

She brushed at the shell.

"And these things are all around, once you get a bit below the surface."

When she was this excited and happy, she just seemed to blossom, leaving any traces of her earlier bad mood far far away.

"And something else," she added, grabbing a second specimen from her pouch. It was a bivalve—one empty shell, looking somewhat like a large Zebra Mussel and several inches long.

"Lydia," I said flatly, "I love you."

She gave a high-pitched giggle. "You only love me for my snails," she said with a pout and I mimed a huge shrug. Then she hunched up with a shiver and hugged herself. "Oh boy," she said. "The contrast is cruel. I'm f-f-freezing now."

I hustled her back to the pile of equipment. "Fine scientists we are," she said with a shivery laugh as we rummaged urgently for one of the towels we had packed so carefully and never unpacked again. I began to rub down her heat-pink and goosepimply body as fast as I could.

Later, we set to unpacking the tent and sorting out our equipment—the small heater and stove, our supplies of food, our equipment for collecting and analysing specimens and samples etc. Several large books on molluscs. The boring, mundane stuff of camping and shells. Then, from her personal bag, she grabbed the small wooden recorder that travelled everywhere she did. She put it to her lips and blew a smooth but intricate phrase—the instrument's clear high tone ringing out eerily across that black lake. The notes coiled across the low Iceland landscape seeming very much at home here, miles from civilisation.

She had been a quiet and unobtrusive musician ever since I had known her—sometimes classical music, sometimes more unusual and experimental stuff. There is often an ideal in music that it gives a true glimpse of the person behind it. This is not necessarily true—music can be as shallow or as deep as anything else—but in her case I liked to think it might be. It was beautiful and very melancholy—riven with a deep sad streak right through it. When I first met her, that sadness was already in residence and she never did really tell me where it had come from or much about her past. I didn't know whether it was the product of some earlier trauma or simply an inherent and natural reaction in the face of the pressures of living in this world.

For a few minutes, she forgot all about helping me with the tent and stood there on a rock enjoying the sounds she was making. Then I set up the stove and began cooking a basic meal and the smells quickly got her attention. After we had eaten, we sat in the tent, trying to reconcile the bright daylight outside with our body clocks that emphatically told us 'evening'. That was another thing that we had known about intellectually that still managed to surprise us in reality. Lydia still had her recorder in her hand. She sat over a sheaf of music manuscript, working on a composition and occasionally blowing a few notes while I immersed myself in details of mollusc anatomy. It was not without a throb of guilt that I had killed that *Lymnaea* specimen—I didn't normally like to operate in this way, but my drive to find out was tremendous now and I had to know what it was, not just speculate. Poking delicately through the snail's organs and anatomy, I still had not been able to match it to any species I had data for, which, if correct, meant either of two things: It was a stray colony of a species from a very long way away—outside Europe—or it was indeed completely new.

In spite of my excitement, I had a slight headache now and I cursed the limited range of food we had brought. It was all very professional—high energy bars, specially formulated drinks, stuff that could be heated up in our little saucepan containing all the proteins, vitamins and minerals that the body needed to perform at its best in the great outdoors—apparently. But even so, there was nothing that could really be called a meal. It's the fundamental flaw with scientifically prepared survival or diet foods like this: they may feed the body but they leave the soul starving. I was suffering withdrawal symptoms for good meat and vegetables, I decided with a smile. And I would quite happily commit a minor crime to get some fresh fruit.

Eventually, I put the *Lymnaea* aside and sat back with a yawn—then slid under my opened sleeping bag, enjoying the feeling of stretching out.

"Well?" Lydia asked, putting down her recorder.

I shrugged—deliberately casual. "I need to check—and then recheck—and then check again. But I think this could be a new species."

She settled down beside me.

"Congratulations," she said softly. I gave a laugh. It's what any naturalist dreams, of course—finding something new and announcing it to the world. And I cautioned myself not to get excited. So many new species turn out to be nothing of the kind. Nature is infinitely more subtle than our neat and precise methods of cataloguing. But even so—a description is a description. Physical properties are physical properties. You can't argue with that.

I stroked her hair—then my own. The water of the lake had done it no favours, I realised. It felt coarse and heavy and salty and it sat on our heads like a dirty mop. That didn't matter though as we cuddled together, comfortably bundled up under the sleeping bags.

"I shall name it *Lymnaea lydiae,*" I murmured.

"Awwww," she said. "I'm not sure I deserve that."

I kissed her.

"My head is really aching," she said.

"Sorry," I murmured, backing away.

"Bollocks," she said with a smile. "Don't you know what one of the best cures for a headache is?"

I was also not feeling 100 percent and a part of me wondered why. Were we doing something wrong here? We were hardly experienced campers after all. Or was it just a mixture of the strange air and our helicopter ride? But the nice glow of companionship soon drove it from my mind. It had been an exhausting day after all and I was quite happy to let myself wrap around Lydia in a warm tangle and pretend it was night.

Sleep though, when it came, wasn't exactly restful. I found myself turning over and over in a slow cartwheel—a spinning vertigo that wasn't quite sleep, wasn't quite awake. Unsure which way was down, unsure whether I was dreaming. And all around was that dark water and the orange-stained rocks...

Next morning, we found Svartavatn's second potentially new species rather more directly—when it bit Lydia on the leg. She was wading in the warm water in her sandals when I spotted a small red dot on the back of her calf...

Once a couple of years ago now and back home in England, an incident occurred that I always remember. A Lydia I then barely knew was lying sprawled out on a rock with her scruffy jeans rolled up to her knees and her feet trailing in the water. This was Dartmoor—a small reddish stained pond lying hidden among the rocky slopes.

"Um," I said. "Do you know that there is a twelve-centimetre horse leech just by your foot?" I asked. She just glanced at it and gave me a lazy smile. Of course, it wasn't dangerous and wasn't interested in her at all, but her complete and utter lack of reaction to that swimming S always stuck with me. I don't know or care anything about stereotypes, but I am sure that not many of the people I have known would have reacted like that.

"Just thought I would mention it," I said, reaching into the water and scooping it up, where it promptly attached itself to my hand. Not biting—merely engaging in battle with its mysterious assailant. I looked at it with interest, deciding then and there that on some weird level I quite liked leeches. They were curious creatures—on the one hand so simple, on the other very well aware of what they were doing and very efficient. With neither Lydia nor the leech aware of it, the three of us had just formed some kind of mutual bond right there that would never really be broken again, no matter what happened. Even if I had never seen Lydia again, that bond would have remained—the way faces sometimes come out of the crowd at you, even for just a few seconds, and make an impression that lasts a lifetime.

I tried to shake the horse leech back into the pond, but it still wouldn't let go—remained clinging to me until I simply held my hand still and let it swim away of its own accord.

The reason I mention this now is that it helps explain why her reaction to that red dot on her calf rather took me by surprise. She twisted round and glanced at it, then gave a kind of whoop and slapped at it furiously, just about turning in a circle in the process. Then she came stumbling out of the water in a rush, looking more unsettled than I could ever remember seeing her before. She ended up standing on the bank, breathing heavily and staring hard at the lake.

"You ok?" I asked.

"Yeah," she muttered. "Sorry—I am feeling a bit highly strung this morning."

She gave a dark frown and turned away sharply, making her way back to the tent. I stared after her, then into the water. I realised that there were a few other red dots drifting there and I caught one in a specimen jar and held it up to the light. And finally what it was became clear. It was a water mite or something very like one. A large one, though still barely seven millimetres across. It seemed little more than a furry red sphere with a cluster of furiously paddling legs at one end. I looked at it, feeling bewildered. I had never heard of anyone being bitten by a water mite before—but then, we were a long way from home.

I quickly followed her and found her sitting in the tent looking glum.

"It felt as though it was sticking a needle into me," she said. "And the needle was taking root and spreading into a whole network of tiny needles. Not really painful—it just… felt strange."

"Nerves," I said. She gave me a sharp look.

"What?"

"Nerves—reacting off each other and sending sensations flashing all through you. Pain seems to come from all sorts of illusory places. Is that it?"

"Oh I see. Yes—something like that."

She squirmed round, trying to see her leg and I leant forward.

"There's nothing to see," I said. "I can't even find a mark. Does it feel of anything?"

"No," she said. "Nothing now."

She gave me that dark look again, leaving me to guess at what specifically was upsetting her and what, if anything, it had to do with me. Then she stood up and reached for her recorder.

"I'm going out for a bit," she said shortly. "Just a little—"

I nodded vaguely and watched her go. Then, a minute or two later, the delicate sounds of the instrument came drifting back from the distance. It seemed unusually eerie now—little fluttering phrases and long winding note sequences that seemed filled with unusual and out of tune pitches. One curious little two-note sound seemed to reoccur—just a little descending tone that was half way between a bird call and a sigh. It would call out over and over through the glowing evening—and in some strange way it sounded like a communication.

I gave a sharp sigh and lay back on my sleeping bag. I also was feeling a bit fragile—my headache was still there—and it was hard not to be upset. Dark moods had been an occasional presence as long as I had known her and they were certainly a communication of some kind—but on a level I was not used to. Maybe a language I never really learnt. Love is a viciously strong force and it is defined by the sense of connection it brings—and, I suppose, awareness. A feeling of awareness of all the layers and complexity and contradictions and mind games and manipulation that naturally form a part of human behaviour. As though you can finally relax and just… *see*. And yet, beyond that is an equal awareness of the basic human isolation. Love only highlights the fact that even the most intimate contact is minuscule in the face of the huge distances between people. The isolation between human beings is like vast voids filled with impenetrable blackness. A blackness through which you might just occasionally glimpse a faint winking light. Whatever lay at the heart of that blackness was a mystery that you could never touch, even though that came with the awareness of your own blackness that surrounded you yourself—your own winking light that no one could ever really see. Other people are a mystery and unknowable—and the only way you can survive life is through some kind of selective blindness to that fact.

These were gloomy thoughts but familiar ones. In spite of my excitement at all that this place offered, even then it flashed through my mind for a moment that it would be nice to get away from here again and go home. Such a thought was rather dismaying, especially when I glanced at the massive shell she had found—but hey, human is human.

Reminding myself that there was no sense brooding, I turned to the water mite that was still swimming inside my specimen jar. At this scale, it was extremely cute—little more than a fuzzy red ball moving purposefully through the water. It looked like some kind of mascot from a Japanese kids cartoon. But why had it bitten? Was it an aggressive or defensive bite? Was it a blood sucker? That made little sense because there was little for it to suck on here when there were no lonely scientists visiting. I wasn't an expert on Hydrachnidiae so I would need to do some serious checking before I could tell what it was. New species? Who knows? But I could fantasise. Isolated specific environments like Svartavatn often do lead to new species after all. And if it was, as part of me inevitably hoped, then I could name that as well. So I tentatively christened it *Lamiapilosus*, which means Hairy Vampire. And as to the second name, there was only one possibility. *Lamiapilosus lydiae*—what else? I added the name to the description I was formulating in my mind. Then there was a sound behind me and Lydia came in again and sat down. I was surprised to see that she was soaking wet under her clothes.

"Do you want to eat?" she asked shortly, with what looked to me almost like hate in her eyes, and I saw her absently rub at her leg. I gave a sharp sigh. No I didn't want to eat—not now.

"Are you alright?" I asked softly. "Is something wrong?"

"Yeah—I'm fine."

"Then why are you looking at me like that?" I asked—still desperately gentle. She gave me a sharp glance.

"Like what?"

"As though you hate my guts for some reason."

She stared in silence for a moment, while I tried to read her face, waiting for some sign of surprise or indignation. But in the end she just sighed.

"I'm sorry," she said abruptly, "I'm not sure I like this place."

"You mean—the air? The strange atmosphere?"

She sighed again.

"Maybe," she said, as though the simple effort of answering was just not worth the trouble. In the end we just subsided into a quiet where the only sound was the ticking of the little heater. She curled up in her sleeping bag and appeared to go to sleep.

Later though, as I was lying in a restless and faintly dizzy half-sleep myself, I felt her beside me and her arms were snaking round my neck and chest. I turned sharply but she just buried her face under my chin.

"I'm sorry," she murmured, and I was startled to see tears in her eyes.

I hugged her tightly.

"I'm being horrible. I was just feeling—so totally rough and fed up—headache. I just…"

She gave up as though realising the uselessness of words like that.

"It's ok," I said. "I just wish I knew how to respond—how to be useful."

"Something in me feels broken," she said. "As though it cracked years ago. Long before I ever knew you. And I can't put it together again."

She stared at me for a moment as though imploring me to rescue her from something. As though all she really and truly wanted was for me to open up her head and cut out the part that was hurting her.

I really wanted to, of course. But I didn't know how. And that lack of knowledge hurt like a knife blade in my own brain.

Next morning—as far as it was ever morning in this place of near-constant daylight and heavy-scented air—she awoke me again when she shifted and sat up.

"Oh boy," she muttered sleepily, trying to rub the exhaustion from her eyes. "Dreams."

I glanced at her, but she said nothing more, simply scrambled out of her sleeping bag and exited the tent, not even looking at me. I stared after her. I couldn't recall ever seeing her this dark before, and frankly it was giving me a creeping feeling that something was wrong. Seriously wrong. Maybe it was paranoia or maybe not, but this isolated wilderness was no place for drama.

I didn't follow her. If she wanted to be alone then she had better be alone. Instead I just busied myself with mundane stuff. I began making a detailed analysis of the Zebra Mussel shell. The inside of the shell was smooth and a little worn but I could just make out the adductor mussel scars and these seemed to correspond dead on with the common and widely distributed Zebra Mussel *Dreissena polymorpha*—just an unusually large and somewhat twisted and rough specimen, as though bent with age. In the end I put it aside, feeling unexpectedly bored with it. Zebra Mussels were common enough—enough to be a nuisance sometimes. And as to why this one was so large, I wasn't even very interested.

In the distance, the call of the recorder came again—just that familiar two-note sound. She didn't seem to be playing anything else now—just calling over and over. There was something desperate about it—as though each call was saying 'Please answer—Please answer'. For a moment I wanted to answer myself, in the hope that my answer would be of some relevance. But then, in the corner of the tent, I spotted the pages of manuscript that she had been working on and I picked them up, hoping for some insight. I was not very good at reading musical notation but I could clearly see that there was something bizarre about this—it was not quite her usual style. There were no barlines—no time signature. And even the notes themselves seemed to be skewed. There were curiously shaped noteheads that must have some specific meaning, but it was not explained. Vaguely scribbled lines criss-crossed the staves. And rough written sentences—*Pain and darkness. Deeper and deeper. As red and blue is water. Crystal fluidity.*

I sat back, trying to remember if this was a new piece or one she had been working on before. One thing I could make out though were two notes—just two quavers—that seemed to repeat at odd moments throughout the pages, and I wondered how these corresponded to the sighing calls she had been making. Lydia's bird call—if there had been any birds around here to talk to.

I put the papers back and left the tent—and the moment I did, like a bubble bursting, the calling stopped. I stared round at the landscape but for a while there was no sign of her. Then I spotted a white shape in the lake and felt a thrill of shock for I really thought she had drowned there. She was lying motionless in the water, naked—her body gleaming pink through the clear dark liquid. Her recorder was half-submerged on her chest and her hair flowed out and down into invisibility below. There was a tension in the air—almost like some inaudible musical note still playing.

I hurried to the lakeside, calling her name, but I got no response.

A few of the red mites were patrolling the water around her, I realised—a few on her skin. Sucking. How long would it take for these things to suck a person empty, I wondered—which was a stupid question as the answer was far far longer than anything relevant here, if indeed it could ever be physically possible. But even so—the eerie black steaming water and the mineral growths, her so beautiful body and these orbiting red dots had a weird and almost unearthly quality to them that kept me silent for a moment.

I called to her a second time—then gave a groan and began stripping off whatever extraneous clothes seemed appropriate, splashed in and started swimming.

She gave me a brief glance then resumed staring at the sky. I stared at her, feeling an increasing dread. She looked as though she was in another world—barely conscious and zoned out. Then, without any ceremony at all, she sank beneath the surface. I watched her form fading down into the dark, feeling a freezing sensation somewhere in my stomach; she blew one rush of bubbles, then nothing. I made a wild grab and fortunately caught her hand, yanking her back up. She hung there as though dead. Was she even breathing?

I towed her to the bank. She made a faint sound of protest, then a sharp cough shook her, spraying water from her mouth. I saw the rough mineral growths jar against her skin as I tried to pull her out, but even that didn't get a reaction and I half dragged, half carried her back towards our tent. Her skin looked red and raw from the heat and the thin claggy water gave her a slimy feel. I placed her on her sleeping bag and she abruptly flopped over onto her face, coughing and spraying out more fluid. Shivering with what might have been cold, or shock, or something else entirely. I checked her mouth, but she appeared to be breathing normally now.

Somehow, through all this, she was still clutching her recorder.

I moved the heater nearer to her and began rubbing her down, since she made no move to do it herself, trying to still the shivering, rub away the goosebumps that blossomed all over her skin. She flinched away though.

"Don't" she snapped, and I withdrew hastily.

She sat there, just shivering and breathing heavily, staring into space.

"What happened?" I asked at last.

She gave me a shaky look. "I don't know," she whispered. "Nothing—why would anything happen? I just went for a swim."

"But you were…"

I suddenly felt uncertain. It was so easy to start questioning memories and perceptions, even very recent ones. Even what felt like near death experiences.

"Are you sure?" I asked stupidly. She didn't even answer, just slowly and shakily rolled onto her side.

"There's something down there, you know," she said at last.

"Down—there?"

"Just a basic scientific deduction. I mean think about it—those mites must have something to feed on. There's something living right down there in the deep part of the lake—something very big. I mean—very… very big."

"That lake could never support anything large, surely?" I said. "What sort of thing are you referring to? Maybe there are fish in there for the mites to feed on? Or..."

"I've seen it," she said dreamily. "It stretches as far as you can see."

I didn't know what to say to that. I remembered my own dreams of turning and turning deep in that water. The unknowable warm depths.

It was a fitting fantasy.

"And you," she said, "need to leave me alone."

"What?"

"I don't appreciate interference," she said. "It's not very nice."

I stared at her, too shocked and frightened to be angry. "You were going down," I whispered, trying to remind myself as much as anything. "You were drowning."

She just sat up again, staring at the tent flap—then she was scrambling up onto her hands and knees.

"Wait," I cried. "Where are you going?"

She made no move to stop and, on shrieking instinct, I grabbed her hand.

"What are you doing?" I demanded.

"I need to go," she said. "I need to go and swim..."

I felt her forehead for signs of a temperature, but instead she felt cold. Cold and clammy. I glanced at the heater but it was on maximum.

Then she abruptly rolled over onto her sleeping bag and curled up into a foetal position. "Oh god," she wailed, tears standing in her eyes. I reached out a hand as though that would be any comfort, but she flinched away.

"Look," I said. "We've got a day left before we are out of here. I don't know what's going on but please—just take it easy till then."

She gave me a stare that made me cringe.

"Ok," she said shortly. "Ok—I'm fine. Really." She clutched the sleeping bag round herself. I drew a deep breath and backed out of the tent, urgently needing some fresh air—as far as any of this air could be called fresh. I stared at the lake, feeling as though the black water of Svartavatn had cast a spell over us both.

As I stared, there was a heavy swirl out on the surface. I couldn't see much, but something had shifted out there. Maybe something alive, maybe some bubble of volcanic gas. Maybe I was just dreaming. I wish I knew. I really wish I knew.

I sat down beside the silent Lydia, thinking furiously. I was scared now—really scared. It was hard to be coldly scientific under these circumstances. My head was painful and swimming, but I had to focus—had to work out what was going on. Maybe it was the bite. I considered that carefully. Could she have been infected with something from that little mite? Could I? I grabbed up the specimen jar and stared at it, my hand trembling, but that little fuzzy sphere told me nothing. She seemed physically normal—I could see no sign of sickness or fever. She just lay still under the sleeping bag, the fabric rising and falling as she breathed.

Somewhere—from the distance or from the depths of my brain, I could hear those two notes calling again—over and over. Some audible ghost in my own head. I clutched my clothes to myself and stared at the heater. It was on maximum but I could hardly feel it and I buried my head in my hands. I was trying to count the hours now—even the minutes— until the helicopter was due to return for us. It wasn't long by normal measure but it promised an eternity of sleepless staring and hope. Hope that she would just recover from all this—just be ok. It was a time for bitter regrets that we had ever come out here that went round and round until I wanted to scream them, pointless and irrelevant though they were. If anything happened, the fault would be mine of course. Not so much for anything I had done or not done, but for that old fundamental inability to connect. That fundamental black void with the single winking light that you can never reach. How can you ever forgive yourself for that when it starts to have consequences?

A couple of hours later, I jolted out of a hazy non-sleep as she sat up again and made for the tent flap—and again I caught her hand, filled with terror.

"Where are you going?" I called. No answer, save for the sounds of Iceland—the wind in the rocks—those calling notes ringing over and over. But that was only a dream. Wasn't it?

"Please don't," I begged. "What are you trying to do?"

I switched my grasp to her wrist and held her fast, then stood staring at her as she sat back down like a sulky teenager, her eyes full of hate.

And at the sight of that expression, I felt something shift ever so slightly in my own brain. "No," I snapped, yanking her back far too violently. "Please—just—here… Wait…" Incoherent words and as I spoke them, huge billowing clouds were rising up in my brain. Clouds of red. Tangled streamers of poison. "Don't look at me like that," I yelled, and for a brief moment, I actually drew back my fist… then let it fall to my side.

After a moment, I bundled her right into her sleeping bag and zipped it up, trapping her inside. Then I grabbed a rope and, my hands still shaking so violently that I could hardly control them, wound it round her, trussing her up until I was sure that she wasn't going anywhere and securing it with a fumbling knot. It felt ridiculous—lethally so. It was a farce, a pantomime. A bad play or cartoon of some kind and I gave a wild laugh. In that cartoon, of course, I would now be the villain—and maybe I was. Maybe I'd always been. Doomed by my inability to every really understand another person. In some hysterical sense of liberation, a part of me did want to just let her go. Let her go and swim. Why shouldn't she if she wanted? *Why shouldn't she?*

After watching her for a while to make sure she was safe, I fumbled among our supplies for the painkillers and swallowed a couple, then curled up and shut my eyes. Some kind of sleep happened, amid the red clouds, but the whole pantomime just followed me there and my dreams were only more intense now. Again that feeling of turning over in a slow cartwheel—of floating downwards through some immense black tube, where light glimmered far below. Gigantic Zebra Mussels clustered all round, so large now that I could almost crawl inside one of those rough brown shells. As I watched, their pallid siphons contracted in unison and ejected clouds of white milk like a silent fanfare. And something moved far below. And through it all came the keening sound of Lydia's two-note phrase on the flute. Over and over—over and over. Would that sound never shut up?

I tried to call up memories. A year or so after our first meeting, after a long time of isolation, we finally came together with a bump. In those early weeks, she had guiltily asked me to sleep in her spare room—climbing in with me for ecstatic sex, then slipping off to her own bed. And even then giving me the occasional dark look and retreating into some hidden place, as though hating the necessity of forming connections with people even in the midst of happiness. Then coming back again, wild with an affection that defeated all paranoia. It was a wild time—a voyage of discovery. And not so much had changed since then. Or at least, so I thought. As time passed, in spite of our sometimes skewed communication, a bond had formed of intense ferocity, even if the priest that married us had been a leech.

And I realised then that I had never actually told her about that.

From waking into dreaming into waking again—it was a repeating cycle. When I woke, it was into a world of pain and deadly tiredness as my head throbbed. I tried to focus—but there was just a vague grey in my eyes and the sound of the wind and calling notes. And even when I forced myself, blinking, I could hardly see anything but shapes and colours. And sleep was a respite. It was a peaceful part of this cycle, for all the nightmares. Painful but static, with the passage of time having no meaning. No day. No night. No sun. No stars. Just a simple flat surface of time that seemed infinite and unchanging.

Finally though, during one indefinable cycle in the sequence, the realisation came that there was something missing and that jolted me up a few more levels in wakefulness. Her sleeping bag was open, the rope I had clumsily used to secure her was unravelled and, when I got a better look, I realised that there were traces of blood on them both. Feeling a sudden huge weight in my stomach—not unmixed with a sense of inevitability—I staggered to the entrance and peered out. A bright low sun of goodness knows what o'clock shone down across the empty landscape.

Just as before, like a bubble bursting, the music stopped.

There were more traces of blood on the rocks outside—in the direction of the lake. They came like a dream. I hurried in that direction, ignoring the rough rock under my bare feet—and a few metres further on, I found the coat I had managed to get on her earlier. It was lying casually in a crumpled heap in the rough grass. I stared at it, feeling increasing panic.

Then a white figure—blurred, standing in the water. I gave a whoop—and she was down and swimming out towards the middle.

There were no surprises now—this was pure inevitability. I didn't dither or have to engage in any internal dialogues. I just ran after her and splashed fully clothed into the hot water. I sprawled down, sending mud and minerals swirling in all directions, ruining years of crystal growth in a second. In a half-drowned tangle, I scrambled out of my coat and swam awkwardly. Below me, the lake bed vanished and I tried not to think about where I was, or just how deep Svartavatn might be. My eyes were burning—I could see nothing of Lydia now. No bobbing head. She had gone down like before, I realised. Sunk. The dark water had shut her off. I splashed out to where I remembered her to be and dived, bracing against the temperature. I could see little, as though I was swimming in black milkless tea, and I felt despair trying to get my attention from some lingering rational part of my mind. But I didn't pay attention to that—to the seeming impossibility of ever finding anything in this black water. I splashed up for another gulp of air, then plunged down again.

And then, there she was. I saw her. A white form floating deep in the water of Svartavatn. In some strange way, this sight was also inevitable and I didn't question it. I stared at her and tried to reach her, but she was still descending. I could see red dots orbiting her body like tiny planets and I knew what they were. When we first arrived, they hadn't been visible—now though they seemed to be everywhere. Maybe they were coming up from somewhere deeper in response to our activity. Now I was reminded of them, I realised that they were orbiting me as well. I hadn't even noticed—even their few needle-like bites.

There were no bubbles coming from her at all.

Then she turned to look at me. I swallowed water in shock, choking on the acrid mineral taste. Had I imagined that? Or was this just humanity's inherent sense of narrative deluding my brain? It was not possible for Lydia to just float away, after all. She must look back one last time. But not with those blank eyes.

But she just carried on drifting downwards, turning over lazily, hair streaming, and getting darker and darker in the dark water. Down below, I thought I could see flashes of light winking on and off in the black distance. I made a frantic effort to follow her but after a few more metres, the vicious heat of the water became too much and I had to stop—self-preservation taking control and sending me hurtling to the surface, to gasp some more of the heavy air and the glaring Iceland daylight.

Of course I went down again. And again. I kept diving as deep and as hot as I could bear, then struggling to the surface. I dived for over half an hour before I finally gave up and drifted to the shore. My body was burning all over. My head felt as though it was blossoming into a flower of pain and no matter how much I gasped in air, it didn't seem to refresh.

When I reached the crystalline rocks, I couldn't even climb out of the lake. I just lay in the shallows, rested my head on an uncomfortable nub and more or less passed out. In my head, I could still see her descending away into the black water, while the red dots orbited. And lights winked on all round, revealing themselves to be the lights of windows and doorways in the wall of this volcanic tube. A vertical city that stretched away downwards forever. And through everything, that same peeping two-note call still rang out—like the voice of a bird from the depths of the earth.

I can't say much more. I have only vague memories now. Time passing. Colours. Shapes. Noises. A shocked helicopter pilot who hauled me on board. Questions. The next coherence was seeing the ground far below as the Iceland wilderness flowed past. And feeling fresh cold air, which I drank like wine.

"Where… is… she?" I murmured. "Where are we going? You have to call for…"

But it was pointless over the sound of the engine.

It was the air.

At least, that's what appears to be the case.

I should have known of course—should have realised that from the first day. There was something strange about that air. The air and the water of Svartavatn were both filled with strange scents—an alien heat and thickness. Later analysis of both revealed a slightly-poisonous slightly-suffocating volcanic cocktail that caused certain glimmers of scientific interest in various places. Svartavatn is now on the scientific map and there is talk of a return expedition to take up where my ill-equipped trip and the crazy and useless recovery/rescue efforts left off. People want to know what is going on in the depths of that weird black lake.

As I lay dully and unforgivingly in my little room in Reykjavik, my specimens were returned to me—the little *Lamiapilosus* mite, now dead in its bottle, the *Lymnaea* snail and the massive Zebra Mussel. I know that many people probably wouldn't understand, but these were a kind of comfort to me, that at least something had come out of that disastrous trip. In the end, they even caused some interest among others who are interested in such things. Sadly, my name *Lamiapilosus* got thrown out because the creature turned out to have relations to another genus of water mite-like creatures but in the end, somewhat to my surprise, my choice of last names was upheld for both. I don't think anyone had the heart to quibble. *Lydiae* was entered into the catalogue of life twice…

Needless to say, Lydia was never found. She's still down there somewhere.

My practical mind sees her with the flesh long-since cooked from her bones by the intense heat lower down—slowly dissolving away to nothing in a place as inhuman as you can ever find, yet probably still supporting life of a kind. Extremophile micro-organisms all the way, revelling in the heat. The less practical side of me still wonders what she thought she had seen down there—that stretched as far as the eye could see. Another brief clue to a vision originating in that small winking light surrounded by blackness that you can never touch. And in my dreams and fancies, she still drifts—and twists and turns and swims—and stares back at me forlornly from her new home where strange lights that might be doorways wink on and off in the wall of that deep tube of water—and where indefinable forms just maybe move with some kind of sentience.

When that expedition is put together at last to return to Svartavatn, I shall ask if I can go along—again, I hope they don't have the heart to refuse. I want to see that strange tube of water again. And I want to see just what lives in its depths.

Queen Rat

As she washed off the mud of an entire day in the Thames, Long-Fingered Lissy was feeling more than a little melancholy. Her muddy trousers, jacket and everything else were in one tub, her day's findings in another, herself in a third, and the water in all three was roughly the same, stained as brown as tea and filling the room with a strong whiff of the Thames. A whiff of corruption, death and sewage that she hardly smelt any more.

It was impossible to get completely clean, but there was no denying that this felt good.

"Pass me the cloth," she said, standing up, feeling the grit and sludge beneath her feet. Her father did so with a brief wordless grumble and she wrapped it around herself then shook out her hair, spraying water droplets everywhere.

"Mind what you're doing," he said, moving his cup.

She was about to respond with something caustic when she heard a voice outside yelling her name. She swore and stepped out of the tub as the door opened, revealing a black and faintly menacing figure in a filthy long velveteen coat and a wide floppy hat. He held a staff considerably taller than himself and had a dark lantern fastened firmly to his chest. The lantern was closed but she could make out a faint crack of illumination. A stink radiated off the man—a stink so strong that it blasted even her rather desensitised nose.

"Evening, Tidy Tom," her father called.

"Oh, Tom," she said. "Couldn't you have tidied up a bit more?"

"I came straight here from the sewers."

"I can smell you did. Well, look away for a minute while I git dressed."

The figure turned about with a rather flamboyant gesture and she reached for her clothes—a well-patched and mended dress rather than her mudlarking gear.

"All right sweetheart, what do you want? I can see you want somethink more than the usual."

He spun around again, removed his hat and his face emerged into the light—a younger face than one might have expected from the outfit, and wearing a wide grin. "Bless your heart but such a day I've had."

"Well I'm glad someone's happy. I'm totally done up."

"No luck?" he asked.

"Oh I've been in luck. Come 'ere and I'll show you."

She hustled Tom over to what she thought of as her workshop—a small desk with various tools and pots. She slung the water out of the bucket of findings and replaced it from her washtub—a process she repeated twice. Then she drew out something large. He opened his dark lantern and shone the bull's-eye of light on it, and whistled. It was solid, glassy, opaque and a vivid sky blue in colour.

"Nice bit o' slag," she said. "No idea what they were smelting to make this. Some new 'sperimental… metal thing. An' this dumped on the bank of the Thames. But I know some people who'll love this. I could make some beautiful jewellery."

"Excellent," he said, then leant forward with a hint of conspiracy. "But look what I found."

"If it's better than this," she said, "it'll win you a kiss."

"Oh, it's much better than that," he said eagerly. "'Ere, look. An' I wouldn't show jist anybody."

He fumbled in his bag and drew something out. There was a flash of gold.

"Ooohhhh," she murmured as he spat and rubbed the filth off. It was a sovereign—a whole sovereign. She stared at it in awe.

"When I change this, I'm going to buy you somethink nice."

"Where did you find it?"

He flashed her a huge grin. "There's the thing—that's why I'm here. I need your help."

"Hm?"

"There's more down there. So much more. I know places down there where the roads are paved with gold," he said. "Enough to make us both rich."

She stared at him dubiously. It was not unknown, she realised, to pick up coins of this value in the sewers, but they were events that tended to be whispered about in breathless excitement. The idea of more of them just there for the taking felt improbable. That wasn't how scavenging worked. Except in dreams.

"Help?" she asked with a frown.

"Yes. Come with me."

She had never ventured into the sewers before, even though the pickings were supposed to be good. Even though among the scavengers, the sewer hunters or toshers were the elites. Even though, when you got down to it, the stench and the shit weren't so different to that of the whole city these days. The sewers had always seemed too enclosed, too suffocating. Too many stories of people savaged to death by rats or flushed out when the flushermen opened the sluices of the tidal containment ponds upstream to wash out the system. Or stranger stories. Legends of rampaging feral pigs in the dark depths or wisps of eerie supernatural legend—female figures that haunted the darkness, now here, now gone again.

And she herself, picking around in the mud, had occasionally stumbled upon the resultant bloated corpses…

"I ain't going down there," she said. "The mud's my place, the sewers yours. And besides, I'm not putting my gas-pipes on any more today."

"It'll be perfectly safe. And I know the place like the back o' my 'and. I know the tides, I know the sluicing times—I know the places to go if anything goes wrong… it'll be safe as the bellows."

"Yes, I'm sure. All right, what is it you found?"

"In there… way, way in there, father than I ever went afore, there's a great big mass o' sewer metal. Biggest I ever seen. Maybe the works dislodged somethink and it all came tumbling down there and piled up. They are digging all around London now—Mr Bazalgette's interceptor sewers an' others. The railways… But serious, I need some 'elp. There's more, but I can't manage it by myself."

"Then git one o' the teams to 'elp you."

"No," he said. "I doesn't trust them. Too many o' them to whack it as well. I…" He nudged her in the ribs. "I'd much rather whack it with you."

She glanced at him, the mischievous grin on his face confirming the small innuendo.

"And who knows," he continued. "Mr Bazalgette has already started work all over. There might not even be any sewers for us when he's done. No smell, they say—but no pickings either. So if there is somethink, I want to find it first."

She smiled dubiously. "I'm doing fine," she said. "No mudlark in London but me is selling blue jewellery. Only I know the finding o' it."

"A place o' your own? Out o' this court forever? Git this thing and we wouldn't care how the wind blows for the rest of our lives."

She froze, listening again to the racket from outside, glanced across at her father sitting at the table staring into his mug. "As much as that?" she whispered.

He shrugged. "Maybe. It's a big one. And I could see the gold. At least enough for a bit of luxury. And I want it afore the other hunters can git it."

She fell silent, idly turning over some of the stones on her desk—the blue slag, as well as some Thames flints. Nice though they were, and regular though the sales were, you couldn't ask much for a piece of Thames slag glass.

"Anything down there as I could make into some rum jewels?" she asked.

"Think any o' the toffs would like some polished sewer metal?"

She hesitated. He was grinning, but that was such an odd idea that it might even work. She had seen some of this material before—rusted and fused deposits that had built up over many years, filled with many different bits and pieces, including money—gold coin. Some people, she knew, had the taste for such unusual things. It was not all diamonds and pearls, antiques or orientalist curios. People collected all sorts, sometimes precisely because they were obscure and different rather than conventionally precious—precisely because the world they were from was alien to their own. She glanced at the ancient brown hacksaw on her desk, imagining it cutting out neat shapes, patterned with many colours of metal, maybe fixed and filled with shellac if needed. Then polished. Would that work? There was a temptation there. There was only so far you could go with blue slag glass.

"I am afeared o' the stink," she grumbled.

"Bless your heart, but it smells as bad out 'ere as it does down there these days."

"Hm."

"No—the stink niver done me no 'arm. Do I look sick?"

She had to admit that he didn't. Tidy Tom was small, wiry, strong and his complexion was good—certainly no pallid spectre.

"It's good for you," he said with a big grin. "Toughens you up. You jist don't git bit by the rats and you'll be fine."

She sighed. "All right, let's go. But if this is a fool's errand I swear I'll batty-fang you."

She grabbed her bag and shook it out, then quickly loaded today's pickings back into the bucket. A couple more pieces of blue glass joining the first—subtly varying colours.

He eyed them with another of those wide grins. "Hey—you owe me a buss."

She wrinkled her nose in disgust. "You stink."

"So do you. So does all o' London. You know, they even had to evacuate the toffs from parliament a while back, it stunk so bad."

She chuckled. "No great loss." She had to admit that was true, however. The air had never felt so foul. A constant inescapable miasma lurking over the river and the surrounding city, the source right there in the mud through which she waded. A soup of shit seasoned by the occasional bone and bloated animal carcass—or even the occasional human one.

"Well, wait till you've 'ad a wash," she said.

"I want to leave now. We'll wait till we're underground," he said with a lewd grin.

"No we damn wont. I'm no bangtail. And I am not going to pay a call on the local dressmaker either." She gave a groan and rubbed her eyes. "What do I wear down there? I have to git my gas-pipes on ag'in?"

"Yes." His grin widened. "You can't wear that lot down in the tunnels. And you got a dark lantern?"

"I have."

"A hammer?"

She hesitated. "Father," she called. "We still 'ave a hammer?"

"Yes," he said, pointing to a corner.

"Put it in your bag," Tidy Tom said. "And bind your knees."

"Why?"

"In case we need to crawl."

"Oh…"

She hurried across the room and dragged open a large basket, taking out a clean pair of trousers. She tugged them on beneath her dress, then dragged the floppy and still rather damp fabric off over her head and tossed it away. Shirt and thick jacket went on. Two cloths added to her bag for her knees.

"You got an 'at?" he asked.

"Not… that kind of 'at."

"We can pay a call at my place—you can have my spare. Jacket as well."

"All right, all right, let's go."

The stench always seemed worse nearer the river, the great brown slithering snake that was the Thames. Eventually the nose got used to smells, but that only lasted until something changed or increased—until you approached its source. Then it would come thundering back, almost a physical sensation in the air, almost a hallucinatory shimmer.

This was a black-on-black but clamouring world, pierced by only the occasional light. Voices, shouting, an endless bustle of people on the move to who knows where and who knows what. The thorns of masts rising up against a shadowy sky, their shapes pained and twisted—dark hulks of boats of all sizes, the tangle of building sites and constructions that filled the city like fungus.

Lissy was feeling a little nervous, however, for Tidy Tom's mirror had revealed a strange figure—almost unrecognisable as a woman, or indeed as anything. She was wearing the full sewer-hunter regalia now—a large floppy hat and long velveteen jacket a few sizes too large with a dark lantern fixed firmly to the chest. She had worn all sorts of things in her life—one had to when relying on whatever one could scavenge or pilfer—and when poking around in the mud, she had to do whatever it took. Trousers were a norm for her at least, in spite of the occasional glance they received. Sometimes, sensational news would filter down about some toffer wearing trousers and causing a flutter or scandal—even getting arrested. But they seemed like news reports from a distant country. She had been wearing trousers in the mud for much of her life. There was little choice. And as far as modesty was concerned, the filth of the Thames was a good barrier against any lecherous glances.

"This is Mr Bazalgette's interceptor," Tom said at last, as they approached another building site. Everywhere things were being built or torn down, the city seeming to change by the day, heaving and festering like a carcass in the sun. In the low light, it looked as though the street had exploded, a massive trench fenced off with wooden railings—and in the depths, hints of brick tunnel—twin slot-black holes leading off into oblivion. It was a time of turmoil, that was certain—and a time of uncertain future as well. Maybe Tom was right that the days of the sewer hunters and even the mudlarks could be numbered—a chilling thought. Thinking of Tom's discovery, she allowed herself a flicker of hope. Maybe something could be gained from this, if handled with sense.

"We—go down here?" she asked, looking round uneasily.

"No. Too well guarded. They really doesn't like us getting into the tunnels now. They say it's too dangerous, though they niver care how we starve or freeze. We'll slip into the old tunnel entrance jist down the river and git through that way."

"Okay," she muttered, feeling an upswell of nervousness.

"Keep your lantern closed," he added as they descended the steps to the Thames. This was familiar territory, of course, and she walked quickly, quicker than most would have.

"Tell me some more," she said. "Are there really wild hogs that live down there?"

He laughed a somewhat theatrical laugh. "Lor' bless you, no. I doesn't believe a word on it."

"And the ghosts?"

"You do see strange things."

"You ever seen the Queen Rat?"

He glanced at her and she could feel him grinning in the dark. "Oh yes. She appears sometimes as a fine lady in the sewers."

"And what would a fine lady be doing down there?"

He gave her a knowing look. "Wouldn't you like to know," he said.

"That's why I asked."

"They say as you won't guess who she really is—except that her eyes, if you catch them with your lantern, they shine like an animal's. And if you see her feet, her toes have claws."

"See her feet?" she asked with a laugh. "So this fire ship is down there, splashing through the shit, in bare feet?"

"Maybe," he said. "And you see a lot more than her feet."

"Yes?"

"They say she—if you guv her a really good time, she'll bring you luck. Plenty o' valuables to whack. But it has to be a really very good time."

Her laughter went a little shrill. "So that's how you found your great hoard? Having a tiff with strange wagtails in the shit?"

"Why would I when there's such a good time on the surface?" he said with a mischievous grin. She brushed that off, despite the moment of warmth his words evoked. Her mood abruptly switched to chill again as Tom came to a halt. Ahead was a mouth of utter black in the wall that fringed the river. A faint sound of trickling water.

"Here we be," he said.

She nodded slowly. "What kind o' windward passage is this?"

"Hold still for a while and listen—and look. You sense anybody around?"

She froze for a while, ears and eyes straining, trying to analyse the familiar background murmur of the riverside city.

"I can't hear nothing."

"Nor can I. Okay—quickly inside."

With barely a sound, in spite of the squelching mud, Tom flitted forward and plunged into the dark. She followed, stumbling awkwardly. A hand took hers. "Walk forward ten paces," he said, and she allowed herself to be led, completely blind, trying not to think about any unexpected obstacles her feet might encounter or what would happen if she fell into whatever it was that was flowing around her boots.

Then they waited again—and a thin ray of light blazed, picking out ancient brick. It was a relief to cut through that utter black and she opened her own lantern and stared around with interest. The tunnel dwindled into the dark—ancient arching brickwork, soft and decayed, or occasionally fallen entirely, leaving rotten sockets behind them. It was pretty much as she had imagined it: a long thin world of wet and rot and stench. A concentrated essence of the stink that hung over London.

There was no time to stand still and stare, though, for Tom was already marching onwards at some speed. She followed without any real difficulty, the two lantern beams lighting up the sewer with a dreamlike quality. Walking here was if anything easier than out on the Thames mud. She knew the ways of the river intimately—knew which surfaces would take her weight and which would have her wading through a deep sucking morass. Here though the ground was a uniform swamp of sewage on brick—some debris but no major surprises.

"You ever seen her?" she asked,

"The Queen Rat?" He shrugged and grinned a dark, theatrical grin. "I might have. Well, maybe. I think I saw her king."

She stared at him in surprise. "You telling the truth?"

"I swear. Some say it's nothink more than some bored toffer or other who goes swanning around down there looking for excitement—you hear stories about what they git up to. But…"

In spite of herself, she felt a prickle and her eyes flashed up and down the sewer. "But what?"

He nodded. "I doesn't know," he said. "But one day… one night…" His voice dropped to a whisper and she looked at him in surprise. "One day, when I was down here, a'walkin the tunnels, I did catch a look o' someone. Somethink."

"Her?" she asked breathlessly.

"Naw. 'twas a man. An' I know that 'cause he was full nakked."

Her eyebrows rose.

"White as cloth, he was. Eyes very dark. And the moment he saw me, he slipped away so quick an' so quiet I thought I'd dreamed him."

She was silent, her skin still thrilling. Tom was a theatrical character and this might well be just another of his tall tales. But here in the utter darkness, it was hard to be sure.

"Close your lantern," he said. "Grating."

She did so, and became aware of a glimmer of light from overhead—a sound of voices and bustle that penetrated eerily into this underworld. She stared up in surprise at this glimpse of the street—a mundanity seen through an impassable crack. Sometimes the light would flash off as a figure passed overhead—the flicker of a pair of male feet or the complete eclipsing of a woman's dress. Passers-by totally oblivious of the watchers below.

"Shouldn't let them see nothink going on down here, in case anyone calls the peelers," he whispered.

She would have liked to pause and watch for a moment but Tom marched on, just fractionally faster than was comfortable, and soon the twin beams again pierced the dark. Conversation flagged and Lissy was starting to wish she'd had no part in this. It would have been nice to be in bed, listening to her parents snoring, then sleeping off a long day's work. This tunnel was unchanging, save for the occasional inlet pipe or overhead grating, necessitating the closing of their lanterns. It felt as though you could walk forever here—and indeed would have to. A continuous nightmare of wet brick. That was, if anything, more disturbing than the smell or the feeling of enclosure.

"How far do we have to go?" she asked at last.

"Way way in," he said. "Deeper in o' where the hunters usually go. Beyond the familiar tunnels."

"Fuck."

"We have to move fast to clear the tide. Normally we'd git in and out afore the tide comes in. This time, we go deeper to places where the water doesn't reach.

"What?" she demanded. "How long is this going to take?"

"We can take a rest in an hour or so. Can even sleep, if you wish."

"You niver told me it would be an all-night job," she said crossly.

"Think about what we might find," he said. "It's worth the effort."

She subsided, grumbling. But she felt surprisingly little urge to back out. Maybe there was indeed something hypnotic about these tunnels. They drew you onwards into another world. She was reluctant to admit it, but she was beginning to see why the sewer hunters were so strangely proud of what they did and where they did it. Even the smell was reasonably static, and by now her nose was becoming numbed to it.

"This had better be worth it," she said, breaking into a run for a few steps to keep up with him.

It was a long walk—very long. Sometimes, the tunnels narrowed frighteningly—at one point they even had to crawl on hands and knees. The reasons why this area was off the usual paths of the sewer hunters were becoming very clear—and the prospect of being caught in this narrow pipe when the flushermen opened the sluices was almost unthinkable.

Eventually, though, the way became easier again and they could rise to their feet. And a few minutes later, Tom came to a stop with a triumphant shout.

Here there was a step in the sewer, where the flow dropped about two feet. And right below the ledge, an amorphous mass. She stared at it, brain ticking over, trying to work out what she was seeing, her experienced mudlark's eye picking out plenty that fired her interest. To most it might have seemed unprepossessing, but there was definitely a gleam in there. Many gleams.

Metal.

Rusty, but very clearly metal.

She drew a deep breath. "Not bad," she murmured, bending down and poking it with her hammer. It must have been building up here for years, undiscovered by the scavengers, slowly growing and fusing almost as though alive. The sewer would sort the materials that it carried much as the tide would in her own river world. The heavier metals would accumulate in certain places, the lighter materials in others. And if you could read that, then sometimes, as here, there was treasure to be found. And how much might this be worth? Hints of copper and brass were promising, but it was the coins that were especially interesting. A few of them would be very welcome indeed. And could some of them really be gold?

"We can carry this out?" Tom asked.

"We can guv it a damn good try," Lissy said quietly.

"We can break it up with our hammers and fill as much as we can."

He swung his hammer and hit the mass a hard blow—a shockingly loud sound that echoed up and down the tunnel. A part of the mass cracked off and a stream of filthy water trailed from it. Tom picked the piece up, studying it. Lissy was trying to visualise what it would look like polished. The colours were interesting—hints of red and inky black, while no doubt polishing would reveal shining metal as well, all merged into a fused and complex mass. There was potential here, assuming she could find a way to clean it up and work it.

Her eyes wandered to her feet, where the water was still flowing strangely dark—some sediment or other released from its prison by the breakage. Her eyes and lantern followed the stain downstream… then she gave a huge yelp of shock. Tom looked at her, followed her eyes, and echoed it, dropping the chunk of metal with a solid splash.

There was a figure standing behind them, pale and naked. Still as a statue, like a paper cut-out, framed by the filthy brick and backed by darkness—watching them with deep black eyes. Lissy gave a faint wail, feeling a preternatural strangeness. Fear froze her into immobility—and Tom likewise beside her. As the terror flowed through her, she aimed the lantern at the figure's feet to check for claws, but they were submerged. For a moment, she wanted to collapse into the shit in obeisance and start praying.

But then, with a faint unlatching breath, something more rational began to surface in her mind. The figure was clearly female, the skin ghostly pale under the dirt that smeared her, but Lissy could recognise small details that spoke of flesh-and-blood reality. A few scars, delicate silky body hair, her chest rising and falling with a speed that indicated tension and wariness. And also her tools—hammer, pick, crowbar, awl and various pouches and bags, all suspended from a tough strap over her shoulder. Her hair was tied up tightly into a solid mass and Lissy could make out the slight pull of each individual strand on her forehead. Why she was naked, she couldn't begin to imagine—but she was definitely human.

"Who are you?" Lissy asked at last.

The woman just stared at them, her facc blank.

"Bloody 'ell," Tom muttered, and Lissy refocused her eyes, realising that more figures were approaching down the tunnel. At a sound behind them they whirled round, to find yet more of these folk; at least a dozen of various ages and sizes. Women. Men. Even children. All naked save for their utility straps or belts—all the same ghostly pale skin. They may not have been supernatural, but terror swept through her again—the terror of being caught, pinned, trapped, by something she really didn't understand.

"Who are you?" Tom echoed, his voice high-pitched. "What do you want with us?"

The only response was a sudden movement—almost a pounce—as white arms lunged out and grabbed them from both sides. Many arms. Tom shrieked—a harsh raw sound that frightened her almost as much as the figures themselves.

"This," one of the men said in a quiet, light voice, "must be ours." He had long hair that had once been sandy-coloured, also tied up. Lissy hadn't a clue what he meant for a moment, then realised he was pointing at the metal deposit.

"Take it," Tom cried, his voice filled with terror. "Sir. Take it. I'll nawt stand in your way."

There was a flash of metal as Lissy was forced down first onto her knees, then flat on her face in the sewage. Tom likewise. It wasn't deep enough to choke her but it splashed around her mouth and chin horrifically.

Then the feeling of something cold and hard and very sharp at her throat. Lissy gave a long, closed-mouthed scream. It was the woman they had seen first, bending over her and staring down with an expression that was simultaneously implacable and… sad. Regretful? Behind her, stood the man with sandy hair. Both of these seemed to radiate an aura of authority—the rest of the group looking to them for directions.

"One must live how one can," the woman said. "This will allow us to buy many things." Her voice was strange—almost gentle. Perfectly enunciated, refined yet tinged with just a hint of the London streets as well—really quite beautiful. Even in that intense moment, it came as a surprise.

A flurry of bangs rang out in the tunnel and Lissy's terrified eyes could just make out some of the pale figures already working at the deposit with hammers and picks, hacking off lumps of fused metal and loading it into bags.

"There is nothing on the surface but a failed, poisonous world," the woman continued, her voice going dull. "So… our need is strong."

"Yes," Tom spluttered. "I agree… ma'am."

"We have no wish to hurt you, but at the same time, we must survive."

"We… we, we'll go," she said, trying to keep her mouth above the sewage. "Please, ma'am…"

"Nah, we can't 'ave you telling anybody," the sandy-haired man said—his voice very different, much more familiar from the streets. It was a startling contrast.

"We won't tell nobody, sir," she wailed. "I doesn't even know who you are."

"Right, sir," Tom said. "The sewers are my world too. You… This is your area? Why would I betray my fellow sewer people?"

"We must preserve ourselves," the pale woman said. "We cannot take risks."

Lissy closed her eyes, waiting for the blade to slice, her stomach feeling as liquid as the shit that sloshed around her.

"But… but… soon the sewers'ill be no more," Tom said. "Do you know this?"

"What are you speaking of?"

"Doesn't you know about the great interceptors, ma'am?"

There was a silence.

"The sewers may soon be cut off entirely," Tom continued, speaking urgently. "No more toshers then. No more sewer hunters. That's me gone. That's you gone—sir. Ma'am. We're fellows here. I can help you, not hinder you. Jist let us go."

More silence, and then the pale woman spoke. "What can you tell us of Mr Bazalgette?"

There was a shifting among the crowd and Lissy was finally allowed to sprawl over and sit up. She felt soaked from top to toe now in the reeking fluid, matter smeared over her coat and oozing within—the stench so strong that it was completely overwhelming her previously deadened nose. She desperately searched for some clean part of her clothes to wipe her face with, but there was nothing. She spat and spat again. Tom was in no better state, but he was staring around with gleaming, urgent eyes.

"I speak the truth," he said. "I'm no friend o' the surface, sir. Ma'am. They tell us what to do all the time yet let us starve and die without a thought. And… This is your area—that's fine, sir. The mudlarks 'ave the Thames, and we sewer hunters don't pick up stuff there. You 'ave the deep tunnels and we'll leave you alone as well. You have to trust us…"

"What of Mr Bazalgette?" the sandy-haired man echoed.

"Plenty," Tom said. "His great plan is to intercept all the sewers so they no longer flow into the Thames. Instead they'll flow east, out o' the city to the new pumping stations. And you ain't getting in and out o' there through a giant steam pump."

There was a hint of worry in the crowd now, Lissy could read it very clearly.

"Yes, sir," she chimed in. "This is a time o' change. Everything. In a few years… who knows where any o' this'll be?"

"Tell us more," the pale woman said.

Lissy just remained sitting in the sewage, listening as Tom talked in surprising detail—flow rates, diameters, rough outlines of the routes of the great new sewers, the new Thames Embankment where trains and sewers would coexist, the marvel of engineering that would soon be the Crossness containment system and outflow…

"Now I doesn't know," he was saying. "I doesn't know whether all ways'll be closed off straight away, or jist the Thames outfalls we usually use. You may know of ways out as I doesn't. But it's certain that one day the sewers'll be out of reach. They build, and build, and build—and it's fine and grand. But our world is fading away, and I doesn't know what else there is for us."

Lissy swallowed. The pale figures were looking much more human now, faces filled with unease and hints of fear. She stared in discomfort at the naked bodies—especially that of the sandy-haired man. He seemed very naked, disturbing her eyes every time they settled on him. Then she glanced at Tom. He appeared to be taking this in his stride at least—talking with both of them, man and woman, as though it was the most natural thing in the world. In a way that she would have to consider later, that caused her heart to beat faster.

To her surprise, the sandy-haired man extracted a cloth from his pouch and handed it to her, and at last she could wipe her face a little cleaner.

"I never saw a woman sewer hunter before," he said.

“Oh… I work the Thames, sir. Mudlark. Though—I also make jewellery o’ what I find. There are heaps o’ slag dumped by the river in the finest colours.”

The sandy-haired man actually smiled at that—and held up his hand. Lissy focused on a bracelet he was wearing—made of woven leather but with a large round stone on it. She stared with interest, trying to make out the colours in the dim flickering light. It was dark—black with swirls and bands of reddish hue, as well as flashes of metallic sheen.

“Is that…?” She waved at the metal mass that some of the pale figures were still excavating and carrying off.

The sandy-haired man nodded and Lissy smiled back, wryly remembering her plan to try making just such jewellery. She didn’t say anything about that, though—that plan was completely dead, at least as far as this expedition was concerned. “It’s beautiful.”

“We occasionally manage to whack some o’ it,” he said. “Though mostly nowt but raw metals an’ the occasional gold.”

She nodded slowly. That made sense. If certain people were fascinated by her slum jewellery from the Thames mud, they’d only be more so from a source such as this. “Um,” she said shyly, “if you wish, sir, I might ’ave some connections. The same people who buy my… river pieces might be very interested in somethink like this.”

“Maybe. Though we ’ave to keep our secrets. As long as we can. Though if what your friend says is true…”

“It’s true,” she said. “I’ve niver known things changing so fast. Railways, canals, sewers… The only thing as doesn’t change is that nobody cares what happens to us.”

“We may have to return to the surface,” the pale woman said. “I fear that would be bad.”

"I… suppose," Lissy said, nodding. "Though, you know, there is always mudlarking."

He nodded slowly.

"If you wish," Tom said, "I can return here on occasion. While I can. And bring you news."

Lissy stared at him in surprise, trying to read his face. Was he putting on a massive act to try and get them to trust him? Or was there something in his eyes that said he meant it? If so, maybe she could see why. It was there in the sense of community among the mudlarks and sewer hunters—the sense that it was them against an unfriendly world. The sense that, whatever may have happened, these pale figures might be closer to them than most others on the surface. They occupied more or less the same place, after all.

And did they believe him? She wasn't sure. Maybe they weren't sure either.

"Aye," the pale man said at last.

"That is a good offer, and we thank you for it," the woman said. "And for everything you have told us."

"You can rely on me," Tom said.

"And we wish you good speed to the outside."

"Thank you," Tom said, "and… I also wish you an undisturbed future—for as long as possible. I wasn't fooling you. You ever need anything on the outside, you come and pay a call on Tidy Tom. Six Napier Court."

Again, Lissy stared in surprise at the familiar, truthful address.

"As long as I'm alive," he added with a hint of darkness in his face. "One shouldn't afear change. It's jist that them as doing the changing have never cared about us."

The pale woman nodded.

Tom cautiously rose to his feet. "So," he said, as though asking permission, "we shall be on our way?"

"By all means," the pale woman said. "Thank you."

He glanced down at his shit-drenched coat and lantern. "Apologies, but would you mind relighting our lamps? They've been flooded."

The pale woman held up her own rough lantern and Lissy met wick with wick. It spluttered for several seconds, then caught alight and she carefully transferred it to Tom's as well.

"Thank you," she mumbled.

With a certain awkwardness, they turned away. "Goodbye," she said, her voice still shaking. The two hurried down the tunnel, Lissy glancing over her shoulders every so often at the figures standing in their island of light, until they rounded a bend in the pipe and the darkness was complete again.

Tom was marching at full speed—so fast that she was almost running to keep up—and they walked for several minutes before he swung into a side passage and sat down heavily on a ledge.

"What are we doing?" she asked, breathing hard.

"No sense running. The tide's still up. Jist a bit."

Long-Fingered Lissy closed her eyes—the thought of much more time stuck here underground seemed barely endurable and tiredness gnawed at her mind. She sat down and pulled miserably at her clothes—but she had no way of cleaning herself. All she could do was rub at the drying filth on her face and try and wring it out of her hair.

If Mr Bazalgette really managed to take all this far far away, then so much the better.

Maybe.

It was not until several minutes later that she finally broke the silence. "I suppose… there is your Queen Rat."

He nodded.

"And… King Rat. Funny that," she murmured. "Makes you think. What actually… where these stories come from. And… other stories as well… who knows what… causes them."

She stumbled to a halt, too tired to express this.

"Her voice," he said.

She nodded slowly. "A fine lady."

There were stories here as well, it seemed. Confusing, impenetrable ones. She remained there listening to the trickle and drip of water, trying to imagine how someone could make the transition from the upper rarefied echelons of society to walking the sewers.

"Did you mean what you said?" she asked. "Would you come back?"

"Maybe I did, maybe I didn't," he muttered. "I… don't fancy 'aving my throat cut. Jist… We in this kind of life 'ave to stick together. An' I'm curious."

She nodded, not sure either. Then Tom abruptly shifted and grinned one of his huge grins in the lantern light.

"Bless your heart but I'll come back," he said. "Course I will. Those sewers are still paved with gold an' no Queen Rat is going to keep me away for long."

A Taste of Canal Burgers

And I'm usually such a careful cyclist. I don't go barging through when I can't see what's ahead. I don't go sailing along trusting the world to get out of my way. I don't even jump red lights, before any idiots start having a go at me. But on that cool spring night…

It was around three A.M.. Cycling London's canal paths at this hour is hallucinatory enough at the best of times—they are narrow unpredictable cracks that plunge through the city, worlds of uneven pavement, alternating light and deep deep dark with low bridges, heavy city always crowding around as close as it possibly can—and a continuous line of moored narrowboats lurking beside you like half-submerged coffins. But tonight the slamming of a door still rang in my ears—a voice sounding stupid and ugly followed me—the memory of words. Bad words. So I guess I was somewhat distracted. Maybe there were even tears in my eyes—the world reduced to a half-blind Gerhard Richter painting of rainy black and orange. At the time, I had no idea what I hit.

I remember balance disrupted. I remember hurtling through the air. I remember a massive presence to my right—water, suddenly seeming like an ocean. I remember my mind very calmly trying to work out what to do to prevent myself impacting that water, working through scenario after scenario in my head, even until the last moment trying to find one that would function. I remember an almighty bang as my bike and my shoulder hit the hull of one of the narrowboats tied up there. I remember a sudden chaos of black and wet. I remember my bike and everything else vanishing from sight. I remember a lot of cold.

I wanted to scream aloud in sheer rage, but of course I couldn't open my mouth. As if things weren't complicated enough and miserable enough in the world, now this had to happen. Which way was up? Which way was down? Could I align myself to either? To my relief, it seemed I could. My feet touched bottom soon enough with a dull soft-hard feeling, as of muddy stonework, and I could stand again. My face broke the surface. I had gone down in the gap between two narrowboats—a few metres of black open water with the stern of the one I had hit looming over me. I looked round in a panic for a way out of this, but I can tell you, a low wall or the hull of a narrowboat may look insignificant when you are standing up above it, but when you are in the water below, it is another matter. I could see nothing but vaguely sinister fluted metal and the jet black hull of what might as well have been a battleship.

And then—I just about got the shock of my life when a face erupted out of the water about a foot away from me.

I think I might actually have screamed. I mean, okay, of course I bloody screamed. What would you expect? Stuck there in the dark, my nerves already twice jangled. Figures on the towpath I could cope with. Even annoyed and sleepy figures on the boats. But coming up from below, out of nowhere—fuck yeah I was scared.

"Ach—careful," it cried.

But it soon got a lot more surreal than that. There was a flurry as the figure struggled—seemed to struggle—with something in the water. Something that slid past my leg with an indefinable feeling. Something that splashed and swirled. And then there was a sharp pain, as though the something had bitten me…

I screamed again, flailing away from it all until I banged into the massive hull behind me.

"Shhh," the figure begged. "You'll wake the boaters. Hang on…"

I just stared, too shocked for any kind of coherence. But by this time the figure was beginning to reformat itself in my mind from 'monster' or even 'mad human who might possibly be a serial killer' to just plain and simple 'woman'. A pale face with hair streaming over her skin in long wet snakes—a pair of transparent swimming goggles that glimmered at me like the blinded eyes of a cave fish. She grabbed a length of cord that hung down from the side of the boat and did something complicated with it—apparently tying it to something. Apparently to *the* something. To whatever it was she was fighting with in the water. Then she was backing away with a small gasp of relief, as though some minor but troublesome chore was completed.

"Are you alright?" she asked, shoving the goggles up onto her forehead.

"How can I be alright?" I cried. "I mean, what's ..?"

"Did you fall in?" she asked with an almost petulant frown. "You scared me half to death."

"What do you think you did to me?" I yelled. "What's the heck's going on here?"

She gave me a weird eyebrows-up look. I drew a long long breath, slapping the drips of water away from my face. It was important not to lose it here—this was not a good place to lose it. Losing it always needed to be saved up carefully for the right time in the right location…

"I cycled into the canal," I said, trying to calm down. "Hit something on the path."

"Fuck," she muttered. "I hope it wasn't my hose…"

"Your what?"

She shook her head.

"For gawd sake, let's get out of here, okay?"

That sounded a good idea, but—

"Over here," she said, half swimming around to the side of the boat away from the towpath—and away from the tethered thing. She felt her way along the hull a short distance, then grabbed something.

"Wait—" I muttered, turning back. "My bike."

"Uh uh," she said, restraining me. "Don't. Don't go that way. I'll get it out for you in a moment. This has all got quite insane enough already."

"If you say so…"

"This way," she said, gesturing. I propelled myself after her, half swimming, half walking over the uneven canal bed. There was something hanging down into the water from the side of the boat, I realised. A rope ladder.

"Go on—up you go."

I grabbed it and climbed, hauling myself up and landing in a squelching heap on the tiny stern deck, surrounded by unidentifiable boat oddments on all sides. It was illuminated by a small lantern—just a tiny island of light in this canal darkness.

"Mind out," she called, following. "And mind my crayfish." I glanced vaguely at some large white plastic tubs beside me, then slithered out of the way feeling like a sodden half-drowned worm.

I stared up her. For a moment I thought she was stark naked, and you know what? After all this, I wouldn't even have thought it odd. But no. Actually she was just wearing a perfectly normal set of underwear. Wet and clingy and almost precisely not what you expect to encounter at night in London. I sat up and focused on finding reality again rather than that. In some kind of search for the normal, I found my wallet in my pocket and opened it, surveying the wet ruin of all my notes and papers. "Sorry about your boat," I managed, my voice quavering. "I think I hit it somewhere on the way down. Is it ok?"

"Oh fuck the boat," she said gruffly. "Are you hurt?"

"Yeah—I—I think I'm okay." I rubbed my shoulder. Nothing seriously wrong there. Then I absently rubbed at my leg—and froze when my hand came away covered with dark fluid. Red.

"Oh gawd," she muttered.

I was trying to remember. That pain had come when—she had—and something—when it almost felt as though…

Teeth.

"What was that?" I demanded. "Something bit me. At least—it felt like it…" I stared at her, a look she returned with a slightly shifty expression. Then I shook my head. "Uh uh—no, it must have been my bike or… or some metal down there." I peeled my trouser cuff upwards and examined the wound, which she helpfully illuminated with a small torch. It looked rough—shallow and rather torn. Two neat parallel gouges, running a nice river of red down my calf. She leant in and took a closer look, then shrugged with a hint of unease.

"Get those things off and I'll dry them. And you'd better get inside. Clean that out a bit."

"My bike?" I mumbled.

"Oh gawd yeah," she said, shoving her goggles over her eyes again. "Where did you fall?"

I waved vaguely at the narrow corner between the stern of the boat and the towpath, then glanced at the cord hanging into the water not far away. Something was definitely swirling there beneath the surface, tugging on it.

"Okay, hang on." She hopped onto the towpath and jumped in again with a surprisingly quiet splash. "Gimme that rope," she whispered, gesturing at one lying in a pile on the deck beside me. I passed one end to her and she vanished underwater—all very routine. Then she was up again and nothing to do but haul the rope in. The bike soon emerged, streaming water, the panniers hanging empty, no doubt leaving their contents behind on the canal bed. I swore under my breath.

"My phone was in there somewhere," I muttered.

And wrapped round one wheel, a length of yellow hosepipe—one end still trailing into the canal.

"Oh gawd," she muttered, looking really unhappy. "I'm… sorry. There's not usually anyone around at this time of night."

"What is it?" I asked with a sigh.

"It's my air supply," she said.

I stared at her feeling stupid.

"For—diving…?"

"Yes."

I glanced down again. The cord was still stretched taut and moving slightly. My leg still bled a nasty little stream.

"Have you been fishing?" I asked dizzily.

"Yes," she muttered, still apprehensive.

"I mean… actually in the water?"

She nodded and shrugged. "I use the hose sometimes to get under the surface so I can feel around. Just pop it in my mouth—not as if I am going very deep."

I stared at her, wondering which of us was the more insane. That trailing yellow worm looked the most ridiculous and unsafe thing I had ever seen in my entire life.

"At three A.M.?" I demanded.

She shrugged again. "Well—you know how it is in London. Always someone wanting to interfere—some stupid regulation or other—"

I shook my head. Whatever it was that she had tethered to the end of that rope was not tiny. It was large enough for the cord to hang taut. It must be a big fish. Maybe even a pike? Had she been pike noodling with her bare hands at three A.M.? In Regents Canal?

Before I could say anything though, she suddenly got into motion. "Come on," she said with a shiver. "Please get those wet clothes off."

"Yes but—"

"We'd better get you warm and dry at least. I'm standing here in my eddies and I doubt you are any warmer. Get those clothes off and get in that fucking shower."

"You have a shower?"

"Of course," she said, waving at the steps down into the interior of the boat. "All the comforts of home, provided you don't mind water everywhere."

"Ok then," I said with an appreciative smile. "Thanks."

I made for the doorway.

"Out here please," she said with a small thin grin. "That boat gets enough fucking condensation. Get 'em off."

I dithered, feeling a little self-conscious.

"Come on," she said impatiently. "There's nobody about. Have you got a face on your aris or something?"

"My what?"

"Arse," she clarified.

I gave a short laugh, aware that there was no real choice about this. The canal wasn't the cleanest place in the world and if I didn't, I would probably have gangrene by the time I got home—or I would have turned into some highly specific kind of toxic superhero. And besides, the wet was already wicking every mote of warmth out of me. With a shrug I stripped off and, with comforting practicality, she took my sodden clothes and wrung them out into the canal before draping them over the side of the boat in a neat line.

"The shower's on the right, just beyond the kitchen area."

I watched her grab my bike and sling it on the roof in one muscular movement, then I turned away and headed inside, stumbling down the steps and through a haze of cluttered interior—and soon found the shower. It was a tiny cubicle, barely big enough for one person to squeeze into, but I must admit the blast of hot water was utter bliss. Bye bye chill and canal stink and good bloody riddance. I lingered in there for a few minutes, scrubbing at the wound, then opened the shower door and peered out, feeling awkward and naked but rather more human again. I found her waiting right outside, still looking very wet and shivering.

"You look better already," she said with a tired almost-smile. "My turn." She gave a shaky laugh. "Lemme in there."

She handed me a nice fat robe and pushed past me as I tried to climb into it.

"Thanks," I said, meaning it. "It really is—very good of you,"

"Don't worry about it."

A moment later, her two items of underwear, or eddies as she called them, came tossing out of the doorway—a neat and accurate throw that took them right into the nearby kitchen sink with a plop.

I sighed and tried to relax. It had all been a bit of a flurry, but now at last I had a chance to slow down and look round the interior of the boat properly—and I have to say it was quite striking. It was more spacious than I had expected since the floor was a little way below the surface of the water. It was a long thin cabin, almost like a train carriage, divided up into several spaces. I was sitting in some kind of lounge with a fitted sofa and chairs, with the kitchen taking up one end of it. In one corner, an old woodstove crackled agreeably, radiating heat. Beyond the shower, a doorway let into what I presume was a bedroom at the front. It was a pleasing space, the walls sloping out, then in again making a roughly hexagonal cross-section. It was cluttered—the basic stuff of human life crammed into a long thin box, as well as some more arty touches. Oddments picked up, things collected, things made.

In short, whatever else it was, it was a home. No doubt whatsoever, a permanent liveaboard home. This was nothing unusual. An ever-increasing number of Londoners were moving onto the water into places like this, squeezed out by the impossible housing market.

I couldn't resist getting up and having a look around. The kitchen seemed well-appointed—and bloody hell, I've seen smaller ones in the cupboards they call London apartments these days. A cooking range and oven, presumably run off a gas cylinder somewhere, a sink, cupboards, drawers—it was indeed all the comforts of home.

Poking around curiously, I soon found myself looking at the sink, which contained a rather unappetising salad of wet underwear, a few vegetable scraps, and something else that I didn't recognise. Three black things that looked like thorns. At first I thought they were some kind of claw. Then I wondered if they were parts of a squid beak. But they weren't. I picked one up and studied it. It was about a centimetre long, hollow and very sharp.

I had no idea what they were.

Then the shower door opened again and I quickly dropped it. She looked out.

"Um—would you mind..." She frowned. "Oh fuck it." She stepped out, stark naked and hurried into the bedroom—only to emerge a few moments later wearing a robe of her own. It looked hand-made—simple brown material held together with vivid red stitches. Definitely a certain artistry blended with the basic utilitarian. She hesitated, suddenly looking awkward.

"Sorry," she muttered. "I am not used to company. You know, it's about four months since I last had someone visit me here. You'll have to bear with me, I am not—I don't think I am very good at this..."

"So long as I am not in the way," I said, desperate to match politeness with politeness.

She sat down by the stove and handed me some antiseptic and a length of bandage, which I applied to and wrapped round my still slightly oozing leg. As with the boat, I now had a chance to look at her properly as well. Her face was quite thin and there was a continual wary expression on it that bothered me. It was a face that seemed to find it hard to smile or relax without keeping something carefully in reserve. A face that has had suspicion beaten into it over a long period. Her age could have been almost anything from worn-out late teens to 30s—it was hard to tell.

"Your clothes are drying outside," she said. "I'll bring them in and put them in front of the fire in a moment. I, I don't know if you need to go home but—"

I frowned.

"I don't—need to, no," I said. That came out sounding much bitterer than I intended and she glanced at me with a flash of curiosity.

"Are you homeless then?" she asked with a casual tone that gave me a small chill.

"No—not really," I said, tossing my head with a slightly daft defensive gesture. "I just—can't go home for a little while."

The curious look continued. I gave a guilty squirm. I suppose there was no choice now. I had doomed myself to explain. "I had a bit of a row," I whispered. "With my, ah—"

"Trouble and strife?"

"Um ..?"

"Other half?"

"Yeah—"

"And stormed out?"

"More like chucked out," I said with a sigh.

She gave a frown. "So that's why you were cycling round the canals at three A.M.. Is she crazy?"

"I should be thanking you," I said caustically. "At least you have saved me worrying about phone calls…"

She gave me an embarrassed look and a tiny smile, one that flickered over her face as though unsure if it was allowed to be there.

"And—you're going back?" she asked.

"I—suppose so. Not much else I can do."

"Well, at least that means there's no hurry. Some bloody sanctuary this is, but—welcome aboard. Make yourself at home, as far as possible in this thing. You want to stay the night?"

I stared at her, not used to such offers out of the blue. Not in these paranoid days.

"Would that—bc okay?"

"Sure—I don't think my sofa is so bad."

"Then—thanks," I said. "You live alone here?"

"Yeah," she said shortly. "Just me and my boat. You know, the cockney for boat is nanny goat—so I guess this is my nanny. Kind of nice."

I glanced up with interest at the reference to cockney slang—and at last I remembered what the term 'eddies' meant. Eddie grundies = undies. The funny thing, though, was that her voice didn't sound cockney. Instead she had a smooth and almost featureless accent, for all her sometimes colourful language. Maybe she was a lost ex-student, unable to find a toehold in the world and thus settling down here in maybe one of the very few lifestyles left that didn't steal your soul.

"Isn't it—lonely?"

She was silent for a while, long enough for me to wish I hadn't asked, then nodded. "Yes. But…" She paused, and then the words came out with unexpected eloquence. "I suppose, sooner or later everyone and everything proves unreliable. Even oneself. Especially oneself. I am better off alone and with what I can hold in my hand."

"Maybe," I said, thinking of my own home without much affection.

"You know, this thing cost about a quarter of just the deposit for one of those swanky flats up there." She waved vaguely at the ceiling and I tried to remember which particular buildings were clustering around. But they all look the same—the same hopeful luxury of any flats near water.

I nodded slowly.

"Sorry," she muttered, sitting up. "I'm not much of a bloody host. Would you—like something to eat? Or—maybe drink? I ought to offer you something hot but I don't really drink tea or coffee, so—"

"That's okay—"

"And... as for food, I haven't much in the fridge, but... Gawd—I'm not... I'm pretty much out of... I've eaten everything I caught and there's only a few bits and bobs left."

She stared at me, an obvious tension in her now—a jittery nervousness that was threatening to become contagious. It was clear she wasn't kidding. She really wasn't used to this.

"Don't worry," I said, trying to be soothing. "It's fine. I'll be..."

"Unless maybe—there's something in the traps outside? Not the crayfish though—they are not ready yet."

"Do you really manage to live off the canal?" I asked, anxious to steer her towards different topic.

"Well—hardly that," she said, "but everything you can find is one less thing you have to buy."

"I always assumed these places were rather dead?"

"You'd be surprised. There's crayfish, and fish. And... and you can find lots of plants. Salad everywhere if you know it. And there's other things around as well, like snails. Earthworms—they make a nice patty, you know."

"Really?" I asked, startled in spite of myself.

"Oh yes. I don't have any though. They need twenty-four hours to prepare. You give them wet flour to eat..."

That was not entirely a disappointment, but somewhere at the back of my mind I had heard of this before. Wild food. The foraging lifestyle. Living off the land. But this was the first time I had run into it in the flesh—and the last thing I expected in the heart of the city, where I would half-imagine any wild food would put you in the hospital.

"I'm—just going to check my traps," she said. "Otherwise…"

"You really don't have to worry," I tried to say again with some desperation, but she was already stumbling up the steps to the stern deck. I followed her and found her standing precariously half way along the outside of the boat, her bare feet perched on a tiny little ledge. She was hauling in a rope, and something soon came up dripping and gleaming in the dark—some kind of box. Then a second one. She came scrambling back and dumped them on the deck.

"Nothing," she said forlornly.

"Please don't worry," I said with a laugh. "I'll be fine—really."

She gave a sigh. "It's easier to find crayfish—but you can't eat them straight away." She lifted the lid off a bucket, and I leant over to take a look. Several small lobster-like creatures rested there placidly in a pool of water—all legs and massive claws. I don't think I had ever seen a crayfish before, except maybe on a menu. They looked dramatic creatures to be wandering round in a London canal.

"Signals," she said. "Not ready to eat yet, unfortunately."

"If I pick one up, will I regret it?"

"Naah—hold it by the body. It won't nip you."

I caught one gingerly, it's hard and spiny shell pricking my fingers. Close up, it was hard to imagine anything more alien, with its weird machine-like face and squirming jointed legs.

"They need to spend some time in clean water," she said. "That's the thing. So they can shit out all the crap they've been eating. A sort of detox diet." She gave a shrill giggle. "You need it in London especially."

"Fantastic," I murmured, returning the creature to the bucket. "I'm amazed there's so much here."

"Oh there's more things here than anyone really imagines," she said with a smile, her nervousness beginning to fade now. "You know—there's several types of crayfish all dicking it out for the title of lord and master of the London canals. All of them invaders. My money's on this guy—the Signals. They are tough and cruel and vicious." She waved at the quiet water. "There's a gang war going on here more brutal than anything the city has ever seen."

"What do you mean 'invaders'?" I asked.

"Oh—you know. Species that shouldn't be here. That have come in from elsewhere. London's full them."

"It is?" I said in surprise.

"Fuck yeah. There's exotic spiders, parrots, turtles, snakes, scorpions—all sorts of things. All over the city. There's even a colony of fucking wallabies in Highgate Cemetery. And even stranger things as well."

"What things?"

She was silent. I was sure her eyes had found the rope that still hung over the side. The rope that still moved with a tautness that was nothing to do with the water. Then her face went dark.

"Nobody knows what's down here. Even those entitled clots who live right up there above us have no idea. Because they won't connect with their own fucking world." I looked up at the expensive and anonymous-looking flats. "They love to pretend this is some kind of nice sweet park just for them. I see them swanning down the towpaths, glowering at the cyclists and glowering at us for daring to run a working boat in their precious waterway—but they haven't a fucking clue what is down here. Human, animal, vegetable, mineral—they haven't a fucking clue. This might as well be another world as far as they are concerned."

"I think I prefer your world," I said. She gave me a sharp look, maybe wondering whether I was serious or just patronising her.

"You—umm—really don't mind this kind of thing?" she asked with some caution, waving at the crayfish and various other tubs scattered around.

"Not at all," I said. And it was true. I knew better than to be squeamish about lifestyle choices, lifestyle necessities, eating crayfish or anything else. Even earthworms.

She was silent for a while, then shook her head with a small smile. "Come on," she said. "Let me see if I can scrape together anything at all from what's in my cupboards. I am sure I can manage something."

"Thanks," I said. She was already descending the steps though. I stared after her—and lingered. I was curious. This was a world that I had barely known existed—a lifestyle utterly alien. Crayfish? Earthworms? And what the heck was at the end of that rope? Out of pure curiosity, I reached out for it and pulled.

Whatever it was, it was reluctant to come, though I could feel it moving on the end of the line. I stared at the black water, my mind taking me closer to the Amazon river now than to Regent's Canal—picturing giant catfish or murky toothy river monsters. Could it really be a pike? If so though, why on Earth had she tied it up like this rather than just brought it on board?

Then, as though I had finally defeated its grip, the thing came up with a rush—so fast that it was almost in my hand before I even saw it. And I think I gave a yelp of shock.

Something big—black—long—thin—spiny—formless—that thrashed very unhappily and immediately tried to wrap itself round my arm.

It was… by no stretch was it a fish. I thought at first it was a snake—but no snake is covered in bristles. No snake has spines like that. Then I caught a hint of soft segmentation and it suddenly classified itself in my mind. Worm. Absurd and insane though it seemed, that's what it was. But this was a long long way from the earthworms she had talked about. This was a grotesque king among worms. A massive predatory bristly monster. I would estimate about four feet long. It moved with a weird sentience, more like the sensitive questing perception of a leech than a fumbling earthworm. This creature, whatever it was, had a certain sophistication about it.

I want to be clear here. I have never had a problem with the small creatures that surround us. I was always fine picking up spiders—even the maybe-or-maybe-not poisonous False Widow spiders that seem to be swarming over London these days. You handle them right, they won't hurt you. I can cope with leeches and slugs and pretty much anything this country can throw at me. But this thing was utterly outside my experience, almost ridiculously so, and anything outside your experience is going to blindside you, at least at first. So no wonder I panicked a little. No wonder I gave a yelping shriek.

There was a clatter of feet on the steps and she stared out—and swore. I looked at her guiltily.

"Be careful," she yelled.

I didn't really need telling. I just let go of the cord, watching it drop into the black water again with a dull splash.

"What the heck is it?" I whispered. She didn't answer, just darted to the side and leant over.

"Fuck's sake," she growled, "I didn't want you to see that."

"Why?"

"Because—"

She hesitated.

"Because—well to be honest I am not sure what it is. Not sure anyone knows about it. It's another of those—things that turn up in London. Like the crayfish. But this is my canal and I don't want complications from those fuckers up above."

She tugged on the rope tentatively.

"You going to tell anyone?" she asked with a wooden glance at me over her shoulder. "Any fucking point my asking you not to?"

"I'm not sure anyone would believe me," I said.

She gave a weary sigh and a massive shrug. "Well—now you've seen it, you want it for dinner? I suppose it would be a bit more substantial than anything I have in the fridge."

I blinked at her.

"With a touch of lemon and a bread crust. They make a great worm burger. Better than earthworms any day."

I still just stared.

"Yeah," she continued with a challenging grin. "You gut 'em, boil 'em, mince 'em up. No need to put them on a detox diet—they are so big you can get the gut right out. Then it's butter, lemon peel, salt and pepper. Then bread 'em and fry 'em. Very tasty—very sweet."

She yanked on the rope again and the creature resurfaced. She hauled it right up onto the deck this time and I hastily retreated to a safe distance. But she just grabbed it behind the spiny head, holding it and securing the squirming tail between her legs.

"No need to look like that," she said.

"I'm not looking like that," I said stupidly. "I mean—"

"Hey—you wouldn't care about fancy French escargot or prawns—so why the heck not? Don't give me that British squeamishness crap. You should see what they sell in Chinese markets."

I cautiously stepped forward again, feeling somewhat reassured now because she seemed to know what she was doing. A closer look revealed its structure, which was very complex. The bristles that covered it were arranged in two tufts on each of the segments, with those towards the head end also armed with the large backwards-pointing thorns. It was among these spines that the cord was tied—seemingly the only way to secure it. As far as I could see, its mouth was nothing more than a gummy fold of flesh, around which four feelers or tentacles flopped like flaccid strings.

And those spines looked familiar. Definitely not teeth or claws. Even less squid beaks. Presumably they were defensive—and very sharp.

"I've seen what they sell at the market in bloody Ridley Road," I said gruffly. "I'm not sure anything can surprise anymore." I shook my head. "Are you serious?"

"Of course I'm fucking serious."

"Okay then. I—I—I—I'll give it a go..." Feeling floaty and ethereal, I followed her—and it—down into the boat. Then I grinned. "When my mad girlfriend asks me what the heck I was doing all night, she'll never ever believe me."

It looked normal enough, but then, anything looks normal when it's made into a patty with a bread crust and cooked a pleasant golden brown.

"Want me to go first?" she asked with dry humour.

I picked one up. There was a challenge here and I didn't want to fail it—not some childish game of who went first but whether I could accept this world and respond to it properly. I was trying very hard not to be spooked by the knowledge of what it actually was and the memory of what it looked like—nor by the sight of her stretching the creature out on a chopping board and whacking the spiny head end off with one quick slice, before opening it up lengthways to remove its highly alien anatomy. She'd handled it with great proficiency and pragmatism, even though it had squirmed for a long time, even when she had finished prepping it. Even when it was little more than a strip of meat. I have a strong stomach and only so much patience with squeamishness, but I wouldn't have blamed anyone for freaking out at that bizarre spectacle.

But understand this: I wasn't forcing myself here. I wasn't trying to prove anything to myself or anyone else. I wanted to try this—it was that simple. Because—hey, it's interesting, right? There's a lot of experiences out there that you've never had, so why fight them when they turn up?

In the end we pretty much chomped on the things simultaneously. And inside the crust was a subtly flavoured filling that my taste buds couldn't quite place. Definitely something unfamiliar about it though. I can attempt to describe it—I can say it was mild and smooth with the faintest hint of scallop and a touch of pork fat, but it is so hard to describe flavours in any meaningful way. I guess you will just have to try it sometime.

"Do you like it?"

"It's… yeah, it's rather good actually." I tried hard to keep a note of surprise out of my voice but I probably failed.

I went for another mouthful. Tasty. And the patty had vanished.

She gave a smile—I think the first real broad comfortable smile that I had seen from her. Picking up a second patty, I looked dreamily out of the window, maybe thinking some crap about how you never know where life is going to take you next. Or other barely acknowledged thoughts like *how long would it take to save up for a narrowboat?* Or maybe just registering the hint of dawn light that was beginning to flood the old canal.

On the towpath, the first commuter cyclist raced past with a brief rattle, eyes on nothing but the slabbed path and mind no doubt on anything but what might be residing in the dark water beside her.

Henge

"No curtains?" Aiko asked.

The landlady shrugged. "This is how she left it."

Matt stared around the bedroom, pointing his camera this way and that. Even after seeing many apartments filled with the diversity and mess of London, this seemed an especially curious one. Not the furniture—that was basic, old and rather minimal, chests-of-drawers with one drawer not quite closing, a wardrobe with doors ever so slightly off symmetrical, mysterious stains on the tabletops—the sort of thing you might find in any London flat that a basic human being could afford. Not the building, which was just another of those once-large blocks that might not have even been residential originally but was now subdivided into tiny apartments, like a game of Tetris. It was the decoration that covered the walls that did it. Hand drawn and painted shapes and figures, scribbled handwritten text that a casual glance couldn't decipher, and the many mirrors that gleamed everywhere. Decoration that made him feel as though he had walked inside some deranged yet intricate and beautiful artwork. It was safe to say that he had never seen anything quite like it before…

And Aiko was right—no curtains. Not even lace. Stark naked glass was the only thing between them and the outside world.

"Of course," the landlady said, pushing open another door, "you'll have to use some imagination. We still need to do the place up—get rid of all this mess, paint the walls. It's only been on the market for a few days and we haven't had time."

She gave a prim sniff, her fat face wrinkling as though tasting something sour.

"Or the money. Her deposit won't begin to cover all this and we can't get any more out of her. She's dead."

Matt and Aiko looked at her warily, trying to read the tone of her voice.

"Dead?" Aiko asked. The landlady sighed.

"Knocked off her bike and squished in Shoreditch Highstreet," she said with some bluntness. There was a silence. Matt covered the increasing discomfort by aiming his camera round the room—the living room, he supposed, since it didn't have a bed in it. Now, with the artwork on the walls, came the realisation that it was a glimpse into the world of one who no longer existed. That was a somewhat haunting thought. There were still a few mundane possessions hanging around as well, giving the whole thing a sharply personal touch.

On the wall opposite the window was the most massive painted design of all—a huge curved squarish shape of interacting lines and colours. He stepped further in and examined it with interest. It was safe to say that this was far more than just scribbles or bad graffiti, and he actually found himself prickling slightly as he looked at it. There was a mirror placed in the middle—a large one—and when he tried to look in it he realised that it was a trick one. It was slightly curved, distorting his image into a twisted form.

"What the heck is all this?" he demanded.

The landlady shrugged with a hint of resentment. "Like I said, this is how she left the place. I'll have to paint it over."

He glanced briefly at her two rather dull grey orbs, then photographed the design a few times, the flash ringing out with a disturbing brightness.

They crossed to the window. More buildings rose up tall on all sides, it seemed. Not far below, about one storey down and just a few slot-black feet from the wall, ancient brickwork supported the massive weight of four railway tracks. The paradox of an elevated railway at the bottom of a city canyon. And even as he watched, there was a rush as a small urban commuter train rattled past, left to right.

He aimed his camera at the view and pressed the button.

Aiko took his arm, looking a little dubious. "It's a bit… shadowy," she murmured. She was right. With the buildings clustered round, there was little direct light down here, save for a couple of thin bars of sun cutting across the tracks. Matt found himself rather liking the view. It was urban and dramatic. It was the side of the city that was the obverse of the glitzy façade—almost the secret side. The utilitarian railway, usually out of sight behind walls or high on arches, here ruled the world and across the way he could see glimpses of other people's lives through windows or strewn on balconies. It was these kinds of details that he loved about the city—not the grand classical buildings or gleaming towers that it liked to show off to the world. He turned back to the painted design on the wall and realised that its placement wasn't chance. Somehow, through some process not immediately apparent, it formed a projection of the window, an arced, stretched square filled with intricate lines and shapes across the old paintwork.

The landlady was pointing out some small cupboard or other into which your life's possessions would be crammed, but he wasn't listening until she said, "Well, there it is. What do you think? I should warn you, places go quickly here. It's a good location."

"Whatever you ask, right?" Matt said with smile containing just a hint of acid. "They come clamouring round?"

The landlady shrugged, not showing any offence. "It's a fair market price," she said. "And places in this building are never empty long."

"That's London," he said, turning away and staring round again. He glanced at Aiko but she was just waiting, subdued. She flashed a dark look at the woman, then a *please can we get out of here* look at him.

"Okay," he said, trying to inject some formality into his voice. "Thank you. I think we have seen all we need to. We will be in touch…"

The landlady shrugged and gave a weary smile. "Okay love, I'll show you out."

"Baka," Aiko muttered under her breath.

"What was her name?" he asked, a few days later.

"Who?"

"The woman who lived here before."

The landlady frowned.

"You know, I can't actually remember what she put on the agreement off the top of my head. People just called her Feather."

He nodded.

"Artist?"

The landlady shrugged carelessly. "I suppose, if you count this lot," she said gesturing at the walls. "As I said, I will get rid of it all before you move in."

"No," he said with what he hoped was firmness. "Leave it."

"Huh?"

He stared into her blank face, which seeded a nasty feeling deep inside. "Clean the place up, fix the kitchen and everything, but don't paint. We will take care of that."

The landlady shrugged. "Well okay, that will save a bit of money."

Yeah, about one forty-fifth of our first month's rent, he thought, but did not say.

"Are you crazy?" Aiko demanded as they walked down the high corridor towards the stairs. "That's her job. Why should we pay to do it?"

He smiled. "Because I don't want to do it at all," he said. "At least not yet. Look at this stuff—it's fucking amazing. And I would like to… photograph it. It reminds me of some of the stuff in the Outsider Art show they put on in Primrose Hill. You remember?"

"Yes, but for how long?"

He shrugged. "I dunno. Just enough to look at it a bit."

Aiko gave a sigh and a smile. "Matt-chan, you are crazy," she said.

"Well, what's wrong with living inside an artwork? Not many can say they've done that."

She tugged at her lower eyelid in a rude *Akanbe* gesture, then gave a shrill giggle. He made to chase after her and they stumbled out of the main door together, ignoring the surprised look from a woman just coming in.

"Why are you suddenly in such a good mood?" he asked.

"I'm relieved," she said. "It is sorted."

"You think the place will be… okay then?" he asked anxiously.

"It's somewhere to put our *oshiri* for a year or so. The rent is five times what it's worth, the kitchen you need to… to cover yourself with oil to get into, but who cares! We won't do any better."

He gave her a wry look, trying to work out if any of that was positive. But maybe she was right. Any place to park their arses for a year or so was a good place.

"Why are there no curtains?" she demanded. "This is a furnished fucking flat. Why are there no curtains?"

"We will have to order some," Matt said, deliberately calm, switching the computer on with the uneasy hope that it still worked after its wild journey across the city. Boxes were all over the floor, some trailing scattered contents—clothes, books, unidentifiable fabric and packing material. The bed and the computer were sorted, but that was about all. And nerves were fraying.

"This Feather person must have been crazy," she muttered. "Look at all these mirrors. There's five in this room alone. Was she obsessed with her own face? A dozen mirrors but no fucking curtains. And the landlady… why can't the landlady get some? The price we are paying, you would think she could…"

Matt rubbed at his forehead fretfully. It was getting dark now and he had had enough. He rubbed her shoulders and sat her down on the bed, ignoring her startled look.

"Never mind," he cried with a grin. "Enough work and enough worry." He plucked a bottle of wine from his bag and smiled. "Let's just drink a quick something to the new place and relax a bit."

She grabbed a glass gratefully and he filled it.

"Cheers," she said, her accent startlingly British. Outside, the low clanking rumble of a freight train passed by and she looked up in annoyance.

"Close the window can you please?" she asked.

"Must I?"

"But… that noise," she protested. "I never thought there would be trains this late."

Matt sighed. The freight trains probably ran throughout the night, and the occasional sound didn't bother him much—less than the ubiquitous noise of traffic and sirens from all around that was the continuous soundscape of the city. But he didn't argue, pulling it closed, grabbing a glass of wine of his own and settling back comfortably on the bed. It slipped his mind soon enough anyway when she switched the light off and dropped on top of him, grabbing him into a hug.

"What do you think?" she asked. "Shall we… what's the word? Break in the new house properly?"

"*Sekkusu wo suru ka?*" he murmured in awkward Japanese, and she gave a shrill giggle.

"Do you have any idea what that sounded like?"

"Um… yeah yeah, maybe I don't want to know."

It was only after things had cooled down again, with Aiko sprawled out comfortably half on top of him, that he noticed the lights on the ceiling and walls. Three or maybe four glowing blocks cast by the various light-sources outside the building. Some orange, one a dim and puzzling green. They formed a complex shape and he found himself staring at it, feeling dreamlike. Patterns in the light… patterns in the dark… and not so different in some ways.

Aiko gave a sigh. "We must get curtains soon," she said. "It is hard to sleep when so much light comes in."

He gave a dry smile in the darkness. "Almost more light at night than during the day." He was trying to imagine where the sources must be to cast such a pattern—and even as he watched, a passing train, left to right, sent a second pattern flashing across them, from one side of the room to another. As it did so, the green light flashed to red, solving one mystery at least. Railway signal.

Aiko sat up, then tramped off to the bathroom, leaving the door open and letting yet another block of light in from the hall. Matt crossed to the window one last time and stared out. There were lamps in the areas surrounding the buildings beyond the railway, some cutting through narrow cracks. There were lighted windows. The signal stood beside the tracks only a few metres down the line to the right. He studied it for a moment, allowing himself to be surprised at just how bright it was, cutting through the London night like a searchlight. Powerful modern LEDs that came close to hurting the eyes.

Against all this city light, the sky was nothing but a hazy darkness with no stars, brighter than the dark spaces down below. Matt smiled and returned to bed, tucking himself down into the covers and trying to shut out the glow.

Then there was a bump as Aiko came back.

"Matt," she wailed. "Can't we please keep that window closed? I have to be up early to cycle to work."

Matt glanced round. "I… sorry, did I open it?" he asked, confused.

Aiko closed it with a thump and scrambled back into bed.

Throughout the night, the lights of the signal flashed to red, then to a less visible yellow against the general glow of London, then to green for go, sometimes followed by a low rumble as something passed by below their window. It was a sound that drifted through Matt's mind as he faded down to sleep almost like the wash of waves on a beach.

◇

Next morning he sleepily watched her scramble out from between the sheets, her small body white-grey in the dim light, her black hair almost invisible.

"Fucking dark," she muttered, fumbling for her clothes. She dressed, carefully avoiding the curtainless window, rattled around in the tiny kitchen for a few minutes then left the flat, closing the door behind her. His imagination affectionately followed her downwards and out into the dawn, heading for her bicycle and then off to work through the quiet streets.

He rolled over and smiled, then forced himself to sit up. There was a lot to do. Boxes still needed attending to—the most important were the ones containing his small artworks and created objects of various kinds. These needed to be back up for sale or auction again as soon as possible—a small but valuable extra income. So until well after mid-day was a spiral of sorting out; he was alternately deep in boxes and fiddling with websites on his computer. Stashing things in cupboards and other boxes, WYSIWYG HTML and awkward auction listing pages. It was a relief to finally reach a natural break, slam the cupboard door with expressive force and open the window. He leant out, taking in the vertical, old-brick-and-glass city around him with a calm-down sigh, a breath as long as the train passing below. A long-distance train, right to left, sloping nose and simmering diesel engines, the massive power of the vehicle reigned in to an almost tranquil roll over the metal tracks as it approached the terminus hidden somewhere deeper into the city. The pale sun was behind the building now, casting a big block-like shadow across the tracks and beyond. He smiled a small smile. This was London. In some ways it was a magical place where everything seemed possible and anything could be waiting round the next corner. In other ways, it was a stinking trap out to get both your body and your soul. And what was life but some kind of avalanche of attempted survival?

The train vanished, carrying its load of people into the core of the world, and he stepped back into the apartment. It was very dark in here, even now at mid-day, and he reached for the light switch. The apartment was so deep down in the city canyons that the shadow seemed eternal. That was just something he was going to have to get used to.

There was no appeal in going back to the boxes, so he started checking the storage spaces instead, poking around in their new home's nooks and crannies. Surveying and analysing. What to go where, where to put what? Interestingly, some of the cupboards were not quite empty. A few things had been missed by the landlady's unfriendly cleaning team and he found himself hauling them out and browsing through them with interest. There were a few items of crockery—just basic life-accumulated mugs and glasses—an ornament or two, a couple of novels by authors he had never heard of, a few indefinable pieces of cloth… and then something else. Shoved almost out of sight at the back of one dark space was a different kind of book. He opened it curiously. It was a simple, cheap hardback journal and it was filled with sketches and handwriting that looked very familiar. From the walls.

Feather.

As he turned page after page, it gave him a slight prickle to realise that he was looking at the work of a dead woman. The art was beautiful, complex and delicate, little sketches with an innocent yet confident roughness about them, detailed diagrams that he couldn't begin to understand, pages of densely written text, more pages of numbers and equations. Feather the scientist? These were interspersed with a handful of sketches that were delicately romantic and sometimes very sexually explicit—maths and porn forming a strange blend. Carefully drawn anatomy and figures engaged in various fun acts, laid out with great precision, and with accompanying notes. Its style reminded him a little of Henry Darger, though with a fixation on the wispy adult rather than the semi-mythological child.

This was Feather's book and as he scanned through it, he found himself more mystified and intrigued. Her death was a totally meaningless conjunction in a busy London street, her life a blank beyond the traces she had left in this room and on these pages. In a way, it was extraordinarily poignant, this seemingly private glimpse of a person unclouded by the need to put on a performance for the world, to pretend that some things didn't matter and some things did. Who on Earth was she? Was she a recognised artist? Or was she another of those outsider souls whose creativity blossomed in complete darkness, seen by no one except maybe a few close acquaintances. Outsider art was something he had always loved and felt close to, maybe precisely because it was so removed from the commercial and the academic, which felt refreshing in contrast to his own continual creative grubbing for the next few quid. Art and money really didn't mix—never ever and ever—and there was a glorious freedom in the thought of creating in complete isolation from the commercial, like Henry Darger, or Alexander Lobanov, or Miroslav Tichý, or Judith Scott had done. And when you saw the curious and wondrous worlds that were created by these most innocent of artists, it was suddenly less easy to define just what was real and what wasn't, to define on what sense and level of reality some event might be taking place.

A few pages later, the book fell open with unexpected ease, revealing a sequence of pasted-in photographs that sent a prickle across his skin. A serious-eyed girl with brown hair staring into the camera lens in what were obviously self-shots. He stared at them, trying to work out why there was the faintest of faint ghost of a feeling that he had seen her before.

The sun never shines here, he read, and smiled. That was true enough. *I have moved into a dark place, but that is okay. One day, the light will come. And in the meantime, I don't mind the dark.*

He turned a few more pages, skipping through a lot of numbers that he didn't understand. Then he was confronted by a complex diagram that he did recognise—it had to be a representation of this apartment. Lines and arrows crossed, some carefully drawn with a ruler, some quick and scribbled, passing back and forth around rooms and from room to room. His eyes flicked up and looked about, but could see nothing on the walls or floor that the lines could represent except for the carefully labelled window. The page opposite was full of more text, but that appeared to be separate.

> Down the road is a small supermarket—Turkish I think—filled with baklava and beef sausages and curious fruit. This food needs sunlight and it tastes weird in my dark flat. I wonder what kind of food is most appropriate? Some rich dark soup maybe, or roast duck with spices? Or food from Scandinavia or Iceland where the sun never rises for months on end. I must find some recipes. There is a pair of young people in that Turkish shop whose eyes follow the weather. When it is bright they seem bright and when it is overcast and shadowy, they are also plunged into gloom. I think they are lovers. Though always dour, when they talk together, the sun rises a little in their eyes. I presume they are unlike me; I am so used to the dark and the grey. I wish I could bring them back here, show them that the dark isn't always bad. But would they understand me?

There was a bang outside in the hallway and he flinched, then glanced at his watch. It was later than he thought. Aiko came in and collapsed dramatically face down on the bed with a huge sigh. He closed the book and looked around the flat with a twinge of guilt.

"That fucking road," she muttered.

"Hmm?"

"The High Street. And now I have to cycle down it every day. It's so busy!"

She gave him a wan look.

"When will the glamorous days come?"

He gave a sympathetic smile.

"At least no work tomorrow," she said.

"Sorry," he murmured, sitting down beside her and rubbing her back where he knew she liked it. "I haven't started cooking anything. I got completely distracted."

"Oh don't worry," she said. "Let's just order something. The plates are still in the boxes anyway, right?"

"Okay then," he said.

"This flat is still dark," she added. "Does it never light up at all?"

"Too many shadows out there," he said. He smiled. "I think we have moved into a dark place."

"*Sleeping in the walls of canyons, sleeping down the well,*" she sang to a tune of her own, before drifting away into a muddle of formless humming. "Did you order curtains?" she asked.

"Uh, no, not yet."

She frowned. Matt coughed. "You had better help me choose. We could sort it now if you want?"

Aiko gave a sigh and rolled over. "After dinner. I am wrecked."

She sat up and jabbed the CD player. Quiet J-pop filled the room—high-pitched fluting voices supported by synthetic music that sounded as though it was played on candy. Then she turned to the computer. "What do you like?"

"Hmm?"

"For dinner?"

His stomach didn't seem particularly excited by any of the usual fast food candidates. Kebab was too prickly, Chinese too circular. Pizza too heavy and cubic. And fried chicken just the usual unpredictable formless blob. Not appetising.

"Come on Matt-chan," she said with a giggle. "Make up your mind. Or shall I order noodles again? Udon noodles for the new house—you know that's traditional?"

"Surprise me," he said with a smile, picking up the sketchbook again. She gave a mischievous grin.

"In London that's dangerous," she said, ducking down to the computer screen and clicking through the web pages. "Battered frog's legs perhaps?" she asked. "Goat curry? Jellyfish salad? It's all here."

Matt shrugged and grinned.

"If you fancy," he said, turning the pages, looking for that mysterious diagram of the apartment and the numbers and equations that preceded it.

On the 25th, the light will come, he read. *I am excited—I think I am right. In the months I have been here I have missed the light. Dec. will reach 13.19.*

"Okay, ordered it," she said, interrupting.

"Ordered what?" he asked, surfacing abruptly.

"You'll see. I will just run into the shower. Watch for the door."

He nodded. *The light will come,* he read again and frowned in puzzlement. That was a very blunt and precise statement. Light = lamp delivery, religious experience, enlightenment, parting clouds. But surely those didn't need pages of scientific-looking measurements and calculations to work out. The diagrams meant little to him and he was still frowning over them when Aiko came dripping back into the room, rubbing herself dry. She peered out of the window for a moment, staring down at the darkening tracks and glaring signal-light, then sat down at the computer again.

"Your turn," she said.

"Mm?"

"Shower. The room is nice and warm and you should be clean."

Matt swallowed his reluctance, put the book down and tramped through to the bathroom. He flicked the light on, but even as he did so, he registered a glowing square on the wall. It was startlingly tall, reaching from the floor, all the way up and round onto the ceiling at one corner. Out of sheer curiosity he switched the light off again and looked at it, then opened the frosted window. The city was full of lights but he couldn't tell which was making this. Or maybe it was more than one, given its size.

He shrugged it off, switched the light on again and took his shower as fast as possible, the water helping to clear the fustiness of an entire day spent indoors. Back in the living room, he found Aiko unpacking trays and packets from a warm-looking white bag. He grabbed the book and sat down with her. What did it mean? The 25th? There was a date on the journal entry, 3rd May 2013. He realised with a certain shock that the entry was less than a month old. Was it the 25th of May? What day was it today? He wasn't sure, but he thought the 25th was still to come. That gave him a strange sensation, a mix of poignancy and a prickle of unease. The dead woman Feather had an appointment of some kind.

And what the hell did Dec. mean?

"Matt?" Aiko interrupted, and he reluctantly put the book down. He would have to check that term on the computer after dinner.

He was not there in this dream, he knew that. Later, he would try to work out just how normal or unusual that was and not really come to any conclusions—but now this was just her, alone as she was so often in this apartment, completely white-naked. She twirled round it, moving with the unselfconsciousness of one not being observed. She didn't care how she moved or what she looked like, and the result was a kind of primal simplicity.

That was how it appeared at first. But then he realised that there were no curtains, that she might not be as unobserved as it first appeared. Outside the window he could see more windows. The girl moved carelessly towards it. If she was putting on a performance, it wasn't one of any standard posturing. She stood there and moved gently, white and very simple. She was dancing, he realised, a complex, performance-art kind of motion with her arms, her entire body swaying slinkily. Outside, a train passed on the far track, left to right, a beast of gleaming metal seeming even more substantial in this dream-state. He watched her reach out to it almost with longing. Windows processed by, and he wondered if they could see her—whether any of the people passing noticed this spectacle of a naked girl dancing for them in her one small window among many.

Matt turned over restlessly, half-awake but still dreaming. Attempting to find himself in all this, he reached out to touch the girl's shoulder, motive uncertain, but the only result was that the whole thing drained away. The rumble of the audience train became a real rumble passing outside in the dark. He woke up to the familiar glow of London. It seemed to be everywhere. He hoped the curtains would arrive soon, because this was like sleeping in some weird light sculpture.

He realised the patterns were changing. He jolted into a higher plain of wakefulness and stared in amazement. The colour shifted subtly—different shades of white and orange. The angle also appeared to change and move, casting a ray into the bedroom that crawled across the floor a moment before changing again, this time into a diffuse glow. It was as though different sources of light were being switched on, moved and switched off in some sequence. He tried to work out how light cast in from outside could achieve this. It came with an unearthly feeling that froze his skin—a sense of the eerie—and he realised that he was actually frightened. The silence seemed absolute. There was no sound anywhere, no traffic outside, no train anywhere near, no sirens, no wind. Just this silent light show.

The light changed again, another ray crawling across the floor and up the wall towards him, expanding as it moved. Almost without thinking, he shifted out of the way, not wanting to be touched by it. Then it winked out, shifting again to a diffuse illumination from the doorway that slowly changed colour.

He abruptly jumped out of bed and ran into the hall. There was nothing to see, just the familiar apartment and the glow from the windows in the kitchen. A low rumble made him pause, his skin prickling again, but it was only a freight train approaching in the distance, right to left, cutting the silence. He exhaled with relief and paced back to bed.

"Matt?" Aiko murmured, barely awake.

"It's okay," he whispered. "Go back to sleep."

"When's the 25th?" he asked next morning.

"Tomorrow," Aiko said casually. "I know that because it is not my day off."

"Ah…"

"Why?"

"I don't know yet."

Aiko gave him a puzzled look. He returned to working on his collages—alt-glam photo prints of Aiko supplemented with select debris and rubbish from where the picture had been taken: brick, gravel, mess, all spray-painted into a nice grungy whole and framed in rough wood. He thoughtfully pasted a miniature road sign in there—just a laminated 'road narrows' warning, which seemed to match her posed body rather well—then set it aside to dry. These were quick, simple things with a certain carefully cultivated aesthetic that could be sold for a handful of pounds on various online communities and auction sites—hardly great art. Hardly—the thought nagged at the back of his mind, like the sketchbook. It seemed years since he had created anything for its own sake and without some kind of commercial agenda. Last night's light show also lingered in his mind. Often he would find himself pausing, his art blurring as his mind wandered back to the way the light had crawled across the floor towards him, and the sense of fear and even revulsion that it had evoked. Matt was not used to thinking the thoughts that were now prickling at his brain or feeling the confusion and uncertainty that swirled within him. The explanation that it was just stray reflections from outside didn't seem enough to dispel the crazy notion that there was something wrong—that some of the lights and reflections cast were impossible.

Mentally plotting the movement of light in darkness quickly brought Feather's diagram back into his mind—the intricate spiderweb of lines running through the apartment. Could she have been wondering the exact same thing? As soon as the current artwork was finished, he picked up the sketchbook again and leafed through the drawings, looking for the right page. Aiko leant over his shoulder and studied first the small, framed collage and then the diagram with a puzzled frown. "What is it?" she asked.

"It's here," he said helplessly waving round the room. "This apartment. But I don't have a clue what it all means."

She studied it with some curiosity, then jabbed her finger at one point where lines converged.

"Mirror," she said, indicating the wall. "And that one there as well."

Matt stared round, following her finger to the big curved mirror at the centre of the artwork opposite the window. He realised she was right. It was only a small part of the whole diagram, but it was there. In fact, now she had pointed it out, it seemed kind of obvious.

"What is all this?" she asked with a smile.

He shrugged. "No idea, but she dated it tomorrow."

"Sounds like a *Kaidan*," she said dryly. "A ghost story. You think she will be back tomorrow to greet us as new tenants?"

That was a bit too close to what was in his head. Aiko pressed a glass of wine into his hand. He took it gratefully and made half of it vanish in one large sip.

"Matt-chan, focus," she said with a grin, rubbing at his shoulder. "We should get on with things, yes? We should take some more pictures? In spite of ghosts."

He nodded with a sigh.

"I'll go and get ready, you set up the lights and screen," she said, and slipped out of the room.

Focus indeed, he thought wearily. That was easier said than done. Aiko would be a while in the bathroom, preparing face and body, so he crossed to the big mirror and stared carefully into it, angling his gaze so he could pan round the room, trying to follow some of Feather's sketched lines. He felt stupid and the task was made even harder by the curve, but the wine was dulling any questioning now. At one point, his reflected gaze encountered another mirror on the other side of the room, and yet another layer of world opened up. In the distance, twice reflected, he could see a third version of the apartment. Just a small square that included part of the doorway and hall beyond. It was hard to make anything out—like looking through a cheap microscope—and he impatiently swung away to turn the light on. As he moved, there was a flash of awareness, the shocking realisation that there was someone standing just inches away…

…as though she had been staring over his shoulder.

He locked his movement instantly and slammed backwards against the wall. Reflections still muddled his brain. Unsure what was real and what was all a scene in some huge hall of mirrors. He closed his eyes furiously, trying to earth himself.

"Feather?" he murmured.

He stared round the empty room, his heart racing. It had seemed so clear—a serious faced girl looking at him with big eyes. It was a sickening sensation, trying to decide whether he had seen a ghost or some flash of hallucination. He glanced at the mirror again, half-expecting to see her lost somewhere in the confusion it contained. But there was nothing. He urgently grabbed the book and found some of the photographs, trying to compare what he thought he had seen with Feather's reality. But they told him nothing he didn't already know. The face was the same. But whether it had come from within or without was anybody's guess.

He sat down and inhaled, still feeling deeply shaken.

"What was that noise?" Aiko asked anxiously, stepping into the room again, wrapped in a towel, her face half-finished. "What's wrong?"

"Wrong?" he murmured. "Nothing—no—nothing's wrong. I'm fine. I just thought..."

"Is that book getting you... spooked?" she asked, picking it up and studying the pages. "Seriously?"

"Well..."

"This is just—she was a bit crazy, that's all. No more than many people—many of your favourite artists. All of us in fact. There's no ghosts here."

"Ah shaddup," he muttered, embarrassed, trying to smile.

Aiko shook her head and tossed the book at him, then stepped back into the bathroom. Trying to calm himself, he flipped onwards through the pages, but the result was a second shock that eroded reality even further. A coupling of three words...

> I had some company today. It is rare—many people are scared of me for some reason. I am the quiet girl whose thoughts they can never know. And those who are not scared of me, I am scared of them. They smell of desperation and decay. But sometimes not. That's why I still go out to the good places—and occasionally find friends. Usually visitors, foreigners, as here. I had my red lights on in the flat. He looked surprised when I served *silungur* (pickled trout) with crusty bread and

> homemade pickled mushrooms—not sure he liked it. Then glasses of port, which seem to me to fit well with this shadowy place. We spent three hours having sex in positions 3, 8 and 10. He was shy at first, but burst out in positive laughter when I told him my classification and showed him this book. That was good. Then we were at the window, naked. The window where I dance. And he told me that this was the line he always rode to travel home. He would always be glancing up at this block as the intercity train accelerated slowly away from the terminal, in case I was dancing. That was nice. One day I will dance for him.

Matt closed the book, feeling his skin prickling even more. *Dance for him…*

Aiko returned to find him staring at nothing and gave him a worried look. She was now wearing a light robe, her face decked with immaculate and colourful make-up.

"Matt," she said uneasily, "I was thinking, maybe the walls should be painted soon," she said. "And make this place ours rather than hers."

He refocused his eyes and stared at her in dismay.

"No," he protested. "We can't…"

"I don't like the way you are since moving here. You seem very… far away sometimes."

He gave her a blank look, honestly surprised.

"Am I?"

"And I want a home. I am sure you would feel better as well."

He put the book aside and stared at the wall, feeling deeply disturbed.

"We can't paint over these," he said, almost feeling a prickle of tears. "That would be… would be…"

There was a silence. He didn't know what to say.

"Matt, come on," she said with a grin, putting her arms around him from behind and kissing his ear. "She's not a ghost still haunting this miserable little apartment—who would haunt this place? And I am working again tomorrow. So we should carry on and finish some things, right?"

He gave her embracing arms a squeeze in return, then reluctantly went to find the green screen.

The next morning, a sharp sensation in his side jerked him out of dreams of following lines and shapes with no destination. He looked around, hunting for reality, but reality was only Aiko standing over him, dressed neatly in her work clothes and grinning. She removed her finger from the well-defined ticklish spot beneath his ribs.

"Matt-chan, good luck," she teased. "Good luck facing the forces of darkness."

He gave a sleepy growl and rolled over. It was too early and the night had been too restless and uncomfortable for him to manage much else. But as soon as she had pattered out of the door, he sat up. There seemed little point in trying to sleep again since restlessness had already set in. His eyes flickered around the room, looking for anything different, but there was nothing. The day seemed bright, so far as he could tell down here in the shadows. Just a normal London day with the normal London sonic backdrop. "Is there anybody there?" he asked, drawing the words out in a theatrical incantation. Then he frowned and screwed up his face, trying to dispel the prickling in his eyes. Feather had mentioned no time in her notes—at least as far as he could tell.

Some unknown thing, in the mind of a crazy artist, might just possibly have been intended to take place at an unknown time on this day that didn't seem any different to any other. And now almost certainly wouldn't. After all, being dead cancels out most things. Even art.

"Feather," he said out loud, "you are a complete fruitcake. I hope you can hear me."

He kicked the bedclothes aside. There was a dull throb of annoyance—almost rage. What was happening to him? There was too much to do to waste time with this.

He busied himself washing up. Checking through the online auctions. Packing a couple of things ready for mailing. Unpacking a few more of life's possessions. Publicising this that and the other. Grubbing a few more of the golden coins needed for survival in the dance of London that was starting to seem wearily like a computer game. And when there was no work left, he paced back to the tiny kitchen and studied the fridge for something to eat. A plate of edamame salad and a Turkish sausage and, with nothing else to do, he found himself looking at the book again while he ate and the day ticked onwards. Somewhere outside, beyond the buildings, the sun was rising higher. The temperature climbed slowly from morning towards the pre-noon. The rush hour, if such a jumbled mess of busyness and gloom could be called anything so precise as an hour, was over and the general throng of the London day was in full progress.

In the absence of any new information, the book made no more sense than it had before—it was either beyond fathoming or totally illusory. Maybe the diagrams meant nothing at all. Maybe Aiko was right and Feather had been a crazy and that was that. Instead of worrying about them anymore, he turned the pages and focused on some of the sex positions she had laid out with such detail. The simple rawness and beauty of those quiet pencil lines was another world entirely. Maybe worth testing out with Aiko, if they could ever find the energy for it at the same time.

But even here the tone of the book only remained happy for a brief while.

> There are places where humanity cannot go, except caged in massive machines. The most forbidden places in the city. The railway tracks run through a mythological land visible only through the windows—a land that can never be touched and rarely be seen. Sometimes I want to go there—to climb up the ancient brick and smell the smell of metal and electricity. Lie there in the dark. Have sex there. But then again, I suppose I am similar in reverse—a similar unreachable world to those that pass by below and spare a glance. It is hard to imagine worlds that can collide less, the one protected by illusions of privacy and the private, the other the forbidden zone of the rails. It makes me wonder whether any human interaction is any closer. How can people ever touch, given the vast distances that fill our heads?

These were melancholy thoughts and he closed the book feeling unexpectedly touched. For all her occasional visitors and her strange communication with the world as it rolled past her window, Feather seemed a symbol of isolation, radiating it out into the world like some kind of disease. It made him think in turn about Aiko, with diffuse thoughts on just how close they were or could ever be, even leaving aside cultural and language barriers. Like many people, they had found a level of trust and intimacy up to a point—but that only went so far. Beyond lay vast reaches of each other that neither of them would ever fathom.

Perhaps in defence against such thoughts, he felt a wash of deep affection, a strong yearning to gather Aiko's small and sharp-edged form into a hug, into some tight and safe place.

The melancholy stasis of his thoughts was soon interrupted, though with no particular drama, by a bump from the living room. Almost like a summons, he thought. In a moment, Aiko was forgotten and he looked at the door, skin prickling all over, trying to get himself back to Earth. He stepped through into the room and the culprit was clearly to be seen. A small lamp was lying on the floor. He picked it up. The window was open, the room stirred by a gentle wind. A shirt he had left hanging from the empty curtain rail was flapping where the lamp had been. Perfectly normal. "Idiot," he muttered. He grabbed the shirt to put it away, but then it dawned on him that something about the room was subtly different. Something intangible, something about the quality of light. Outside were just the usual buildings silhouetted against the morning sun and gleaming tracks. Nothing unusual there.

But then he saw it.

A thin sliver of sunlight, just a few centimetres wide, was cutting into the window frame. A wedge of thin white. He stared at it, eyebrows clenched, and as he looked it seemed to move. Slower than a snail, it expanded across the wood, almost seeming to crawl, and reached the edge. He spun round as the pale bar hit the opposite wall of the room. He realised that it perfectly matched one edge of the painting. He looked at the sketchbook again and it clicked. Dec. must be declination—the seasonal angle of the sun above the equator. And even as he watched, the light was still moving, growing. It was carefully planned and almost mystic. Feather the scientist—that's what this was.

For a moment he stared out across the tracks, trying to work out where the light was coming from—no doubt some random chink of wall and roof that happened to let a small gleam through. But he quickly gave up and sat down on the bed and watched as it moved slowly across the design in a perfect diagonal path. The light meshed with the patterns on the wall, forming new patterns, revealing regular shapes that hadn't existed before. Lines and planes and triangles. Then it reached the mirror and something even more remarkable happened. It was pale—the hazy yet strong London sun—but it gleamed back across the room, focused by the concave surface and squarely striking a second mirror, which in turn reflected it out of the room and into the hall. The reflections amplified the intensity and he could clearly see it catching more mirrors, only to be reflected yet further. Some of them were splitting the beam, or scattering it across the walls, some acting only as reflectors. The whole apartment was coming alive with light in a carefully worked out, meticulously plotted pattern that surrounded him with a pale and almost unearthly illumination.

The rest of the world seemed to have stopped. The silence was absolute, deafening. All the trains on the London railways had come to a halt, every police car and London bus had stopped, every person on the streets walked in silence. Memories of his horror at the crawling light came back to him and he smiled. There was nothing alarming about this—it was magic pure and simple. He glanced around, sure he wasn't alone. He could almost feel a figure sitting beside him on the bed, staring as raptly as he at the fulfilment of her art but, he was sure, understanding it far more. A prickle of proximity on the skin. There was a meaning hidden here that went beyond just putting on a pretty show, that was very clear. But he also knew that he had no chance of working it out. Maybe that didn't matter. He wanted to reach out, squeeze a hand if there was one to squeeze. Some brief communication of the luminous wonder that was being enacted.

The original light eventually passed off the mirror and the room faded to dark again. There was just a last shape on the wall reaching towards the edge of the design, and as it touched it, it began to pass from view. He felt a stab of panic. It was slipping away—he hadn't even photographed it. Something so ephemeral that it could never be recaptured. But those thoughts faded away again almost as soon as they arose and instead he sat filled with a glassy relaxation as the gleam shrank until it was nothing more than a thread that followed the curving edge of the pattern, almost down to the millimetre. Then it was gone, the performance over. The dull grey of the city canyon returned.

He drew a deep breath, then glanced blearily round the room, almost convinced that there had been a movement that went with the vanishing, a faint awareness of jeans and brown hair. But of course there was nothing. He drew a deep breath, feeling that prickling sensation of waking from a particularly intense dream. Maybe the sun would be back again tomorrow, he wasn't sure. This couldn't be the only moment of the year when it would pierce the complex geometry of the buildings. But he felt certain that never again in this turning of the year, would it fit so perfectly into the artwork this room had become.

"Feather," he murmured, "that was quite amazing, you know that?"

Outside, London was starting to impinge on his awareness again. A wail of sirens somewhere in the distance signalling some drama or other. A mundanity that was not very welcome. He sighed and blinked and peered out of the window again, watching an intercity train pass by, left to right, slowly heading for who knows where.

Aiko arrived back from work and found him lying on the bed. She poked him crossly.

"Wake up," she said. "I'm hungry."

Matt blinked at her hazily, as though trying to remember who she was, then smiled and sat up.

"Sorry," he said. "I didn't realise it was so late."

"What have you been doing?" she demanded. He smiled again.

"Oh nothing much. Just watching the ghosts…"

The next morning, there was a ring at the doorbell announcing the delivery of a large soft package—curtains. Simple lace plus heavy red fake-velvet-type. Good for keeping the light out. Matt put them up in a few minutes, but not without a complex feeling, almost, but not quite, of regret.

"Sorry, Feather," he murmured aloud. "Don't blame me."

And that night, as they lay together, one arm of each trailing over the other, it was indeed much darker. Matt's sleep-hazed eyes followed the last few glowing patterns imprinted on the room, some still moving with that incalculable motion. New patterns that matched nothing on the wall, distorted and corrupted by hanging fabric. The green glow of the railway signal… the orange and white of the city lights… lines and squares. As he watched, trying not to analyse anything and trying to repress a slight prickle of unease, one cubic gleam came crawling slowly across the bed sheets towards them. It arrived at Aiko's face and stopped. He saw her twitch slightly, frown in her sleep, then turn over, but the light remained, illuminating her ear and cheek.

Then it winked out…

www.ingramcontent.com/pod-product-compliance
Lightning Source LLC
Chambersburg PA
CBHW020307030826
48979CB00029B/2294/J

* 9 7 8 1 9 1 3 7 6 6 2 6 9 *